THE IMMORTAL HIGHLANDER

"Seductive, mesmerizing, and darkly sensual, Moning's hardcover debut adds depth and intensity to the magical world she has created in her earlier Highlander books, and fans and new readers alike will be drawn to this increasingly intriguing series." —*Library Journal*

"All readers who love humorous fantasy romance filled to the brim with fantasy-worthy Highlanders will find Moning's latest to be a sensuous treat." —*Booklist*

"Nonstop action for fans of paranormal romance."
—*Kirkus Reviews*

THE DARK HIGHLANDER

"Darker, sexier, and more serious than Moning's previous time-travel romances . . . this wild, imaginative romp takes readers on an exhilarating ride through time and space."
—*Publishers Weekly* (starred review)

"Pulsing with sexual tension, Moning delivers a tale romance fans will be talking about for a long time." —*Oakland Press*

"*The Dark Highlander* is dynamite, dramatic, and utterly riveting. Ms. Moning takes the classic plot of good vs. evil . . . and gives it a new twist." —*Romantic Times*

KISS OF THE HIGHLANDER

"Moning's snappy prose, quick wit and charismatic characters will enchant." —*Publishers Weekly*

"Here is an intelligent, fascinating, well-written foray into the paranormal that will have you glued to the pages. A must read!" —*Romantic Times*

"*Kiss of the Highlander* is wonderful. . . . [Moning's] story-telling skills are impressive, her voice and pacing dynamic, and her plot as tight as a cask of good Scotch whisky." —*Contra Costa Times*

THE HIGHLANDER'S TOUCH

"A stunning achievement in time-travel romance. Ms. Moning's imaginative genius in her latest spellbinding tale speaks to the hearts of romance readers and will delight and touch them deeply. Unique and eloquent, filled with thought-provoking and emotional elements, *The Highlander's Touch* is a very special book. Ms. Moning effortlessly secures her place as a top-notch writer." —*Romantic Times*

"Ms. Moning stretches our imagination, sending us flying into the enchanting past." —*Rendezvous*

BEYOND THE HIGHLAND MIST

"A terrific plotline . . . Gypsies and Scottish mysticism, against the backdrop of the stark beauty of the Highlands . . . an intriguing story. Poignant and sensual." —*Publishers Weekly*

"This highly original time-travel combines the wonders of the paranormal and the mischievous world of the fairies to create a splendid, sensual, hard-to-put-down romance. You'll delight in the biting repartee and explosive sexual tension between Adrienne and the Hawk, the conniving Adam, and the magical aura that surrounds the entire story. Karen Marie Moning is destined to make her mark on the genre." —*Romantic Times*

TO TAME A HIGHLAND WARRIOR

"A hauntingly beautiful love story . . . Karen Marie Moning gives us an emotional masterpiece that you will want to take out and read again and again." —*Rendezvous*

THE IMMORTAL HIGHLANDER

KAREN MARIE MONING

A DELL BOOK

THE IMMORTAL HIGHLANDER
A Dell Book

PUBLISHING HISTORY
Delacorte Press hardcover edition published August 2004
Dell mass market edition / August 2005
Dell mass market reissue / July 2008

Published by
Bantam Dell
A Division of Random House, Inc.
New York, New York

This is a work of fiction. Names, characters, places, and incidents either
are the product of the author's imagination or are used fictitiously. Any
resemblance to actual persons, living or dead, events, or locales is
entirely coincidental.

ISBN 978-0-440-24504-9

Printed in the United States of America

www.bantamdell.com

OPM   10   9   8   7   6   5   4   3   2   1

For Elizabeth — if we weren't sisters, we'd be cats.
Sister cats. You can borrow my hat anytime.

Damn, *it's good to be me.*

—Adam Black , on being Adam Black

Tuatha Dé Danaan: (tua day dhanna)

A highly advanced race of immortal beings that settled in Ireland thousands of years before the birth of Christ. Called by many names: Children of the Goddess Danu; the True Race; the Gentry; the Daoine Sidhe; they are most commonly referred to as the Fae or Fairy. Although frequently portrayed as shimmering, dainty creatures of diminutive size that flit about exuding effervescent good humor and a penchant for mild mischief, the true Tuatha Dé are neither so delicate nor so benevolent.

—FROM THE O'CALLAGHAN *Books of the Fae*

Adam Black:

Tuatha Dé Danaan, a rogue even among his own kind. His favored glamour is that of an intensely sexual Highland blacksmith with a powerful rippling body, golden skin, long black hair, and dark, mesmerizing eyes. Highly intelligent, lethally seductive. Alleged to have nearly broken The Compact on not one, but two occasions. He is, by far, the most dangerous and unpredictable of his race.

WARNING: EXERCISE EXTREME CAUTION IF SIGHTED.
AVOID CONTACT AT ALL COST.

—FROM THE O'CALLAGHAN *Books of the Fae*

PROLOGUE

Adam Black stood in the central chamber of the stone catacombs beneath The Belthew Building and watched as Chloe Zanders stumbled about, searching for her Highland lover, Dageus MacKeltar.

She was weeping as if her very soul were being ripped apart. Incessant and piercing, it was enough to split a Tuatha Dé's head.

Or a human's, for that matter, he thought darkly.

He was getting bloody tired of her constant wailing. He had problems of his own. Big problems.

Aoibheal, queen of the Tuatha Dé Danaan, had finally made good on her long-running threats to punish him for his continued interference in the world of mortals. And she'd chosen the cruelest punishment of all.

She'd stripped him of his immortality and made him human.

He spared a quick glance down at himself and was

relieved to find that, at least, she'd left him in his favored glamour: that of the dark-haired, muscular, irresistibly sexy blacksmith, a millennia-spanning blend of Continental Celt and Highland warrior, clad in tartan, armbands, and torque. On occasion she'd turned him into things that didn't suffer the light of day well.

His relief, however, was short-lived. So what if he looked like his usual self? He was human, for Christ's sake! Flesh and blood. Limited. Puny. Finite.

Cursing savagely, he eyed the sobbing woman. He could barely hear himself think. Perhaps if he informed her that Dageus wasn't really dead she would shut *up*. He had to find a way out of this intolerable situation, and fast.

"Your lover is not dead. Cease your weeping, woman," he ordered imperiously. He should know. Aoibheal had forced him to give of his own immortal life-essence to save the Highlander's life.

His command did not have the intended effect. On the contrary, just when he was certain she couldn't possibly get any louder—and how such a small creature managed to make such a huge noise was beyond him— his newly acquired eardrums were treated to a wail that escalated exponentially.

"Woman, cease!" he roared, clamping his hands to his ears. "I said *he is not dead*."

Still she wept. She didn't so much as glance in his direction, as if he'd not spoken at all. Furious, he skirted the rubble littering the chamber—debris from the battle that had taken place there a quarter hour past between Dageus MacKeltar and the Druid sect of the Draghar, the battle he should *never* have intervened in—and stalked to her side. He grabbed the nape of her neck to force her gaze to his, to compel her silence.

His hand slid right through the back of her skull and came out her nose.

She didn't even blink. Just hiccuped on a sob and wailed anew.

Adam stood motionless for a moment, then tried again, reaching for one of her breasts. His hand slid neatly through her heart and out her left shoulder blade.

He went still again, wings of unease unfurling in the pit of his all-too-human stomach.

By Danu, Aoibheal wouldn't! His dark eyes narrowed to slits.

Would she?

Jaw clenched, he tried again. And again his hand slipped through Chloe Zanders's body.

Christ, she had! *The bitch!*

Not only had the queen made him human, she had cursed him with the threefold power of the *féth fiada*!

Adam shook his head disbelievingly. The *féth fiada* was the enchantment his race used when they wanted to walk among humans undetected. A Tuatha Dé customarily invoked but one facet of the potent, triumvirate spell—invisibility. But it could also render its subject impossible for humans to hear and feel as well. The *féth fiada* was a useful tool if one wished to meddle unobserved.

But if cursed with it permanently? If unable to escape it?

That thought was too abhorrent to entertain.

He closed his eyes and delved into his mind to sift time/place and return to the Fae Isle of Morar. He didn't care who the queen was currently entertaining in her Royal Bower; she would undo this *now*.

Nothing happened. He remained precisely where he was.

He tried again.

There was no swift sensation of weightlessness, no sudden rush of that heady freedom and invincibility he always felt when traversing dimensions.

He opened his eyes. Still in the stone chamber.

A snarl curved his lips. Human, cursed, *and* powerless? Barred from the Fae realm? He tossed back his head, raking his long dark hair from his face. "All right, Aoibheal, you've made your point. Change me back now."

There was no response. Nothing but the sound of the woman's endless sobbing, echoing hollowly in the chill stone chamber.

"Aoibheal, did you hear me? I said, 'I get it.' Now restore me."

Still no response. He knew she was listening, lingering a dimensional sliver just beyond the human realm. Watching, savoring his discomfort.

And . . . waiting for a show of submission, he acknowledged darkly.

A muscle leapt in his jaw. Humility was not, nor would ever be, his strong suit.

Still, if his choices were humble or *human*—and cursed and powerless, to boot—he'd eat humble pie until he choked on it.

"My Queen, you were right and I was wrong. See, I *can* say it."

Though the lie tasted foul upon his tongue.

"And I vow never again to disobey you."

At least not until he was certain he was secure in her good graces again.

"Forgive me, Queen Most Fair."

Of course she would. She always did.

"I am your most humble, adoring servant, O glorious Queen."

Was he laying it on too thick? he wondered idly, as the silence lengthened. He noticed he'd begun to tap a booted foot in a most human manner. He stomped it to make it be still. He was not human. He was nothing like them.

"Did you *hear* me? I apologized," he snapped.

After a few more moments, he sighed. Gritting his teeth, he dropped to his knees. It was universally known that Adam Black despised being on his knees for any reason, for anyone.

"Exalted leader of the True Race," he purred in the ancient, rarely used tongue of his kind, "Savior of the Danaan, I petition the grace and glory of thy throne." Ritual, ancient words of formal court manners, they signified as nothing else could, his complete and utter obeisance. And ritual demanded she reply.

The contrary bitch didn't.

He—who'd never before suffered the passage of time—now felt it acutely, as it stretched too long.

"Damn it, Aoibheal, fix me!" he thundered, lunging to his feet. "Give me back my powers! Make me immortal again!"

Nothing.

Time spun out.

"A taste," he assured himself. "She's just giving me a taste of this, to teach me a lesson."

Any moment now she would appear. She would rebuke him. She would subject him to a scathing account of his many transgressions. He would nod, promise never to do it again, and all would be made right. Just like the thousands of other times he'd disobeyed or angered her.

An hour later nothing was right.

Two hours later and Chloe Zanders was gone, leaving him alone in the silent, dusty tombs. He almost missed her wailing. Almost.

Thirty-six hours later and his body was hungry, thirsty, and—a thing nearly incomprehensible to him— tired. The Tuatha Dé did not sleep. His mind, customarily razor-sharp and lightning fast, was getting muddled, sluggish, shutting down without his consent.

Unacceptable. He'd be damned if any part of him was doing a single thing without his consent. Not his mind. Not his body. It never had and never would. A Tuatha Dé was always in control. Always.

His last thought before unconsciousness claimed him was that he was bloody well certain he'd rather be *anything* else: stuck inside a mountain for a few hundred years, turned into a slimy, three-headed sea beast, forced to play the court fool again for a century or two.

Anything   but...so...disgustingly...pathetically... uncontrollably...hum—

1

Summer, Gabrielle O'Callaghan brooded—
always her favorite season—had absolutely sucked this
year.

Unlocking her car, she got in and slipped off her sun-
glasses. Shrugging out of her suit jacket, she nudged off
her heels and took slow, deep breaths. She sat collecting
herself for a few moments, then tugged free the clip re-
straining her hair and massaged her scalp.

She was getting the start of a killer headache.

And her hands were *still* shaking.

She'd nearly betrayed herself to the Fae.

She couldn't believe she'd been so stupid, but, God,
there were just too many of them this summer! She
hadn't spotted a fairy in Cincinnati for years, but now,
for some bizarre reason, there were oodles of them.

Like Cincinnati was some kind of great place to hang
out—could a city *be* more boring? Whatever their

unfathomable reason for choosing the Tri-State, they'd appeared in droves in early June, and had been ruining her summer ever since.

And pretending she didn't see them never got any easier. With their perfect bodies, gold-velvet skin, and shimmering iridescent eyes, they were a little hard to miss. Drop-dead gorgeous, impossibly seductive, dripping pure power, the males were a walking temptation for a girl to—

Brusquely she shook her head to abort that treacherous thought. She'd survived this long and was darned if she was going to slip up and get caught by one of the erotic—*exotic*, she corrected herself impatiently—creatures.

But sometimes it was so hard not to look at them. And doubly difficult not to react. Especially when one caught her off guard like the last one had.

She'd been having lunch with Marian Temple, senior partner at the law firm of Temple, Turley and Tucker, at a posh downtown restaurant; a very critical lunch, during which she'd been interviewing for a postgraduate position.

A soon-to-be-third-year law student, Gabby was serving a summer internship with Little & Staller, a local firm of personal injury attorneys. It had taken her all of two days on the job to realize she was not cut out for representing pushy, med-bill-inflating plaintiffs who were firmly convinced their soft-tissue injuries were worth at least a million dollars per ache.

At the opposite end of the legal spectrum was Temple, Turley and Tucker. The most prestigious firm in the city, it catered to only the most desirable clients, specializing in business law and estate planning. What carefully selected criminal cases they chose to represent were renowned, precedent-setting ones. Ones that made a difference in the world, protecting fundamental rights and addressing intolerable injustices. And those were the cases she hungered to get her hands on, even if she had to slave away for years, doing research and fetching coffee to get to them.

She'd been stressed all week, anticipating the interview, knowing that TT&T hired only the cream of the crop. Knowing she was competing against dozens of her classmates, not to mention dozens more from law schools around the country, in a cutthroat bid for a single opening. Knowing Marian Temple had a reputation for demanding nothing less than high-gloss sophistication and professional perfection.

But thanks to hours of aggressive practice interviews and pep talks from her best friend, Elizabeth, Gabby had been calm, composed, and in top form. The aloof Ms. Temple had been impressed with her scholastic achievements, and Gabby had gotten the distinct impression that the firm was predisposed to hire a woman (couldn't be too careful with those equal-opportunity statistics), which put her ahead of most of the competition. The lunch had gone swimmingly, until the moment they'd left the restaurant and stepped out onto Fifth Street.

As Ms. Temple was extending that all-important invitation to come in for a second, in-house interview with the partners (which was *never* arranged unless the firm was seriously considering making an offer, joy of joys!), a sexy, muscle-bound fairy male sauntered right between them in that infuriatingly arrogant I'm-so-perfect, don't-you-just-wish-you-were-me way they had, so close that its long golden hair brushed Gabby's cheek like a sensual ripple of silk.

The intoxicating fragrance of jasmine and sandalwood surrounded her, and the heat radiating off its powerful body caressed her like a sultry, erotic breeze. It took every ounce of her considerable self-discipline to *not* inch backward out of its way.

Or worse—yield to that incessant temptation and just pet the gorgeous tawny creature. How many times had she dreamed of doing that? Copping one tiny forbidden fairy-feel. Finally finding out if all that golden fairy skin really felt as velvety as it looked.

You must never betray that you can see them, Gabby.

Thoroughly discombobulated by the fairy's proximity, her suddenly nerveless hand lost its grip on the iced coffee she'd taken from the restaurant in a to-go cup. It hit the sidewalk, the top flew off, and coffee exploded upward, drenching the impeccable Ms. Temple.

At that precise moment, the fairy turned back to look at her, its iridescent eyes narrowing.

Panicked, Gabby focused all her attention on the sputtering Ms. Temple. With the enthusiasm of near-hysteria, she plucked tissues from her purse and dabbed frantically at the spreading coffee stains on what had been, moments before, a pristine ivory suit that she had a sick feeling cost more than she made in a month.

Babbling loudly about how clumsy she was, apologizing and blaming everything from eating too much, to not being used to heels, to being nervous about the interview, in a matter of moments, she managed to completely blow the image of cool, composed confidence she'd so painstakingly projected through lunch.

But she'd had no choice.

In order to make the fairy believe she hadn't seen it, that she was just a clumsy human, nothing more, she'd had to act like a complete spaz and risk sabotaging her credibility with her prospective employer.

Sabotage it, she had.

Swatting away Gabby's frantically dabbing hands, Ms. Temple smoothed her ruined suit and huffed off toward her car, pausing to toss stiffly over her shoulder, "As I told you earlier, Ms. O'Callaghan, our firm works with only the highest-caliber clients. They can be demanding, excessive, and temperamental. And understandably so. When there are millions at stake, a client has every right to expect the best. We at Temple, Turley and Tucker pride ourselves on being unflappable under stress. Our clients require smooth, sophisticated handling. Frankly, Ms. O'Callaghan, you're too flighty to be successful with our firm. I'm sure you'll find an appropriate fit elsewhere. Good day, Ms. O'Callaghan."

Feeling like she'd been kicked in the stomach, Gabby watched in stricken silence as Ms. Temple accepted her spotless Mercedes from the valet, dimly registering that the fairy, blessedly, was also moving on. As the sleek pearl-colored Mercedes merged onto Fifth Street and disappeared into traffic—the job of her dreams flapping farewell on its tailpipe—Gabby's shoulders slumped. With a gusty sigh, she turned and trudged down the street to the corner lot where simple law students not-destined-for-success-because-they-were-too-flighty could afford to park.

" 'Flighty,' my ass," she muttered, resting her head on the steering wheel. "You have no idea what my life is like. *You* can't see them."

All Ms. Temple had probably felt was a slight breeze, a moderate increase in temperature, perhaps caught a whiff of an exotic, arousing fragrance. And if, by chance, the fairy had brushed against her—although they were invisible, they were real, and were actually *there*—Ms. Temple would have rationalized it away somehow. Those who couldn't see the Fae always did.

Gabby had learned the hard way that people had zero tolerance for the inexplicable. It never ceased to amaze her what flimsy excuses they dredged up to protect their perception of reality. "Gee, I guess I didn't get enough sleep last night." Or, "Wow, I shouldn't have had that second (or third or fourth) beer with lunch." If all else failed, they settled for a simple "I must have imagined it."

How she longed for such oblivion!

She shook her head and tried to console herself with the thought that at least the fairy had been convinced and was gone. She was safe. For now.

The way Gabby figured it, the Fae were responsible for ninety-nine percent of the problems in her life. She'd take responsibility for the other one percent, but *they* were the reason her life this summer had been one crisis after another. *They* were the reason she'd begun to dread leaving her house, never knowing where one might pop up, or how badly it might startle her. Or what kind of ass she'd make of herself, trying to regroup. *They* were the reason her boyfriend had broken up with her fifteen days, three hours, and—she glanced broodingly at her watch—forty-two minutes ago.

Gabrielle O'Callaghan harbored a special and very personal hatred for the Fae.

"I don't see you. I don't see you," she muttered beneath her breath as two mouthwatering fairy males strolled past the hood of her car. She averted her gaze, caught herself, then angled the rearview mirror and pretended to be fussing with her lipstick.

Never look away too sharply, her grandmother, Moira

O'Callaghan, had always cautioned. *You must act natural. You must learn to let your gaze slide over them without either hitching or pulling away too abruptly, or they'll know you know. And they'll take you. You must never betray that you can see them. Promise me, Gabby. I can't lose you!*

Gram had seen them, too, these creatures other people couldn't see. Most of the women on her mom's side did, though sometimes the "gift" skipped generations. As it had with her mom, who'd moved to Los Angeles years ago (like the people in California were less weird than fairies), leaving then–seven-year-old Gabrielle behind with Gram "until she got settled." Jilly O'Callaghan had never gotten settled.

Why couldn't it have skipped me? Gabby brooded. A normal life was all she'd ever wanted.

And proving damned difficult to have, even in boring Cincinnati. Gabby was beginning to think that living in the Tri-State—the geographical convergence of Indiana, Ohio, and Kentucky—was a bit like living at the mystical convergence of Sunnydale's Hellmouth.

Except the Midwest didn't get demons and vampires—oh, no—they got fairies: dangerously seductive, inhuman, arrogant creatures that would take her and do God-only-knew-what to her if they ever figured out that she could see them.

Her family history was riddled with tales of ancestors who'd been captured by the dreaded Fae Hunters and never seen again. Some of the tales claimed they were swiftly and brutally killed by the savage Hunters, others that they were forced into slavery to the Fae.

She had no idea what actually became of those foolish enough to be taken, but she knew one thing for certain: She had no intention of ever finding out.

——————

Later Gabby would realize that it was all
the cup of coffee's fault. Every awful thing that happened to her from that moment on could be traced directly back to that cup of coffee with the stunning
simplicity of an airtight conditional argument: If not for
A (said cup of coffee), then not B (blowing job interview), hence not C (having to go into work that night),
and certainly not D (the horrible thing that happened to
her there)...on to infinity.

It really wasn't fair that such a trivial, spur-of-the-
moment, seemingly harmless decision such as taking an
iced coffee to-go could change the entire course of a girl's
life.

Not that she didn't hold the fairy significantly culpa-
ble, but studying law had taught her to isolate the critical
catalyst so one could argue culpability, and the simple
facts were that if she hadn't had the cup of coffee in her
hand, she wouldn't have dropped it, wouldn't have splat-
tered Ms. Temple, wouldn't have made an ass of herself,
and wouldn't have lost all hope of landing her dream job.

If not for the cup of coffee, the fairy would have had
no reason to turn and look back at her, and she would
have had no reason to panic. Life would have rolled
smoothly on. With the promise of that coveted second interview, she would have gone out celebrating with her
girlfriends that night.

But because of that nefarious cup of coffee, she
didn't go out. She went home, took a long bubble bath,
had a longer cry, then later that evening, when she was
certain the office would be empty and she wouldn't
have to field humiliating questions from her fellow interns, she drove back downtown to catch up on work.

She was behind by a whopping nineteen arbitration cases, which, now that she didn't have a different job lined up, mattered.

And because of that calamitous cup of coffee, she was in a bad mood and not paying attention as she parallel-parked in front of her office building, and she didn't notice the dark, dangerous-looking fairy stepping from the shadows of the adjacent alley.

If not for the stupid cup of coffee, she wouldn't have even *been* there.

And that was when things took a diabolical turn from bad to worse.

2

Adam Black raked a hand through his long black hair and scowled as he stalked down the alley.

Three eternal months he'd been human. Ninety-seven horrific days, to be exact. Two thousand three hundred twenty-eight interminable hours. One hundred thirty-nine thousand six hundred eighty thoroughly offensive minutes.

He'd become obsessed with increments of time. It was an embarrassingly mortal affliction. Next thing he knew, he'd be wearing a watch.

Never.

He'd been certain Aoibheal would have come for him by now. Would have staked his very essence on it; not that he had much left to stake.

But she hadn't, and he was sick of waiting. Not only were humans allotted a ridiculously finite slice of time to exist, their bodies had requirements that consumed a great deal of that time. Sleep alone consumed a full quarter of it. Although he'd mastered those requirements over the past few months, he resented being slave to his physical form. Having to eat, wash, dress, sleep, piss, shave, brush his hair and teeth, for Christ's sake! He wanted to be himself again. Not at the queen's bloody convenience, but *now*.

Hence he'd left London and journeyed to Cincinnati (the infernally long way—by plane) looking for the half-Fae son he'd sired over a millennium ago, Circenn Brodie, who'd married a twenty-first-century mortal and usually resided here with her.

Usually.

Upon arriving in Cincinnati, he'd found Circenn's residence vacant, and had no idea where to look for him next. He'd taken up residence there himself, and had been killing time since—endeavoring grimly to ignore that, for the first time in his timeless existence, time was returning the favor—waiting for Circenn to return. A half-blooded Tuatha Dé, Circenn had magic Adam no longer possessed.

Adam's scowl deepened. What paltry power the queen had left him was virtually worthless. He'd quickly discovered that she'd thought through his punishment most thoroughly. The spell of the *féth fiada* was one of the most powerful and perception-altering that the Tuatha Dé possessed, employed to permit a Tuatha Dé full interaction with the human realm, while keeping him or her undetectable by humans. It cloaked its wearer in illusion that affected short-term memory and generated confusion in the minds of those in the immediate vicinity.

If Adam toppled a newsstand, the vendor would

blithely blame an unseen wind. If he took food from a diner's plate, the person merely decided he/she must have finished. If he procured new clothing for himself at a shop, the owner would register an inventory error. If he snatched groceries from a passerby and flung the bag to the ground, his hapless victim would turn on the nearest bystander and a bitter fight would ensue (he'd done that a few times for a bit of sport). If he plucked the purse from a woman's arm and dangled it before her face, she would simply walk through both him and it (the moment he touched a thing, it, too, was sucked into the illusion cast by the *féth fiada* until he released it), then head in the opposite direction, muttering about having forgotten her purse at home.

There was nothing he could do to draw attention to himself. And he'd tried everything. To all intents and purposes, Adam Black didn't exist. Didn't even merit his own measly slice of human space.

He knew why she'd chosen this particular punishment: Because he'd sided with humans in their little disagreement, she was forcing him to taste of being human in the worst possible way. Alone and powerless, without a single distraction with which to pass the time and entertain himself.

He'd had enough of a taste to last an eternity.

Once an all-powerful being that could sift time and space, a being that could travel anywhere and anywhen in the blink of an eye, he was now limited to a single useful power: He could sift place over short distances, but no more than a few miles. It'd surprised him the queen had left him even that much power, until the first time he'd almost been run down by a careening bus in the heart of London.

She'd left him just enough magic to stay alive. Which

told him two things: one, she planned to forgive him eventually, and two, it was probably going to be a long, long time. Like, probably not until the moment his mortal form was about to expire.

Fifty more years of this would drive him bloody frigging nuts.

Problem was, even when Circenn *did* return, Adam still hadn't figured out a way to communicate with him. Because of his mortal half, Circenn wouldn't be able to see past the *féth fiada* either.

All he needed, Adam brooded for the thousandth time, was one person. Just one person who could see him. A single person who could help him. He wasn't entirely without options, but he couldn't exercise a damned one of them without someone to aid him.

And that sucked too. The almighty Adam Black needed help. He could almost hear silvery laughter tinkling on the night breeze, blowing tauntingly across the realms, all the way from the shimmering silica sands of the Isle of Morar.

With a growl of caged fury, he stalked out of the alley.

Gabby indulged herself in a huge self-pitying sigh as she got out of her car. Normally on nights like this, when the sky was black velvet, glittering with stars and a silver-scythe moon, warm and humid and alive with the glorious scents and sounds of summer, nothing could depress her.

But not tonight. Everyone but her was out somewhere having a life, while she was scrambling to clean up after the latest fairy debacle. Again.

It seemed like all she ever did anymore.

She wondered briefly, before she managed to push the depressing thought away, what her ex was doing tonight. Was he out at the bars? Had he already met someone new? Someone who wasn't still a virgin at twenty-four?

And *that* was the Fae's fault too.

She slammed the car door harder than she should have, and a little piece of chrome trim fell off and clattered to the pavement. It was the third bit of itself her aging Corolla had shed that week, though she was pretty sure the antenna had been assisted by bored neighborhood kids. With a snort of exasperation, she locked the car, kicked the little piece of trim beneath the car—she refused to clean up one more thing—and turned toward the building.

And froze.

A fairy male had just stalked out of the alley and was standing by the bench in the small courtyard oasis near the entrance to her office building. As she watched, it stretched out on the bench on its back, folded its arms behind its head, and stared up at the night sky, looking as if it had no intention of moving for a long, long time.

Damn and double-damn!

She was still in such a stew over the day's events that she wasn't sure she could manage to walk by it without giving in to the overwhelming urge to *kick* it.

It.

Fairies were "its," never "hims" or "hers." Gram had taught her at a young age not to personify them. They weren't human. And it was dangerous to think of them, even in the privacy of her thoughts, as if they were.

But heavens, Gabby thought, staring, he—*it*—was certainly male.

So tall that the bench wasn't long enough for it to

fully stretch out on, it had propped one leg on the back of the bench and bent the other at the knee, its legs spread in a basely masculine position. It was clad in snug-fitting, faded jeans, a black T-shirt, and black leather boots. Long, silky black hair spilled over its folded arms, falling to sweep the sidewalk. In contrast to the golden, angelic ones she'd seen earlier that day, this one was dark and utterly devilish-looking.

Gold armbands adorned its muscular arms, showcasing its powerful, rock-hard biceps, and a gold torque encircled its neck, gleaming richly in the amber glow of the gaslights illuming the courtyard oasis.

Royalty, she realized, with a trace of breathless fascination. Only those of a royal house were entitled to wear torques of gold. She'd never seen a member of one of the Ruling Houses before.

And "royal" was certainly a good word for him, er... it. Its profile was sheer majesty. Chiseled features, high cheekbones, strong jaw, aquiline nose, all covered with that luscious gold-velvet fairy skin. She narrowed her eyes, absorbing details. Unshaven jaw sculpted by five-o'clock shadow. Full mouth. Lower lip decadently full. Sinfully so, really. (*Gabby, quit* thinking *that!*)

She inhaled slowly, exhaled softly, holding utterly still, one hand on the roof of her car, the other clutching her keys.

It exuded immense sexuality: base, raw, scorching. From this distance she should not have been able to feel the heat from its body, but she could. She should not have gotten a bit dizzy from its exotic scent, but she had. As if it were twenty times more potent than any she'd encountered before; a veritable powerhouse of a fairy.

She was never going to be able to walk past it. Just wasn't happening. Not today. There was only so much she was capable of in a given day, and Gabby O'Callaghan had exceeded her limits.

Still...it hadn't moved. In fact, it seemed utterly oblivious to its surroundings. It couldn't hurt to look a little longer....

Besides, she reminded herself, she had a duty to surreptitiously observe as much as possible about any unknown fairy specimen. In such fashion did the O'Callaghan women protect themselves and the future of their children—by learning about their enemy. By passing down stories. By adding new information, with sketches when possible, to the multivolume *Books of the Fae*, thereby providing future generations greater odds of escaping detection.

This one didn't have the sleekly muscled body of most fairy males, she noted; this one had the body of a warrior. Shoulders much too wide to squeeze onto the bench. Arms bunched with muscle, thick forearms, strong wrists. Cut abdomen rippling beneath the fabric of its T-shirt each time it shifted position. Powerful thighs caressed by soft, faded denim.

No, not a warrior, she mused, that wasn't quite it. A shadowy image was dancing in the dark recesses of her mind and she struggled to bring it into focus.

More like...ah, she had it! Like one of those blacksmiths of yore who'd spent their days pounding steel at a scorching forge, metal clanging, sparks flying. Possessing massive brawn, yet also capable of the delicacy necessary to craft intricately embellished blades, combining pure power with exquisite control.

There wasn't a spare ounce of flesh on it, just rock-hard male body. It had a finely honed, brutal strength that, coupled with its height and breadth, could feel overwhelming to a woman. Especially if it were stretching all that rippling muscle on top of—

Stop that, O'Callaghan! Wiping tiny beads of sweat from her forehead with the back of her hand, she drew a shaky breath, struggling desperately for objectivity. She felt as hot as the forge she could imagine him bending over, hard body glistening, pounding…pounding…

Go, Gabby, a faint inner voice warned. *Go now. Hurry.*

But her inner alarm went off too late. At that precise moment it turned its head and glanced her way.

She should have looked away. She tried to look away. She couldn't.

Its face, full-on, was a work of impossible masculine beauty—exquisite symmetry brushed by a touch of savagery—but it was the eyes that got her all tangled up. They were ancient eyes, immortal eyes, eyes that had seen more than she could ever dream of seeing in a thousand lifetimes. Eyes full of intelligence, mockery, mischief, and—her breath caught in her throat as its gaze dropped down her body, then raked slowly back up—unchained sexuality. Black as midnight beneath slashing brows, its eyes flashed with gold sparks.

Her mouth dropped open and she gasped.

But, but, but, a part of her sputtered in protest, *it doesn't have fairy eyes! It can't be a fairy! They have iridescent eyes. Always. And if it's not a fairy, what is it?*

Again its gaze slid down her body, this time much more slowly, lingering on her breasts, fixing unabashedly at the juncture of her thighs. Without a shred of self-consciousness, it shifted its hips to gain play in its jeans, reached down, and blatantly adjusted itself.

Helplessly, as if mesmerized, her gaze followed, snagging on that big, dark hand tugging at the faded denim. At the huge, swollen bulge cupped by the soft, worn fabric. For a moment it closed its hand over itself and rubbed the thick ridge, and she was horrified to feel her own hand clenching. She flushed, mouth dry, cheeks flaming.

Suddenly it went motionless and its preternatural gaze locked with hers, eyes narrowing.

"Christ," it hissed, surging up from the bench in one graceful ripple of animal strength, "you see me. You're *seeing* me!"

"No I'm not," Gabby snapped instantly. Defensively. Stupidly. *Oh, that was good, O'Callaghan, you dolt!*

Snapping her mouth shut so hard her teeth clacked, she unlocked the car door and scrambled in faster than she'd ever thought possible.

Twisting the key in the ignition, she threw the car into reverse.

And then she did another stupid thing: She glanced at it again. She couldn't help it. It simply commanded attention.

It was stalking toward her, its expression one of pure astonishment.

For a brief moment she gaped blankly back. Was a fairy *capable* of being astonished? According to O'Callaghan sources, they experienced no emotion. And how could they? They had no hearts, no souls. Only a fool would think some kind of higher conscience lurked behind those quixotic eyes. Gabby was no fool.

It was almost to the curb. Heading straight for her.

With a startled jerk she came to her senses, slammed the car into drive, and jammed the gas pedal to the floor.

———

Darroc, Elder of the Tuatha Dé Danaan's High Council, stood atop the Hill of Tara on the Plain of Meath. A cool night breeze tangled long copper hair shot with gold around a face that was exotically beautiful but for the scar marring his chiseled visage. It was a scar he might easily have concealed with glamour, but chose not to. He wore it to remember, he wore it so certain others would not forget.

Ireland, once ours, he thought bitterly, staring out at the lush, verdant land.

And Tara—long ago called *Teamir* and before that christened *Cathair Crofhind* by the Tuatha Dé themselves—once testament to the might and glory of his race, was now a tourist stop overrun by humans accompanied by guides who told stories of his people that were abjectly laughable.

The Tuatha Dé had arrived on this world long before human myths purported they had. But what could one expect from puny little creatures whose lives both began and sputtered to an end in the merest blink of a Tuatha Dé's eye?

When first we found this world, we had so much hope. Indeed, the name they'd chosen for Tara—*Cathair Crofhind*—meant " 'twas not amiss"; their choice of this world to be their new home.

But it had been amiss, egregiously amiss. Man and Tuatha Dé had proved incompatible, incapable of sharing this fertile world that bore so many similarities to their own, and his race, once majestic and proud, now hid in places humans had not yet discovered. Having only recently learned to harness the power of the atom, humans would not present a serious threat to the Tuatha Dé for some time.

Yet time passed swiftly for his kind, and then would his people be forced to flee again?

Darroc refused to live to see such a day.

Banished. The noble Tuatha Dé had been relegated to leftover places, just as they'd been forced out once before, an aeon ago. Outcast then. Cast out now. The only difference was that humans were not yet powerful enough to drive them offworld as they'd been driven from their beloved home.

Yet.

They hadn't been able to take Danu—the other races had been too powerful—but they could take this world and conquer it. Now. Before Man advanced any further.

"Darroc," a voice interrupted his bitter musings. Mael, the queen's consort, appeared beside him. "I tried to slip away from court sooner but—"

"I know how closely she watches you and expected it would be some time," Darroc cut him off, impatient for news. A few days in Faery was months in the human realm where Darroc had been waiting at their appointed meeting place. "Tell me. Did she do it?"

Tall, powerfully developed, with tawny skin and a mane of shimmering bronze, the queen's latest favorite nodded, his iridescent eyes gleaming. "She did. Adam is human. And, Darroc, she stripped his powers. He can no longer even see us."

Darroc smiled. Perfect. He could ask for no more. His nemesis, that eternal thorn in his side, mankind's most persistent advocate, was banished from Faery, and without him, the balance of power at court was skewed in Darroc's favor at long last.

And Adam was helpless, a walking target. Mortal.

"Know you where he is now?" asked Darroc.

Mael shook his head. "Only that he walks the human realm. Shall I go hunting for you?"

"No. You've done enough, Mael," Darroc told him. He had other Hunters in mind to track his quarry. Hunters not quite as loyal to the queen as she liked to believe. "You must return before she discovers you gone. She must suspect nothing."

As the queen's consort disappeared, Darroc also sifted time and place, but to a different realm entirely.

He laughed as he went, knowing that although Adam was wont to champion mortals, the vainglorious prince of the *D'Jai* would hate being human, would despise being trapped in the body of one of those limited little, fragile creatures whose average life span was so horrifically brief.

He was about to find it far briefer than average.

3

Adam was so caught off guard that it didn't occur to him to do a series of short jumps and follow the woman, until it was too late.

By the time he'd tensed to sift, the dilapidated vehicle had sped off, and he had no idea where it had gone. He popped about in various directions for a time, but was unable to pick it up again.

Shaking his head, he returned to the bench and sat down, cursing himself in half a dozen languages.

Finally, someone had *seen* him.

And what had he done? Let her get away. Undermined by his disgusting human anatomy.

It had just been made excruciatingly clear to him that the human male brain and the human male cock couldn't both sustain sufficient amounts of blood to function at the same time. It was one or the other, and the human male apparently didn't get to choose which one.

As a Tuatha Dé, he would have been in complete control of his lust. Desirous yet coolheaded, perhaps even a touch bored (it wasn't as if he could do something he hadn't done before; given a few thousand years, a Tuatha Dé got around to trying everything).

But as a human male, lust was far more intense, and his body was apparently slave to it. A simple hard-on could turn him into a bloody Neanderthal.

How *had* mankind survived this long? For that matter, how had they ever managed to crawl out of their primordial swamps to begin with?

Blowing out an exasperated breath, he rose from the bench and began pacing a stunted space of cobbled courtyard.

There he'd been, lying on his back, staring up at the stars, wondering where in the hell Circenn might have hied himself off to for so long, when suddenly he'd suffered a prickly sensation, as if he were the focus of an intense gaze.

He'd glanced over, half-expecting to see a few of his brethren laughing at him. In fact, he'd hoped to see his brethren. Laughing or not. In the past ninety-seven days he'd searched high and low for one of his race, but hadn't caught so much as a glimpse of a Tuatha Dé. He'd finally concluded that the queen must have forbidden them to spy upon him, for he could find no other explanation for their absence. He knew full well there were those of his race that would savor the sight of his suffering.

He'd seen—not his brethren—but a woman. A human woman, illumed by that which his kind didn't possess, lit from within by the soft golden glow of her immortal soul.

A young, lushly sensual woman at that, with the look of the Irish about her. Long silvery-blond hair twisted up in a clip, loose, shorter strands spiking about a delicate heart-shaped face. Huge eyes uptilted at the outer corners, a pointed chin, a full, lush mouth. A flash of fire in her catlike green-gold gaze, proof of that passionate Gaelic temper that always turned him on. Full round breasts, shapely legs, luscious ass.

He'd gone instantly, painfully, hard as a rock.

And for a few critical moments, his brain hadn't functioned at all. All the rest of him had. Stupendously well, in fact. Just not his brain.

Cursed by the *féth fiada,* he'd been celibate for three long, hellish months now. And his own hand didn't count.

Lying there, imagining all the things he would do to her if only he could, he'd completely failed to process that she was not only standing there looking in his general direction, but his first instinct had been right: He *was* the focus of an intense gaze. She was looking directly at him.

Seeing him.

By the time he'd managed to find his feet, to even remember that he had feet, she'd been in her car.

She'd escaped him.

But not for long, he thought, eyes narrowing. He would find her.

She'd seen him. He had no idea how or why she'd been able to, but frankly he didn't much care. She had, and now she was going to be his ticket back to Paradise.

And, he thought, lips curving in a wicked, erotic grin, he was willing to bet she'd be able to *feel* him too.

Logic dictated that if she was immune to one aspect of the *féth fiada*, she would be immune to them all.

For the first time since the queen had made him human, he threw back his head and laughed. The rich, dark sound rolled—despite the human mouth shaping it—not entirely human, echoing in the empty street.

He turned and eyed the building behind him speculatively. He knew a great deal about humans from having walked among them for so many millennia, and he'd learned even more about them in the past few months. They were creatures of habit; like plodding little Highland sheep, they dutifully trod the same hoof-beaten paths, returning to the same pastures day after day.

Undoubtedly, there was a reason she'd come to this building this evening.

And undoubtedly, there was something in that building that would lead him to her.

The luscious little Irish was going to be his savior.

She would help him find Circenn and communicate his plight. Circenn would sift dimensions and return him to the Fae Isle of Morar where the queen held her court. And Adam would persuade her that enough was enough already.

He knew Aoibheal wouldn't be able to look him in the eyes and deny him. He merely had to get to her, see her, touch her, remind her how much she favored him and why.

Ah, yes, now that he'd found someone who could see him, he'd be his glorious immortal self again in no time at all.

In the meantime, pending Circenn's return, he now had much with which to entertain himself. He was no longer in quite the same rush to be made immortal again. Not just yet. Not now that he suddenly had the opportunity to experience sex in human form. Fae glamour wasn't nearly as sensitive as the body he currently inhabited, and—sensual to the core—he'd been doubly pissed off at Aoibheal for making him unable to explore its erotic capabilities. She could be such a bitch sometimes.

If a simple hard-on in human form could reduce him to a primitive state, what would burying himself inside a woman do? What would it feel like to come inside her?

There was no doubt in his mind that he would soon find out.

Never had the mortal woman lived and breathed who could say no to a bit of fairy tail.

Gabby didn't take her foot from the accelerator until she'd squealed into the shadowy alley behind her house at 735 Monroe Street. Then she slammed on the brakes so hard she nearly gave herself whiplash.

She'd run every red light between Cincinnati and Newport, half-hoping a cop would pull her over (despite the warrant out for her arrest for unpaid parking tickets, as *if* she could afford to pay them once they'd doubled, with amnesty-day still four months away, and really, if the city would put sufficient parking downtown, a person wouldn't be forced to *invent* parking spaces). Throw her in jail. Lock her away where maybe the thing wouldn't be able to find her.

Most days she loved living in Kentucky, in her quaint historic neighborhood of old Victorians and Italianates, wrought-iron fences, climbing bougainvillaea and magnolia trees, a mere mile across the river from Ohio. It was convenient to work, to school, to the bars, to everything that mattered. But tonight it was much too close for comfort. Then again, Siberia would have felt too close for comfort at the moment.

Parking as close to her house as possible, she snatched up her purse, leapt from the car, raced up the steps, unlocked the back door with shaking hands, slammed it shut behind her, locked it, slid the dead bolt, then collapsed in a limp little heap on the floor.

She stared unseeingly around the dark kitchen, ears straining, listening intently for any hint that it had somehow managed to follow her. How she wished she had a garage! Her car was just sitting out there like a big dilapidated powder-blue X: *Here hides Gabby O'Callaghan. A sitting duck. Quack, quack.*

"Oh, God, what have I done?" she whispered, horrified.

Twenty-four years of hiding, of maintaining a flawless façade, undone in a single night.

Gram would be so disappointed.

She was so disappointed. She'd stood there gaping— no, ogling the thing. And she'd justified it by feeding herself the flimsy fib that she was only staring so she could accurately identify it in the O'Callaghan *Books of the Fae,* or describe it if it wasn't already in there.

As if.

Do you find them attractive? Moira O'Callaghan had asked a fourteen-year-old Gabrielle over orange-ginger tea in the kitchen late one night, nearly ten years ago.

Gabby had blushed furiously, not wanting to betray the depth of her hopeless infatuation. While her high school friends dreamed of actors and rock stars and seniors with cars, she dreamed of a fairy prince that would come swooping into her life and carry her off to some exotic, beautiful land. One that would somehow transcend the innate cold-bloodedness of its kind, all for love of *her*.

Do you? Gram pressed sternly.

Ashamed, Gabby had nodded.

That's what makes them so dangerous, Gabrielle. The Fae are no better than the Hunters they send after us. They are inhumanly seductive. "Inhuman" is the word you must remember. No souls. No hearts. Do not romanticize them.

She'd been guilty of it then. She'd not thought herself guilty of it still. With the passing of her teen years, she thought she'd laid many things to rest, including her foolish infatuation with a fantasy fairy prince.

Not.

With a groan of abject misery, she forced herself up from the floor. Cowering in a limp little heap wasn't going to accomplish anything.

If you ever betray yourself, Gram had told her too many times to count, *if one of them ever realizes you can see them, you must leave immediately. Don't dare waste time packing, just get in the car and go as fast and as far as you can. I'm leaving you money in a special account to be used only for that purpose. It should be more than enough to see you to safety.*

Gabby clutched the edge of the kitchen counter and closed her eyes.

She didn't want to leave, damn it. This was her home, the home Gram had raised her in. Every corner was filled with precious memories. Every inch of the century-old, rambling Victorian was dear to her, from the slate roof that was always springing a new leak, to the spacious, high-ceilinged rooms, to the archaic hot-water heating system that knocked and rattled, but steamed so cozily in the winter. And so what if she couldn't afford to heat most of the house and had to wear layers of clothing unless she was within a few feet of a radiator? So what if it still didn't have central air and the summers were swelteringly hot?

On occasion she'd been awfully tempted to dip into her escape-the-fairy fund, but she'd resisted. Things would change once she graduated and got a real job. Her finances wouldn't always be so precarious. Even an entry-level position with a law firm would enable her to start paying off her pile of student loans and begin much-needed renovations.

She spent most of her time in the octagonal turret anyway, either in the library on the first floor or in the upstairs bedroom she'd redesigned for herself when Gram had died. With all the windows open on a summer night and the ceiling fan softly whirring, she could bear the heat. Besides, she loved lying in bed looking out over the sprawling lush gardens (despite the rickety wrought-iron fencing that desperately needed to be replaced). The mortgage had been paid off years ago. She'd planned never to leave, had hoped to one day fill up the too-silent rooms with children of her own.

And now, just because one dratted fairy—

Wait a minute, she thought, her eyes flying open, *it didn't have fairy eyes, remember?* In her panic, she'd completely forgotten about its strange eyes. They'd been a single color. Black as midnight. Black as sin but for those golden sparks.

Definitely not fairy. The Fae had iridescent eyes that changed quicksilver-fast, spanning all the colors of the rainbow. Shimmery and quixotic. Never black-and-gold.

In fact, she thought, nibbling her lower lip pensively, it had displayed several baffling anomalies: its eyes; its human attire—really, a fairy in jeans and a T-shirt?—usually the Fae wore garments fashioned of fabrics unlike anything she'd ever seen; and its seeming emotion.

Could she be so lucky? Frowning, she replayed the entire encounter in her mind, trying to isolate any other anomalies. Was it possible that the creature she'd seen wasn't a fairy but something else?

Heartened by the possibility, she turned and hurried through the dark house toward the turret library. She needed to consult the O'Callaghan *Books*.

Comprised of nineteen thick, tediously detailed volumes that dated back to the fifth century, the *Books* were dense with fairy lore, sightings, overheard conversations, and speculation. Faithfully preserved by her ancestors, added to over the centuries, the tomes were stuffed to overflowing with fairy fact and legend.

In there somewhere would be information about the creature she'd seen tonight.

Perhaps, she clung determinedly to the optimistic thought as she hastened down the hallway, the thing didn't even signify in the fairy scheme of things. Perhaps it had no greater desire to bother her than she had to bother it.

Perhaps she was worrying for no reason at all.

     And perhaps, she thought dejectedly many hours later, dropping a dusty volume in her lap as if burned, *the moon was made of cheese*.

It *was* a fairy.

And not just any fairy.

It was the worst fairy of all.

And desire? It had it in spades. To bother her? Oh, she'd be lucky if that was all it did. Torture her, play with her for its own amusement, drop her in the midst of some medieval Highland battle and watch her get trampled by snorting warhorses: Those were all possibilities, according to what she'd just read. If it stayed true to form—the thought made her shiver—it would seduce her first. Try to, she amended hastily. (The fact that, according to what she'd read, no mortal woman could resist it was a thought she refused to ponder overlong. That arrogant, vainglorious fairy was *not* getting a piece of Gabby O'Callaghan.)

Rubbing her eyes, she shook her head. *Leave it to me*, she brooded, *to never do anything by halves*. It wasn't enough to merely betray herself to the Fae, she had to go and do it to the most notorious one of all.

A silver-tongued seducer, it was said to be so devilishly charming that mortals didn't even realize they were in danger until it was much too late. It went by Puck, Robin Goodfellow, and Wayland Smith, among countless other names.

A rogue even among his own kind . . .

When she'd begun searching, she'd been afraid it might take her days to wade through the rambling tomes and discern the identity of the creature she'd seen, assuming it was even in there. The earliest volumes were written in Gaelic, which—despite Gram's valiant efforts to teach her the old tongue—Gabby still couldn't speak, and could scarcely muddle her way through reading.

The *Books of the Fae* were a nightmare to sort through, written in myriad and often illegible scripts, with notes crammed into the margins of every page, cross-referencing other notes crammed into other margins on equally difficult-to-decipher pages.

More than once Gabby had complained to her grandmother that someone "really needed to set up an index and organize these damn things." And more than once Gram had smiled, given her a pointed look, and said, "Yes, someone should. What's stopping you?"

Though Gabby would have done nearly anything her beloved grandmother had asked of her, she'd determinedly avoided *that* task.

She'd buried herself instead in modern-day law books that were far less disturbing than ancient tomes that brought to life an exotic world which her continued existence and hope for a normal future depended upon her ability to ignore.

After hours of fruitless searching, Gabby had finally noticed another book, one she couldn't recall having seen before, a slimmer volume tucked back in a corner, as if it had inadvertently gotten pushed behind the other books and forgotten. Curious, she'd reached for it, brushing thick dust from the cover.

Highly intelligent, lethally seductive . . .

Bound in soft black leather, the tome she'd nearly overlooked contained the information she sought. Her ancestors had taken the subject matter so seriously that they'd devoted a separate volume to it.

Unlike the other volumes, which were written in disjointed, sporadic journal fashion and dealt with whatever fairy had recently been sighted, the slim black book addressed only one, and flowed in chronological order, complemented by numerous sketches. Also, unlike the other volumes that were simply labeled by Roman numerals, this one merited its own title: *The Book of the Sin Siriche Du.*

Or, loosely translated from Gaelic—she was capable of that much—the book of the darkest/blackest elf/fairy.

She'd found the creature she'd seen tonight: Adam Black.

The earliest accounts of it were sketchy, descriptions

of its various glamours, warnings about its deviltry, cautions about its insatiable sexuality and penchant for mortal women (*"so sates a lass, that she is oft incapable of speech, her wits muddled for a fortnight or more."* Oh, please, Gabby thought, was that the medieval equivalent of screwing her brains out?), but by the approach of the first millennium, the accounts became more detailed.

In the mid–ninth century—near 850 A.D.—the thing had gone on a rampage, meddling with mortals for the seemingly sole purpose of inciting fury and causing battles to break out all over Scotland.

Thousands had died by the time it was done amusing itself.

Numerous sightings had been made of the thing watching, smiling, as blood ran on countless battlefields. For a time it hadn't been just O'Callaghan women who'd seen it; it had made no effort whatsoever to hide itself, and her ancestors had gathered the tales of those myriad sightings, recording them in great detail.

By far the most dangerous and unpredictable of his race . . .

No other fairy had ever dared such blatant, cold-blooded interference with humankind.

The clock on the mantel chimed the hour, jarring her. She rubbed her eyes, startled to realize that the night had sped by and it was already morning. The first rays of sunlight were pressing at the edges of the drapes that, late last night, she'd pulled tightly across the windows. She'd been up for well over twenty-four hours straight; it was no wonder her eyes felt so gritty and tired.

His favored glamour is that of an intensely sexual Highland blacksmith. . . .

Her gaze drifted back to the book in her lap, opened to a sketch of the dark fairy.

Uncanny. It was the very image that had occurred to her when she'd first spotted it. Was it possible, she wondered, that there really was such a thing as genetic memory? Knowledge passed from one generation to the next, imprinted in one's very DNA? It would go a long way toward explaining why the moment she'd laid eyes on it all kinds of alarms had gone off inside her. Why she'd thought instinctively of a blacksmith, as if in the deepest, darkest reaches of her soul she'd instantly recognized her primordial enemy. Enemy to countless O'Callaghan women before her.

The sketch didn't begin to do it justice, though it captured the unmistakable essence of it. Sighted in medieval times and sketched at a place in the Highlands called Dalkeith-Upon-the-Sea (where it had allegedly killed a young Gypsy woman), it was all muscle and arrogant sexuality, clad in a kilt, standing at a forge near a copse of rowan trees, before a magnificent, medieval castle that loomed in the background. Strong hand wielding a smith's hammer, its arm was flexed in midswing. Its hair was flying about its face in a dark tangle that fell to its waist. Its lips were curved in a mocking smile.

She'd seen that smile tonight. And a worse one still. One far more . . . predatory. If possible.

Her gaze fixed on the heavily inked and underscored admonition beneath the sketch:

AVOID CONTACT AT ALL COST

"Oh, Gram," she whispered, a sudden, hot burn of tears stinging her eyes, "you were right."

She had to leave. *Now*.

Twenty-two frenetic minutes later, Gabby had changed into jeans and a tank top and was ready to go, running on pure adrenaline, in lieu of much-needed sleep. She couldn't leave the precious books behind—she didn't know if or when she'd be able to return, and they simply had to be preserved, by God, she *would* have children to pass them down to one day—so she'd packed them.

While she'd been at it, she'd been unable to resist tossing in a few other items she simply couldn't bear to leave: a soft cashmere afghan Gram had completed shortly before she died; a photo album; a much-loved locket; jeans, a few shirts, panties, bras, and shoes.

She'd firmly turned off her tears, a leaky faucet for which she simply couldn't afford a plumbing bill right now. Later, in some other city, in some other house, she would grieve the loss of her childhood home and virtually all her possessions. Later she would try to figure out if she dared resume her own name and finish law school at another college. Later she would take stock of all she'd so foolishly thrown away in one night with a single look. Later she might admit that her mother had been right about her all along: She *was* a fairy-abduction waiting to happen.

Now she stood at the back door with two suitcases and a backpack crammed full.

Though the banks would open soon, she didn't dare waste any more time. She would stop somewhere in the late afternoon, in whatever state she'd managed to get to by that point, liquidate the special account, and find a safe place where she could lose herself and become someone else.

She took one last look around the kitchen she'd learned to bake cookies in, the kitchen in which she'd cried over her first boyfriend (and her latest—the bastard), the cozy room in which she and Gram had shared so many long talks, so many hopes and dreams.

Damn you, Adam Black, she thought bitterly. *Damn you for making me leave.*

The sharp clarity of anger helped blast away some of the fear fogging her mind. Squaring her shoulders, she slung the backpack over her shoulder and picked up her suitcases.

She was smart. She was strong. She was determined. She would outrun it. She *would* have her chance at a normal life: a career, a husband, and babies. So what if it meant changing her name and starting all over? She would succeed.

Chin up, resolve firm, she opened the door.

Powerful body filling the doorway, it stood there, lips curved in a dangerous smile.

"Hello, Gabrielle," Adam Black said.

4

Adam arrived at 735 Monroe Street prepared for the woman to be a bit skittish.

After all, she'd run from him earlier, obviously intimidated by his overwhelming masculinity and epic sexuality. Women often had that reaction to him, especially when he was stripping off his pants. Or kilt, depending on the century.

He was also prepared, however, for her inhibitions to drop swiftly, as did all women's when they got a good, close-up look at him.

After that, many simply launched themselves at him in a full-frontal assault of sexual frenzy. He'd been entertaining himself with just that possibility, his entire body tight with lust, while tracking her down with the information he'd obtained in the room called "Human Resources" at Little & Staller.

But nothing in his vast repertoire of experience had prepared him for Gabrielle O'Callaghan.

The bloodthirsty little hellion didn't react like any woman he'd ever encountered. She took one horrified look at him, drew back her arm, hauled off, and smashed him in the face with some kind of satchel she was holding.

Then slammed the door and locked it.

Leaving him on the doorstep, bleeding. Bleeding, by Danu, blood trickling from his lip!

Well, he'd just gotten confirmation that she was indeed fully immune to the *féth fiada*, or she'd not have been able to bust his lip. It wasn't quite how he'd imagined learning it.

His eyes narrowed, his teeth bared in a snarl.

Where the hell had that come from? He'd *never* been hit by a woman. None had ever raised a hand against him. Women adored him. Couldn't get enough of him. Fact was, they worshiped him. What the bloody hell was her problem?

Damned Irish. One could never predict the tempers of those fiery, moody Gaels. Obdurate as stones, they passed through the centuries untouched by evolution, as hotheaded and barbaric today as they'd been in the Iron Age.

He arched a brow, trying to fathom her reaction. He glanced down at himself. No latent part of the queen's curse had kicked in, mutating him into something hideous while he'd not been paying attention. He was still his usual irresistible self: the sexy, dark-eyed, muscle-bound Highland blacksmith who drove women wild.

After a moment's reflection, he decided that she just

wanted to play rough. Liked her men dominant, aggressive, and dangerous.

He shrugged. Fine. After three hellish months of being cursed, three miserable months of celibacy, he was feeling all that and more.

He could use an outlet.

Gabby was at the front door, her hand closing on the doorknob, when the back door exploded open, spraying slivers of door frame and bits of dead bolt everywhere.

Metal and wood screeched protest as two-hundred-plus pounds of furious fairy blasted through it.

Knowing she had the lead by mere precious seconds, she turned the knob and yanked the door open, only to feel the thud of its palms on either side of her head, smashing it shut again.

Impossible! No way it could move that fast!

But it had, and now she was trapped: hard door in front, harder fairy behind.

For a few frantic moments she ducked and twisted, trying to escape, but it moved with her, seeming to anticipate her every feint and joust, bracing its hands on either side of her, caging her in with its powerful body.

Unable to evade, she went still as a cornered animal. Dozens of things to say collided in her mind, all of them beginning with a pathetic little "please." But she was damned if she was going to beg; it would probably *enjoy* that.

She bit her tongue and kept her mouth firmly shut. If she was going to die, she would die proud. Stiffening stoically, she prepared herself to meet whatever grisly end it had in store for her.

But an end, she realized swiftly, wasn't what it had in mind at all.

Grazing its jaw against her hair, it growled low in its throat, and there was no mistaking the hungry, sensual edge to the sound.

Oh, God, she thought wildly, *just like the* Books *said, it's going to try to seduce me before it kills me.*

It snared her hands and, though she struggled wildly, she was no match for its immense strength. Stretching her arms above her head, it flattened her palms against the door and molded all that rock-hard fairy body to hers.

Gabby's eyes flew wide.

Her first forbidden, absolutely electrifying fairy-feel. And with it, the answer to a question she'd been trying desperately not to wonder about for years.

No—they were not like mortal men.

At least not any *she'd* ever felt. *Whuh.*

She swallowed. Hard. Despite the clothing between them, her skin positively sizzled where Adam was pressed against her. Heavens, she thought dimly, what would it feel like to rub her naked body up against a fairy? Might she go up in erotic flames?

"Is it rough love you're wanting, then, Irish?"

For a moment Gabby's brain was simply incapable of processing the content of what it had said, overwhelmed by sensation: the steely maleness of it prodding her behind; the spicy, masculine scent of it; the sultry heat it was giving off; the seductive, deep, strangely accented voice. She was melting, knees going buttery-soft . . .

She inhaled a deep fortifying breath and forced herself to focus on the voice: rich Irish cream tumbling over broken glass, cultured, smoky, velvety. Thick with an exotic accent that her floundering mind realized was probably that of an ancient Celt. An accent she'd be willing to bet no living person had heard spoken in thousands of years. Filled with rolling *r*'s and softly dropped *g*'s and peculiarly shaped vowels.

Then the content of its question belatedly penetrated and so offended her that all she managed was "Huh?"

"Name your fancy, woman," it purred, lips braising the edge of her ear, sending shivers rippling up her spine. "Is it bondage? A bit of spanking?" A slow, hard, sensual thrust against her bottom punctuated the last question. "Or just a good, hard fucking?"

Gabby opened and closed her mouth several times, but no sound came out. Then, blessedly, outrage stiffened her spine and freed her tongue. "Ooh! None of the above! My *fancy* is for you to remove that…that… *thing* from my butt!"

"You don't mean that," came the deep, self-assured reply. Accompanied by another sinfully erotic movement of its hips.

Could it *be* more arrogant? "I do too. I'm serious. Get it off me!" Before she did something really, really stupid, like pressed back against it the next time it rubbed.

Aw, come on, Gabby, this is the most turned on you've ever been in your entire life, a devilish inner (suspiciously fourteen-year-old-sounding) voice provoked. *What could it hurt to finally get a little taste of fairy? You've already blown it.*

It's here to kill us! she countered fiercely.

We don't know that. Silence, then a plaintive: *And if it is, do you* really *want to die a virgin?*

Gabby was horrified to realize that for a moment she actually entertained that question as a legitimate avenue of inquiry. Reasonable. Sane even. How sad it would be to die a virgin.

Oh, grow up, she seethed, regaining her senses, *this is not a fairy tale. There's not going to be a Happily-Ever-After here.*

Happy now? came the hopeful query.

She was losing it. Completely.

It tried to turn her then, and she fought a momentary, pointless little battle with it, making herself heavy and stiff in its grasp. She knew it was stupid, that she was just stalling for time, but she'd stall for all the time she could get. Feeling it behind her was bad enough; being forced to look at it while it was touching her would be downright devastating.

It picked her up and rotated her. Literally plucked her from the floor and spun her about, depositing her on her feet again.

She fixed her gaze at eye level: its sternum. Damn the thing for being so big and making her feel so tiny and helpless. At five foot four, she was accustomed to having to look up at people, but the darkest fairy was at least a foot taller than she was, and nearly twice her mass.

It slipped a finger beneath her chin. "Look at me." Again, that dark, strangely accented voice caressed her. There should be a law against men—fairies—having such voices, she thought grimly.

She kept her chin firmly down. She knew how inhumanly erotic it was. She also knew—the little argument she'd just had with herself showcased the point well—that she had a lifetime of dangerous fairy-fascination corked up inside her. And that cork was too highly pressurized.

"I said," it repeated evenly, a hint of impatience edging its tone, "look at me, Gabrielle O'Callaghan."

Gah-bry-yil was how it pronounced her name. What its gorgeous accent did to her last name was simply beyond describing. She'd never known her own name could sound so sexy.

No way was she looking up.

There was a moment of silence, then it said mockingly, "Willy-nilly, peahen. I thought the Irish were tougher than that. What happened to the wench who bashed me a good one and made me bleed?"

Her head whipped back and she stared up at its dark, chiseled face: *Fairies didn't bleed.*

There was blood on its lip. Crimson drops dripping from the corner of that full sensual mouth, making it look even more elemental and dangerous.

Blood? Gabby gaped, trying to comprehend what she was seeing. Was it a fairy or wasn't it? The *Books* had said it was! What in the world was going on?

"You put it there. I'm giving you the chance to get it off before I decide to claim vengeance instead." Its dark, smoldering gaze dropped to her mouth and fixed there. "Your tongue will serve well. Come, a kiss to make amends."

When she scowled and didn't move an inch, it gave her a coolly smug smile. "Oh, come, *ka-lyrra*, taste me. We both know you want to."

Its supreme arrogance (no matter that it was entirely right about her wanting to taste it) pushed her over the edge. She'd been up for twenty-four hours straight and was emotionally exhausted by what had been the most horrid day in her entire life. She was beginning to feel strangely numb, almost beyond caring.

"Go to hell, Adam Black," she hissed.

For a brief moment it looked completely taken aback. Then it tossed its dark head back and laughed. Gabby shivered as the sound coursed over her, rolled through the room, echoing off the high ceilings.

Not human laughter. Definitely not human.

"Ah, Irish, I'm already there." It cupped her jaw in one big hand and forced her head back, locking gazes with her. "Know what that means?"

Gabby shook her head tightly, in as much as she could with her face clamped in its implacable grasp.

"It means that I've got nothing left to lose." Pressing the pad of its thumb against her bottom lip, it forced her mouth open, and began lowering its head toward hers. "But I'll bet you do. I'll bet you've got all kinds of things to lose, don't you, Gabrielle?"

5

Far too many things to lose, **Gabby thought** glumly.

Her virginity. Her world. Her life. And—if it had its wicked way—probably in precisely that order.

At the very last moment, just before its lips claimed hers, its grip on her face relaxed slightly and she did the only thing she could think of: She head-butted it.

Snapped her head back, then forward again, and bashed it square in the face as hard as she could.

So hard, in fact, that it made her woozy and gave her an instant migraine, making her wonder how Jean-Claude Van Damme always managed to coolly continue fighting after such a stunt. Obviously, movies lied. She wished she'd known that before she'd tried playing action hero.

Fortunately, it appeared she'd hurt it more than she'd hurt herself, because she recovered faster.

Fast enough to land a direct hit with her knee to its groin while it was still looking dazed.

The sound it made as it doubled over sent pure panic lancing through her veins. It was a sound of such affront, of such animalistic rage and pain, that she really, *really* didn't want to be around by the time it managed to recover.

As it sank down to the floor, groaning and cupping itself, she dashed past it, making a frantic beeline toward the back door. There was no point in bothering with the front door. She'd never be able to outrun it on foot. She needed her car.

She darted through the living room, skittered around the table in the dining room, and burst into the kitchen.

Looming ahead of her—freedom—an open rectangle of doorway, splashed with morning sun.

She could still hear it cursing, three rooms away, as she reached the threshold. The hell with her luggage, she thought, leaping over it, she'd be lucky to escape with her life and she knew it.

Vaulting through the open doorway, she—

Slammed into Adam Black's rock-hard body all over again.

She screamed when it caught her roughly, lifting her up until her feet dangled helplessly above the ground. The expression on its stunning dark face was icy and terrifying.

It crushed her against its body, tightening its arms around her until the air was whistling as she tried to suck it into her lungs. And she knew, if it tightened its powerful arms just a little bit more, her oxygen would be cut off completely.

It kept her like that for long painful moments, and she went perfectly still, face buried in its neck, its torque pressing into her cheek, willing herself to be soft and limp, to exude a nonthreatening air. She sensed instinctively that she'd pushed it to the brink, and if she evidenced even the slightest degree of resistance, it would respond with even greater force.

Her body wasn't going to be able to withstand greater force.

So it was true, she thought dismally as it held her immobile, the Fae *could* move about in the blink of an eye. One instant it had been lying on the floor three rooms behind her, the next it was in the doorway in front of her. How on earth was she going to escape something that could move like that? What else could it do? Suddenly her mind was stuffed to overflowing with all Gram had ever taught her about the Fae, all the horrifying powers they possessed. The ability to mesmerize humans, control them, bend them to their every whim.

Could she *be* in any deeper shit?

After what seemed an interminably long time, it drew a deep, shuddering breath.

Just as she was drawing a shaky breath to start apologizing, or more accurately, begin begging for a swift and merciful death, it said with silky menace:

"Now it's not just my *lip* you'll be needing to kiss if you're wishing to make amends with me, Irish."

Five minutes later Gabby was securely tied to one of her dining-room chairs with her own clothesline.

Wrists bound behind her to the ladder-back chair, ankles snugly roped to the legs.

Dispiritedly she wondered how it was possible that a person's life could go so thoroughly to hell in a handbasket in so short a time. Only yesterday morning the biggest worry on her mind had been what to wear to her interview. Whether Ms. Temple might think a black suit too severe, a brown one too modest, a pink one too frivolous. High heels too flirty? Low heels too butch? Hair up or down?

God, had she really worried about such things?

Mornings like this certainly put one's life in perspective.

Dragging a chair around to face hers, Adam Black dropped into it, legs spread, elbows on its knees, leaning forward, mere inches from her. A long silky fall of midnight hair spilled over its muscular shoulder, brushing her thigh. The thing clearly had no concept of personal space. It was much too close. Just as she thought that, it raised a hand toward her. She flinched, but it only grazed her cheek with its knuckles, then slowly traced the pad of its thumb over her lower lip.

She tossed her head defiantly, averting her face. A finger beneath her chin forced her to turn back.

"Ah, yes, I like you this way much better." Its dark eyes glittered, sparking gold.

"I don't like *you* any way." Jaw jutting, she tipped her nose skyward. Dignity, she reminded herself. She would not die without it.

"I think I got that, Irish. Best bear in mind you're at my mercy. And I'm not feeling particularly merciful at the moment. Perhaps you should endeavor to *keep* me liking you."

She muttered something she rarely said. A thing Gram would have washed out her mouth with soap for.

Its eyes flared with instant heat. Then it laughed darkly, wiping blood from its lip with the back of its hand. "That's not what you were saying a few minutes ago."

"That's *not* how I meant it and you know it."

Its laughter stopped abruptly and its gaze turned cold. "Ah, but I'm afraid I'm a very literal man, *ka-lyrra*. Don't say that to me again unless you mean it. Because I will take you up on it. And I won't give you the chance to take it back. Just those two words. Say them to me again and I'll be all over you. On the floor. Me and you. Say it. Go ahead."

Gabby gritted her teeth and stared down at the hard-wood floor, counting dust bunnies. *No more than you deserve, Gabby*, Moira O'Callaghan chided in her mind. *I raised you better than that.*

Great, she thought mulishly, now everyone was ganging up on her. Even dead people.

The finger was back beneath her chin, forcing her to meet its shimmery gaze. "Got it?"

" 'Got it,' " she clipped.

"Good." A pause, a measuring look. "So tell me, Gabrielle O'Callaghan, what exactly is it you believe my people do to the *Sidhe*-seers?"

She shrugged nonchalantly—in as much as she was able, tied so securely—not about to admit to anything. A shee-seer, it'd called her, the archaic name for what she was. She'd encountered it in the *Books of the Fae*, but never heard it spoken aloud. "I have no idea what you're talking ab—"

It made an impatient noise and laid a finger to her lips, shushing her. "Irish, don't dissemble with me, I have no patience for it. The *féth fiada* doesn't work on you, and you called me by name. I admit, when first I caught you looking at me, I was perplexed, but there's no other explanation for your behavior. It's why you fought me. You know all about my race, don't you?"

After a long moment Gabby swallowed and nodded tightly. She had well and truly betrayed herself, first by being caught looking at it, then by telling it to "go to hell" by name. It knew. And it was clearly not in the mood for games. "So what now?" she asked stiffly. "Are you going to kill me?"

"I've no intention of killing you, *ka-lyrra*. Though indeed there was a time a *Sidhe*-seer's life was forfeited if caught, my people haven't spilled human blood since The Compact governing our races was negotiated." It swept a fall of hair from her eyes and tucked it behind her ear, its hand lingering, tracing the curve of her cheek. "Nor do I plan to hurt you, unless you hurt me again, at which point all bets are off. As of this moment I'm willing to wipe the slate clean between us, consider your hostility a misunderstanding. Allow that a wee thing like you—believing your life in jeopardy—would feel driven to fight dirty against a man like me. However, if you hurt me again, you'll pay tenfold. Understand?"

Gabby nodded stiffly, wishing it would stop touching her. The mere brush of its hand made her skin tingle, made all the muscles in her lower stomach clench. How dare the embodiment of her worst nightmare come packaged as her hottest fantasy?

It leaned back in the chair, swept its hands through its long dark hair, then laced its fingers together behind its head. Its powerful arms rippled with the movement, cut shoulders bulging beneath the black T-shirt, massive biceps flexing, gold armbands glinting in the morning sun spilling through the tall windows. It took immense effort to keep her gaze firmly fixed on its face, keep it from sweeping down over all that fairy perfection.

The *Books of the Fae* contained dozens of tales about how, in the days of yore, on nights when the moon hung fat and full against a violet dusk and the Wild Hunt ran, young maidens had raced into the forests, hoping to be taken by one of the exotic Fae males. Had gone willingly to their doom.

Gabby O'Callaghan would never be such a fool. Whatever it had in store for her, she would fight it every inch of the way.

"A *Sidhe*-seer," it said, dark gaze scrutinizing her intently. "It never occurred to me to look for one of you, that any of you might still be about. Aoibheal believes the Hunters eliminated the last of you long ago, as did I. How many others of your bloodline have the vision?"

"I'm the last." For the first time in her life she was grateful she had no other family members who shared her curse. There was no one else to protect; only her own survival was at stake.

While it studied her, she pondered its words. *Ah-veel,* it had said: the High Queen of the Seelie, Court of the Light. *Hunters:* The mere word iced her blood. As a child they'd been the bogeyman in her every closet, the monster beneath her every bed. Handpicked by the queen and dispatched to hunt the *Sidhe*-seers, they were ruthless, terrifying creatures that hailed from the Unseelie King's hellish realm of shadow and ice. She might not know all the Fae by name—there were too many, and they donned too many different glamours for that—but Gram had taught her about the most powerful ones at a young age.

"Your mother is no longer alive?"

"She doesn't have the vision." *Stay away from my mom, you bastard.*

"Then how did she protect you?"

Gabby flinched inwardly. *I can't protect her, damn it, Mother! How can I protect her from something I can't see?* Jilly had shouted at Moira O'Callaghan on that dark, snowy night so long ago. Three days later her mother was gone.

"Who taught you how to hide from us?" it pressed. "Not that you did a very good job at it." A smirk curved its sensual lips. "But then, women never have been able to keep their eyes off me."

"Oh, you are *so* arrogant. I just couldn't figure out if you were a fairy or not," Gabby snapped.

A dark eyebrow arched. "And you thought the answer to that question might be found in my pants? That's why you were looking there?" Its dark gaze shimmered with amusement.

"The only reason I looked there," she said, flushing, "was because I couldn't believe you would just so blatantly . . . re-rearrange your—your . . ." She trailed off, then hissed, "What *is* it with men? Women don't do things like that! Move their . . . their personal parts about in public."

"More's the pity. I, for one, would find it quite fascinating." Its gaze dropped to her breasts.

The raw sexual heat in its gaze made her nipples tighten. Made her shiver. How could its mere gaze have as much tactile impact as if it had dragged a velvety tongue across her skin? "It was your eyes that threw me," she gritted. "I thought all fairies had iridescent eyes. I was off-kilter, trying to figure out what you were."

"My eyes," it said lazily, gaze raking slowly back up to her face. "I see. So how is it you learned to hide?"

Gabby blew out a breath. "My grandmother was also a *Sidhe*-seer. She raised me. But she's dead now. I'm the last." She couldn't resist asking, "So why don't you have iridescent eyes? And why do you bleed?"

"Long story, *ka-lyrra*. And one you're about to get very involved in."

At that, another shiver kissed her spine. "You're really not going to kill me?" she said warily. She was exhausted; mentally, physically, and emotionally wrung out. Her head was still pounding from head-butting the fairy, and she was desperate for reassurance, any reassurance. Even if it came from her enemy.

"Oh, no, *ka-lyrra*," it purred silkily. "That would be such a waste. I have far better uses for you than that."

Well, she'd gotten her "reassurance."

Too bad it wasn't even remotely reassuring.

6

Far better uses indeed, **Adam thought**, leaning back in his chair, watching emotions skitter across her delicate features like sunlight rippling across a loch. Anger warred with exhaustion, frustration dueled with fear.

By Danu, she was beautiful. But beauty alone had never been enough to pique his interest. Passion was his magnet. Mortal fire drew his immortal ice.

And what a fiery thing she was. Defiant. Brave. Aggressive. The golden glow of her immortal soul illuming her from within was more vibrant, more intense than most humans, a hot amber aura surrounding her, marking her as a veritable tempest-in-a-teapot of passion. Half his size and still she'd fought him like a wild thing, a hissing spitfire with a lethally hard head and deadly knees; and although he'd just suffered more pain in the past half hour than he had in his entire existence, he was not particularly displeased. Pissed off in a fundamentally male way, but not displeased.

He had his very own *Sidhe*-seer. One who made him burn with lust. Touching female flesh while in a human body was exquisite. He'd been right: Sex in human form was going to be incredible, a new experience, a rare thing in an immortal's existence, and all the sweeter for it. Merely crushing her against the door, feeling her generous, sweet ass cushioning his cock had made his body shake with desire.

Shake. Him. He'd never trembled in his life. Never suffered even the mildest involuntary shudder.

A shameless voyeur, he'd spied on lovers uncounted over the millennia, avidly watching them, studying their bedplay. He'd watched giants of men, hardened warriors with scarred bodies and iced hearts, men made brutal by war and famine and death, tremble like inexperienced boys from the mere touch of a woman.

He'd never understood it. He'd wanted to understand it. He did now.

The press of her hips against his heavy loins had flooded him with raw, primal aggression. Never had he felt such an overwhelming imperative to mate. Never had he had such a vicious, raging hard-on.

And even now, despite his residual pain, he hungered to touch her. Resented the very air that separated their bodies. Needed to feel her again. Shifting in the chair, he moved his knee between hers so it was brushing her inner thigh, not missing how her leg instantly tensed. Ah, much better. For a moment he couldn't drag his gaze from the ripe press of her round breasts against the soft fabric of her shirt. Christ, he couldn't wait to get his mouth on them.

But not by force. He might tempt, lure, and manipulate,

but none could accuse the consummate seducer of resorting to something so banal as force. Not him. It was a point he prided himself on. Those who fell prey to his machinations fell of their own accord. When they chose to take what he offered—and they always did—any black marks on their souls were their own.

A *Sidhe*-seer. He'd never have even thought to go searching for one.

Gabrielle O'Callaghan was a wild card of the finest sort, a possibility Aoibheal hadn't taken into account when she'd levied the *féth fiada* against him, believing them all long dead.

As had he.

The last *Sidhe*-seer he'd encountered had been over two thousand years ago, in the first century A.D., deep in a towering, lush forest in Ireland; a wizened and withered old crone. He'd not bothered to alert the Hunters; she'd been courting Death's kiss anyway. He'd sat and told her tales for a time, answered her many questions. A few years later he'd returned, gathered her fragile, dried-up husk of a body in his arms, and taken her to a secluded beach on the Isle of Morar. She'd died looking out at an ocean so intensely, brilliantly aquamarine that it made humans weep. She'd died with the scent of jasmine and sandalwood in her nostrils, not the stench of her filthy one-room hut. She'd died with a smile on her lips.

But this one—could he have been more blessed by Fate? Young, strong, defiant, beautiful. And why not? Fate was a woman, and women always aided Adam Black. As would this one once he'd allayed her misgivings.

She'd been raised to fear and despise his kind and would require a thorough seduction. Once, the mere fact that he was Fae would have inspired unstinting obedience, but the world had changed much since such times, as had the nature of women. They were stronger, far more independent. No longer were they willing to spend their lives hidden in a forest, forswearing the bearing of progeny lest they pass on the vision and, one day, have to watch the grim, nightmarish Hunters slay their offspring.

Ah, yes, times had changed, as the Tuatha Dé had changed, too, been forced to change when Queen Aoibheal had accepted the terms and many limits of the sacred Compact on behalf of their race. No longer were they permitted to spill human blood, lest The Compact be voided, and any Tuatha Dé who violated it condemned to the grimmest fate for one of their kind: a soulless death. Although, should the queen or any of his race, for that matter, hear hint of the existence of a *Sidhe*-seer, the Hunters would still be instantly dispatched, they would no longer be permitted to slaughter their prey.

However, Gabrielle O'Callaghan didn't know that, as the terms of The Compact were secret from all mortals but the MacKeltar, a Highland clan of ancient bloodline descended from the first Druids, and sole keepers of Man's end of the treaty.

Hence, when he'd appeared at her door, she'd believed she was fighting for her life. Adam shook his head. Even on his worst days in his worst centuries, when he'd been the worst kind of immortal, ungoverned by any Compact, he'd not have killed this one. Played hard and rough with her? Certainly. Killed her? Never.

Ka-lyrra, he'd called her, not realizing just how accurate it was. The *ka-lyrra* was a creature native to his homeworld, Danu. Silky-pelted, exquisitely marked, with huge, phosphorescent eyes, velvety paws, and a striped, tufted tail, its delicate beauty tempted, but its bite was dangerous, even to a Tuatha Dé; not killing but causing madness of considerable duration. Few were they who could woo it; few were they who dared to try.

Indeed, the appellation suited her. She was certainly maddening; only the second mortal woman he'd ever encountered who hadn't melted into a puddle of accommodating, adoring femininity for him. Even the crone *Sidhe*-seer had been girlishly flirtatious with him. At the end, he'd gifted her a glamour of beauty and taken her last breath with a kiss.

"Well?" she snapped, jarring him from his reverie. "What 'uses'?"

Adam studied her. Anger had won the battle for control of her facial muscles, drawing her lips in a delicate sneer, flaring her nostrils. Still, apprehension shadowed her lovely eyes. He didn't want her fearing him. Fear would interfere with his plans to experience human sex with her and use her as his intermediary to regain his immortality. "I told you I have no intention of harming you, and I meant it. I merely seek your aid with a small problem."

She eyed him suspiciously. "You seek my aid? How could I possibly aid an all-powerful fairy?"

"I'm not all-powerful at the moment." Now she would begin to relax.

"Really? Do tell."

Her eyes narrowed a bit too calculatingly for his taste. Relaxed was one thing, but he had no intention of walking around on constant guard against those treacherous knees. "I may not be all-powerful, Gabrielle," he said softly, "but even diminished, I am far more powerful than you. Indeed, far more powerful than most humans.

Need you a reminder?" He stretched lazily in his chair, fully aware of how his body rippled and flexed.

She growled, actually growled low in her throat at him.

"I didn't think so," he said, lips curving faintly. Small and currently helpless as a kitten, she sported a lion's share of ferocity; her lush, five-foot-four-inch body jam-packed with six feet of temper. "Listen well, *Sidhe*-seer . . ."

Gabby listened well indeed while he talked, eyes narrowing, taking meticulous mental notes.

What he told her fanned the spark of hope in her heart into flame. Not only was he not all-powerful, but he was actually trapped in mortal form.

All that splendidly masculine body is human? cooed a breathy, traitorous voice in her mind.

Oh, shut up. How was it possible that a fourteen-year-old version of herself was still skulking around inside her head?

And not only was he flesh and blood—which explained why he'd bled and didn't have typical fairy eyes—but he'd been cursed by the full triumvirate power of the *féth fiada*, which, he told her, made it impossible for humans to perceive him. Effected illusion and affected memory, weaving chaos like a cloak around him. Except for her—descended from an ancient line of *Sidhe*-seers on whom Fae magic didn't work the way it was supposed to.

Further compounding his problems, he could no longer traverse realms. He was stuck in the human one.

Gabby couldn't believe he was telling her all this. He was revealing, without reservation, that he posed no otherworldly threat to her. That he couldn't carry her off, couldn't summon the Hunters. And he was stripped of his fairy magic to boot!

Though he refused to answer when she asked for what offense the queen had punished him, she didn't press. She didn't really care. What mattered was that, in his current condition, he posed no greater threat than any other human man—albeit an extraordinarily large and strong one.

She was going to survive. She really wasn't going to die today! After all, he couldn't kill her; she was all he had, the only one who could see him. He *needed* her.

That realization went a long way toward calming her nerves. She wasn't dealing with impending death, she was dealing with impending battle, and those were two very different things.

Wait a minute, she thought suddenly, frowning as her mind latched on to an inconsistency: He claimed to be powerless, but was still able to move in the blink of an eye like a fairy. How could that be? She needed to know precisely what she was up against. "I thought you said Aoibheal stripped your powers. Why can you still move like a fairy?"

He shrugged. "It's the only power she left me—the ability to sift short distances."

"Why would she leave you anything at all?" she pressed, wondering if he was telling her the truth.

"I suspect," he replied dryly, "so buses wouldn't run me over while I was trying to adjust to my new form. She wishes me to suffer, not die."

"But she left you nothing else?"

He shook his head and gave her a chiding glance. "Don't think to escape me, Gabrielle. I won't permit it. It would be unwise to think me"—he paused a moment, as if choosing his next words with care, and smiled faintly—"impotent...in any way."

"And why do you want me to talk to this Circenn Brodie person?" she forged on, refusing to acknowledge his thinly veiled threat. *Think him impotent?* With all that testosterone and virility dripping from his pores? Ha. She'd as easily mistake the Sahara Desert for the North Pole.

"Because he has the power to return me to the Fae realm."

"Is he a fairy too?" She stiffened instantly. No more fairies. There was no way she was going to reveal herself to another one, especially not one that possessed all its powers.

"Half-Fae. But he chooses to reside in the mortal world."

Still too dangerous, even if only a half-blood. "And after I act as your intermediary and he takes you back to Faery, then what?"

"Then all will be made right, and I'll be invincible again."

She rolled her eyes. "I meant, what happens to me? While you may be the most important thing to your egotistical little self in your narcissistic little world, guess what—so am I in mine."

His eyes glittered and he laughed. Tossed back his dark head, white teeth flashing, muscles in his corded neck flexing, and she bit back a soft, appreciative moan. His body might be human, but it was dusted with Fae exoticness, from his incredible gold-velvet skin, to those eyes that flashed with shimmering gold sparks no human had, to his flat-out intimidating sexual presence. Potent, larger-than-life Fae essence bottled—and not quite capped—in a mortal body. And a perfect mortal body at that.

Simply deadly. A pure fairy could not have tempted her so. She would have kept telling herself it was a "thing." But now that she knew he was all human male beneath that black T-shirt and those snug, faded jeans, he seemed like an entirely different—*Eew!*

Her spine went rigid as the back of her chair. She snapped up straight so violently that she nearly toppled herself over.

How long had she been thinking of it as "he" and "him" in her mind?

Oh! She wanted to spit, to scrape the foul taste of her own betrayal off her tongue! Had her grandmother taught her nothing? She closed her eyes, shutting it out, painstakingly rebuilding its it-ness in her mind.

After a few moments she opened them again. *It* had not yet answered her. "I said," she repeated, "what about me?"

"Anything you want, *ka-lyrra*," it purred. "You have but to name it." Its gaze raked over her body appreciatively, hungrily, those dark eyes promising the fulfillment of any fantasy she might harbor in her deepest heart. It wet its lower lip with its tongue, caught it with its teeth, then gave her the slowest, sexiest smile she'd ever seen. "Whisper in my ear, Gah-bry-yil, your deepest desires, and I shall make them yours."

Yeah, right, she thought acerbically (stoically refusing to ponder, for even a moment, its offer of unlimited sexual fantasy that was making her stomach feel kind of sick, but not in a sick way at all), it would forget about her in a heartbeat. The moment it was its impervious, all-powerful, immortal self again.

But she'd be willing to bet no *other* fairy would. If it

was, indeed, Aoibheal herself who'd punished it, barring it from the Fae realm, wouldn't she want to know exactly how Adam Black had gotten back to Faery without her royal consent?

And that would lead the formidable queen to Circenn Brodie (assuming this Brodie person didn't just immediately hand Gabby over) and ultimately to Gabby herself. And then the Hunters would come thundering down on nightmarish hooves to steal her away and—if they no longer killed mortals as it claimed—she could look forward instead to a lifetime of servitude to a host of arrogant, cold demigods.

That was *so* not going to happen.

"What if I don't?" she asked stiffly, bracing herself for the worst.

It arched a dark brow. "What if you don't what?"

"What if I don't help you?"

"Why would you not aid me? Such a small thing I ask of you. Merely to speak to someone."

"Oh, please. Betray myself to more of your kind and fling myself on Fae mercy? As if *that's* not an oxymoron. Believe you'd just let a *Sidhe*-seer walk away and live out her life in peace? I'm not that stupid."

It leaned forward, elbows on its knees, all amusement vanishing from its features, leaving its chiseled visage quietly regal, dignified. "I give you my word, Gabrielle O'Callaghan," it said softly. "I will protect you."

"Right. The word of the blackest fairy, the legendary liar, the great deceiver," she mocked. How dare it offer its word like it might actually mean something?

A muscle leapt in its jaw. "That is not all I have been, Gabrielle. I have been, and am, many things."

"Oh, of course, silly me, I left out consummate seducer and ravager of innocence."

Its eyes narrowed. "I have not ravaged yours. Though I smell it on you. And though I could with little effort, as I am twice your size."

Oh! Surely it couldn't smell that she was a virgin, could it? A mere technicality, at that. Flushing, she snapped, "And what guarantee do I have that you won't?"

A dangerous smile sparked an equally dangerous glint in its eyes. "None. In fact, I guarantee you I will. But I'll grant you this pledge: When I do, it will be because you're asking it of me. Standing in front of me. Asking me to fuck you."

Its words slammed into her like a brick wall, almost knocking the breath out of her, as it had meant them to. It had masculine intimidation down to a fine art. She inhaled sharply, preparing to snap back, to deny, to insist it would be a cold day in hell, but it surged up from its chair and stood, towering over her.

"Enough. Do you intend to aid me or not, Gabrielle?"

Gabby swallowed hard, sifting frantically through her meager options. Damn it all, if she helped it, she just *knew* she'd end up taken by the Fae. There was no way they'd let her walk away free. No way. They hadn't spent thousands of years hunting down and destroying the *Sidhe*-seers, only to let one go now. Especially not one young enough to spawn a whole future line of *Sidhe*-seers.

And what if they decided to take her mother too? What if they refused to believe Jilly truly didn't possess the vision she'd bequeathed to her daughter? Happily remarried with three stepchildren, her mom would never forgive her! Not that they had the best relationship as things stood, but she had no desire to make things any worse.

And what if, discovering that *she'd* eluded them—that they'd been wrong about the last of the *Sidhe*-seers being wiped out—the Fae began to hunt them again in earnest. Gabby had no doubt that somewhere in the world there were others like her, hiding, keeping their heads down, trying to live normal lives. There were entries in the *Books of the Fae* that made vague reference to other bloodlines similarly cursed, claiming that once there had been many. Gabby wasn't fool enough to think that only the O'Callaghan women had figured out how to survive. What if her betrayal caused them all to become persecuted anew? If even one other *Sidhe*-seer was ferreted out and captured because of her, she would bear the responsibility for their grim fate.

What a mess she'd made of things!

I give you my word, it had said, *I will protect you*. But Gabby'd not been raised by Walt Disney, she'd been spoon-fed fairy tales of the darkest kind since birth. She was incapable of trusting it. And even if, by some bizarre chance it actually meant what it said, it couldn't defend her against the queen. Aoibheal held the throne above all four Houses of Fae royalty, and wielded the greatest power of all. If Aoibheal wanted her, Aoibheal would get her. Period.

She had no choice but to fight and resist until the bitter end.

Bracing herself for its rage, for whatever awful thing it would do to her once she asserted her refusal, she tipped her head back, and back more, to meet its imperious gaze.

"No. I'm not going to help you." She sucked in a shallow breath and held it anxiously.

It stared down at her an interminable moment, gaze inscrutable, saying nothing, doing nothing.

And she waited, nerves strung like tiny wires being ruthlessly pulled by a puppeteer to near-breaking point.

She braced herself to be hit. She fully expected it to hurt her, to attempt to coerce her with physical violence; perhaps even just short of death, and she prayed she would be strong enough to endure. It *was* a fairy after all. It had no conscience, no soul. She expected it to do whatever it had to do to get its way.

She expected anything but what it did next.

Inclined its head.

Bent to her feet and untied them.

Reached its powerful arms around her, its gold armbands cool against her skin, its silky hair brushing her cheek, its spicy scent enveloping her.

And freed her hands.

As she sat, too confused and afraid to move, it stepped back and rose to its full height, a faint smile playing at its firm, sensual lips.

And vanished.

7

Gabby went to work.

Running on zero sleep and pure nerves, fueled by an icy shower, two Starbucks double-shot espressos, and a need for normalcy, any normalcy.

Maybe her life was falling apart around her ears, but she could pretend it wasn't.

Besides, despite her exhaustion, she knew she'd never be able to sleep. She was too on edge, too afraid of what it was going to do next, for she had no doubt that it would do *something*. Had she remained at home by herself, she would have driven herself crazy, her overactive imagination conjuring an endless array of hideous fates for herself.

Initially, when it had vanished, she'd considered resorting to her first plan: hopping in her car and running while the running was good. But somehow she just knew, deep in the marrow of her bones, that running wasn't going to accomplish anything. She wasn't sure she believed its claim that it had no other Fae powers but the ability to sift place. She certainly wasn't fool enough to think that, considering she was the only one who could see it, it had truly gone away and intended to leave her alone.

No, it would never have left her alone if it hadn't been unequivocally certain of its ability to find her again. Which meant running would be a waste of time and energy best conserved for the battle to come. Besides, she'd reasoned, if she was going to stand and fight, she was better equipped to do it on familiar turf. Here at least, they were in her world, and she knew her way around.

Why hadn't it hurt her? Why hadn't it used its immensely superior strength to bully her, to bend her to its will? It could have so easily. She was stymied by its reaction, or rather, its lack of one. It could have done anything it had wanted to do to her as she'd sat there helplessly tied up, but it hadn't even so much as uttered the slightest villainous threat.

It had vanished. Simply vanished. And it had been smiling. And that made her deeply, deeply uneasy. Like it had something far worse planned for her than mere force.

What could be worse than force?

Like waiting for the other shoe to drop, not knowing when or where it would come.

"O'Callaghan, where in the hell are the Brighton contentions?" her boss, senior partner Jeff Staller, demanded, looming over her tiny desk in her cramped cubicle strewn with files and law books and crumpled wads of legal briefs that just weren't coming together. "That case was supposed to be filed last week. We're never going to get a September hearing date now."

Gabby's head shot up. Startled, she almost knocked over her fourth espresso of the day. Bleary-eyed, she glanced at the clock. It was two-thirty already. "I'll have it for you by four o'clock," she promised.

"You were supposed to have it for me by four o'clock yesterday, but you didn't bother coming back in to work after lunch. Reason for that?"

She kept her eyes trained on the clock, reluctant to meet his gaze, aware she wasn't the most convincing liar. "I . . . uh, got sick. I got really sick. I had sushi for lunch."

"You said you were going to Skyline for chili."

Damn the man for having a mind like a steel trap. Didn't he have anything better to do than remember where she'd said she was going to eat? She *had* muttered something about Skyline when she'd passed him on the way out, not wanting him to know she was interviewing around. Knowing he'd work her ten times as hard for it. Unless the firm one was interning for believed them an eventual hire, they were downright brutal with the workload.

"I changed my mind at the last minute," she said glibly. "I'm sorry I didn't phone in, but I was so sick I could hardly move. You know how food poisoning is." She forced herself to tip her face up and meet his glowering gaze, knowing she looked a fright from lack of sleep and stress, and that the dark circles beneath her eyes would reinforce her lie.

"*I'm* lying and deceitful?" a deep, exotically-accented voice purred behind her. "Guess we have something in common, Irish."

Her head whipped around. So there it was; the other

shoe was dropping. Sprawled insolently on the file cabinet behind her was Adam Black, all preternatural insouciance and grace. Gone were the sexy faded jeans. Now it sported snug black leather pants and a black silk shirt, complemented by gold armbands and torque. New, *very* expensive-looking boots, too, she noticed, briefly distracted into wondering where/how it got its clothes. Probably just stole whatever it wanted, cloaked by the *féth fiada*, she thought disparagingly. Figured. Thief.

Still, it was impossible not to notice that he—*it*—looked Old World elegant and simply to-die-for. *Careful, Gabby, could be prophetic.*

"We have *nothing* in common," she hissed.

"What?" Jeff said blankly. "O'Callaghan, what are you talking about?"

Gabby winced, turning back to her boss. He was frowning, his gaze darting between her and the filing cabinet. She cleared her throat. "You and I, I meant," she blurted hastily. "What I meant was that *you* probably wouldn't have even gotten sick, but my digestive system is really sensitive, it always has been. The least little thing sets it off, especially raw fish that hasn't been properly prepared, and I should have known better than to trust sushi from a street vendor, but I was hungry, and it looked good, and, listen, I'm really sorry, but I swear it'll be on your desk by four." *Breathe now, Gabby.* She breathed and punctuated it with the brightest smile she could muster, which not only felt more like a grimace but came out rather lopsided as well.

Stony-faced, impressed neither by her explanation nor the way she'd managed to mutilate a smile, he growled, "Too late. I'm due in court in ten minutes and won't be back in time to log it. It had better be on my desk when I come in in the morning. And the Desny case. *And* the Elliot contentions. Got it?"

"Yes," Gabby said, gritting her teeth.

As he turned away, she shot a furious look over her shoulder at the fairy on the files. It winked and flashed her a lazy sexy smile.

"And, O'Callaghan . . ."

Gabby's head swung back around.

"While you're at it, let's see what kind of case-precedence you can establish for the Rollins case. On my desk by Monday morning."

Only when he'd disappeared into his office did Gabby let her shoulders droop and her head fall onto her desk with a soft thud.

"Why do you do this, Irish?" came the velvety purr from behind her. "It's a glorious day outside. The sun is shining. The world is a vast adventure begging to be had. Yet you sit in this cramped little box and take orders. Why?"

She didn't even bother raising her head. She was just too tired to be afraid anymore. Fear required energy, and she'd depleted her reserves hours ago. "Because I have to pay the bills. Because not all of us get to be all-powerful. Because this is life."

"This isn't life. This is hell."

Gabby raised her head and opened her mouth to dispute that, then took a good look around. It was Thursday. It would take her the rest of the day to finish up the Brighton arbitration. All of tomorrow to wrap up the Desny and Elliot contentions. And digging up case-precedence for the Rollins trial? Well, she might as well just drag a cot into the office for the weekend. Yes, she thought dismally, life at Little & Staller *was* hell.

"What are you doing here?" she said wearily. "Did

you come to torture me? Bully me into compliance? Just get whatever it is over with, okay? Kill me. Put me out of my misery. Or don't. I have work to do." She puffed her bangs from her eyes with a sigh, refusing to look at it.

"Brutality is the refuge of the dull of mind, *ka-lyrra*. Only a fool conquers when he might instead seduce."

"Great. A fairy that reads Voltaire," she muttered. "Go away."

"A fairy that knew Voltaire," it corrected mildly. "And don't you get it, Gabrielle? I'm a permanent part of your life now. We'll be doing everything together. I'm *never* going away."

The other day upon the stair, I saw a man who wasn't there. He wasn't there again today; how I wish he'd go away!

The nonsensical rhyme looping madly through her brain was one she'd learned from Gram as a small child. She'd never thought that one day she'd be living it. Trapped in it. Forced to coexist with a being no one else could see but her.

But she was. And afraid that already half her coworkers thought she was nuts. Despite her efforts to ignore Adam Black, on too many occasions the fairy had provoked a response from her, and she'd not missed the funny looks other interns had been casting her way.

Midnight. She was in bed fully clothed, blankets snug to her chin, clenched in tight little fists. Afraid to sleep, for fear she'd wake up and find it in bed with her. Or worse, not wake up in time. At least this way she figured it would have to undress her before it could make good on those heated, erotic glances it had been giving

her all day, and surely that would jar her into wakeful-
ness before it got too far.

It had dogged her steps the entire afternoon.
Watched everything she did. (Well, almost everything.
It'd been civil enough to stay out of the rest room when
she'd turned around and bared her teeth at it before
slamming the door in its face.) It had taunted, provoked,
brushed its big, hard body against hers at every opportunity, and in general lounged about looking like the epi-
cally horny fairy it was reputed to be, dark and sinfully,
shiver-inducingly sexual. She'd stayed at the office long
after everyone else went home, until nine o'clock, trying
to get a handle on her caseload, so tired and distracted
that everything was taking her ten times as long as it
should have.

And she might have stayed later had Adam Black not
vanished, only to reappear with a sumptuous dinner pilfered from Jean-Robert at Pigall's, of all places. Of
course it had exquisite taste in food. And why not, when
it could steal everything it wanted? She'd like to wear the
féth fiada herself, long enough for a few hours of mad-
cap penalty-free shoplifting at Saks Fifth Avenue, maybe
a mosey up to Tiffany's.

In silence, the tall, muscular, leather-clad Fae had
spread a stolen linen on her desk, arranged her meal of
roasted salmon braised with a heavenly-smelling sauce,
a decadent cheesy-potato dish, a side of roasted vegeta-
bles, crusty bread with honey-butter, and no less than
three desserts. It had produced, with a flourish, a single,
velvety Stargazer in a tall, shimmering vase and poured
wine into a delicate lead-crystal goblet.

"Eat, Gabrielle," it had said softly, moving to stand
behind her, briefly resting its hands on her shoulders.
Then one big hand had slipped up, cradling her skull,

while the other had begun gently massaging the nape of her neck. For a treacherous moment, she'd nearly melted into the magic of those hands.

Plastering a fierce scowl on her lips, she'd tipped back her head to verbally lambaste it, to tell it precisely where it could stuff its stolen goods, but it had vanished again. She hadn't seen it since.

She knew now what it planned to do to her, and it was far crueler than force. It was going to be in her life every day, driving her crazy, provoking her, exhausting her. It was going to be, not cruel and brutal, but gentle and teasing and seductive, almost as if it somehow *knew* of her secret obsession with the Fae. And when she was in a weakened state, it would ply its seduction on her, hoping to subvert her to its aim.

No, it wouldn't use force; she should have seen that coming. Hadn't the *Book of the Sin Siriche Du* made it clear that the thing lived to seduce and manipulate? She supposed brute force was a thing an immortal, all-powerful fairy wearied of in a mere few centuries. She could just hear it saying, *Too easy, where's the fun in that?*

Force she could deal with: It would make her fight, rage, perhaps even die resisting it. Force would fuel her hatred of it and make her more stubborn.

But seduction from that sexy dark fairy?

She was in a world of trouble, and she knew it.

Sad thing was, it hadn't even had to look very far for a weakness to exploit. She liked nice things. She was rarely able to have them, what with her meager income barely covering her most essential living expenses and tuition. She was just as much a sucker for good food, pretty flowers, and expensive wine as any other girl. Though she'd berated herself the entire time, she'd nonetheless eaten the fabulous meal after Adam Black had left, knowing she'd never be able to afford Jean-Robert at Pigall's on her own. After she'd finished the last succulent bite of chocolate-macadamia truffle tart smothered in whipped cream, she'd been so disgusted with herself that she'd given up and packed it in for the night.

And she had a dreadful suspicion that it was only getting warmed up.

The world is a vast adventure begging to be had, it had said as she'd sat in her gray cubicle surrounded by oodles of other gray cubicles in a gray office building, pushing paper, or rather, being pushed by paper that daily thieved more of her life; she rarely saw the sun anymore because it had yet to rise when she went in to work and had often set by the time she got home.

A *vast adventure* . . . Had she ever felt that way, excited by all the possibilities life might hold?

No. She'd always felt compelled, driven to be responsible. To get the best grades. To have a respectable career. To excel at said career. To be kind to small children and old people and animals. To do everything right. *You don't need to prove anything, Gabby*, Gram had chided her years ago. *You're perfect just the way you are.*

Right. That was why her mom had left. Because she was so perfect. If she'd been any more perfect, Gram might have left too.

With a grunt of exasperation, Gabby punched her pillow and rolled over. Her sweats got twisted, the underwire of her bra dug into her skin, and her shirt rucked up. One sock was annoyingly half-on and half-off, a disgustingly doopy feeling. She never slept in clothes and, despite the open windows and the rhythmic paddling of the ceiling fan, it was hot in her turret bedroom. Sweat was trickling down between her breasts and her hair was clinging damply to her neck.

"I'm going to *kill* you, Adam Black," she muttered tiredly, closing her eyes.

Then opened them again, wide, electrified by the thought.

It was in mortal form.

Holy cow.

It *could* be killed.

And wouldn't that just solve all her problems?

"I only want four of you," said Darroc, barely concealing his distaste. He didn't know why he even bothered to hide it; the Unseelie Hunters were far too barbaric, too brutish, to care.

"A score of us will find him more swiftly, Darroc," said Bastion. The oldest and most powerful of the Hunters, he shifted his leathery wings, glancing hungrily around at the lush, rolling fields.

Darroc watched Bastion's nostrils flaring at the scent of the human realm. He'd chosen to release the Hunter from his icy prison—that grim, hellish Fae realm to which the Unseelie had been condemned—and bring him to the Hill of Tara to remind him of all the Unseelie had lost. Also to ensure that the Unseelie King, who at times supported Aoibheal and at other times didn't (and none could ever predict when, not even her) did not overhear. Though the King of Darkness rarely emerged from his dark fortress in the bleakest of reaches within his realm of shadow and ice, Darroc had no desire to draw the notice of the formidable . . . creature.

"Haste is not the issue, stealth is. A score of you in the human realm is too risky, and our plans might never come to fruition. Seek you to roam the earth freely again, Hunter, as you did before The Compact?"

"You know I do," growled Bastion.

"Do as I say and it will come to pass. Disobey me and it will never happen."

"The Hunters obey no one." Dark wings rustled angrily.

"We *all* obey, Bastion, and have since The Compact was sealed," said Darroc, striving for patience. The Unseelie tried his patience at the best of times, and these were not. They were dangerous times, and he didn't need the danger compounded by rogue Hunters who refused to obey his commands. "A thing I'm trying to change. Will you follow my orders, or am I to assume you are content in your realm? Trapped. Stabled like lowly beasts."

Lips drawn back in a scowl, Bastion nodded once, tightly. "Very well. Four of us, no more. Have you any idea where he is?"

"Not yet. Aoibheal has forbidden his name to even be spoken at court, hence my spies have been able to tell me nothing. Go first to Scotland, the Highlands. He once sired a son there." Unfortunately, Darroc knew little more than that. He had no idea if the child had even survived to maturity. Those Tuatha Dé Adam might count as friends had never been friends of Darroc's, and Aoibheal kept her own counsel where the prince she'd been so wont to indulge was concerned. If not for Mael, he'd have known nothing at all of Adam's fate. He—a bloody Elder of her High Council—kept in the dark. Still, a number of his race hadn't been seen for several mortal months, coinciding with a time shortly after Adam's banishment to the human realm. He had no doubt he would soon find one of his brethren who knew exactly where Adam was, if the Hunters didn't find him sooner.

"And when we find him?"

Darroc smiled. He could sense the Hunter's restlessness, his hunger for a return to old times and old ways. It mirrored his own. He felt every bit as caged on the Fae Isle of Morar as did the Hunters in their prison-realm. "You may kill him, *but*"—he placed a forceful hand on Bastion's arm—"you must make it appear an accident. As if he died of mortal causes. Removing Adam Black is only the first step in my plan, and the queen's suspicions must not yet be aroused. That means no hint of anything remotely Fae anywhere near his body. Human wounds only. Do you understand?"

"Yes."

"Can you make the other three understand and obey you?"

"I will choose well." Bastion shifted impatiently.

"Then, name your three, and I will bring them here," said Darroc.

Bastion's flame-colored eyes flashed as he called forth his Hunters.

8

Gabby awoke just before dawn. For one blissful moment her body was awake, but her mind was still muzzily cocooned by dreams, and she thought it was a day just like any other. Normal, peaceful, filled with trivial issues and manageable concerns.

Then, *wham-bam!* memories battered her: She'd blown the job interview, betrayed herself to a fairy, had a week's worth of work to do today, and her life was a living hell.

Groaning, she rolled over, trying desperately to fall back asleep so she wouldn't have to face it all yet.

No such luck.

Adam Black was in the shower.

She could hear him, er—*it*—splashing around in there.

A mere dozen paces down the hall from her bedroom.

A tall, dark, sexy, and *very* naked fairy. Right here in her house. In her shower. Using her soap and towels.

And it was singing. Sexy voice, too, with that strange, husky Celtic accent. Nothing less than an old Sophie B. Hawkins song: *Damn, I wish I was your lover, I'd rock you 'til the daylight comes . . .*

I just bet you would, a teenage voice sighed dreamily inside her mind.

"I need a gun," Gabby whispered.

"I need a gun," Gabby told Jay as she stepped into her cubicle.

Placing her cup of coffee on her desk, she tucked her purse in a drawer, dropped into the chair, smoothed her skirt over her hips, then spun about, facing the aisle. "Where does a person buy a gun, Jay?"

Jay Landry, co-intern and inhabitant of the cube catty-corner to hers, slowly spun his chair around and glanced at her searchingly. "Gabby, are you feeling all right? Jeff said you were sick. Are you sure you're better? You've been acting funny."

"I'm fine," she said, legs crossed, one foot briskly tapping air. "I just wondered where a person might buy a gun."

"What do you want it for?" he hedged.

"I don't feel safe living where I live," she lied baldly. It wasn't as if she could possibly get caught and tried for what she was planning to do, she reassured herself. In order to establish murder, one had to have not only a weapon but a body. And since nobody but her could actually *see* the body-to-be, *voilà*—no crime. Besides, it was self-defense, through and through.

"Take a karate course."

She rolled her eyes. "And what do I do for the next however-many-years it takes before I manage to become remotely proficient at that?"

He shrugged. "Make your boyfriend move in."

"I don't *have* a boyfriend anymore," she said peevishly.

He didn't look at all surprised. "Probably because you work so much, Gabby. I bet he got sick of you being married to your job. I would. You know"—he glanced around and cautiously lowered his voice—"Jeff wouldn't push you around so much if he didn't know you'd take it. He knows you'll spend the whole weekend researching the Rollins case. He knows you'll bust butt trying to prove yourself. And what's *he* planning to do this weekend, you ask? I'll tell you. I overheard him making plans this morning to meet some buddies and spend the weekend golfing at Hilton Head. He'll be out catching some rays, drinking some beer. While you sit here in your—"

"All right, already," Gabby bristled, temper spiking. But first things first: one dastardly fairy out of the way, *then* she'd deal with Jeff Staller and his sneaky little golfing plans. "This is not about me, or my ex-boyfriend, or our boss. This is only about where I can get a gun."

"You're scaring me. And I'm not telling you." Jay turned back around, nose to his computer screen.

"Oh, for heaven's sake, I'll just look in the phone book if you won't help me."

"Fine. Then I can't be implicated as any sort of accomplice."

Law students could be *such* sticks-in-the-mud about

potential liability issues, Gabby thought, sniffing, as she turned back around to her desk.

And gritted her teeth. Adam Black was perched on the low, half-wall of her cubicle, clad in leather pants again—these a deep charcoal and positively buttery-soft-looking, and her gaze got stuck on them for a moment—white T-shirt stretched across his massive chest, and yet another pair of expensive-looking slate-gray suede boots. He was holding the Yellow Pages in one big hand. His black hair spilled in a shimmering fall of silk to his waist, with a plait swinging at each temple. Merely looking at him made her mouth go dry, her palms sweaty. Made every hormone in her body leap to quivering, delighted attention.

"Is it to be war between us, then, *ka-lyrra*?" he said softly.

Snatching the phone book from his hand, she hissed, "It already is. It has been since the moment you invaded my life."

"What?" Jay said behind her.

"Nothing," she tossed over her shoulder.

"It doesn't have to be, Irish. Things could be good between us." Hand still outstretched, he captured a silky fall of her hair, sliding it between his fingers. His eyes narrowed, darkening with desire. "I like your hair down. You should wear it this way more often. Masses of silky stuff for a man to bury his hands in." He made a soft purring noise deep in his throat that was so erotic it made her nipples tighten. Dropping from his perch atop the half-wall, he sat back on the edge of her desk, facing her, legs splayed on either side of her chair. It put her at eye level with his groin, with a heavy swollen leather-clad bulge that simply could not be missed.

Jerking her gaze to his face, she hissed, "You're not a man, you're a *thing*."

Oh, *who* was she trying to convince?

It just wasn't humanly possible for a woman to look at Adam Black and call him an "it." It was wearing her out, trying to. Diverting her attention from larger issues, like figuring out how to get rid of him. *Give it up, O'Callaghan*, she told herself, exasperated. *It's hardly worth the effort, considering how consistently you're failing. Devote the effort to better causes. Causes you might succeed at.*

"And it's only down," she continued frostily, not about to miss an opportunity to air her backed-up grievances; it had been *such* a sucky morning, "because you were hogging the upstairs bathroom, and I couldn't get my hair dryer or any of my clips. I couldn't even get my toothbrush. And you ran me out of hot water." She'd showered downstairs (hastily and with the door locked—as if that were much of a barrier against a being that could "sift place"—still, it had given her an illusion of security, and Gabby was willing to settle for illusion, being that her reality was so depressing) in water that had raised chill bumps all over her skin. Then she'd tugged on panty hose and a suit, reluctantly skipped breakfast, and dashed out, determined to avoid him for as long as possible.

"Gabby?" Jay's voice, sounding genuinely worried.

Without looking back, Gabby snapped, "I'm on the phone, Jay; I have my headset on."

"Oh. Sorry." Relief evident in his voice.

"Truly, Irish, I vow you lie more than—and nearly as smoothly as—I. And plotting murder? It gives me pause, makes me wonder just what kind of nefarious human I've gotten myself mixed up with."

"Oooh, how dare you act like *I'm* the—"

But she didn't get to unload even the teeniest piece of her mind, for the infernal fairy had vanished again.

Bristling, she tossed the Yellow Pages aside (not much point in buying a gun now that he was forewarned; besides, she doubted she had the stomach to point a gun at something that looked so human and pull the trigger, not to mention having to dispose of the body. Though no one else could see it, she could hardly leave its body lying about in her house or office—*eew*) and pulled out the Desny case. She might as well get as much work done as possible, because she knew Adam Black would be back.

Must be nice, she seethed, to just be able to "pop out" whenever you didn't feel like continuing a conversation. She knew a lot of men who'd give their right arms for *that* unique talent.

Flipping on her computer, she mentally filed murder away as a last-resort option. If things got really bad, she'd force herself to find the stomach to do what she had to do. (That she didn't already consider things "really bad" should have set off more than a few alarms, but her mind had moved on to other concerns.)

Opening the file, she prepared to refresh herself with the case. And froze, blinking down at fully completed contentions. Had she finished them last night and just been so tired she'd forgotten?

No way. She wasn't that good when she was tired. She peered. It wasn't even her handwriting. She had terrible penmanship, and this was beautiful script, striking, bold, flowing.

Arrogant, actually, if penmanship could be called that. Nothing indecisive about this slanted, self-assured script. Frowning, she began to read.

A few minutes later, she was still reading, muttering "I don't *freaking* believe it" beneath her breath.

It figured that when she actually wanted to see him, he left her alone. He stayed away most of the day. Making her wonder what dastardly deeds he was up to. The office was empty again by the time he appeared around seven-thirty, right behind her, so close he was practically on top of her, carrying bags from—oh, God, no—she briefly closed her eyes, *please no*.

The Maisonette. Five-star dining, no less.

But Gabby had prepared herself this time. She'd snacked on candy throughout the entire day (no hardship there), just to make sure she wouldn't be hungry and tempted by anything he might offer.

Still, the Maisonette? Grr. She shook her head brusquely and refused to even look at the bags, refused to wonder what scrumptious stolen delicacies lurked therein.

She moved hastily away from him. When he deposited the bags on her desk, she grabbed a thick, rubber-banded accordion file and threw it at him, hitting him smack in the chest. "How?" she demanded.

"How what, *ka-lyrra*?" Catching the file, he placed it gently on her desk.

"How did you do my work? *When* did you do my work?"

He shrugged, one powerful shoulder rippling. "I don't need as much sleep as you."

"So you're telling me that in a few hours last night you personally wrote the contentions for *seven* of my cases?"

"Nine. Then I realized two of them weren't yours, so I discarded them."

"How do you know enough about what I do to even argue liability?"

"Oh, please." He sounded highly insulted. "I've been alive for thousands of years and watching humans for most of it. I read a few of your other cases. It was easy to pattern them appropriately. Human law is simple: You blame anything but yourselves. I merely accused everyone and everything mentioned in the file but for the person you were representing, and backed it up with whatever evidence I could twist to support my allegations."

Gabby tried not to laugh. She did. Tried hard. But he'd gotten his subtle little dig in with such a perfectly bland expression, and had so thoroughly summed up what she hated about handling personal injury cases, after only a few hours of working on them, that she couldn't help it. A little snort escaped her. And it turned into a laugh. And she might have continued laughing except a slow smile curved his lips and his dark eyes glittered. He stalked toward her, caught her by the waist with his big hands, and stared down at her.

"This is the first time I've seen you laugh, Gabrielle. You're even more beautiful when you laugh. I hadn't thought it possible."

Her laughter died abruptly and she jerked away from him. But it was too late, his hands had already left their fiery imprint on her body, like a heated, erotic brand. "Don't flatter me. Don't be nice to me," she gritted. "And do *not* do any more of my work for me."

"I was merely trying to help. You looked so weary last night."

"As if you care. Stay out of my life."

"I can't do that."

"Because I refuse to sacrifice my whole world just to help you regain yours," she snapped bitterly.

"No," he said evenly, eyes narrowing. "Because I don't like your boss. I don't like the way he looks at you. I don't like the way he treats you. I don't bloody like a bloody frigging thing about the prick. And when I'm myself again, I will rectify the situation."

Gabby went still. Adam Black looked and sounded angry. Genuinely angry. About how she was being treated. His face was dark and thunderous, his eyes snapping with golden sparks.

Oh, that was deadly. That was cruel. Acting like he had feelings. Like he gave a damn. Especially when she really didn't have anybody else in her life that did. Clearly he would do anything in order to seduce her to his aim—even mimic emotion and pretend concern. After all, wasn't that why it was called seduction? Because the victim was lulled into a feeling of false safety and well-being? And how could that be engendered except through the pretense of caring?

No soul. No heart. Ergo, no emotions, she reminded herself.

Snatching up her purse, she flipped off her computer and stomped out of her cubicle.

They'd even been really *good* contentions, she was still brooding irritably, an hour and a half later, as she dumped the laundry basket on her bed and began sorting her clothes into loads. Immersing herself in routine helped her pretend the *sin siriche du* himself wasn't currently downstairs in her kitchen, drinking single-malt scotch straight from the bottle (fifty-year-old Macallan, no less) and typing away on her laptop, surfing the Net.

By the time she'd gotten home, he'd already been there, with the stage lavishly set for his next seduction. Five-star dinner spread out on her dining room table, a vase of long-stemmed roses perfuming the air, drapes drawn and candles lit. Fine crystal sparkled on the table, crystal she *knew* she didn't own. Silverware she'd never seen before, fine china too.

She'd tipped her nose skyward and started to stalk past him toward the stairs. He'd moved into her path, brushing his body against hers. Then caught her by one arm.

He'd turned her to face him and just stared down at her in silence for the longest time before finally releasing her. She'd said nothing, not about to give an inch. Not even when he'd dropped his dark chiseled face forward until his lips had been a mere breath from hers, using his blatant masculinity in an attempt to cow her. Stoically resisting the overpowering temptation to wet her lips in a timeless invitation, she'd stood her ground, levelly meeting that dark gaze, refusing to believe that there might be anything other than cold-blooded calculation in his eyes. And if, for a moment, she'd thought she'd seen a hint of humanity, of male frustration, of genuine desire, of tempered impatience in their goldsparked depths, it had been a trick of the flickering candlelight.

Nothing more.

His legal briefs had been better than anything she'd ever written. Brilliant, charismatically persuasive, incisive. She had no doubt she'd win every arbitration he'd written. She'd been envious reading them, wishing she'd thought of that argument or seen that subtle, keen twist. Two of the cases he'd argued were ones where she *knew* the person she was representing bore negligence in excess of fifty-one percent (they were being filed because they were "friends of friends," and her smarmy boss owed a few people favors—probably in exchange for golf privileges at some fancy club), yet after reading Adam's argument, even *she* would have decided in favor of her guilty client.

He was that good.

I've been alive for thousands of years, he'd said. She shivered. Ancient. Adam Black was ancient. And had probably done everything there was to do, at least once. Why should it surprise her that he could do her job so well? He was a being that could travel through time and space. Maybe he had no soul and no heart, but there had to be a pretty damned formidable intellect behind those dark, shimmering, intensely alive eyes.

She sorted her wash automatically, hands moving, brain whirring away. Whites. Lights. Darks. Darks. Darks. Lights. Darks. Whites—wait!

His *T-shirt*?

He'd actually had the gall to toss his dirty shirt in her laundry basket? Wadding it up in her fist, she turned around to go tell him exactly what he could do with his dirty clothes. Then stopped.

Then started again. Then stopped.

Nibbling her lip, she had a brief and very heated argument with herself.

With an exasperated sigh, she raised his shirt to her nose and inhaled deeply, closing her eyes.

Could a man smell any more like sin?

Hint of jasmine and sandalwood and a spray of night

surf. Scent of darkness and spice and sex. Forbidden things, unholy things, things that prayers were meant to cover in that part about *deliver us from temptation and protect us from all evil*.

He was never getting his T-shirt back.

Much later, after Gabby had gone to bed, Adam ducked his head inside her turret bedroom. She was sleeping soundly. Good. The petite *ka-lyrra* worked too hard. Permitted others to push their responsibilities off on her. He would put an end to that. Life was short enough for a mortal. They shouldn't work so much. Play more. He would teach her to play. Once he was again immortal, she would never work, want for nothing.

All the windows were open and a fragrant night breeze was blowing in, rippling across the thin sheet beneath which she slept. Moonlight spilled across the bed, casting her long hair spun-silver, her slumbering features warm pearl.

Fully clothed, he noticed, with a sardonic smile. Wise woman. If she'd been foolish enough to sleep nude, he'd not have contented himself with the minor mission for which he'd come. The mere thought of her nude beneath that sheet . . . ah, he was sexually obsessed with her. With her full, round breasts, the endless temptation of her soft, womanly ass, her lush carnal lips, her hair, her eyes, her hands. Her fire.

Even her virginity turned him on. Filled him with a primal possessiveness, knowing he would be the first man to push himself inside her, to fill her up, to touch her in all those dark, heated, intimate ways. He would seduce her so thoroughly that she would no longer be able to conceive of herself apart from him; she would be his for the taking, anytime he wanted, anywhere, and in any way he chose to take her, able to deny him nothing.

He knew she'd expected force from him. He'd seen it in her eyes when she was tied to her chair yesterday, so defiantly telling him "no."

How little she understood of what he had planned for her.

Yesterday morning, after she'd gone in to work (which hadn't surprised him; his tenacious *Sidhe*-seer would no more relinquish control of her world than he willingly would of his), he'd thoroughly acquainted himself with her home, learned everything about her he could. He'd examined what kind of books she liked to read, what kind of clothing she wore, what lingerie got the bliss of cupping her breasts and slipping between the curves of her bottom, what soap and scents caressed her silken skin. He'd examined photographs, opened her luggage, and studied what things she'd deemed too precious to leave behind when she'd packed to run. And each discovery had made him want her all the more; she was shiny and bright and ripe with mortal hopes and dreams.

The *Books of the Fae* had been a laugh. Well, except for the volume that so grievously maligned him. But he'd been rectifying that.

The slender tome had made him out to be the foulest of the Fae. It had portrayed him as a consummate liar, a trickster and deceiver, a cold-blooded, arrogant seducer who cared for nothing but his pleasure in the moment.

It was no wonder she'd fought him so fiercely, no wonder she'd so swiftly dismissed his word. The Devil himself hadn't fared worse in literary history.

Still, he could do without words; he would speak to

his *Sidhe*-seer through his actions—select, carefully chosen ones. He'd learned long ago that it was the tiniest of details that seduced, the most delicate of touches that brought the mightiest to their knees.

Christ, he thought, staring down at her, she had to be hot in all those clothes. Her house was overly warm, even on the first floor where he'd been working online. Another thing he would do something about for her.

He'd had no luck finding anything about Circenn's whereabouts in any of those databases humans were so fond of compiling, but he'd not truly expected to. His half-Fae son could be not only anywhere but any*when*. It was entirely possible he'd taken his wife and children back to the Highlands, to his own century and a simpler way of life, where he might stay indefinitely.

But no matter, Circenn would show up eventually.

And the day had been productive in other ways; he'd planted many seeds that were already taking root. Not the least of which was a simple shirt.

She'd done her laundry tonight; he'd heard her.

But there'd been no explosion. No shouting, no insistence that it would be a cold day in hell before she washed his clothes. Not that he'd intended her to. He discarded clothing once he wore it and took new.

Stepping deeper into her room, he silently slid open a dresser drawer. Then another. And another. Until there it was. His T-shirt. Neatly folded in her bottom drawer, hidden beneath a pair of sweats.

A smile curved his lips.

He closed the drawer and walked over to her closet, opened it, and glanced down at her laundry basket. As he'd thought, she'd not washed what she'd been wearing today. A pair of panties disappeared into his pocket.

"Quid pro quo, *ka-lyrra*," he murmured softly. "You get a piece of me; I get a piece of you."

He shut the closet door and stared down at her again. His body was strung tight with lust so intense that the mere wanting of her was a thing to savor. All his senses were inflamed, and he was suddenly feeling things that, if ever he'd once felt, he'd long ago forgotten.

By Danu, he thought, inhaling sharply, he felt *alive*. Vibrantly, acutely, perhaps one might say...passionately alive. The simplest of experiences were suddenly so savory, so rich in nuance and complexity. Merely choosing his clothing each morning at Saks held new fascination for him, as he selected them with an eye toward her reaction, learning what she liked to see on him. What made her eyes widen, her pupils dilate, her lips part just a bit.

Leather. She definitely liked leather.

He knew what he would see on her, once he'd smoothed that bristly spine of hers.

Nothing.

Her nipples hard and wet, glistening from his tongue. Her bare ass cupped in his hands as he raised her to his mouth. That same ass flipped over and raised for—

A low growl built in his throat. Clenching his teeth, he forced himself to step away from her bed. Not yet.

She would soon come to understand that he was not what she thought of him. That there was much more to Adam Black than the bloody, blasphemous, idiotic *Book of the Sin Siriche Du* downstairs alleged. He'd spent several hours today rewriting it, crossing out entire sections, simply ripping out other pages and inserting new ones.

It occurred to him as he slipped from her room that, supposing Circenn never came back, seducing

Gabrielle O'Callaghan might not be a half-bad way to pass a mortal life.

At least until Aoibheal returned for him and made him immortal again.

Before he left, he turned off her alarm clock. He had no intention of letting her go to work tomorrow.

9

"Stay away! Don't touch me!"

Gabby woke hard, in a full panic, scrambling up and back, plastering herself against the headboard of her bed, eyes wild.

Adam stood a few feet away, one dark brow arched, a tray balanced on one hand. "Easy, *ka-lyrra*, I but brought you breakfast. I was about to put it on the edge of your bed and shake you awake."

Gabby pressed a hand to her chest, trying to slow the pounding of her heart. "You scared me! Don't sneak up on me like that. What are you doing in my bedroom? Get out of my bedroom."

"I didn't 'sneak.' I said 'good morning' three times. Louder each time. I practically bellowed it at the last. You sleep like the dead, Irish. Be easy. How many times do I have to tell you that I'm not going to hurt you? If I'd wanted to, I would have done my worst by now." He placed the tray on the edge of the bed and picked up a cup, offering it to her. "Double-shot espresso. I've noticed you like to kick yourself awake in the morning." He smiled lazily. Sexily.

Gabby blinked slowly. Life was so not fair. Her heart had begun to slow but was now speeding back up all over again, for entirely different reasons.

There Adam Black stood, nearly six and a half feet of sleek hard body, wearing nothing but a pair of faded jeans slung low on his hips, gold armbands, and a torque. The jeans lent him the air of a modern man, but the arm cuffs and neckpiece, coupled with his strange dual-colored eyes, reminded her that he was a being whose origins predated Christ. Probably by thousands of years. He probably even predated Newgrange. For that matter, maybe he'd built it.

And, oh, but he took her breath away. His wide shoulders and hard chest were sinfully sculpted, his abs rippled and lean. He had those twin ropes of muscle ripping the sides of a six-pack that led straight down to his groin, disappearing into those low-slung jeans, advertising the fact that he could no doubt move said groin for hours without stopping and in ways that could make a woman whimper in ecstasy.

And all of it was covered with that luscious gold-velvet fairy skin. She curled her hands into little fists, battling the overwhelming impulse to cop that eternally denied fairy-feel.

Knowing that he would let her pet him, that in fact he would strip off those jeans in a heartbeat and stretch that hard body over hers and drive into her, made it all the more difficult. With immense effort, she dragged her gaze up to his face.

But looking at his face was no better. His hair was a

fall of sleep-tangled midnight silk, his eyes were half-awake, sensually hooded. His face was unshaven, dusted with black stubble; he was a beautiful, rough-around-the-edges, early-morning-sexed man.

"Exactly how old *are* you?" she asked grumpily, trying to put him back into the perspective of an inhuman being. He looked about thirty, with tiny faint laugh lines at the corners of his eyes.

He shrugged. "Somewhere between five and six thousand. It's a bit difficult to keep track of when one moves about in time as frequently as I have. Aoibheal is nearly sixty thousand. I am a mere child by my race's standards."

"I see." *Whuh.* Definitely inhuman. Unfortunately, discovering his age didn't seem to have diminished her attraction to him in the least. In fact, it seemed somehow, perversely, to have heightened it.

He waved a hand at the breakfast tray. "A croissant perhaps? No? How about some fruit?" He proffered a bowl of freshly cut strawberries, mangoes, and kiwi. "Aren't you hungry? I wake up starved." He sounded mildly offended by the fact.

Oh, she was hungry, all right. Unfortunately, the only thing in her bedroom that she wanted to eat was him.

Suddenly she was fourteen again. And there he was, her fantasy fairy, in her bedroom, no less, serving her breakfast in bed. Her gaze fixed on his gold torque and she had to know. "*What* are you, anyway?" she demanded irritably.

He cocked his head. "I'm a Tuatha Dé Danaan." Dark brows drew together in a frown. "You know that."

"I meant," she clarified peevishly, "your torque."

"Ah." Those slanted brows relaxed. "I'm the last prince of the *D'Jai* House."

"P-p-p-*prince*?" she sputtered.

"Yes." His eyes narrowed. "Problem with that?"

She didn't trust herself to speak.

"I'm not elitist, if that's what concerns you. I bed commoners all the time." A faint, provocative grin.

"I just bet you do," she muttered. "But not this one."

"Not yet," he agreed, far too mildly for her comfort.

"And I'm not a commoner. We don't have those kinds of class divisions anymore."

"Actually," he agreed with her, "that's true. You're *not* a commoner." He dropped onto the foot of her bed and tucked one leg under the other, sitting cross-legged.

"What do you mean?" she asked warily, watching him carefully. Braced for him to try something. But he made no move toward her, just sat there perfectly at ease on the end of her dainty bed in her frilly, feminine bedroom: a big dark giant of a man, surrounded by lacy pillows and silky embroidered throws, and all the girly-stuff just made him look that much more masculine.

"Drink your coffee and I'll tell you," he bribed.

An awful suspicion occurred to her. "Why do you care if I drink it? Is it drugged or something?"

He rolled his eyes, picked up the cup, took several sips, then handed it back to her. "Of course not, Irish. I merely want your day to start well. I want you to be happy."

"Yeah, right." But the aroma of fresh-ground coffee teased her nostrils, and something deep inside her sighed hugely and capitulated without further argument. She took the cup and sipped. Heavenly. Hot and dark and sweet, just the way she liked it. He'd even gotten the amount of sugar right. When he glanced away for a moment, out the window, she turned the cup to where he'd sipped, and closed her mouth on the rim.

Coffee in bed—when had anyone ever brought her that? Never, that's when. And exactly the way she liked it, with exactly what she usually had for breakfast. A croissant and fruit, so she could justify all the candy she tended to snack on the rest of the day, not to mention her weakness for cheese-smothered french fries. And Skyline coneys. And everything else that went straight to her hips. But so long as she had her healthy meal first thing in the morning each day, she felt good about herself for the rest of it.

"Okay, so how am I not a commoner?" He'd piqued her curiosity. Here was a man, er, fairy, who knew more about history than any living person, and from firsthand experience. What might he be able to tell her about her ancestors?

"You're a *Sidhe*-seer. In days long gone, in ancient Ireland, thousands of years before the birth of your Christ, they were prized among humans and treated as royalty, for they alone could protect the people from the Unseen. The mightiest warriors in all the lands competed in tournaments for the privilege of a *Sidhe*-seer's hand in marriage. Many a man died trying to win such a maiden. She answered to no one, not even human kings, so highly was she regarded. A *Sidhe*-seer lived in the finest of comfort and, in exchange for her protection, was protected and cared for by her people all the days of her life."

Wow, Gabby thought, what a far cry from her life. She—who had such a hard time keeping a boyfriend—would have once been fought over by warriors. She wouldn't have been considered a freak but would have been valued for her curse. Rather than being ridiculed or carted off to a loony bin if someone found out, she would have been respected, born to a family whose fortunes would have been bettered by having her. Born to a mother who would have been proud.

"Even now you continue the tradition," he said softly.

"What do you mean?"

"The *Sidhe*-seers were also *brehons:* lawgivers to their people. Though human law has become a very strange thing indeed, it is what you chose as your life's work. Blood will tell."

Gabby was silent a moment, sipping her coffee and looking at him over the rim of it.

He's getting to you, O'Callaghan, a faint inner voice warned.

No he's not, she retorted silently. *What harm is there in having coffee and talking about history with him?* She hadn't had anybody to talk to about fairy-things since Gram died. Four years was a long time. She hadn't realized how much she missed it.

This is how he's seducing you.

Hardly. He hasn't even tried to kiss me again. She was almost beginning to wonder why not. How long since he'd exploded through her door—two days? Three? Four? Heavens, she was beginning to lose track of time.

But he's doing it all deliberately, to slip past—

Gabby shook her head sharply, terminating the paranoid voice. Her defenses were fine. Ramrod straight and fully erected. She was in control. Caffeine was beginning to hum through her veins, soothing her nicely. It was cozy to sit tucked in bed and talk. "Tell me more about my ancestors," she said, reaching for the croissant.

Gabby stood under the shower feeling de-liciously relaxed. She'd hit it first this morning and planned to use every last drop of hot water herself. She lathered, exfoliated, and shaved, until her skin felt silky smooth and eminently touchable (not that she was planning to let anyone touch it or anything).

It was Saturday, and though she usually worked a full day on Saturdays, she'd decided not to go in. Not because of him; it had nothing to do with Adam Black. She'd just realized she was long overdue to send a message to her boss. It was time she made it clear that she was not his personal slave and was not going to sacrifice her weekends for him.

Hence the Rollins research wasn't going to get done. And if he had a problem with that, he could fire her. She knew he wouldn't. Interns were slave labor, they came cheap. And although she wasn't as brilliantly persuasive as a fairy that was thousands of years old, she still managed to win a sweet eighty-two percent of the arbitrations she filed. No, he wouldn't fire her.

A *brehon*, she thought, lathering shampoo in her hair. Adam had told her much about old Irish law; regaled her with tale after tale about his experiences with, and knowledge of, the ancient Celts. She almost felt as if she'd spent the morning slipped back in another time.

He was, she grudgingly admitted, fascinating. Possessing a dry, often dark sense of humor, he was a veritable font of information about virtually anything and everything.

Perhaps, she mused, eyes narrowing pensively, if she spent more time with him, coaxed him to tell her more about himself, she'd find a weakness she could exploit, a vulnerability she could turn to her advantage.

The more time you spend with him, the more chance you give him to seduce you.

Yeah, well, she really couldn't see any other options.

He'd moved in. The blackest fairy was playing house with her, and she was pretty sure he wouldn't be leaving anytime soon, unless she could find some way to make him leave.

Keep your friends close, Gabby, Gram had always said, *but your enemies closer still.*

"So, what did you do that got you into so much trouble with your queen?" Gabby embarked on her new plan without preamble as she entered the kitchen. He was standing at the sink, eating leftovers from the Maisonette.

Adam swallowed the last bite of cold filet mignon and shrugged. Christ, this having to eat five, six, even seven times a day to keep his body running at peak efficiency was absurdly time-consuming. Still, it was pleasurable, the feeling of hunger, and the sating of it. Taste was every bit as heightened in human form as lust was. In fact, all human sensations were more intense than a Tuatha Dé's. It hardly seemed fair. There were some things about being human that he was going to miss when he was immortal again. "Irrelevant, *ka-lyrra*," he evaded.

Of all the things she might have asked, that was the one thing he didn't want to talk about. Even after all these months, he still wasn't sure why he'd done what he'd done. He'd known Aoibheal would have to punish him. He'd known this would push her too far. He'd known that defying her, questioning her authority in front of her entire court and the High Council, would force her to call him to account in ways more severe than she'd ever done before.

And still he'd done it.

There'd been no reason for him to. Dageus MacKeltar had clearly defied his most sacred trust and deserved to be punished. He'd broken The Compact between their races by using the time-traveling power of Scotland's standing stones for personal reasons—to save his twin brother's life—an action punishable by any means the queen so chose.

And she'd chosen, at the demand of her High Council, to subject him to trial by blood, which meant the Hunters would be sent to kill those closest to him, and if he used even the slightest amount of forbidden magic to save them, the Hunters would carry out a systematic destruction of the Keltar clan from the sixteenth century forward.

Long had the MacKeltar preserved the peace between their races, upholding The Compact and performing the feast rituals on Imbolc, Beltane, Lughnassadh, and Samhain that kept the walls between Man and Fae realms intact. Now they were to be destroyed for breaching the ancient treaty.

And something inside Adam had reared its asinine head and opened his mouth, and the next thing he knew he'd been bargaining for the mortal's life *at any cost*. Irreverently, flippantly, wagering it all.

He'd been spying on the MacKeltar clan for millennia; the queen's edict forbidding any Tuatha Dé to go within one thousand leagues of MacKeltar land in the lush Highlands of Scotland had only tempted him all the more (and as ever, she'd granted him leeway; she'd not liked it, but she'd tolerated it).

He'd watched the petite, brilliant physicist Gwen Cassidy on her journey through time as she'd fallen in love with Drustan MacKeltar. He'd spied upon sensual, eclectic, and not-quite-ethical-when-it-came-to-artifacts Chloe Zanders as she'd lost her heart to Dageus, despite the younger MacKeltar twin being possessed by the evil souls of thirteen dark Druids at the time.

And the thought of watching them all die had filled him with a dark restlessness akin to one he'd not felt since the ninth century.

Name your price, he'd coolly told Aoibheal.

And then, when Dageus MacKeltar had lain dying, she'd named it. And Adam had placed his hands on the mortal's heart and given of his immortal essence to restore him to life. He'd thought that the temporary sapping of his immortal strength and power, which would have left him weak for centuries, was to be his price, but she'd taken it even further and made him human, powerless, and cursed.

"So what makes you so sure she'll just forgive you?" Gabby asked, jarring him from his thoughts.

He shrugged again. "She always does. Besides, she wouldn't be able to stand eternity without me."

She snorted and shook her head. "Oh, I see. I keep forgetting how irresistible you are."

"No you don't," he said easily, flashing her a grin. "I see the way you look at me."

"What I don't understand," she pressed hastily on, cheeks pinkening faintly, "is why you don't just talk to one of the other fairies hanging around. The *féth fiada* doesn't work on them, does it? Or don't they want to help you either?"

For a moment Adam was so astonished that he thought he mustn't have heard her correctly. "What—other—fairies—hanging—around?" he enunciated each word tightly. Surely Aoibheal hadn't taken that from him, too, had she? Made him no longer able to even perceive his own kind? The *féth fiada* alone wouldn't have done that to him. It rendered its wearer invisible, but it didn't render anything else invisible to the wearer.

They're not your own kind anymore, an inner voice reminded. *You're human. They're Tuatha Dé, and humans—except for the* Sidhe-*seers—can't see the Fae.*

Bloody hell, he could be so stupid sometimes! He'd thought the reason he'd not seen any others of his kind was because she'd forbidden them to spy on him. But no, it was because she'd made him human through and through.

They'd been watching him all along, no doubt endlessly amused by his humiliation. "I said, 'what other fairies?' " he gritted.

Gabby blinked at his tone. "All of them. Any of them. There are oodles—" She broke off abruptly. "Oh, God, you didn't know, did you?"

"How many Tuatha Dé are in this city besides me?" he growled.

She took a step back. "Well, really just a few, hardly even half a dozen, maybe not even that many, and actually, come to think of it, I haven't seen any at all in over a week, which makes sense because one of them said a while back that they were all planning to leave—"

His hand shot out and closed on her upper arm. "Don't lie to me, *Sidhe*-seer."

"I refuse," Gabby snapped. "I will not, I repeat—*abso-freaking-lutely-will-not*—talk to one of them for you. Hell will freeze over first. We're not even talking about half-Fae like this Circenn person you wanted me to talk to, these are the real deal, fairies with the power to summon Hunters. Iridescent-eyed, soulless, deadly fairies."

His smile was chilling. She'd just *had* to throw in that "soulless" bit. What was it with women and their hang-up about souls, anyway? Couldn't they find something else to obsess about? Like the phenomenal sex he could give them, the money, the fame, the complete fulfill-ment of their every desire, anything they wanted. But no, it was all souls, souls, souls. "Fine. Refuse. I'll simply walk around talking to you in public places until one of them figures out you can see me. How many did you say are just 'hanging around'? 'Oodles,' was it? On every street corner perhaps? How long do you think it will take for me to smoke you out? A day? Two? A week? The way I see it, you have two choices: agree to help me and se-cure my protection—and I vow that I will do my utmost to keep you safe—or refuse and be revealed to *all* the Fae. And if you choose that, I won't lift a bloody finger to help you, Gabrielle. So choose well."

"You won't do that. You need me! You—"

"I will go find another *Sidhe*-seer. I've no doubt there are a few others still around," he snarled. He knew he was no longer seducing, was fully into the forcing arena, but fury had the same effect on his body as lust; it made him primitive. He would not be mocked by his own kind, spied on and humiliated by his own race. And with her "soulless" jibe still ringing in his ears, he was no longer in the mood to play the charming seducer. She thought he was black? She hadn't even seen pale gray. In fact, she'd seen nothing but lily-white Adam Black so far.

Besides, it was only a matter of time before she was discovered anyway. They'd come to spy on him, to watch him be human and humbled, and he was surprised they hadn't noticed her already. They must be keeping a bit of a distance, perhaps uncertain how long the queen in-tended to sustain his punishment, and wary of being too close, in case he suddenly regained his power. As they should be, he thought viciously. "So?" he demanded. "What will it be, Irish?"

"I need to think," she said tightly.

"You have one hour."

10

Well, that had to be the shortest-lived plan in history, Gabby thought peevishly, as she paced back and forth across her bedroom, periodically glancing at the clock that was devouring her precious minutes tick by greedy tock.

Right—she was going to learn about him, lure him into revealing a weakness. A whopping two questions into her dazzlingly expert interrogation, thrown off-kilter by his comment about the way she looked at him, she'd blurted the first thing that had popped into her mind, only belatedly realizing that he hadn't known. Hadn't had any clue that the city was thick with other fairies. She'd just assumed that he was either too proud to ask them for aid, or they'd already refused to help him. Never had it occurred to her that he couldn't even see them.

She just kept digging herself in deeper.

And he was right. It wouldn't take long, as he'd threatened, for him to smoke her out. Merely being spotted walking down the street with him would give her away to any watching Fae.

She could either willingly help him, hoping he'd truly protect her (and that he could somehow save her from the formidable Aoibheal), or refuse and be abandoned to other Fae, who she knew wouldn't lift so much as a smugly superior finger to help her. At least this way she had the hope of getting a fairy indebted to her, if that counted for anything among fairies.

Better the devil you know than the devil you don't know was another of Gram's favorite adages.

"Barely," she muttered.

Puffing her bangs from her eyes with a frustrated breath, she pivoted and paced to the window. Propping her elbows on the sill, she stared blindly out, eyes narrowed, thinking hard.

He'd been furious. Up until now, every seeming emotion he'd displayed since she'd first encountered him, she'd instantly discounted as mimicry, mere trickery, part of his calculated seduction.

But what she'd just seen had looked all too real. Intense, deeply felt, and genuine.

She'd seen not just anger, but wounded pride, and something else, something deeper that had seemed to flash involuntarily through his eyes when she'd made her comment about "iridescent-eyed, soulless, deadly fairies."

Was it possible, she wondered, bemused by the notion, that since he was in a human body he was actually experiencing human emotion? That all the emotions she'd thought she'd seen had been real not faked?

She had no idea what was possible and not possible

when a fairy was in human form. She'd never stumbled across anything like this in the O'Callaghan *Books*. And—she glanced at the clock again—she highly doubted he'd give her any extra time to do some searching.

She could only pray that he *was* feeling, and feeling enough to make him keep his word to protect her, because, unfortunately, her back was to a wall.

Like it or not—and she didn't—she was going to have to help Adam Black.

"**Okay, I'll do it, but we need to discuss** terms," she said flatly as she walked back into the kitchen.

He'd showered and dressed while she'd been up in her room and was once again leather-clad and sexy as all get-out, long legs outstretched, boots propped on the kitchen table, arms folded behind his head. He no longer looked angry but was once again coolly, almost lazily, at ease.

"A wise decision, *ka-lyrra*." His dark gaze swept her from head to toe, a palpable, erotic caress that reminded her that, no matter how dead-set she was against him, her traitorous body was all for him. He inclined his head regally. "I am pleased you will aid me, and will consider your terms."

She bristled at his princely demeanor but refused to be baited. Her terms were critical. "First, I will only approach a solitary Fae. I'll reveal myself to no more of your kind than I have to."

He shook his head. "You won't find a solitary Fae. Have you seen any alone since they arrived in your city?"

Gabby thought about it for a moment. Now that he

mentioned it, no, she hadn't seen any alone. They were always in groups, or at least pairs. Even the one that had walked between her and Marian Temple, blowing her dream job, had only broken away from a small group that it had rejoined when it moved on.

"Why is that?" Her brows drew together in a frown. There was so much she didn't understand about the Fae.

"Tuatha Dé do not walk the human realm alone. Actually they don't walk alone much anywhere. Only the occasional rogue Fae will do so."

"Like yourself?"

"Yes. Most of my kind have no fondness for solitude. Those who walk alone are not to be trusted."

"Really," she said dryly.

"Except for me," he amended, with a faint, insouciant grin.

"I'll approach a pair, no more. Minimal exposure is my goal."

"Understood."

"And you will guarantee not only my safety from your kind, but the safety of my future children. You must promise me that I can live out the rest of my life in peace, safe from being taken by the Fae, or having anyone I love taken. Can you do that?"

"Yes."

"How?" she snapped.

Another lazy, appreciative glance down, then up, her body. "You'll have to trust me, *ka-lyrra*. All I can give you is my word. And though you doubt me, once given, it's inviolate. It's securing my word that's so difficult. But you have it. As you've had since the day we met."

She supposed that was all she was going to get. Anything she did from this moment forward was going to require a leap of faith in some direction. She sighed gustily. "Fine. But you just better understand that, number one, I know how stupid it is to take the word of the *sin siriche du*, but I don't have any other choice; and number two, if you don't keep it, I'll make your existence a living hell any way I can, and if I get killed somehow, I'll come back as a ghost and haunt you. For *all eternity*. And if you don't think I could, you don't know the first thing about O'Callaghan women. We persist. We never give up." Well, her mom had, she amended darkly, but she wasn't including her mom.

He smiled faintly, bitterly. Her refusal to trust him chafed. He might mislead a bit, rely on disinformation and evasion from time to time, but on those rare occasions he gave his word he stood behind it.

"Come, *ka-lyrra*, you can threaten and malign me while we're sifting place."

When he rose and moved toward her, extending his hand, she backed up hastily.

"I am so not doing that vanishing thing you do." She was firmly in the Dr. McCoy camp when it came to the transporter room on the *Enterprise*. There would be no beaming Gabby O'Callaghan up, down, or anywhere. She liked her feet firmly planted on the ground.

He arched a brow. "Why not?"

"I have no desire to be . . . whatever it is one has to be, to be . . . translated . . . through wherever it is you go," she said. "No thank you. I'll stay right here in my world."

He shrugged. "We'll drive then." He waved his hand toward the back door, gesturing that he would follow.

The playful curve of his lips coupled with his suspiciously swift capitulation should have warned her.

She opened the door, stepped out onto the top step, and froze. He stopped behind her, but just barely, crowding her with his big body. Was that his chin grazing the top of her head, his unshaven jaw against her hair?

She took several slow deep breaths, then, "Okay, what happened to my car?"

"That *is* your car."

"I may not know much lately," she gritted, "but I do know what I drive. I drive a falling-apart Toyota. A disgustingly powdery-blue one. With lots of rust and no antenna. *That* is not my car."

"Correction. You used to drive a falling apart Toyota, B.A."

Had his lips just brushed her hair? She shivered, and though she knew better than to ask, she did it anyway. "Okay, you got me, what's 'B.A.'?"

"Before Adam. After Adam, you drive a BMW. I take care of what is mine. That Toyota wasn't safe."

Figured the arrogant beast would define himself as the dawning of an epoch. "I'm not yours, it was too, and you can't just go around stealing—"

"I didn't. I filled out all the paperwork myself. And there was a ridiculous amount of paperwork. What is it with you humans and paperwork? You have so much time you can afford to squander it? We have all the time in the world, and you won't catch us doing paperwork. You are now in every possible regard the legal owner of that car. And no one will ever be able to prove otherwise. The *féth fiada* has many advantages, Gabrielle."

"I will *not* drive a stolen car," she snapped as he slipped a hand around her from behind, offering her the keys.

"It's not stolen," he repeated patiently, softly, close to her ear. "According to the dealer's records, it was paid for in full. They wouldn't take it back even if you tried to give it to them. And if you refuse to drive it, am I to assume that means you've changed your mind about traveling my way?"

As his other hand began to slip around her waist, his body brushed against hers, and there was no mistaking the thick, hard ridge grazing her jean-clad bottom. Heavens, did that thing never subside? The rest of him might be mortal, but his immortal erection certainly didn't seem to have gotten the memo. Snatching the keys from his hand, she jerked away.

Nibbling her lip, she glared at the spot where only last night her dilapidated little Corolla had sat. In its place was a brand-new BMW. And if she wasn't mistaken, it was one of those high-end roadsters. It was red. And shiny. It had all its trim and everything. And it was a *convertible*.

I take care of what's mine, he'd said. And a purely feminine part of her had felt a shiver that was more delicious than chilling.

Oh, yes, she was going to hell in a handbasket.

But as far as handbaskets went, she thought glumly, it was an awfully nice one.

"Cincinnati," said Mael, appearing abruptly at Darroc's side.

"What? You've found him?" Darroc turned, startled. He'd not expected such swift developments.

"Yes. Apparently he's looking for his half-blood son there."

"You're certain of this?"

"I haven't been to the human city myself, but Callan saw him there only a few days ago. He'd sensed the presence of many Tuatha Dé sifting to that dimension and wondered at it. He confirmed that Adam is there. And that he can't see us at all."

Darroc smiled. The power a Tuatha Dé used when sifting dimensions left a residue other Tuatha Dé could sense. Though imprecise, though it scattered swiftly with the passage of time, the residue, when fresh, could be tracked to a general area.

"Excellent, Mael. You've done well."

Adam Black was going to die. And Darroc was going to watch. He would command the Hunters to take it slow, to strike first only to wound . . .

Her handbasket was, to be precise, a BMW Alpina Roadster V8.

Complete with climate-controlled leather seats, navigation system, Harman Kardon stereo, handless phone, and an engine that simply purred with sleek, state-of-the-art muscle.

Gabby guided the ultimate driving machine into the parking garage beneath Fountain Square, eased into a parking space, and turned it off with a sigh of genuine relief. One of the nice things about her Corolla was that she'd never been afraid she might wreck it; it wouldn't have looked much different if she had. Nor had she ever worried about getting a speeding ticket, because unless she caught a serious back wind, she was lucky to hit sixty in it.

But this thing; oh, this car was almost as dangerous as the fairy who'd stolen it.

Unsnapping her seat belt, she slipped her purse over her shoulder, got out of the car, waited impatiently while he disentangled himself (the roadster wasn't an easy fit for a man of his brawn), then pressed the little button on the keypad to engage the alarm.

When she'd first slid into the plush leather seats of the dreamy car, she'd popped open the glove box and damned if there hadn't been a tidy little registration in there, free of lien, with her name on it.

And the bill of sale: $137,856.02.

No doubt about it, her life had plunged from the realm of the absurd into the downright surreal. She'd just driven a car that cost more than a lot of people's houses did. And already a tiny part of her was busy making the case that, considering she was risking her life, surely she was entitled to some recompense? It was only a car, right? And nobody would ever know. It wasn't as if she were hurting anybody. He'd said so himself: How was she ever going to convince anybody to take it back when it sure looked like she was the legal owner? And there were no outstanding parking tickets on it. No warrant for her arrest. Which begged the interesting question: "What did you do with my car?"

"Drove it into the Ohio River," he said mildly.

"Oh." Well. Nothing she'd not been tempted to do herself a time or two. Looked like she was stuck with the BMW if she wanted to get to work next week. Assuming she lived through the weekend.

"Hurry up," she said, impatient to get on with things. She couldn't shake the ominous feeling that her life had only begun its downward spiral and worse things were yet to come.

As they stepped from the dark garage into the momentarily blinding sunlight and began walking toward the square, Gabby scanned the busy streets, searching for fairies. The sidewalks were teeming with people moving en masse down toward the river in the general direction of the stadium. Must be a baseball game, she decided, briefly torturing herself with the thought of normal, pleasant things like hot dogs and beer and pretzels, family outings, and the sharp crack of ball against a bat.

Once again people were out doing things, socializing and having fun, while she was frantically attempting to rectify the latest fairy debacle.

"Just what am I supposed to say when I find these beings?" she asked irritably.

"Tell them that I'd like an audience with the queen at the next new moon."

"The next *new moon*?" Scowling, she stopped walking. "Why not today? When *is* the next new moon?"

He shrugged. "The last one was a few days ago. We missed it." At her pointed glare, he added, "She only grants audiences once per cycle of the mortal moon."

"You've got to be kidding me."

He was, but not about to admit to it. He'd realized in the car—while watching her hand close around the leather-bound stick shift, and mentally substituting his own leather-clad stick shift that seemed to have gotten firmly lodged in overdrive—that if they were successful today, he'd lose his human body.

He'd gotten strangely all-too-humanly panicked. His stomach had actually felt queasy and he'd nearly insisted she turn around. The only thing that had stopped him was that he knew that if she knew that he wanted to stay human just so he could have sex with her, she'd go beg every fairy she could find to take him away this very instant.

And one of them might.

Aoibheal had no such ridiculous schedule, but what his petite *ka-lyrra* didn't know, she couldn't use against him. He would get her to tell them to come collect him at the next new moon. He'd easily have her in bed long before then. Get to sate his curiosity before reclaiming his rightful place.

"I am not going to be stuck with you until then," she was saying.

He smiled. By Danu, she was sexy when she was angry: eyes sparkling, nostrils flaring, breasts rising and falling with her tight, angry breaths.

When he made no reply, she flung an exasperated hand in the direction of a bench some distance away, in the middle of the square. "Oh, just go sit over there, okay? They tend to hang out on the square sometimes. I think they like to people-watch, or I suppose *fairies* would say human-watch."

When he opened his mouth to disagree, of no mind to sit so far away from her, she placed her palm flush to his chest and gave him a little push toward the bench. It was the first time she'd touched him of her own accord. And he'd not missed the tiny hesitation after she'd placed her hand on his body before pushing. As if she had savored the feel of his chest beneath her hand. Her barriers were dropping. Fascinating.

"You can't sit here with me or every fairy that sees us together will know I can see you. I get to choose who to reveal myself to," she gritted. "When I see the ones I want, I'll wave you over."

"As you wish, Gabrielle."

11

It was late in the day before Gabby spotted a pair of Fae she was willing to approach. The ballgame-goers had long since swept back through downtown, retrieving their cars (the Reds won; she'd heard the fireworks), and the sun had ducked low behind the skyscrapers that hemmed Fountain Square, gilding the silvery-windowed walls fiery rose and slanting tall early-evening shadows across the square.

During the interminable wait she'd realized the Fae were, indeed, watching him. Many appeared throughout the course of the day. But since he was just sitting there doing nothing, most of them went away after only a short time. She supposed he wasn't being very entertaining.

Finally, she spotted her two. She chose them because they weren't as blindingly beautiful as the rest, and she hoped, rather like people, the less attractive ones weren't quite so . . . well, were more approachable.

A male and a female, both blond and shimmery-eyed, were standing near the bench Adam was sitting on, deep in conversation. Rather than waving him over, she decided to join him and get it over with.

"What? Haven't you seen any?" Adam asked, as she approached.

Did that husky, Celtic-accented voice sound almost . . . cheery? She shook her head at the idiotic notion, deciding the sun must have baked her brains during the long, tedious afternoon.

"They're right there," she told him, pointing.

"Where?" He looked where she was pointing and muttered a string of curses. "Christ, I can't believe I can't even see them. Are they looking at me?"

"Not at the moment. And they're there," she said, trying to correct his gaze, "standing about ten feet to your left, less than a foot from the trash can." She drew a deep breath, bracing herself to approach them, when suddenly the male fairy turned and looked at her.

"Hello," she said politely. "I'd like to speak with you a moment. I need to—"

"I do believe it sees us, Aine," the male fairy spoke over her, with a haughty lift of a brow.

It? Gabby thought, nostrils flaring. *It* was calling *her* an *it?* The nerve. The unmitigated gall. She was human. She had a soul. It wasn't and didn't. If anyone was an it, it was it, not her.

"Oh, get over yourselves already. I'm just here to pass on a message. Adam Black wants me to tell you . . ." Gabby blinked and trailed off. They'd turned their backs to her and were paying her no attention whatsoever, carrying on a hushed conversation that she couldn't over-hear.

Then the male fairy nodded, and suddenly both fairies vanished. There one moment, then gone.

Exhaling gustily, Gabby clenched her hands into lit-tle fists and turned to Adam. "Are all of you so damned arrogant?"

"What do you mean? What are they saying?"

"They're not saying anything. They're gone. They called me an 'it,' said something to each other, and van-ished."

His eyes narrowed. "If this is some kind of trick . . ."

"It's not," she said impatiently. "I swear, they were here. I was trying to talk to them, and they just van-ished."

"What did they look like?" he demanded.

She described them, adding that the male had called the female "Aine."

Rolling his eyes, he groaned. "I know her."

"And?"

"She's a princess from Aoibheal's line, the First House of the D'Anu, and the only thing royal about her is how much of a pain in the ass she is. But she'll help me. She'll be back."

"Are you sure?"

He nodded. "Yes, Aine has always had a bit of a thing for me. Perhaps more than a bit. Actually," he said with a long-suffering sigh, "she's obsessed with me."

Figured, Gabby thought irritably. Even other fairies weren't immune to his seduction. What did that say about a human woman's chances? There should be a vaccine against Adam Black. And all women should be given it at birth.

"Sit," he said, gesturing to the bench beside him.

"It won't be long. She'll be back. Aine will refuse me nothing."

Gabby began to sit, then stopped. Another fairy had suddenly appeared over by the fountain, alone. A solitary one. Just what she'd been hoping for all afternoon. Just what Adam had said she'd never find. "Well, you were wrong," she grumbled, feeling inexplicably irked about Aine-who-would-refuse-him-nothing, "because there's a fairy over there, all by himself."

Adam surged to his feet, inhaling sharply, audibly. "What? Where? No, wait—don't point, *ka-lyrra*. Don't even look at him again. Or at me. Move away, give me your back, then tell me what he looks like," he hissed.

Gabby glanced at him. She couldn't help it—he sounded so alarmed.

"Don't *look* at me," he hissed again softly. "Do as I said."

Jarred by the urgency in his voice, Gabby obeyed, moving away. Turning, giving him her profile, she rested her hands on a low stone wall that encircled an arrangement of sculptured shrubs and flowers and pretended to be enjoying the view. Dropping her head forward so her hair shielded her face, she said clearly, softly, "He's tall. Copper hair, gold highlights. Black torque and armbands, wearing—"

"White robes and he has a scar on his face," Adam finished for her.

"Yes."

"Gabrielle, walk away from me this instant and don't look back. As fast and far as you can. Do it. Now."

But, damn the woman, he should have known she wouldn't obey a direct order again. The first time must have been a fluke; she obviously didn't have an obedient, malleable bone in her body.

She looked back at him, searching his face, her brows drawn in confusion.

And was that a touch of concern in her lovely green-gold eyes? Concern for *him*? Though he was pleased to see the first hint of such weakness, at the moment, it could prove her undoing. She'd just described Darroc and, if Darroc got his hands on him in his current condition, well... he wouldn't be having an audience with Aoibheal—ever again. And if Darroc got his hands on Gabrielle... Adam tensed, refusing to complete the thought. Bloody hell, he hadn't anticipated this! "Go," he growled.

But even as he said it, he saw her face change. She was no longer looking at him; her gaze had fixed on a point slightly to the right of and behind him. Her mouth had dropped open, her eyes had gone impossibly wide, and her face was bloodlessly white.

"H-h-h—*huuuunh—huuuunh—*" she gurgled.

Adam reacted instantly, able to think of only one thing that might put that look on her face and make her tongue trip all over an *H*.

Hunters.

"G-g-g—" she tried again.

And if there were Hunters in the same place as Darroc, they hadn't come for her. At least not first. There were thousands of years of bad blood between him and the High Council Elder, and he could think of little Darroc would enjoy more than watching the Hunters rip him to pieces while he was in mortal form. Then and only then would he turn his attentions to the *Sidhe*-seer. And his petite *ka-lyrra* wouldn't stand a chance. In Darroc's hands, every dark and twisted fairy tale she'd ever been told would come true.

He launched himself at her.

Christ, they were surrounded by danger that he couldn't *see*! How was he supposed to protect her? Whose stupid bloody idea had this been, anyway?

As his hands closed on her shoulders, something whizzed past his arm with a soft whine. Snaking an arm around her waist, he twisted and ducked, pulling her into the shelter of his body, wincing as something burned the back of his shoulder.

Closing his eyes, he held her tightly and sifted place in a general southerly direction, pushing to the farthest limits his diminished power could carry him. The moment he rematerialized, he instantly sifted again, arms locked around her.

Railroad track. Sift. Grocery store. Keep moving. Roof of a house. Sift. Cornfield. Sift. Cornfield. Sift. Cornfield. Sift. Cornfield. Bloody Midwest. Sift. Atop the steeple of a church with no way to balance on the narrow slippery spire.

They began to fall, plummeting past crosses and gargoyles, and he hastily sifted them in midair. He kept moving, faster and dizzyingly faster, without pausing for a breath, trying desperately to put as much distance as possible between his enemy and his wee, much-too-mortal *ka-lyrra*.

Gabby was sure she was screaming at the top of her lungs, but nothing was coming out.

Adam Black's arms weren't just tight around her body; he'd managed to wrap himself around her like a living shield.

But that wasn't what was making her choke on a scream. It was that she kept materializing and dematerializing. Sort of. One moment she existed, and then she didn't exist, and then she existed again. She didn't like it one bit. Each time she was in a different place. Stores. Parking lots. Cornfields. A lot of those. Suddenly on the peak of the slender, pointed spire of—*ack!*—a church, and *falling*! As the pavement rushed up to meet them, they were suddenly, blessedly, somewhere else.

After a while, she just closed her eyes and prayed, trying really hard not to think about much of anything, especially not how wrong the *Books of the Fae* had been about the Hunters.

They'd been even more horrifying in the flesh, if that was what they were made of, than the O'Callaghan *Books* had said. Naturally, there were no pictures of them, because any O'Callaghan who'd seen them had been taken. What little description was given, likened them to a classic version of the Devil, hoofed, winged, and horned. And they were, sort of, but even worse. Tall, leathery-skinned, with glowing orange eyes like windows into hell, they had wings, sharp teeth, and long, lethal claws. And she wasn't certain, but she thought she'd seen a tail. The only thing she didn't understand was why, when they were so obviously capable of ripping their prey to shreds with their bare ... er, handlike appendages, they'd been shooting at them with human guns.

When finally they stopped in a grassy clearing, Gabby couldn't speak for several long moments. She was, she realized, soaked from head to toe. Water was gushing from her hair, plastering it to her face. She stood shaking in his arms, leaning back into the strength of his hard body, gulping one deep breath after another.

"Are you all right, *ka-lyrra*?" he said close to her ear.

"All right? All *right*?" Exploding from his grasp, she spun around to face him. Scraping the sodden hair from her face, she shouted, "Do I *look* all right? Of course I'm not all right. My life is falling apart around my ears and you ask me if I'm all right?"

Mascara was dripping down her cheeks, splattering on her shirt. She backed away from him, eyes narrowing. Her shoes squished with the movement and, as she peered uncomprehendingly down at them, a tadpole emerged from the leg of her jeans and flopped about on the ground.

"*Eew!*" She pointed a shaking finger at it. "A tadpole. I had a tadpole in my pants!"

"Lucky tadpole," he murmured. Then, "When one sifts place, *ka-lyrra*, one comes out on top of whatever currently occupies that space. Which isn't much of a problem if one also has all one's other powers. But I don't. We hit a lake somewhere around the ninety-seventh hop. And, contrary to popular belief, I don't walk on water."

Frantically running her hands up and down her drenched jeans, feeling about for any more creepy-crawlies, she hissed, "Oh, I hate you. I hate you." So maybe she sounded like a child having a temper tantrum, but really, she seethed, ever since she'd met him she'd just been having one unsettling, disturbing, bizarre experience after another. She'd nearly had a heart attack on top of that church. Just when she'd begun to think she was getting the hang of it, that it wasn't quite so awful being deconstructed then reconstructed again and again and again, she'd been gagging on foul-tasting, smelly, fishy, mossy water.

"No you don't," he said softly.

"I *drank* some of that lake! I might have choked on a fish or a frog or a...a...a turtle!"

"It is wisest to keep one's mouth shut while sifting."

She skewered him with a frosty stare. "Now you tell me." Damn the fairy, anyway. There she stood, feeling ragtag and bedraggled, and he only looked more beautiful wet, all drippy and shimmery gold-velvet, his hair a wet tangle to his waist.

"Come, Gabrielle," he said, extending his hand, "we must keep moving. They can track me by what little magic I'm using to sift, but only to a general vicinity. We need to keep sifting, to spread out their search."

"Is there anything *else* it's wisest to do that I should know about before we just pop off again?" She tucked her hands behind her back so he couldn't grab her and just sift rather than answering her. Besides, she needed a minute to brace herself for the next bout of traveling in a manner that defied all the known laws of physics.

"You might try kissing me. Better my tongue than a frog, no?" Dark eyes sparking gold, he reached for her.

"Close contest," she growled the lie, backing away, hands still tucked behind her back. She glanced pointedly at the flopping tadpole.

"What?"

"Take it back."

"You're kidding, right?" he said disbelievingly.

"Do we have time?"

He considered that. "Yes, but—"

"Then, no I'm not."

"That lake was three hops ago," he said impatiently.

"If you don't take it back it's going to die, and while you may think it's just a pathetic little thing with an abbreviated little life that hardly even signifies in the fairy scheme of things, I'll bet in the tadpole scheme of things it's really looking forward to becoming a frog. Now take it back. A life is a life. I don't care how tiny an almighty fairy thinks it is."

One dark brow arched and he inclined his head. "Yes, Gabrielle." Scooping up the tadpole in one big hand, gently enough that it gave her pause, he popped out.

While he was gone Gabby scraped the slimy moss from her purse (which she was rather stunned to find still looped over her shoulder), unzipped it, and inspected the contents. For a novel change, she was glad she could afford only cheap purses—the fake leather had proved waterproof. Fishing out her compact, she scrubbed away the remnants of her makeup and plucked algae from her hair, ruefully acknowledging that things were now pretty much as bad as they could get.

She was not only still stuck with Adam Black, but other fairies now knew that she could see them, and some rogue fairy—according to Adam, one of those not to be trusted—had also found her out and in the thick of it all somebody had summoned the Hunters.

She shuddered at the memory. One moment she'd been staring at Adam, trying to figure out why he sounded so tense and urgent, the next, horrific creatures from her worst nightmares had materialized out of thin air behind him.

And they'd had guns, which she found bizarre enough, but even more strangely, they'd been shooting—not at her—but *him*. What on earth was going on?

Dabbing away a last smudge of mascara, she went still. He'd not been able to see them. All he'd been able to see was her face, and she knew how horrified she must have looked. She'd been incapable of forming a single word; the blood in her veins had turned to ice, freezing her solidly in place. Had it not been for Adam, she'd have stood there squawking silently, helplessly, until the Hunters had done whatever it was Hunters did to *Sidhe*-seers. She'd tried desperately to say "Hunters" and "guns" but hadn't been able to spit out a syllable.

And what had he done? The last thing she'd have imagined. He'd lunged forward without hesitation to shield her. Wrapped his powerful body around hers. Knowing that something awful was behind him, he'd not instantly sifted himself to safety. He'd used his mortal, no-longer-invincible body to protect her. He could have simply translated himself elsewhere and abandoned her, which was exactly what she expected from a cold-blooded fairy.

He only did it because now he needs you even more. He has to protect you. You're his eyes for the enemies he can't see.

"The tadpole has been returned to its watery home, *ka-lyrra*." Adam materialized before her, shaking like a great wet beast, water droplets flying everywhere. He cocked his dark head, absorbing her serious expression. "All will be well, Gabrielle. I won't let anyone harm you. Not today. Not ever."

"Because now you need me more than ever," she said bitterly. "You *have* to keep me alive."

He cocked his head and regarded her for a long, measuring moment. "In case you've forgotten, I tried to make you leave the moment you told me about the lone Tuatha Dé. I said, to be precise, 'Walk away from me this instant and don't look back. As fast and far as you can.' You chose not to heed me. And I could always find another *Sidhe*-seer, Gabrielle. I read your books. One of them lists the names of the bloodlines in Ireland that carry the vision. All the bloodlines."

"It does?" Gabby was horrified. Where? How had she missed it? Why had they ever been written down? Oh, *why* hadn't someone burned those pages long ago?

He nodded. "In the first tome, scribed in the ancient tongue. Pages of names. So you see, I don't need you. I know human ways far better than my enemies. I could easily conceal myself long enough to track another one down."

"Then, why don't you?" she asked faintly. And how would she survive if he did?

"I endangered your life. I will fix it."

Gabby blinked up at him. His voice was tight, his accent more clipped than usual and, were he a normal man, she would have thought he was furious with himself for having placed her in jeopardy.

Oh, for crying out loud, her inner fourteen-year-old snapped, *even for a Fae prince he sounds furious with himself for having placed you in jeopardy. Cut him some slack, would you?*

She stood, mouth open, a dozen different questions vying for her tongue, but he shook his head.

"Not now. We must go. There will be a place to talk soon enough. This is not it. Come."

Gabby stood, tucking her purse securely over her shoulder. As she moved to join him, she suddenly noticed that the water trickling down his wet shirt held a reddish tinge.

"Are you hurt?" she exclaimed, reaching for his arm.

He twisted away with a shrug. "It's nothing—"

"Let me—"

"Leave it. I'm fine. I rinsed it out in the lake. It's not deep. Come, Irish. Hand. In mine. Now."

When she just stood there, frowning worriedly up at him, he said, "I have no intention of expiring before I'm made immortal again. Rest assured, if I say it's of no consequence, it isn't." He paused a moment, then added softly, "And you needn't fear, Gabrielle. I destroyed them."

"The Hunters?" she said blankly. "No you didn't."

"The pages that name the *Sidhe*-seers. You shouldn't make things so easy for my race. They can be without mercy, dangerous."

"Unlike you, that oh-so-nice-guy-Adam-Black?" The caustic comment slipped from her tongue before she could stop it.

He shot her a look of impatient rebuke. "Try to see past your preconceptions, Irish, would you? Try seeing *me*."

Okay, now that messed with her head. Made her feel like she was being judgmental and petty. She wasn't judgmental, she was merely going by the facts, and the facts were —

Well, the facts were ... er, that she wasn't entirely certain what the facts were at the moment.

Damn it! Why couldn't things just be black and white? Human good, fairy bad. Simple! That was what she'd been raised to believe.

Had he really destroyed those pages betraying all the *Sidhe*-seers? Why? Why would he even expend the effort?

For that matter, why had he so gently retrieved the flopping tadpole from the ground and returned it? There was no doubt that he had; he'd been freshly drenched again. He could have just lied (after all, lying was supposed to be his second nature) and told her there was no time. She would have believed him; she had no idea what Hunters were capable of.

And he *had* told her to walk away the minute she'd spotted the lone fairy. Had he truly meant to send her away for her own protection, at his own risk?

What kind of fairy did such things?

A legendary seducer and deceiver?

Or ... halfway decent fairy? *Was* there such a thing?

At a complete loss, she slipped her hand into his.

His big hand swallowed hers, making her feel dainty and feminine. She tipped her head back, looking up at his chiseled face. His eyes were dark, his jaw set. And he looked so very ... human.

As they began to sift, she was ambushed by the realization that, though she knew she wasn't safe *from* him, she felt strangely safe *with* him.

They didn't stop again until well after nightfall. Actually, she mused muzzily, it felt nearer to dawn. She'd lost track of the passage of time during their discombobulating passage through place.

He sifted them onto a passenger train just outside of Louisville, Kentucky, explaining that they now needed to travel by human means for a while, to ensure the Fae couldn't track them. Assuring her that the Hunters would be tangled up for quite some time in the net of magic-residue he'd left behind.

She was once again so tired she could barely function. When he guided her through the cars until they found a nearly empty one, then took a seat by the window and pulled her in next to him, she sank limply down. Since Adam Black's advent into her life, her sleep schedule had become the biggest joke. Judging by the faint streaks of orange and pink on the horizon beyond the glass, it appeared she'd again been up nearly twenty-four hours straight—and again they'd been some of the most traumatic hours she'd ever endured.

Unable to find a single solid point of reference to latch on to in the recent epidemic of otherworldly events, she decided to deal with it all later and yielded to exhaustion, slumping down in the seat, chin nodding toward her chest.

And when he pulled her across the seats, stretched out his long muscular legs and drew her into his arms, she only gave a weary little sigh and curled up against him. Her jeans were still damp, she had no blanket, and could use the body heat.

Still, that was no excuse to press her cheek to his chest and inhale deeply of his spicy masculine scent. She did it anyway.

"You aren't falling for me, are you, Irish?" he purred, sounding amused.

"Hardly," she muttered.

"Good. I'd hate to think you were falling for me."

So would she. Oh, God, so would she.

12

Adam shifted position carefully, trying to take the pressure off his shoulder without disturbing Gabrielle.

She was sleeping in his arms. Had been for hours, easy as could be. Her face, in repose, was sweet, youthful, innocent, and utterly beautiful to him. He traced a finger down her cheek, studying the subtle, soft planes, wondering at what made beauty. In thousands of years he'd still not figured it out. Whatever it was, she had it in spades. She was warm and earthy and vibrant, unlike the coolly flawless females of his race. She was fiery autumn and spring thunder, while Tuatha Dé women were a silvery winter that went on and on. She was just the kind of lass a Highlander might take to wife; laugh with and argue with and make love to for the rest of his life.

She sighed in her sleep and curled closer, nestling her cheek against his chest. He understood what was responsible for the sudden change in her demeanor, what had caused the lamb to slump down in exhaustion against the wolf. Not trust, no, not from his fiery *Sidhe*-seer (though he was beginning to see some signs of thawing); circumstances alone had driven her into his arms. Until late this afternoon she'd perceived him as her greatest threat. Now there was a greater threat, and he was suddenly her only ally against it.

No matter the reason, he liked feeling her soft and yielding to his strength. Unconscious, vulnerable, entrusted to his care while her mind was steeped in dreams. He liked it a great deal. Enough, in fact, that he—who had no patience with physical discomfort—would put up with pain rather than wake her. Fortunately, the bullet had only grazed him, presenting no significant threat to his mortal form.

Hunters carrying guns. He rubbed his jaw and shook his head. When she'd told him what she'd seen, during the few pauses he'd permitted them while sifting place, he'd been incensed.

At himself.

What a fool he'd been. A week ago, he'd thought his most pressing problem a severe case of frustration and boredom. Then he'd found Gabrielle, and his most pressing problem had been how best to seduce her.

Now his most pressing problem was how the bloody hell to keep them both alive.

It didn't take Tuatha Dé genius to understand the significance of Hunters carrying human weapons. Not in the presence of Darroc.

How swiftly he'd forgotten all he'd left behind in Faery upon being banished from that realm—the complications, the tensions, the incessant court intrigues—but he'd been thoroughly wallowing in his aggravation at being human. What a fool he'd been to forget Darroc for even a moment. The bad blood between him and the High Council Elder stretched back four and a half millennia, to a time before The Compact between Fae and Man. To a time before the deadly spear and lethal sword his race had brought with them from Danu — two of the four Hallows, and the only weapons capable of doing injury to or even killing an immortal — had been removed from Faery and secreted away. All the way back to that day Adam had taken up the sword and laid open Darroc's face, giving him the scar he still sported.

He'd like to pretend he'd tried to kill Darroc for a noble reason, but the simple truth was they'd been fighting over a mortal woman. Adam had seen her first. But the queen had summoned him back to court for some nonsense or another, and Darroc had gotten to her first. Knowing full well Adam had wanted her.

Darroc had killed her. There were those among his race who believed that beauty and innocence could truly be savored only via their destruction. There were those among his race who, in that lawless time before The Compact, when they'd first arrived on this world and were scouting it, not yet having settled it, had fed like scavengers on the passion they could elicit from a human during sex, not caring that it killed the mortal in the process. He'd seen what Darroc had done to her when he'd returned. Gone was the laughing, teasing young maiden who'd been so vibrantly alive. Sadistically broken and forever silenced. Her death hadn't come easy. And for no bloody frigging good reason. Her murder had been an act of bitter, senseless violence. Adam had done his fair share of killing in that lawless time, but for reasons. Always for reasons. Never just for the pleasure of it.

The loathing spawned between him and Darroc that day had never waned. Leashed by the queen, under threat of dire recompense (a soulless death at the queen's hand, no less), they'd taken their vicious battle into the arena of court politics, an arena in which Adam had perfected his powers of subtlety and seduction, tools he'd used to defeat Darroc on many occasions. The Elder, too, had changed with time, perfecting a cunning that equaled his brutality. While Darroc secured a seat on the queen's council, Adam managed to secure her ear in other ways. He and the Elder were by far the most powerfully persuasive figures at court, staunchly on opposing sides, and with Adam gone ... well, he had no doubt that already the complacent courtiers were being turned to the Elder's aims. How long, he brooded darkly, before Darroc managed to turn some of them against Aoibheal herself? Was she aware of the danger she'd created by casting Adam out?

So Darroc had tried to kill him, he mused. And with guns at that. Had he been trying to make it look as if Adam had gotten caught in stray fire from some human dispute? Knowing Darroc, he would play the odds that once Adam was gone, the queen would be able to prove nothing if Adam's body sported only man-made wounds.

Though Adam mocked human law, Tuatha Dé code was equally convoluted. Without solid proof, the queen would never punish one of their own. Their numbers were no longer increasing as they'd once been. Though he'd once told Circenn he was virile in Tuatha Dé form, it had been but one of many, many lies he'd told his son. Few of them could still sire offspring, and although the Tuatha Dé didn't exactly die, sometimes they ... went away.

Gabrielle stirred in his arms, jarring him from his

thoughts. She shifted, tucking her knees up, snuggling closer to his body. She was curled on her side between his legs, cradled against his chest, and he sucked in a sharp breath, shuddering, as the generous, sweet curve of her hip nestled against his cock. Which was, as ever, ready and willing. That part of his body was simply un-controllable, apparently functioning in accordance to a single law of nature: She existed—he got a hard-on.

Christ, he wanted her. Force had never seemed such a tempting option, yet force would make him no better than Darroc.

He would accept nothing less than her willing sur-render.

But, bloody hell, it had better be soon. He was cur-rently only human. With a Tuatha Dé's conscience. Or lack thereof.

Gabby stretched gingerly, taking careful note of every muscle in her body that ached.

That would be all of them.

She was crinked from head to toe and dream-befuddled, with absolutely no idea where she was.

She opened her eyes warily.

Adam Black was staring down at her, his dark gaze unfathomable.

"Good morning, *ka-lyrra*," he purred with a slow, heart-stoppingly sexy smile.

"Highly debatable," she muttered. Any morning that had him in it was bound to be many things, but good was hardly the first adjective she'd choose. Dangerous? Yes. Endlessly tempting? Yes. Eventful. Perhaps even fas-cinating. But not good.

"I'd have procured coffee for you but you're on top of me, and I was loath to disturb your slumber."

He looked as if he were about to say more, but she didn't give him the chance. She was too appalled by her discovery that he was reclining back against the window and she was sprawled uninhibitedly on top of his big, warm body, astride one of his powerful thighs (with something hard against her belly that she was trying really, really hard not to think about), her breasts crushed against his chest, and oh—her hand was curled in his hair! As if she'd been petting him or something in her sleep! "Sorry," she said hastily, disentangling herself, snapping upright, and scooting away.

He came with her, his hand closing around her wrist like a steel band. "Not so fast, Irish."

"Let me g—" Gabby froze. She'd managed to get off him and was sitting up all right. But something was wrong. It took her a moment to figure out what it was. Someone else was sitting in her.

Sitting *in* her.

She opened her mouth to scream but he clamped a hand over it. He rose, pulling her up with him, and half-carried, half-dragged her from their seats. Holding her tightly, he pulled her down the aisle through car after car until they came to an empty one.

Only then did he let her go.

Wide-eyed, she backed up against a seat and stared at him. Her mouth opened and closed repeatedly.

"Easy, *ka-lyrra*. It's just the effect of the *féth fiada*."

Her tongue unstuck. "What are you *saying*?" she wailed. "Am I cursed now too? Did you let somebody curse me while I was sleeping? Is it contagious or something?" She thumped him in the chest with a fist. "How could you *do* this to me? I trusted you!"

He arched a dark, slanted brow. "You did? Imagine that, and me the *sin siriche du* and all, only your mortal enemy."

"Oooh! I don't mean that I trust you, like with important things, but I thought at least I could count on you to—"

"You're not cursed, Gabrielle," he soothed. "It's merely that when I touch you the curse affecting me encompasses you as well. I wasn't sure exactly how it was working until the lady sat in you, and then it was too late."

"I thought I was immune to it," she cried.

"You are. The *féth fiada* doesn't *work* on you. But it works *on* you."

"Not getting this," she hissed, running her hands up and down her body, making sure she was really real.

"As with any other object in the human realm, when I touch you you get drawn into the enchantment that surrounds me. You become invisible and noncorporeal to other humans. Until I stop touching you. Hence, you were sat in. I tried to warn you but you pulled away too quickly. I didn't dare release you while you were being occupied, because I'm not certain what would happen if I did."

Gabby blanched. "You mean, you think if I became corporeal again while someone was in me . . ." She couldn't finish the thought.

He nodded. "That someone might be ... er, incorporated. But then again, they might not. It might work like sifting, where things come out on top of each other. Wouldn't that be a laugh? Can you imagine the look on that woman's face if you'd suddenly appeared on top of her? Unless . . ." he mused thoughtfully, "with a *Sidhe*-seer it's so difficult to predict; Fae power doesn't work the way it's supposed to around you, which is what we find so unacceptable about your kind. Perhaps some part of the confusion element would—"

"I don't think it would be a laugh at all," Gabby snapped. "It felt really bad to be sat in. Like I was a ghost or something."

He nodded. "I know."

Her eyes narrowed. "So help me understand this. When you're touching me, I can't be seen or felt by any other humans?"

"Right."

"But the Fae can still see us?"

"Right."

"But when you're touching me, and I'm not solid to other people, I can still feel everything else. And I could feel you. So am I actually there, or not?"

"It's difficult to explain, *ku-lyrra*; I have no human terms. Your race does not yet possess ones sufficient to discuss in any useful detail"—he broke off, frowning, searching for words—"well, this is a near approximation, though not really at all: complex, element-specific, event-contingent, multidimensional shifting in, er... you'd say 'spacetime,' but give it thirteen dimensions instead of four. Humans have simultaneity issues and don't deal well with breakdown. Your concept of the universe is not yet advanced enough, although your scientists have been making progress. Yes, you're real. No, humans can't feel you." He shrugged. "The *féth fiada* doesn't affect animals either. Cats and dogs can see and feel us just fine, which is why they often seem to be staring fixedly at nothing, hissing or barking for no apparent reason."

"Uh-huh. I see. Adam?"

"Yes?"

"If you ever let somebody sit in me again, in any freaking dimension, you won't have to worry about the Hunters, I'll kill you myself."

His dark eyes glittered with amusement. A full foot shorter than he, lesser by at least a hundred pounds, she was bristling up at him, undaunted. Only one other mortal woman had similarly stood her ground before him. Over a thousand years ago, in another time, another world, in ninth-century Scotland. Circenn's mother, Morganna: the only woman to whom he'd ever offered immortality.

Let me die, Adam. I beg of ye, let me die, a smoky feminine burr swirled through his mind.

He tossed his head viciously, shaking the voice away. That was a memory best left in those dark times where it belonged.

Striking without warning, giving her no chance to react, he fisted a hand in the fabric of her shirt, pulled her close, ducked his head, and brushed his lips to hers. Though at the merest touch of his mouth to hers, his cock surged painfully in his jeans and his body raged for more, he kept the kiss light.

Merely rubbing his lips back and forth over hers, with a husky little purr.

The hand not holding her shirt clenched into a tight fist at his side as he battled the urge to crush her to him, shove his tongue into her mouth, drop her back onto a seat, strip her jeans down, and thrust himself between her thighs.

But he gave her only the barest taste of a kiss. Savoring the erotic friction. Feeling her lips soften beneath his. Relishing the tiny catch in the back of her throat.

Then letting her go.

When he released his grip on her shirt, she stumbled

back slightly, looking utterly dazed, much to his satisfaction. Her lush mouth was soft, her green-gold eyes startled and confused and very sleepy-sexy aroused. And he knew if he reached for her again, she'd not fight.

Good.

He wanted her wanting. Wanted her wondering why he'd not taken more. Wanted her primed for the next time he reached for her.

Hunger for me, ka-lyrra, he thought silently, *get addicted to me. I will be both venom and antidote, your poison and your only cure.*

Aloud he only said softly, "Yes, Gabrielle."

13

They disembarked that evening in Atlanta,
Georgia, and "checked into" a hotel Adam-Black–style.

Only for the night, he said, as they needed to keep
moving. But tonight they would shower, rest, and eat
"real" food (by which she guessed he meant his usual
fare: five-star dining).

He certainly did have exquisite taste, Gabby thought,
as she wrapped her long wet hair in a fluffy towel and
stepped out of the shower. Along with absolutely no
qualms about taking the best of what he wanted. The
bathroom she was standing in was nearly the size of her
turret bedroom at home, and a designer's dream. Cream
marble shot with rose and adorned by gold fixtures, it
had a walk-in marble shower with a built-in bench that
sported top-of-the-line toiletries, as well as a decadent
soaking tub.

She snorted, recalling how effortlessly he'd "appropriated" their luxury accommodations. He certainly did know his way around the human realm. He'd left her standing in the domed entrance to the hotel, gaping at the abundance of glittering crystal, antique furnishings, and Old World elegance, feeling—despite the attempt she'd made on the train at freshening up—the epitome of I've-been-dunked-in-a-lake-and-slept-in-my-smelly-clothes grunge. He'd stalked off for the reservations counter while the doormen had stood sniffing disdainfully at her, and gone to work, invisible and undetectable, at an unoccupied computer terminal.

A few moments later he'd returned with printed reservations in his hand. He'd taken her arm (which had caused the doormen to stiffen and blink suspiciously at the space she'd only an instant before been occupying) and guided her past them, into the elevator, up to the twenty-third floor.

I'd have gotten the penthouse, he'd told her with a vaguely apologetic air, *but it's occupied. This is second best. If you like, we can go to a different hotel.*

As if. She'd never seen such exquisite accommodations before. The suite had three sumptuous rooms: a large, opulent bedroom with ornate mirrors, richly brocaded chairs, patterned-silk wallpaper, a real fireplace, and a magnificent canopied king bed; a dining room with an elegant table and leather chairs positioned before a sleek wall of windows that overlooked the city; and a living room with an oversized pullout sofa bed, a plasma TV, two sitting alcoves, and a small attached wet bar/kitchenette.

Why did you bother with reservations? she'd asked *Why didn't we just sneak into the room?*

*If it were only me, I would have, but since I won't be holding your hand nonstop—unless of course you'd like me to—*he'd purred with a sexy smile and a glance in the direction of the shower, *it's simpler this way. More convenient for you.*

He'd pushed her toward the bathroom, told her he would return in one hour, then vanished.

After he'd gone, she'd suffered a momentary, nearly immobilizing flash of panic—what if the Hunters somehow managed to find her while he was gone?—but it dissipated swiftly, leaving her astonished to realize that she truly trusted him to keep her safe, at least from everything besides himself.

After raiding the wet bar for snacks, she'd taken an inquisitive peek inside the bathroom and begun stripping where she stood, leaving her dirty clothes in a pile outside the bathroom door. She'd lingered in the marble shower for twenty glorious minutes, letting the three steaming, jetting pulses—one above, one on each side—work magic on her cramped, sore muscles.

Now, slipping into a thick, downy-soft, white courtesy robe, she stepped out into the bedroom.

Her gaze fell on the bed. The only bed. Looked like she'd be sleeping on the pullout sofa.

He'd kissed her.

Out of the blue and without warning. Grabbed her by the shirt, yanked her close, and lowered that sinfully sexy mouth to hers. And when he'd done it, her lips had been slightly parted. (Okay, so maybe she'd parted them a teeny bit more at the last moment.) She'd expected him to take advantage of it, to thrust his tongue deep, to take her in a demanding, hungry, hot, and slippery kiss. She'd expected a full assault on her senses. She'd expected that kiss to escalate into a hot, steamy make-out session.

Not.

A chaste little kiss. Hardly even a kiss at all. Not that she would have *invited* his kisses, but—since he'd gone ahead and taken one and she was already damned for permitting it—was it too much to ask that he commit to it? Exercise a little follow-through?

But no, he'd just stood there, not even really touching her except for the handful of shirt he was holding (and he hadn't even tried to cop a feel of her breast while his hand was right over it; what kind of man passed up such an opportunity?), cocooning her in that erotic, spicy scent of jasmine and sandalwood, brushing his full, sexy lips against hers so lightly that it had made her want to scream. Or bite him.

That tiny little touch, that thing that hardly even qualified as a kiss, had left her feeling hot and achy and miserable.

She'd just stood there, dazed, looking up at him, knowing she should have put up at least a token fight, for heaven's sake!

Wishing he'd do it again. The right way.

And, damn it, he'd known exactly what effect he'd had on her; the pure masculine satisfaction in his eyes had been unmistakable.

With a little growl of irritation, she rubbed her mouth with the back of her hand and forced her mind away from that abysmal, aggravating, humiliating kiss, to what she'd learned over a pilfered lunch on the train.

Which wasn't much. No one could ever accuse Adam Black of overdisclosing. He either didn't like to talk to humans about Faery, or he didn't like to talk to *her* about Faery, because she'd had to pull teeth to get anything out of him at all. And what she'd gotten was, she figured, not even the tip of the iceberg.

The beautiful, scarred, copper-haired Fae she'd seen was Darroc, a High Council Elder and an ancient nemesis of Adam's. He believed Darroc had armed the Hunters with human weapons to make his death look like an accident, as if he'd inadvertently gotten caught in a spray of mortal gunfire. He believed Darroc was planning an attempt to usurp the queen's power and, as they'd ever been on opposing sides, was taking advantage of the opportunity to get Adam out of the way once and for all.

And that was the sum total of what she'd managed to learn. He'd refused to tell her what plan he had for saving them, only that he did, indeed, have one. He'd refused to discuss why he and Darroc despised each other so greatly, though when he'd spoken of him his deep voice had resonated with fury, forcing her to finally admit that part of what she'd been raised to believe was simply wrong: Fae *did* feel emotion.

She could no longer deny it anymore. The evidence was right there in front of her eyes, and the *brehon* in her could not ignore evidence no matter how much she might like to. She could no longer tell herself that he was experiencing feelings because he was in human form and subject to the human condition. No, Adam and Darroc had hated each other for millennia, she'd heard it in his voice, and hate was emotion. Strong, deep emotion. Emotion he'd experienced in his Tuatha Dé form.

The O'Callaghan *Books* clearly said, as Gram had confirmed, that Fae were incapable of any emotion. Large or small. That they were cold, icy, arrogant, unfeeling. Nor was there any mention of politics or feuds or any of those human-sounding things going on in Faery—as if the Fae were actually very much like humans. How could the books have been so wrong?

Gee, maybe because they were written by the O'Callaghans who'd escaped the Fae. By ancestors who never interacted with one, never even spoke with one. Would you believe the report of an investigator who'd never even interviewed his subject? Present such a shoddy bit of "proof" in a case? The prosecution would have a field day with it!

Oh, such thoughts were shaking her foundation at the very core. She blew out a gusty breath.

Try to see past your preconceptions, Irish, would you? he'd said.

Damn it all, he was blasting through them, one by one.

After she dried her hair, Gabby used the hotel phone to check her messages at home. Her mom had called four times to remind her that she'd promised to fly out to California for her stepsister's graduation next weekend, and she'd really like to talk to her before then.

Gabby sighed. She hardly even knew her stepsiblings. In fact, she had been to California only twice in the past five years and couldn't understand why it was suddenly so important to her mom that she attend a stupid highschool graduation. But lately her mom seemed to be coming up with all kinds of excuses to get Gabby to fly out for a visit.

She may not be perfect, but she's the only mother you're ever going to have. You need to give her a chance, Gram had said a hundred times.

I gave her a chance. I was born to her. That's a chance. She left.

Gabby, you need to try to see things from her—

No.

As she sat in a hotel room in Atlanta, she could still hear her mom's voice from all those years ago as clearly as if she were seven again, awakened by a need to go to the bathroom, standing in her nightgown at the top of the stairs in the drafty, winter-chilled house, clutching a tattered stuffed unicorn, clinging to the carved post in the dark.

She's fascinated by them! She thinks they're beautiful and wants to go live with them!

She's a child, Jilly. She'll grow out of it.

Then, you'll have to help her grow out of it, because I can't. I can't deal with this.

That night, had her vision been an appendage she could have hacked off with a knife, she would have. *Stay, Mommy. I'll be good. I promise. I don't mean to see them.*

Gabby squeezed her eyes shut. Inhaled deeply, exhaled slowly.

Then glanced at the clock and picked up the phone. It was dinnertime in California; her mom would be at work at Trio's, the restaurant she managed.

She dialed the home number, to get the answering machine. She left a terse message explaining that something had come up and she wouldn't be able to attend the graduation, but she'd send a gift and call in a few weeks. Feeling guilty, as she usually did where her mom was concerned, she added, "Maybe I can fly out for Christmas this year, okay?"

Assuming she was still alive.

Outside the suite, Adam sat with his back against the door, shifting restlessly, impatient for a shower himself, and to further Gabrielle's seduction.

They could have slept on the train, in a passenger compartment with berth and bath, but he wanted her to taste more of the life he could give her, even without his full powers. Seduction required the appropriate stage, and luxury always made a splendid one. Besides, he wanted to do a bit of "shopping." Trust would be a hard thing to win from her, but he could and would begin binding her to him this night with sex and gifts—those were his strengths, the things he could give better than any other man.

He knew she liked the suite. He'd seen it in her eyes. He'd seen also her instant wariness when her gaze had fallen on the only bed. He'd removed himself for a time to give her a chance to acclimate, wanting her shower-warmed and relaxed, her guard down (inasmuch as she would ever drop her guard) when he returned.

A glance down the hall at the clock above the elevators told him it would be soon: fifty-two minutes down, eight to go.

Though he was certain they were safe stopping—the four Hunters Gabby had seen would have a hard time tracking them in modern cities with their millions of inhabitants and confusing man-made scents, and could only cover so much ground—he wasn't about to leave her alone.

Now that he was sifting place again—despite the tangle he'd left in Kentucky and all the Fae-residue in Cincinnati—he guessed they had a full day, at most two, before Darroc arrived in the general vicinity. Which was an acceptable risk, for by morning they would be gone. But this night, this one stolen night, would be his first.

Then he would implement the plan he'd formulated on the train.

It was now imperative he secure an audience with Aoibheal. She had to be apprised that Darroc had brought forth *her* Hunters from the Unseelie realm, something not only forbidden but costly to do, as the Hunters were mercenary to the core and handsomely retained by Aoibheal in exchange for powers and privileges.

Adam knew of only one thing Darroc might have promised them to turn them from the queen's service. The one thing the Hunters knew Aoibheal would never give them: freedom from their realm of shadow and ice. A return to the old ways.

Which meant that Darroc was planning an attempt to overthrow the queen, and soon. And Adam had no doubt that, should Darroc come to power, not only would The Compact be immediately voided, the Unseelie would be freed and it would be war between the realms. Man would be plunged into a Dark Age the likes of which they'd not seen in millennia.

He could no longer afford to waste time waiting for Circenn to resurface. It was no longer a case of him seeking an audience merely because he was fed up with his punishment. The queen was in danger, his *Sidhe-*seer was in danger, the future of all the realms was in jeopardy, and he was going to have to *force* Aoibheal to appear.

When she'd first made him human, he'd toyed with this idea initially but had decided against it. Not only had he lacked the intermediary necessary to make it work, he knew the queen's fury would know no bounds if he did such an unthinkable thing.

But now, he thought darkly, he had a reason. Faery was doing precisely what he'd always suspected it would do without him—falling apart.

In the morning, they would leave for Scotland.

And there, on the first day of August, on the feast of Lughnassadh, a mere ten days hence, one way or another, by fair means or foul, Adam would do the unthinkable.

A thing no other Tuatha Dé in existence would ever even consider doing.

The queen would be incensed at first, but upon realizing why he'd done it, upon discovering Darroc's treachery, she would be pleased and grateful. She would swiftly reinstate his power and restore his immortality. He probably wouldn't even have to apologize (for things that he *shouldn't* have to apologize for anyway). And all would be well once more.

But tomorrow would be soon enough to contemplate such matters. Tomorrow would be all about becoming immortal and regaining his powers again.

Tonight—he spared another glance at the clock, his dark face lighting with a smile to see that her hour was up—tonight was all about being as human as a man could possibly be.

"Are you ready to shop, *ka-lyrra*?"

Gabby blinked and turned toward the door. Adam stood in the doorway to the living room, leaning against the doorjamb, wearing only a towel. She looked hastily away. But it was too late, the image was burned into her mind. Wet, glossy black hair slicked back from his face, magnificent chest and arms, powerful legs. Itty-bitty towel. Eternally present heavy bulge lifting said itty-bitty towel.

A tiny, dreamy sigh escaped her. She camouflaged it hastily with a cough.

"I didn't hear you come back," she said stiffly, fixing her gaze on the TV. She'd been sitting in the living room, flipping stations, waiting for him to return. Unable to bear the thought of pulling dirty, smelly jeans back on over her clean skin, she'd hand-washed her clothes in the tub, hoping they'd be dry by morning. Now she was seriously regretting it. She needed more than a robe on around him. She needed a full suit of armor. And so did he, she thought peevishly. How dare he just saunter about flaunting all that golden, muscular, masculine splendidness?

"I sifted directly into the shower."

"There's another robe in the bathroom," she informed him tightly.

"I know. I ripped it down the back when I tried to put it on. Men aren't built like me in your century, are they?"

Oh, for heaven's sake, Greek gods aren't built like you, she thought irritably.

"Come," he repeated, joining her by the sofa and tugging her up by a hand. "Let's go."

Taking a deep breath, she stood and forced herself to look directly into his face, denying herself even the tiniest skimming glance over his body. His gaze met hers, then dropped to the cleavage at her lapel. He wet his lip and gave her a slow smile, white teeth flashing in his dark face. The pink tip of his tongue danced against his teeth for a moment, sexy and playfully inviting.

"What are we shopping for?" Oh, God, she thought dismally, had that been *her* breathy voice? Had the fourteen-year-old part of her psyche taken over control of her vocal cords?

"Clothing, unless you're comfortable wearing nothing but that robe for the next few days," he said silkily. "I'm certainly fine with it."

She cleared her throat. "Shop. Now. Let's go."

He closed his hands possessively on her waist. His dark head fell forward and with his lips but a breath from hers, he said, "Where? Gucci? Versace? Macy's? What would you like, Gabrielle? What can I give you? I would deny you nothing."

His touch was scorching, even through the fabric of her robe, and she could feel his fingers toying with her belt. He smelled good, too, of soap and spice and sexy man. She was excruciatingly aware of her nudity beneath the robe. And of his. Her heart began to pound erratically. "Macy's is fine," she said hastily.

"Is there anything else you want?" he said softly. "Anything at all?"

She closed her eyes. "Gee, let's see, could you get out of my life and fix everything you've screwed up?"

He laughed and sifted place.

She thought she heard a "never" just before she was deconstructed. The next thing she knew she was standing, in her robe and bare feet, in the dark, locked offices of Macy's.

"What are we doing here?" she asked, staring blankly at dozens of computers and monitoring screens.

"Unless you want to hold my hand while you're trying things on, *ka-lyrra*, I'm deactivating the security cameras so you don't show up on them. I may not have to worry about it, but you do."

Heavens, he thought of everything, taking measures to protect her future, as if he had no doubt that she would survive their current nightmare and *have* a future. Assuming she did, the last thing she wanted was to be caught on Macy's security cameras. Surviving the Fae, only to end up prosecuted for shoplifting, would be too ironic. Not to mention the havoc a criminal record would wreak with her career plans.

A few minutes later, apparently satisfied with his work, he transferred them into the main part of the store. She was relieved to discover that their unique mode of travel was no longer making her feel quite so nauseated.

"Stay here," he said, then vanished. He was back in a moment, holding two large leather satchels in his hands. From Gucci, no less. "I'll be nearby. We leave for Scotland tomorrow. Gather what you require. And, Gabrielle, the weather is different there; the nights get cool in the Highlands this time of year."

"Sc-Sc-Sc—" she sputtered, but he was gone again. *Scotland? The Highlands?* What on earth for? Damn it, what was he planning? And why hadn't he told her? How dare he just drag her all over the world without letting her in on their plans. Key phrase there being "their plans." It was her life too.

She stood for a moment, befuddled and pissed off, then with a brisk shake of her head decided to focus on the task at hand. Later she would confront him and insist on full disclosure. Right now she just wanted more clothing on. Fast. Those few moments of being in his arms while they'd both been so nearly nude had been a test of self-discipline she'd very nearly failed. Every ounce of her body had ached to melt into those strong arms. To run her tongue down that hard, muscled chest and over those sexy rippled abs. To maybe even slip her hand beneath his towel and find out if he really was as huge—*oooh*—she *had* to stop thinking like that!

She glanced around, trying to absorb the fact that she was in Macy's after hours, undetectable, with apparent *carte blanche*. Distantly, embarrassingly distantly, her conscience squawked. She silenced it by reasoning that if later she felt guilty, she could always send an anonymous donation, and headed off to explore all the fashions she'd never been able to afford.

In the end, however, she eschewed high-price couture and settled for things that made sense. The slinky designer dress with the sexy spiked heels that made her sigh so wistfully would only be perceived by him as an invitation, and, really, who knew how many more lakes she might be dunked in?

So into her satchel went instead a dozen panties; three bras; jeans; sweats to sleep in; shirts, socks, sweaters; cosmetics and assorted toiletries; two belts; and—her only concession to temptation—a gorgeous fleece-lined suede jacket that seemed very Highland-ish to her.

But apart from that single expensive item, she stayed away from the high-dollar racks. Luxury was all well and good for a Fae prince, but what would she do with a pair of six-hundred-dollar Gucci boots? She'd be afraid to walk in them. Probably trip and break an ankle or something, and wasn't there some old fairy tale about stolen shoes that punished the thief? She knew better than most people that fairy tales had a twisted way of coming true.

She slipped into jeans and laced up tennis shoes. A sturdy pair of hiking boots went into the satchel.

She was done before he was. Figured. And when he returned, he was wearing dark, tattooed Armani jeans, with a sheer white silk tee and six-hundred-dollar Gucci boots.

Which also figured.

14

A week ago dinner would have been left-over pizza of indeterminate age fished from her barren fridge at home, by herself, while brooding about her nonexistent love life.

Tonight it was dinner from Bacchanalia in a sumptuous suite via invisible carryout, with a dinner companion who was the stuff of fairy tales. Literally.

Sitting across the elegant dining table from a tall, dark, Armani-clad fairy prince, Gabby stuffed herself on buttery lobster, pasta, and salad, followed by chocolate cheesecake and strawberries with champagne. Heavenly. Normally she'd have counted calories (she probably would have still eaten it all, but at least she'd have counted), but since she had no way of knowing how short her life might be at this particular juncture, she wasn't about to deprive herself in whatever remained of it.

She was just about to open her mouth to demand to know, in detail, what his plans were when he said softly:

"Why are you still a virgin, *ka-lyrra?*"

She blinked, an instinctive "it's none of your business" springing to the tip of her tongue, but just as swiftly bit it back. Perhaps if she answered some of his questions he'd be more responsive to hers. Besides, he was part of the reason her love life sucked, and it would feel good to get it off her chest. It wasn't as if she could complain to her girlfriends about the misery of being a *Sidhe*-seer. "In case you haven't noticed, I have a big fat handicap."

His dark brows drew together in a frown and his gaze swept her. "I see none. What kind of handicap?"

She pushed her chair back, tucking her feet up beneath her. "Duh. I see fairies."

"Ah. How is that a handicap?"

"I want a normal life. I want an average, everyday, full life. That's all I've ever wanted. A husband, a job I'm passionate about, and children. I want the dream, Happily-Ever-After and all."

"So, how does your seeing those of my race hinder that?"

She gave a gusty little sigh. "I've had two serious relationships in my life. Each time it got to the point that I was ready to get intimate, all I could think was that if I got pregnant, my child would most likely see fairies too. Which I'm okay with, I can live with that. The problem is, could the man in my life? Do I tell him I see a world he can't see? And that I'll have to protect our children from it? And that he's powerless to help? Or do I withhold that information and deal with it, if and when it becomes an issue, and hope it never does?" She smiled faintly, bitterly. "I told my last boyfriend the truth. I decided it was the only honorable thing to do, and that if he really loved me, he'd be able to handle it. Do you know what happened?"

Adam shook his head, his dark gaze unnervingly intent.

"First he thought I was joking. Then when I kept trying to make him understand—I even showed him the *Books of the Fae*—he completely freaked out. When I wouldn't drop it, when I wouldn't say that I was kidding, when my 'delusion persisted to manifest itself,' as he so charmingly put it, he told me I'd been working too hard and needed professional help. Shortly after that he dumped me. By e-mail, no less, the breakup choice of spineless, sniveling cowards. I tried calling but he wouldn't answer. I left messages, he wouldn't return them; he blocked my e-mail address; he wouldn't even answer his door. We'd known each other for three years and had been dating for half of that. He's a law student in my program. One of my girlfriends told me last week he was telling our mutual friends that I had a nervous breakdown."

"You didn't love him," Adam said flatly.

"What?" She was startled, wondering how he'd determined that so swiftly and matter-of-factly.

"You didn't love him. I've been—seen mortals in love, grieving someone they lost. You're not one."

With a faint, wry smile, Gabby conceded the point. "You're right. I wasn't crazy, head-over-heels in love with him. But I cared about him. A lot. And it still hurts."

"I'm sorry, Gabrielle."

She shrugged. "I can't say I didn't know what to expect going in. O'Callaghan women never have successful relationships. My dad left my mom when I was four. I hardly even remember him. Just a vague memory of a man with a scratchy beard and a loud, angry voice. The only reason my mom's second marriage works is because she can't see fairies and she never had any more children. Her husband has no clue that she's anything other than perfectly normal. And as long as I stay out of the picture, he never will. Gram never married. She settled for the children part of her dream. Got pregnant and didn't tell the father. It's not like ancient times when *Sidhe*-seers were revered and men fought for their hands. In my time, people don't believe in things they can't see. And me? I saw my first fairy, so Gram told me, when I was three years old. I pointed and smiled at it. Fortunately, it was Gram who'd taken me out in the stroller that day, because if Mom had, she wouldn't have even known what I was looking at and I probably would have been captured then. That was when they knew for sure that, though the vision skipped my mom, it hadn't skipped me. I didn't get to leave the house again until I was ten years old. It was that long before Gram was convinced I could go out without betraying myself."

Adam leaned back in his chair, watching her across the table. He'd begun this conversation with his question about why she was still a virgin, intending to turn her mind to sex and smoothly segue into seduction. But she'd ended up turning his mind away from it, toward different thoughts of her. He'd not considered what being a *Sidhe*-seer might mean for a twenty-first-century woman.

It was not so different from the old crone's life in the isolated forest as he'd thought. It still meant hiding, and not just from the Fae but from her own kind too. It meant a life of never quite fitting anywhere. She was right, what man would believe her? And, assuming any did, what man would tolerate such an affront to his masculinity—being unable to protect his own?

She'd actually been making quite a valiant stab at things: building a career, dating, and keeping the Tuatha Dé oblivious to her existence.

Until he'd come along and exploded through her back door, betraying her to the worst denizens of Faery.

"When I'm immortal again, I'll fix everything for you, *ka-lyrra*. You'll never have to fear again."

She wrinkled her nose as if to say "Yeah, right." "Speaking of which, what *is* your plan? If you're going to be dragging me all over the world, I think I have a right to know what we're doing."

He shook his head. "The less you know for now, the safer you are. If by some chance you're taken from me, my plan may be the only way I have of getting you back."

She shivered, paling. "You mean if the Hunters get me, don't you?"

Adam nodded. "Yes. Knowledge you don't possess can't be lifted from your mind by another of my race. Wait until we're in Scotland, I'll tell you there."

She shivered again. "Okay. But can you at least tell me where in Scotland we're going?"

"To sacred ground, where those of my race are forbidden to go. MacKeltar land. We'll be safe there."

"So I take it we're not going to try to find this Circenn Brodie person any longer?"

Adam watched her intently as he replied, "I can no longer wait for my son to resurface."

"Y-your *w-what*?" she sputtered, looking at him with an astonished expression.

"My son. Circenn is my son."

She sat up straight in her chair, frowning. "You mean, by a human woman? That's why he's only half-Fae? You had a child with a *human woman*?"

He nodded, concealing his smile behind a swallow of

wine. She sounded both offended and . . . reluctantly fascinated. Fascinated was good, very good. Precisely what he wanted to hear.

"When? Recently?"

"Long ago, *ka-lyrra*."

"*How* long ago? And stop making me pull teeth, Adam. I answered your questions. If you expect me to answer any more of them, you'd better start talking to me."

She looked as if she were about to leap up from her chair, grab him by the shoulders, and shake him. He might have antagonized her further, to goad her into doing it for the excuse to pull her into his arms, but he was too charmed by the fact that she'd just called him "Adam." Though she'd said his name on other occasions, this was the first time she'd used it so casually in conversation. He'd been waiting for it to happen. It was a milestone, revealing a deepening acceptance of him. He was no fool; he knew he'd been an "it" to her at first. Then the *sin siriche du*, or the blackest fairy, then his full name, Adam Black.

But now he was just Adam. He wondered if she had any idea what she'd just betrayed.

"Circenn was born in 811 A.D.," he told her. "He lived in his time until the early 1500s, when he met a woman from your century. They now live in your time."

Her eyes widened. "I don't think I even want to know how that happened. It would just give me a headache."

She was silent a moment and Adam fancied he could almost see questions whizzing behind her green-gold eyes as she pondered which one to ask next. He was pleased by what she chose.

"So does that mean any children you have are also immortal, even if they're only half-fairy? Not that I personally care," she added hastily. "I was just thinking it might be interesting to add to our books."

The only person who would be adding anything to those idiotic books was him; it was time the O'Callaghans got a few things right. "No, Gabrielle, only a full-blooded Tuatha Dé is born immortal. I gave my son an elixir that my race created so we could grant select humans immortality." She didn't need to know that he'd done it without his son's knowledge or consent. Or that Circenn had hated him when he'd found out what he'd done. Had, in fact, spent most of the next six centuries or so refusing to speak to him, refusing to acknowledge him as his father. His son could hold a grudge with the best of immortals.

"You can make people *immortal?*" she said faintly. "As in, they live forever?"

"Yes. I made his wife immortal too." How long ago had that been? He'd been tripping around in time so much of late that many centuries had passed for him, but for her—three mortal years or so? A distant shadow clouded his mind at the thought. The elixir of life had a particularly unsavory side effect; one he'd told neither Circenn nor Lisa about. Half-Fae children were born with souls (apparently half a dose of humanity was enough to merit the divine), and Circenn, with his more tenacious constitution, had a few more centuries before it would happen. It took roughly a millennium to affect a half-Fae. Pure humans, on the other hand, like Lisa, lasted but a few years. Lisa had little time left at all. The golden glow illuming her would soon sputter out, leaving her as void of a soul as any Fae.

"Did you make Circenn's mother immortal too?"

Abruptly Adam wanted out of the conversation. Pushing himself up from the table, he began bagging up leftovers. What food remained they would eat in the morning before catching a plane. He wanted an early start. "No."

"So she's dead?"

"Yes."

"Why didn't you offer her—"

"I did," he ground out, cutting her off.

"And?"

"And Morganna wouldn't take it."

"Oh." Her eyes narrowed, then widened, as if something had just occurred to her. "When did Morganna die?"

"What the bloody hell does that have to do with anything?" he snarled.

She eyed him warily but persisted, "When?"

Adam shoved the last tray of pasta back in a bag. It burst through the other end. Irritably, he folded the paper over it and shoved it under an arm. "In 847."

She was silent a long, reflective moment, then, "Why wouldn't she—"

He shot her a savage glare, eyes narrowed, teeth bared. "Enough. My life is not an open O'Callaghan Book, *Sidhe*-seer, to flip through as you wish and make all manner of bloody idiotic interpretations. The Tuatha Dé do not speak of Tuatha Dé matters to"—he gave her an icy sneer—"mere mortals."

"Well, mister-mere-mortal-yourself," she bristled right back at him, "maybe you'd better get used to it, because whether or not you like it, you need at least one of us 'mere mortals' to help you become a pompous-asshole-fairy-thing again."

He tried to maintain his icy stare, but his lips curved despite his efforts and he shook with silent laughter. A pompous-asshole-fairy-thing. The indignity of it. Had any of his race ever been called such a thing? Nothing cowed the woman. Nothing. "Point made, *ka-lyrra*," he said dryly. As he gathered the bags and turned to head for the kitchen, he added over his shoulder, "For the record, I've just told you more than I've told any other human in a very long time."

"How long?" The moment she said it, Gabby wanted to kick herself. But she wanted to know. Wanted to know who the last woman . . . er, human, was who had truly known Adam Black.

He stopped and turned back to look at her. When his obsidian gaze met hers, Gabby suddenly felt a little chill in her blood. Sometimes he looked so human, while at other times there was a frightening incongruity to his face, as if something terrifyingly old and completely inhuman were looking out at her from behind a Halloween mask of a youthful human face. And for a brief, strange moment she had the feeling that, were she to somehow lift that mask, she might find something very much like a . . . like a Hunter beneath it.

He made a small sound then, a tired sound. Not a sleepy sound, but an immortally weary one. Then he turned and resumed walking away.

She heard the refrigerator door open and close. Then silence. Then his deep, rich burr floated softly through the suite, "Since 847, Gabrielle."

It was one in the morning by the time Gabby pulled out the sofa bed, still mulling over what Adam had revealed. She'd not missed the significance of the dates. Morganna had died mid–ninth century, had refused his offer of immortality and, right around that time, Adam Black had been seen by not just

O'Callaghans but oodles of others, on a violent rampage through the Highlands.

Over Morganna?

Had Adam Black gone into a rage when he'd lost her? And if so, why had he permitted her to die? He'd been all-powerful; he could have forced her to stay alive, forced her to take his "elixir of life" (which was a mind-boggling concept in and of itself!).

Who *was* Morganna? What had she been like? Why had she refused it? How long had Adam spent with her? Had she lived her whole life with him? Woken up each morning with a Fae prince beside her in bed? Been spoiled every day by his crazy excesses, gone to sleep sated each night in his arms?

What had been so special about her that he'd tried to make her immortal?

"I could really hate that woman," she muttered beneath her breath.

Adam Black had had a relationship with a mortal woman, fathered a son with her, tried to make her live forever.

And Gabby was feeling... oh, for heaven's sake, she thought, exasperated, jealous. Envious that *she* kept denying herself, but Morganna hadn't. No, Morganna had taken what he offered, plunged right into it, taken all of it. *She'd* touched him and kissed him and gone to bed with him. *She'd* played with all that silky dark hair, felt it sweeping over her naked body. *She'd* tasted gold-velvet fairy skin, had sizzling hot fairy sex with him. Even borne his son.

And when she died, he'd razed the Highlands. In his grief? Or had it merely been the petulance of a child denied his favorite toy?

Who cares? I wouldn't mind being that man's favorite

toy for a lifetime, a teenage voice cooed dreamily. *Beats the hell out of the boyfriends you keep picking. Why settle for normal when you could have a life full of fairy tail?*

"Shut up," she muttered. "I'm having a hard enough time without you tossing your two cents' worth in. And spare me the juvenile puns."

Scowling, she punched the pillows, plumped them, then snapped the blanket out, spreading it over the sofa bed. She'd just gotten it arranged when he came up behind her, slipped his hands around her waist, and pulled her back against him, her shoulders to his rib cage. The heat of his big body scorched her through her clothing and she could taste his exotic spicy scent on each shallow breath she drew.

"Did you never wonder, Gabrielle?" he said softly, ducking his mouth close to her ear.

"Wonder what?" she managed, holding very, very still. He'd left just a tiny bit of space between their lower bodies, a tantalizing, tempting amount of space. She would *not* let her traitorous body bridge it. Would not let herself lean into him, searching with her bottom for that rock-hard arousal he always had. She realized then, with a bit of a start, that she *liked* that he was always hard around her. She'd grown accustomed to his incessant seduction. It was a heady thing, to know that the *sin siriche du* was so turned on by her. And the fact that he was so turned on fed her own desire. Being the focus of such intense lust from such an intensely beautiful man/fairy was the most potent of aphrodisiacs.

God, he was dangerous. But she'd known that from the beginning. He'd come packaged with O'Callaghan warning labels: *Avoid contact at all cost.* Didn't get much clearer than that.

"In all your years of watching us, of being forbidden

to look at us, and having to pretend you couldn't see us, did you never wonder what it would be like to touch one of us?" He slid his hands slowly up from her waist, and she knew he was giving her time to pull away, wagering that she wouldn't, and God help her, she knew she should, but she couldn't seem to get enough breath to do so. Her heart was pounding like a sledgehammer against the wall of her chest.

There was a long tense moment where neither of them moved or spoke.

Abruptly, he filled his hands with her breasts.

The breath she'd been trying to gather exploded from her lungs in a hiss. Her skin sizzled beneath the fabric of her shirt, as nerve endings arced to instant, insatiable life. She could only imagine how incredible it would feel to have his bare hands on her bare skin; those big, strong blacksmith hands all over her body. With that extra brush of Fae he had, she fancied she might go up in flames from the sheer erotic heat of it.

He made an edgy sound that was so animalistic and full of sexual hunger that her knees nearly buckled, and she swayed for a moment. His grip tightened on her breasts, causing her to draw in a long ragged inhalation, but he didn't offer her the full support of his body; he still kept himself, from the waist down, that slight, provocative distance away. "You have beautiful breasts, *ka-lyrra*. I've been wanting to fill my hands up with these since the moment I saw you. Plump and full and soft and . . ." he trailed off with a little purring noise deep in his throat.

Gabby closed her eyes; her breasts felt tight in his hands, swelling from his touch. His unshaven jaw rasped against her hair, then against her cheek as he nudged aside her hair. The sleek wet heat of his tongue traced a velvety trail down the side of her neck, sending shivers of sensual delight skittering up her spine. She was going to pull away, to stop him. Any minute now . . .

"Did you never fantasize about us? Tell me you didn't. Say, 'No, Adam, I never even thought about it once.'" He laughed huskily, wickedly, as if endlessly amused by the thought, his thumbs tracing light circles on her breasts, just beneath her nipples, on the soft underside where she was so sensitive. Her nipples were so hard they were poking through both her bra and her shirt, hungry for touch.

He closed his fingers on the puckered peaks at the precise moment that he bit down on the nape of her neck, and she clenched her teeth to keep from crying out. He knew, damn him, he *knew*. Her secret fantasies, the inner, eternal battle she waged. He knew all about it.

"Why so quiet? Why won't you say it, Gabrielle?" A pause. "Because you did think it. Many times." A sleek glide of his tongue down her neck. Another gentle nip on the tender, sensitive cord that ran from her neck to her shoulder, making her whole body shiver with desire. A delicious light pinch on her nipples. "Is it so hard to admit? I know you did. You wondered what it would be like for one of us to take you to bed. To strip you naked and make you come so many times that you couldn't even move. To give you so much pleasure that it left you limp and exhausted, unable to do anything but lay there while your Fae lover fed you from his hands, tended you, and rebuilt your strength so he could do it to you again and again. So he could ride you slow and deep, take you fast and hard from behind. So he could lift you astride him and feel you shudder on top of him when you came. So he could lick and taste and kiss every inch of your body until nothing else existed, until all else ceased to matter but what he was doing to you, the completion only he could give you."

She was panting softly. Damn him. She'd imagined all those things and more. And his words were painting much too vivid pictures in her mind's eye: Adam doing all those things to her. Being lifted astride him; on her hands and knees for him as he thrust into her from behind . . .

God, she thought feverishly, had she *always* been picturing him? Try though she might, she couldn't recall the face of the dream prince that she'd so lovingly detailed in her teen fantasies. Either he'd blasted it right out of her memories, replacing her imaginary lover with *his* dark eyes, *his* hard body, *his* seductive voice and devastating touch, or it had always been him.

Pull away, O'Callaghan, you know this will get you nothing but screwed—and not just physically, the inner, very faint voice of reason warned.

Right, in just a minute . . .

"You fantasized," he continued, his voice low and hypnotic. "You may be virgin in body, but not in mind. I feel the heat and passion in you; there's a fury of it inside you. I felt it the moment I saw you. You're not normal. You'll never be normal. Give it up. Stop trying to fit in a world that will never accept you. Nobody can understand you the way I can. You're a *Sidhe*-seer. You want to spend your whole life denying it? What you see. What you are. What you want. Sad way to live and die."

There was silence for a moment while he just held her, hands gone still on her breasts, breath warm against her neck, unmoving.

She knew this was her moment to rescue herself. To

rage at him. To tell him he was wrong, that he didn't know the first damn thing about what he was talking about.

But she couldn't, because he did.

Everything he'd said was true. She wasn't normal, and no matter what she did, she would never be normal. She'd been torn between worlds all her life, trying to ignore the one and fit into the other—both equally futile ventures—wondering if all there would be for her in the end was the kind of life Gram had lived. A baby, no husband, a big empty house. Telling herself it would be enough, if that was what had to be. In the meantime, giving it her best shot, trying to make things work with a boyfriend.

But no boyfriend had ever been able to compete with the fantastic Fae males she'd been seeing since childhood. No human boyfriend had ever been able to vie with a world that was intrinsically so much hotter and brighter and more sensual. And not with any boyfriend had she ever truly been able to be herself. And the sad fact was, a large part of why she was still a virgin was because she didn't want a man, damn it, she wanted a fairy. She always had.

And she was tired of wondering what it would be like with one, of forcing herself to look away, to turn away, to never touch. Tired of repressing all those sinfully seductive fantasies.

The silence stretched between them.

Abruptly one hand slipped from her breast and cupped her snugly, intimately, between her legs, grinding her bottom back against his erection.

An incoherent little cry burst from her throat.

He answered with a spate of words in an ancient,

unfathomable tongue that tumbled with the rough ve-
hemence of curses from his lips. Then in that ancient,
exotically accented English of his, he growled:

"You wondered what it would be like to fuck a Fae.
Well, here I am, Gabrielle. Here I am."

15

The last vestiges of her resistance eroded with his words.

Here I am.

Take me; do anything you want with me, in essence. And she wanted. Oh, God, did she want. She'd been wanting for a lifetime. Her fantasies about the Fae had always been basely sexual, and though she rarely used the f-word, on his lips, it was pure seduction. Something about the way his accent and deep burr shaped it made it sound, not harsh, but sexy and inviting, secret and forbidden and enticing. It didn't sound crude when he said it; it sounded like an invitation to dance a timeless dance that was innately earthy and animal, for which he would make no excuses and offer no apologies. Raw man, raw sex, was what he offered, in a world airbrushed into soft focus by his sheer beauty and seduction.

Of course, later, after the intense no-holds-barred-marathon-sex, her fantasy prince always fell for her in her dreams...but not until the frenzy of mating had been met. Not until lust's due had been paid. If it could ever be fully paid with a Fae.

She melted back against his body.

He sensed it instantly, the precise moment she yielded. He spoke in that strange tongue again, the masculine triumph in his voice unmistakable. She was lost and he knew it.

She expected him to turn her in his arms, crush her against him, but once again, he defied her expectations.

Hand still snug between her legs, pressing her relentlessly back against his hard-on, he splayed his other hand against her jaw and turned her head, guiding her lips to his. Standing behind her, he kissed her. She'd not have believed it possible to kiss at such an angle, but she'd never kissed anyone as tall as he was, and not only was it possible, it was bizarrely, intensely erotic. Dominant. Possessive. A kiss of branding and claiming. She was captured hard against his body, his big hand warm between her legs, his silky hair falling over her shoulder, his mouth sealing over hers.

She whimpered against his lips, but it was lost to the hot glide of his tongue, probing deep, retreating. Mating, escaping. Playing with her, dancing a slow, torturous, blatantly sexual dance.

Somewhere he'd learned—oh, probably a few thousand years ago, she thought with a tiny, almost hysterical bubble of laughter—exactly how much to give a woman before taking away, exactly how to keep a woman on a brittle desperate edge, merely with his kisses. The moment she melted into it, he would change it, take it some other way, give her less. Then come back for more the second she was about to scream. With him behind her, she had no control over the kiss. He had it all, and was exploiting it mercilessly. One hand on her face, one between her legs, holding her immobile while he tortured her with his lips.

Intense, breath-stealing, mind-numbing kisses, then gone. A soft, sultry brushing with that full lower, sulky lip of his, creating a delicious erotic friction that made her ache far more than it satisfied. More deep, toe-curling kisses, but not lasting long enough . . .

And, oh, God, if he devoted the same languorous, teasing attention to all parts of a woman's body, she was never going to survive him. She'd be an incoherent mess before he even got to the important ones.

And speaking of the important ones, she thought peevishly, he could start moving his other hand any-time now. She wiggled in his implacable grip, trying to communicate the wordless message. She was so close, had been since the moment he'd slipped that big hand between her legs, hovering on the edge. If he'd just move his hand the tiniest bit!

But if he understood her silent plea, he chose to ig-nore it. His hand remained implacably there between her legs, keeping her excruciatingly aware of her warm, wet readiness, of that sensitive bud begging for fric-tion, for even the smallest movement, but stayed mer-cilessly still. He had her trapped between two things that could bring her endless erotic pleasure, and was giving her nothing of them. Only the tantalizing prom-ise, but nothing to ease the intolerable pressure build-ing inside her.

Kisses. Slow and long, hot and hard. Tongue gliding satiny and sleek, tangling, withdrawing.

They were kisses to die for, she thought feverishly, trying to get more of him in her mouth, trying to suck his tongue deeper, refusing to release his lower lip when he pulled away with a soft laugh. She tried desperately to arch against his hand, but each time she managed to gain a tiny range of motion, he shifted his hand, backing off the pressure. Testy with impeded desire, she nipped at his lip.

"Bloody hell, Irish, you after blood? Trying to kill me?" he said with a soft, rough laugh.

"*Me?* Quit teasing! Kiss me deep! And anytime now you could move—"

He shushed her complaint with his kisses. Small laps, nibbles, kisses at the corners of her mouth, a long slow pull of her bottom lip. Deep again, then away. More torture. He kissed, she realized then, as perhaps only an immortal would. Kissed like a being that had all the time in the world, lazily but thoroughly, savoring every subtle nuance of pleasure, drawing it out, prolonging it. No clocks ticked in his world, no hours sped by. There was no work to get up for tomorrow, nothing more pressing than the passion of the moment. He existed as an immortal lost to immediacy, and being kissed with such in-the-now intensity was devastating. And she had a terrible suspicion that he might dole out the orgasms the same way—only letting her have one when he'd milked from her every bit of anticipation and need that he could.

She was drowning in sensation, the feel of his mouth on hers, the swollen hardness of him against her bottom, the heat of his big hand between her legs.

Then suddenly he broke the kiss and the hand cupping her jaw slid to her waist, raked up inside her shirt, and popped the clasp of her bra. He closed his big hand over one of her bare breasts. She shuddered in his arms, her body bucking forward against the hand between her legs.

"Adam," she gasped. "Move your hand!"

"Not yet." Coolly, unyielding.

"*Please!*"

"Not yet. Has any mortal man ever made you feel like this, Gabrielle?" he purred, a hint of savagery in that smooth deep voice. "Did any of your little boyfriends ever make you feel this way?"

"*No!*" The word exploded from her when his fingers closed abruptly on her nipple, pinching the hardened peak.

"No mortal can. Remember that, *ka-lyrra*, if you think to go back to your silly human boys. Do you know how many times, how many ways, I'm going to make you come?"

"I'd settle for just one if I could have it right now," she hissed, so intensely aroused that she was bordering on hostility. She'd never felt this way before, had no idea how to handle it.

Laughter spilled around her, husky, erotic, alien, dark, purely Adam Black.

"You aren't falling for me, are you, Irish?" he purred against her ear, that infernal hand finally moving up to toy with the button-fly of her jeans.

"Hardly," she forced out, her whole body straining with need as she waited breathlessly for his hand to slip inside her pants. With each button that popped, a tiny shudder shook her.

Her eyes fluttered closed and her head plopped limply back against his chest as his hand slid into her jeans and, palm to her skin, he pushed beneath her panties.

The moment his hand touched her bare skin her knees went out from under her.

As she started to go down, he snaked an arm tightly around her waist, holding her up.

"Good. I'd hate to think you were falling for me."

She didn't miss the amusement in his voice, nor the absurd reality that she'd indeed just quite physically fallen, from a mere touch. And he hadn't even grazed her clitor—

"*Oooh!*" A *whoosh* of air escaped her and she didn't even bother trying to stand anymore, just let him have her weight. Dimly, she could hear him panting against her ear, his breathing rough and labored, as if he'd been running for a very long time. Her climax was right there, she was on it, about to go over . . .

"Christ, Gabrielle, you make me—"

"Well, now, isn't this pretty," a deep voice mocked. "Looks like she's primed and ready for me. I can't wait to finish what you've started. Remember how we used to do that, Adam? How you and I used to share? Or is that yet another of those things you like to pretend never happened along with those few thousand years you pretend you never lived? Does she know what we can do to her? Have you told her how we used to play with mortals?"

Gabby jerked violently in Adam's arms, that oh-so-desperately-needed orgasm dying an instant death, though none of the attendant arousal did. Her throat worked convulsively as the sardonic voice penetrated her sensual stupor. She tried desperately to shake it off, to speak through it, to warn Adam that Darroc had found them again, but her treacherous vocal cords had locked up on her every bit as completely as they had back on Fountain Square. She was frozen from head to toe, rooted in place.

As she stood, unable to manage even the smallest squawk of warning, she was stunned and relieved to realize that somehow he knew.

Yanking his hand from her jeans, he turned her roughly in his arms and pulled her against him, snarling viciously. "Bloody *hell*."

Gabby's eyes fixed with horror on the tall copper-haired Fae standing just beyond Adam's shoulder. Head tilted back, she stared up at Darroc.

Its iridescent eyes a cool shade of ice, it pursed perfect lips that held a twist of cruelty and blew her a mocking kiss over his shoulder.

Her mouth opened on a scream.

But they were already sifting.

They sifted place for hours.

At first she was still in such a sensual daze that she could hardly even think, didn't even bother trying to speak. Her whole body was caught in a suspended, painful state of erotic awareness that was taking much too long to dissipate.

Well, at least one part of the *Book of the Sin Siriche Du* had been accurate, she brooded, the part about: *so sates a lass that she is oft incapable of speech, wits muddled.*

For not even fear for her life, it seemed, had much of a dampening effect on the storm of desire Adam had stirred in her.

Then again, she half-suspected she might be getting a little numb to fear; repeated exposure and all.

Still...the passion he'd awakened in her was like nothing she'd ever felt before. Nothing she'd ever thought possible to experience. Quite simply, being touched by Adam Black made her whole body feel gloriously, intensely, addictively alive.

It was just as she'd always feared: a few Fae kisses and a woman was lost.

And it wasn't as if she were a novice where kisses were concerned. She'd kissed a lot. In fact, she suspected she'd kissed a whole lot more than most women. Because she was a virgin and men were... well, men, her dates had put extraordinary effort into foreplay with her, each determined to be The One That Scored, like it was some kind of competition.

Hours of expert, seductive kissing, and she'd always seen her dates firmly to the door.

Yet after a few kisses from Adam, she'd not only been hovering absurdly close to orgasm, she'd been about to fall—literally—into bed, or rather on the floor, or any damn where he'd wanted her.

He was addictive. It had been bad enough looking at him and wondering what he would be like in bed, but now she had a clear idea, and she was never going to be able to look at him again without thinking about it. In great detail. Now that she'd gotten a taste of him, she was finally able to put into words what she'd sensed about him from the very beginning, what had been wreaking havoc with her senses since day one: Adam Black was more man than most *men*.

He was strong and sensual and certain of himself, an uninhibited hedonist, every last glorious gold-velvet inch of him. He adored sex, savored it, everything about it. He was controlling, yet in a way that fed a woman's fantasies. He would be, she now knew, a whole lot dominant in bed and a little bit dirty. He would take her every way she'd ever imagined and, she was quite certain, a few ways she probably hadn't.

He would be inventive and inexhaustible and utterly devoted to pleasure.

There was now no doubt in her mind that he *could* do as he'd said: leave her so limp, so dazedly and thoroughly sated that she'd not even be able to summon up the strength to feed herself, to lift her head from the pillow, or the floor, or wherever else he chose to leave her when he was done with her.

A woman could hurt herself on Adam Black in bed.

And out of it, O'Callaghan, that faint inner voice warned.

Oh, yes, she didn't bother arguing. *And out of it.* And that was something she needed to devote careful thought to, and not while he was touching her either. And she would, just as soon as things settled down a bit.

Not that she was making excuses for herself, but as crazy as her life had gotten, she was pretty much being forced to constantly react, not getting a chance to think things through and act.

She didn't need to dredge up one of Gram's many pertinent adages to understand what a dangerous way that was to live.

But, heavens, she thought, with droll exasperation, it would certainly help her think more clearly if she could just figure out what her odds of survival were. When one didn't know how much longer one might live, discipline and self-denial had a funny way of flying right out the window alongside calorie-counting.

It was quite some time before her body calmed from its wild fever-pitch arousal enough that she was able to relax in his arms while they sifted. Even then, she did it very carefully. Avoiding contact with that part of him that was still rock-hard and would only make her feel so miserably turned on again. She noticed that he, too, was trying to avoid contact for a change, and when she inadvertently brushed against him at one point, he made a harsh sound and snarled, "Don't *touch* that. It *hurts*. Christ, I'm not made of stone."

"Sorry," she said instantly, though inwardly an utterly feminine part of her beamed, delighted to know she wasn't the only one having such a hard time recovering. That she wasn't the only one their intimacy had affected so intensely. (And he certainly felt like he was made of stone, at least *there* anyway.)

She was shocked, sometime later, to find they were back in the hotel room, where Adam grimly snatched up their luggage. She opened her mouth to ask what in the world was so important that he'd risked returning for it—really, clothes and toiletries were eminently replaceable—but he'd sifted place again and she'd learned her lesson about keeping her mouth shut while doing so. (Fortunately they encountered no lakes on their itinerary this time; she was grateful they weren't near the coast, materializing in shark-infested waters would have been way worse than being dunked with tadpoles.)

They continued sifting until she'd completely lost track of time, then boarded another passenger train.

Once on the train, he took a seat and pulled her down to sit between his legs, though maintaining space between their lower bodies. He drew her shoulders to his chest, wrapped his arms around her, and rested his jaw against her hair.

She was startled to realize he was shaking. It was almost imperceptible, but there was a deep tremor running through his powerful body.

"What's wrong, Adam?" she asked nervously. What could make Adam Black shake? Did she even *want* to know? Had she missed something? Were they still not safe yet, even after all their frenzied sifting?

"What's wrong?" he growled. "What's *wrong*? Bloody hell, I screwed up, that's what's wrong! Do you know how lucky we were that he let me see and hear him? If he hadn't, there's no telling what might have happened. Christ, I'm not used to this being-powerless shit; I'm no frigging good at it." A long pause, then a muffled oath. "I should never have stopped for the night, Gabrielle. I shouldn't have stopped until I had you in Scotland and knew you were safe. I was a bloody arrogant fool."

Arms snug around her, he lapsed into stony silence.

Gabby blinked and fell silent herself. Her heart did a dangerous little flip-flop inside her chest. *I was a bloody arrogant fool*, he'd said. Not words she'd ever expected to hear from your average imperious Fae.

But then, nothing about Adam was proving to be what she'd been raised to expect from the average imperious Fae.

And the line in her mind between man and fairy was getting ever more blurred.

Closing her eyes, she leaned back into him, telling herself to try to get some sleep while she could, because it was anyone's guess when or where she might get to sleep next.

She'd just begun to drift off into a light doze when he shook her gently; they disembarked and caught a shuttle to the airport.

"A flight's leaving now, *ka-lyrra*," he said, scanning departures. "There's no time for me to play with their computers and get you a ticket. You'll have to hold my hand. Come. We must hurry to catch it."

Scotland. They were going to Scotland. Right now.

Blinking, stupefied by what her life had become, she slipped her hand into his.

Invisible, they passed through security and made for the gate. She glanced up at his profile. His jaw was set, his eyes narrowed and focused straight ahead, and he was walking so fast that he was practically dragging her.

His pace didn't slow until they'd boarded the plane.

It was Monday, she thought with a kind of distant wonder as she sank into a window seat beside him, holding tightly to his hand.

She should be home, at work. She should be getting ready to make her stand with Jeff. She had dry cleaning to pick up, plants that needed to be watered, a dentist appointment this afternoon, and dinner plans with Elizabeth tonight.

Instead, she was on a plane, cloaked by the *féth fiada*, temporarily noncorporeal, about to fly halfway across the world, being chased by otherworldly demons, and half-seduced by an otherworldly prince. Would have—if she had to be brutally honest with herself—probably been wholly seduced, if not for the interruption of said otherworldly demons, and wouldn't *that* have made a fine mess of the already fine mess in her head?

It was a measure of how surreal her existence had become that, in the midst of all she could be worrying about, indeed, *should* be worrying about, her most prevalent concern was that she really, really hoped everyone had already boarded, and they would just stay in their own seats and not sit in her.

You were firing questions at me today, trying to get inside my head.
You asked if I believe in God.
I told you of course I do — I've always had a strong sense of self.

Your house is quiet now, you're sleeping upstairs and I'm alone with this blasted, idiotic book that purports to tally the sum of my life, and the fact is, maybe I do. But maybe, ka-lyrra, your God doesn't believe in me.

— FROM THE (GREATLY REVISED) BLACK EDITION OF
THE O'CALLAGHAN *Book of the Sin Siriche Du*

16

Scotland. The Highlands.

In Adam's opinion, there was no finer place in all the world. He'd passed much of his existence sporting a human glamour amid her lush vales and rocky tors. He'd lived for a time, back in the seventh century, in the guise of a battle-scarred warrior, with a Highland clan called the McIllioch, eaten and "tooped" and fought beside them. And when one of their many battles had grown too fierce, he'd bequeathed a Fae gift upon the McIllioch males, saving their line from extinction.

He'd set up his smithy here and there, for a time at Dalkeith-Upon-the-Sea, for a time at Caithness, among too many other places to name. He'd infiltrated the Templars when they'd fallen, guiding them to Circenn at Dunnotar, to be used in battle by Robert the Bruce, and then to the Sinclair at Rosslyn, where to this day their fantastic legacy endured.

And the Keltar, well, he'd been fascinated by that Highland clan of Druids since the day they'd been chosen to negotiate and uphold The Compact with the Tuatha Dé, but he'd been especially fascinated by the twin MacKeltars, Dageus and Drustan—dark, powerful, sometimes barbaric—sixteenth-century Highlanders who'd forsaken love, only to find it in the bleakest hours of their existence.

And now he was in human form, driving into those mountains at the side of a human woman, about to meet those very Keltar in the flesh.

What would they make of him? Would his reception be fair or foul? He was, after all, of the race that had made the Keltars' lives so difficult; one of those responsible for generations uncounted of MacKeltar being feared, touted as "pagan" and "evil" for continuing to adhere to the Old Ways when Gaul abandoned their Druids first to the Romans and then to the equally tender mercies of Christianity.

Would they know of him? Would his reputation have preceded him? Would Dageus have any memory of Adam healing him? The mighty Highlander's heart had stopped beating completely by the time Adam had knelt beside him on the Isle of Morar.

Would the Keltar, like Gabrielle, be reluctant to trust him? Reluctant to do what he needed them to do, or rather, *not* do?

Rubbing his jaw, he stared out the window of the rental car, forcing himself to put aside thoughts of whether those two would welcome or revile him— what mattered was that they'd crossed the queen's wards several leagues back, and Gabrielle was now on protected ground—he'd deal with whatever else came to pass. He'd spent most of the time in transit over the ocean mentally kicking his own ass for what had happened in Atlanta: Because he'd been so selfishly intent on seducing her, on binding her to him, he'd imperiled her life. *Stupid, smug bastard; you're not invincible anymore.*

Rather than winning her, he could have lost his *Sidhe*-seer in that hotel room forever. Her fragile, precious life could have been snuffed out, freeing her soul to go places he could never follow, not even with all his powers restored. Merely thinking about it made his human body start knotting up all over again. Bad thing about being human and having so much muscle was that all that muscle could get tense. He'd gotten his first headache on the plane. He had no desire to get another one. Ever. Nor did he appreciate the sick feeling in his stomach no quantity of food had managed to assuage. Nothing but holding her tightly had seemed to help.

Exhaling slowly, he forced his attention outward, to the countryside, a vista of which he never tired.

At that moment, the car veered sharply to the left, then back just as sharply, and Adam bit back a smile, knowing she'd probably hit him if she saw it. Gabrielle had insisted on driving (if one could call it that) when they'd acquired the cramped, compact rental vehicle, arguing that the effects of the *féth fiada* enshrouding him might cause accidents were he to drive. Unaccustomed, however, to driving on the "wrong" side of the car, on the "wrong" side of the road, she was having a time of it.

For heaven's sake, if the sheep would just stop catapulting themselves onto the road, I might have a chance!

she'd snapped the last time he'd laughed. *They come out of nowhere, like they're dropping from the sky.*

Poppycock. Sheep trundle. Slow as snails. If you'd quit rubbernecking, trying to look everywhere at once, you'd see them coming, he'd teased. By Danu, he adored her fine-featured face, the expressions that flitted across it, her temperament. She had an inner fire that begged provoking, just for the pleasure of watching it burn.

Right. I'm supposed to drive past Loch Ness and not look at it? What if Nessie pops her head up and I miss it? You've been around for thousands of years. I've never been to Scotland. They should keep the damned sheep off the road. Put up fences. Why are there no fences in Scotland? Don't they believe in protecting the tourists? And what's wrong with two-lane roads? Have they never heard of two-lane roads?

If it's not two lanes, ka-lyrra, how are you having such a hard time staying on your side of it?

She'd bared her teeth in a ferocious little scowl and he'd had to bite the inside of his mouth to keep from laughing. Or dragging her into his arms and kissing her, which would have certainly resulted in a wreck.

Okay, one and a half lanes, she'd begrudged irritably. *I'm trying to stay on my three-quarters of a lane of it.*

And with a haughty glare, she'd promptly gone back to trying to look everywhere, while avoiding sheep and driving wrong-sided twice-over, spending more time off the road than on.

And he was back to trying not to laugh.

He relished her reaction to the land he'd long loved best, far more than Ireland, perhaps more even than anyplace on all of Danu. He could give it no rhyme or reason, Scotland and her people just did something to

him. Always had. If Gabrielle's inability to keep her
eyes (and the car) on the road was any indication, Scotland was exerting the same ineffable pull on her too.

And how could it not? Late summer was breathtak-
ing in the Highlands, the hills dappled with the colors
of the waning season: the deep reddish-purple of bell
heather, the pale pink cross-leaved heath, the heart-
shaped silver heads of sillar shakles. It would be a few
weeks yet before ling and heather truly began to paint
entire hillsides with their purple-pink haze, and he
found himself hoping they'd still be there to see it.

He'd like to see Gabrielle running through a field of
heather; he'd like to strip her naked and push her down
in it and have his wicked way with her.

And he would, he promised himself. Soon. Now that
she was safe.

It wouldn't be long before they were at the Castle
Keltar. The lights of Inverness were even now fading
away in his side-view mirror.

Inverness.

Morganna.

It was near here that she'd lived so long ago, at Castle
Brodie.

And suddenly, in that side-view mirror there were no
roads, no hotels or shops, no diners or pubs, nothing
but wide-open, unspoiled land stretching beneath a
vast blue sky . . .

I love you, he'd told her, astonished himself when
the words had fallen from his tongue. But Circenn had
just been born and was wrapped in blankets, cradled in
her arms—his *son.* She'd been sweat-glistening, damp-
haired, exhausted, and glowing with an innately female
radiance. And something had come over him. He'd

said it, and it had been too late to recant. And, bloody hell, how swiftly he'd wished to recant.

She'd torn her gaze reluctantly from the bairn and tipped her face up.

And she'd laughed.

If he'd had a soul, it would have sliced right through it.

Her laughter had been soft and wry, and all the more abrasive for it. For in it, there'd been a touch of pity.

Ye canna love, Fae. Ye have no soul.

So much for Adam Black's words. Had any woman ever believed them? Or merely bowed to his irresistible sensual lure, fallen prey in body but never in heart? Once, he'd not cared. But time and contact with humans had done strange things to him, changed him, made him begin to wonder about things he'd never wondered about before—and sometimes he felt like he imagined Gabrielle must: straddling two worlds, one foot here, one foot there, no place that felt like home.

How do you know I can't love? he'd hissed. So casually she'd thrown the words back in his face, words he'd never said before. Words he'd never said again. *Define love, Morganna.*

She'd been silent for a time, staring down at the tiny infant snuffling wetly in her arms.

Love means ye'd die for that person a thousand times o'er, she'd finally said, gazing down at the newborn. *Ye'd give the verra last drop of all ye had to give to tarry at their side but one moment more, to behold them alive and hale and happy.*

That's not fair, he'd countered. *You know I don't have a soul. If I die, I cease to exist forever. If you die, you go on. To some other time, some other place, some other*

*world. I become dust. Nothing more. You can't hold me
to the same criteria.*

*Ye wish to play at being like us but nae held to the
same accounts? If ye truly love someone, Fae princeling,
ye'd give the verra last drop of all ye had to give—
whate'er it may be. And ye'd nae squabble o'er differ-
ences.*

*Maybe it's you who can't love, Morganna. Maybe
when you love someone it means you'd be willing—not
to die—but to give up your immortal soul for them. So
maybe it's your failing, not mine.*

And so the argument had begun. The timeless, eternal, never-changing argument between them. Until
the unique Tuatha Dé bond forged between a Fae male
and human woman the instant a child was conceived
had become more painful than pleasing. Until they'd
both built walls to keep the other out.

By Danu, how many times had they had that fight? A
hundred? A thousand?

Right up to the day she died. And he'd stood over her
deathbed, trying to get her to take the damned elixir of
life, as he'd been trying to get her to since she'd been
seventeen; but like a fool, in a rare moment of abjectly
stupid honesty all those years ago, he'd told the young
Morganna of its unsavory side effect: that immortality
and immortal souls could not coexist.

That once she took it, in a short number of years all
trace of that by which she defined her humanity would
be gone. That soft golden glow surrounding her would
fade day by day, until nothing of it was left. Until she
was as void of that divine inner flame as any Fae.

She would change, they always did.

But better a soulless Morganna than a dead one.

Never, Adam. Let me die.

He could have taken away her memory of his admission. He could have forced her to take the elixir. He could have made her believe anything he'd wanted her to believe.

But what he'd wanted her to believe was that he was worth it.

Would it be so bloody bad to be like me? he'd thundered. *Am I such a foul being, then, without a soul, Morganna? Have I not been good to you? What is it you want from me I've not given you? What have I failed to do, be?*

"Adam, there's something I don't get. Why didn't Darroc just kill us?" Gabby asked abruptly, jarring him from his dark reverie. "He had the advantage of surprise. He could have shot you in the back, or hit you over the head or something."

He blinked, rubbing a hand over his eyes. Christ, those memories had come suddenly and without warning, crashing over him so intensely that he'd forgotten where he was for a few moments. He'd been back there, hating her for dying. Hating her for looking down on him until the very end for lacking that with which she'd had the grace to be born.

Hating all humans, with their holier-than-thou souls, lumping all mortals together as one unilaterally vile species. And finally remembering that he was, after all, a demigod—so fuck them!—he had walked through the Highlands for a time as Death himself.

Jaw clenched, he shoved the whispers of times-gone-by back into that dark corner of his mind he never willingly visited. His *oubliette*, his place of forgetting. Layers upon layers of memories dropped into the pit and left there, stretching back thousands of years. To immerse in it would be to invite madness. Yet another lie he'd told Circenn was that learning too much too quickly caused madness among their kind, when the truth had been a subtle variation of that: It was not knowing when to forget that did.

"You don't know Darroc, *ka-lyrra*," he said. "He likes to play with his prey before he kills it. He wouldn't take the risk while I was touching you because, if he didn't knock me out or kill me instantly, I could sift us to safety. He didn't bother to conceal himself and the Hunters this time with the *féth fiada*, because he wanted me to see him and hear him. He was trying to antagonize me, to get me to turn on him, to separate us. After what he saw, I'd wager he now wants you as much as he wants me."

"Why?"

He glanced at her. She'd twisted her long hair up in one of those clips that she was so fond of, and there was a little spiky tail sticking straight up, poking the roof of the car, bobbing perkily as they bounced and careened over the rough road. She had on her soft suede jacket with the fleecy lining, the collar turned up, framing her slender neck. The early-evening sun was a fiery ball sliding down behind Ben Killan, gilding her dainty profile as she nibbled her lower lip.

And she was the bonniest damn thing in all the Highlands, far more than the blooming bens and sparkling burns.

She was funny and stubborn and sexy and smart and packed with human passion, and she did something to him he couldn't explain. Kissing Gabrielle, he'd decided back in the suite, with his arms full of her lush softness, was as close to tasting heaven as a man without a soul could hope to get. She'd responded to him with all the explosive passion he'd sensed in her the moment he'd laid eyes on her, rising swiftly to the edge of climax. He could so easily have brought her to it after they'd been interrupted, could have been merciful and relieved the tension in her body while they'd sifted, or even later on the train or plane.

But he'd not been about to let her off so lightly. He liked the thought of her stirred to painful awareness of him. Hurting with it, just like he was, constantly, painfully aware of her. They would suffer together. When he finally gave her that first orgasm, it would be followed by a dozen more. By his cock in her, deep to the hilt. Branding her his own.

His human body, it seemed, had pulled a MacKeltar trick; it had looked at her and growled: *mine*. And there was no going back. For either of them. If she hadn't figured that out yet, she would soon.

"To get to me. He's a twisted bastard. He likes to take from me. Especially mortal women. I had to play a deep game to keep him from finding out about Morganna. But he knows about you now, and he's not going to stop coming."

She opened her mouth, then closed it again. Then opened it, "Would it get to you, if he took me?"

He glanced at her, but she wouldn't look his way. There'd been a strained note in her voice. For a novel change, her gaze was fixed firmly on the road ahead. The question was important to her. And to him. "Yes, Gabrielle," he said with quiet intensity. "It would."

"Oh." She was silent a long moment. Then, "Are you sure we'll really be safe at this place we're going to?"

He smiled faintly. She was as bad as he was when it came to skirting issues and changing subjects. No matter. There was time. He would see to it that there was more than enough time.

"We already are; we've passed the wards. The queen is alerted the moment a Tuatha Dé crosses her wards and comes within a thousand leagues of Keltar land, and those wards identify the trespasser. This is the one place Darroc can't come without revealing himself to Aoibheal. If he did, the game would be over, and he's not about to let that happen. Besides, he has little familiarity with the human realm, and if I know Darroc, he'll focus on what must have brought him to Cincinnati. He'll keep trying to find Circenn."

"Will the queen know that *you've* crossed her wards?"

"The wards were designed for a Tuatha Dé, which I am no longer, so I don't think so."

"You didn't think Darroc would find us so quickly."

It wasn't a question, but he answered it anyway. "I underestimated him; I didn't think he'd dare bring forth more Hunters. There's no way he could have found us so quickly with only the four Hunters you saw with him in Cincinnati. But he summoned more."

"How many more?" she said, glancing at him, eyes widening with alarm.

"You don't want to know." When he'd turned her in his arms to face him, he'd been looking over her shoulder. A full score of Hunters had materialized right behind her, just waiting for the moment he would turn to Darroc and stop touching her. Crammed wing to dark wing, looming over her. He'd never seen so many Hunters together in one place, outside of their Unseelie prison. Even he'd found that dark legion mildly disconcerting.

More than disconcerting. The mere thought that

they might get their claws on Gabrielle had done something to the human heart inside his chest, had made it feel as if it were...seizing up, being squeezed in a giant, crushing fist.

"Were they behind me?" she asked warily.

She didn't miss a thing. He nodded.

"Uh...more than...er, a dozen?"

"Yes."

"You're right," she said hastily. "I don't want to know." Another lengthy pause. "You know...um, what Darroc said about you and him playing with mortals..."

A muscle leapt in his jaw. "What about it, Gabrielle?"

"Was it, er...true?"

"No," Adam lied. "Darroc lies. He was just trying to fill your head with nonsense. Cause dissension between us, do the old divide-and-conquer thing."

"Really?" She looked at him, green-gold eyes wide, searching.

"Really." He met her gaze levelly, willing her to believe him, hating that the one time she was looking as though she might, he was lying. But who and what he'd once been was not who and what he was now, and he'd not be tried and convicted for ancient crimes.

She nodded slowly, then, "So," she changed the subject briskly, "are you sure that these MacKeltars we're going to see will believe me? Even though they won't be able to see you?"

"Ah, *ka-lyrra*, I'm not sure there's anything the MacKeltar wouldn't believe. They've pretty much seen it all."

"We've lost him, Darroc," said Bastion. Darroc stared at the Hunter in icy silence. Watching

Adam with his little human had reminded him of the times long ago when they'd ridden the Wild Hunt together, when they'd hunted like brother-gods, invincible and free, ruled by nothing and no one. They'd been inseparable, known each other's thoughts as well as their own. Mortals had been nothing more to them than lowly beasts, good for a chase, amusing to play with, to set upon each other and watch them enact their silly tragedies.

But Adam had changed. He'd been corrupted by contact with humans. And he'd turned on his own kind over one of them. On *him*, Darroc, who'd once favored Adam as he'd favored no other.

Adam had become protective of humans, spending most of his time among the short-lived creatures. It was inconceivable to Darroc that any sentient entity could prefer humans to the Tuatha Dé.

He'd waited for Adam to return to the fold, to indulge and get over his perverse fascination. But millennia had passed and Darroc had come to see Adam for the abomination he was.

Incensed to discover Adam dallying passionately with the human, he'd let himself and his Hunters be seen. He'd *wanted* his scarred face to be the last thing Adam saw as he lay dying, as he watched Darroc break his woman.

But Adam hadn't responded to his taunts in his usual way. No, he'd reacted as if Darroc didn't even matter, as if his taunts couldn't touch him, as if only the safety of his pathetic little mortal was of any concern.

For the second time in as many days, Adam had used his body to shield his human and sifted out before Darroc could stop him.

And now the *sin siriche du* (who was no longer worthy of such a noble appellation) was out there somewhere with full knowledge that Darroc had loosed the Hunters. And Darroc knew Adam knew exactly what that meant: that he was planning to challenge the queen.

Which meant he had to find Adam again and fast. Before the clever *D'Jai* prince devised some way to get Aoibheal's attention, even powerless as he was. Darroc could no longer afford the luxury of drawing out his death. When next he saw Adam Black, his demise would have to be swift. He couldn't let his thirst for revenge jeopardize his ultimate goal.

Still . . . he might keep the woman for a time. She liked Fae males? He'd show her what Fae males could do to human women. He'd show her what Adam really was somewhere deep inside though he tried to deny it. Tuatha Dé: a god. And she *would* worship before she died.

"Don't look at me like that, Darroc," the Hunter growled, jarring him from his thoughts. "We were ready. We could have slain them in a human heartbeat. *You* insisted on separating them and taking them alive. Is this about regaining our freedom, or your vengeance?"

"Both," said Darroc flatly. "And it's none of your concern. Tell me, where did you last have their scent?"

"At a human airport."

"Their destination?"

The Hunter shifted leathery wings. "There were too many humans about. Their scent had been scattered by the scent of too many others by the time we arrived. We were unable to determine it."

Darroc cursed viciously.

"Let me call forth more Hunters. We'll find them again," said Bastion.

"The Unseelie King would note their absence," said Darroc. "He's no fool."

"But he is currently seeking his amusement elsewhere. None have seen him for quite some time," replied Bastion.

Darroc pondered the bit of information.

If only the Unseelie King could be relied upon, could be sought for counsel or alliance, but the King of Darkness was like no other of their race, so ancient that Aoibheal, at just under sixty thousand, may as well have just drawn her first breath. It was rumored that the Unseelie King counted his existence by many *hundreds* of thousands of years; some whispered it to be even more. And was, more often than not, quite mad. Few ever so much as glimpsed him, and none knew his name or true form. He'd created his own realm within the shadow-realm of the Unseelie prison, a fortress that was said to house entire galaxies, a dark, vast dominion sown with traps for the unwary, into which none that he knew of had ever entered uninvited and returned.

For that matter, none had ever entered *invited* and returned, save the Seelie queen on two occasions. Even she gave the King of Darkness wide berth.

Still . . . if he was occupied elsewhere, Darroc could certainly use more Hunters. "How long since last the king was seen?"

"Two score and ten," said Bastion.

A tidy bit of time, a risk worth taking. "Another score of you, no more," Darroc conceded. "Find Adam's son. I believe he will try to use him to get word to the queen. We must prevent that from happening. Saturate both

Cincinnati and the Highlands. When you locate his half-blood bastard, summon me. And if you happen to find Adam, do not approach. I want to be there when he dies."

Bastion nodded, sharp teeth gleaming.

17

Drustan MacKeltar tossed back a swallow of scotch and glanced around the table with a satisfied smile.

In the past year the MacKeltars had pretty much seen it all.

And, God willing, we've seen the last of it, he thought fervently.

After so many calamitous events, life was peaceful and sweet, all he'd ever dreamed and more. He wanted naught more than to immerse himself in simple pleasures for the rest of it. Like a meal shared with those he loved, before a crackling peat fire laid with sheaves of fragrant heather.

His gaze skimmed his dining companions: There was Gwen, his beloved wife, brilliant physicist, and radiant mother of their precious two-month-old twins, prattling happily away to Chloe about—of all things—the schools their children might one day attend.

And there was Chloe, his brother's cherished wife, an antiquities expert and bookish scholar. They'd just learned last week that she would soon be adding to the MacKeltar clan, and she'd been glowing ever since, as had her husband, Dageus.

Ah, and there was Dageus, his twin, younger by three minutes, and best friend.

It had been months since that night in The Belthew Building, when Dageus had battled and defeated the modern-day sect of the Draghar, who'd been determined to resurrect their ancient namesake. Dageus's eyes were once again sunny and clear, and he was full of easy laughter. Drustan couldn't recall ever seeing him happier.

Initially, Dageus had spoken of building his own castle on the northern third of the MacKeltar estate, but Drustan had swiftly put an end to such foolish talk.

The castle Dageus had overseen construction of for Drustan and Gwen—the fabulous home that had been a labor of his love for them, and bespoke it in every beautifully crafted detail—contained over a hundred and twenty rooms. It had been designed to house an entire clan, and Drustan intended for it to do just that.

He'd not lost his brother twice before to bid him any kind of fare-thee-well now. Clans weren't like modern-day families. Highland clans stayed together, worked together, played together, and raised their children together. Conquered their own little corner of the world and stuffed it to overflowing with their unique, proud heritage.

Hence Dageus and Chloe had taken up residence in

the castle, settling happily into a suite in the west wing, opposite Drustan and Gwen in the east.

And each eve without fail, at seven sharp, they met to dine (their wives insisted they dress for it, and he would have donned any blethering thing she'd asked to see his wee Gwen in such dresses and sexy shoes as twenty-first-century women wore), and the stone walls of the castle were filled with laughter, fine conversation, and the warmth of love.

Cocking his head, Drustan glanced up at the portrait of his father, Silvan, and his next-mother, Nell, hanging above the fireplace. He fancied Silvan's painted brown eyes twinkled merrily and Nell's smile curved more sweetly. Aye, life was rich. After all their trials and tribulations, it had settled into a peaceful cadence, with no life-or-death complications, no oath-breaking, no time-traveling, no curses, no evil Druids or Gypsies or crazed seers or Tuatha Dé.

He was looking forward to a very long stretch of unbroken peace and quiet. The rest of his life would serve well.

He pushed aside his plate and was about to suggest they adjourn to the library, when their butler, Farley, came blustering in, white hair bristling, his tall, hunched frame now ramrod straight. Something had clearly ruffled him.

"Milord," Farley said with a disgruntled *humph*.

"Mister MacKeltar," Drustan corrected for the umpteenth time, with a this-is-really-wearing-thin-but-I'm-determined-to-be-patient smile. No matter how many times he told Farley that he was not a laird, that he was simply Mr. MacKeltar, that it was Christopher (his modern-day descendant who lived up the road in the oldest castle on the land) who was actually laird, Farley refused to hear it. The eighty-something-year-old butler, who insisted he was sixty-two and who had obviously never before buttled in his life until the day he'd arrived on their doorstep, was determined to be butler to a lord. Period. And he wasn't about to let Drustan interfere with that aspiration.

If not for Gwen, Drustan might have been more adamant about correcting him, but Gwen doted on Ian Llewelyn McFarley, and had since the day he'd arrived, followed by so many other McFarleys to be employed in and around the castle that Drustan was no longer certain some days if it was Castle Keltar he lived in or Castle Farley.

If might made right, he thought wryly, it was Castle Farley by sheer numbers alone. At last count he employed fourteen of his butler's children and spouses, seventeen grandchildren, and there were twelve wee greats on the premises, from toddler to teen. The McFarleys were a prolific bunch, reproducing like the clans of yore. Drustan looked forward to trying to catch up. He would certainly enjoy the trying, he thought, gaze raking possessively over his wee, sensual wife.

"Aye, milord MacKeltar."

Drustan rolled his eyes. Gwen snorted into her napkin.

"As I was trying to tell you, milord, 'tis a visitor you're having and, though mayhap 'tis not my place to say so, she's a most"—*sniff*—"improper lass. Not at all like young Miss Chloe here"—huge, infatuated smile—"or our delightful Lady Gwen. Verily she puts me more in mind of that one"—he nodded toward Dageus—"when first he arrived. There's something not right about her, not right at all."

Drustan felt a sinking feeling in the pit of his stomach. Peace and quiet was on the agenda. Naught more. He glanced questioningly at his wife.

Gwen shrugged and shook her head. "I haven't invited anyone, Drustan. Did you, Chloe?"

"No," Chloe replied. "What's not right about her, Farley?" she asked curiously.

An annoyed *humph*. A few *ahems*, then a thoroughly miffed, "She's a fine enough lass, that is, when one is able to actually look at her, but"—he broke off with a deeply aggrieved sigh and cleared his throat several times before continuing—" 'twould appear she's having, er . . . solidity problems."

"What?" Gwen said, frowning. " 'Solidity problems'? What on earth does that mean, Farley?"

Drustan inhaled deeply, exhaled slowly. He didn't like the sound of this. Solidity problems did not bode well for the serenity of the occupants of Castle Keltar.

" 'Tis precisely as I said. Solidity problems," Farley reiterated, obviously loath to commit further to describing their unexpected guest.

"Oh, my," Gwen said faintly. "You mean, she's solid and then she's not? As in, she becomes invisible?"

"You'd not be hearing such a thing from me," Farley said stiffly. " 'Twould make one sound quite addled, such an assertion."

"And she's asking for *me*?" Drustan said irritably. How could that be? The only people he knew in the twenty-first century were those he'd met through Gwen, or since settling in on the MacKeltar estate. He'd certainly not made the acquaintance of anyone with solidity problems. Verily, he would have avoided such a person like the grimmest plague. He'd had enough of spells and enchantments to last a dozen lifetimes.

"Nay, she's asking for that one." Farley nodded at Dageus.

"Me?" Dageus looked startled. Glancing at Chloe, he shrugged. "I have no idea, lass."

Exhaling gustily, Drustan stood. So much for peace and quiet and simple pleasures. How foolish to think a Keltar Druid's life might ever be normal. In any blethering century. " 'Twould seem we'd best find out," he said. "Somehow I doona think we'll be so fortunate that this lass with 'solidity problems' might go non-solid in a permanent fashion and leave us all in peace."

When he made for the great hall, Dageus, Gwen, and Chloe were close on his heels.

Gabby stood in the entrance of the castle, shaking her head, stunned.

Adam hadn't bothered to tell her that the MacKeltars lived in a magnificent, sprawling castle with round turrets and square towers, enclosed by a mighty stone wall, and replete with medieval portcullis and barbican, the great hall of which alone could have swallowed her entire eleven-room Victorian.

Nor had he given her any warning that she might have wanted to run a brush through her hair or powder her nose and try to make herself presentable to . . . to aristocrats or . . . peerage or whatever manner of lordly people occupied castles.

Nope, just another abrupt dropping of Gabby O'Callaghan, sleep-deprived and unkempt, into yet another unfathomable situation, wholly unprepared.

She tilted back her head, examining her surroundings. An intricately carved balustrade encircled the hall on the second floor, and an elegant double staircase swept down from opposing sides, met in the middle, and descended in one wide train of marble stairs. It was a staircase out of a fairy tale, the kind a princess might sweep down, dressed in an elegant gown, on her way to a ball.

Brilliant tapestries adorned the walls, plush rugs were scattered about, and colorful stained glass embellished the many tall windows. The furnishings in the hall were massive carved pieces, detailed with complex Celtic knotwork. There were two fireplaces, both large enough for grown men to stand in, faced by high-backed chairs tufted with rich brocades, and arranged beside gleaming accent tables.

Corridors shot off in all directions, and she couldn't even begin to imagine how many rooms were in the place. A hundred? Two hundred? Complete with secret passageways and a dungeon? she wondered fancifully.

It wasn't until they'd begun climbing the long winding private drive to the estate that Adam had finally divulged the fascinating, though sketchy, bit of information that the MacKeltars were descended from an ancient line of Druids that had served the Tuatha Dé Danaan for aeons—and were the sole upholders of Man's side of The Compact between human and Fae.

"The Compact?" she'd echoed, stunned.

The O'Callaghan *Books* held scant information about the legendary treaty. She was beginning to realize that if she survived all of this, she was going to be able to add a wealth of information to the volumes for future generations—more and more *accurate* information—than anything they held to date.

Perhaps she'd even get to see the sacred . . . er, thing, whatever The Compact was—she didn't even know what it was supposed to look like. And how much, she wondered, ablaze with curiosity, might the MacKeltars be able to tell her about the Fae? As upholders of the treaty, they should know a great deal. She couldn't wait to pick their brains.

She snorted softly, not missing the irony of her thoughts. She'd spent her entire life determined to hide from all things Fae, refusing to open the *Books*, turning studiously away, and suddenly she was eager to know as much as possible about them.

The O'Callaghan *Books* had been wrong about many things.

And she needed to know just how many things, and just how wrong.

Only then might she be able to make some sense of the dark, seductive Fae prince who had blasted into her life and turned it so completely upside down.

She glanced up at him. He was standing silently, his gaze focused ahead, his big body still and tense. Was he uncertain of their welcome? It was difficult for her to fathom Adam being uncertain of anything.

She was tipping her head back to inquire, when two men entered the great hall and the question flew right out of her head.

They were simply two of the most gorgeous men she'd ever seen. Twins, though different. They were both tall and powerfully built. One was taller by a few inches, with dark hair that swept just past his shoulders and eyes like shards of silver and ice, while the other had long black hair falling in a single braid to his waist, and eyes as gold as Adam's torque. They were elegantly dressed in tailored clothing of dark hues, with magnificent bodies that dripped raw sex appeal.

Oh, my, she marveled, *they don't make men like these in the States.* Were these typical Scotsmen? If so, she was going to have to get Elizabeth over here somehow. A connoisseur of romance novels, Elizabeth's favorites were the Scottish ones, and these two men looked as if they'd just stepped straight off one of those covers.

"Try not to gape, *ka-lyrra*. They're only human. Mortal. Puny. And married. Both of them. Happily."

So much for fixing Elizabeth up, Gabby rued, glancing up at Adam His hand was resting possessively in the small of her back, and he was looking down at her with an unmistakably irritated expression that looked a bit like . . . jealousy? The *sin siriche du*—jealous of two human men? Over her? The notion seemed so unlikely to her as to be impossible; nonetheless, it made tiny breaths clot up in her throat.

"I'm not gaping," she managed to say, and really she wasn't, because as soon as she'd looked back at Adam, she'd realized that though the two men might be gorgeous for humans, they were nothing compared to him.

Take those two men, merge them together, sprinkle them with Fae dust, brush them with ten times the simmering sensuality and elemental danger, and that's Adam Black, she thought.

"Dageus, are you seeing . . ." the taller of the two began, with a disgruntled note in a voice deep and laced with a thick, soft burr.

"Rather like the faint, misty outline of a lass, Drustan?" his golden-eyed twin finished for him, with the same sexy accent.

"Aye," the one called Drustan said, scowling.

"Aye," Dageus agreed.

"Oh!" Gabby exclaimed. She'd forgotten about Adam's hand at the small of her back (deadly man, he'd gotten her so used to his constant touching that she was now more likely to notice its absence than its presence!).

Then again, how could the MacKeltars see her at all? she wondered, frowning. Because they were Druids? Heavens, she had so many questions!

Slipping away from Adam's touch, she hastily apologized to the two tall, dark men. "I'm so sorry. I keep forgetting that I disappear when he's touching me, because nothing disappears for me. I guess we probably gave your butler a bit of a fright." At their blank looks, she forged on. "I'm Gabrielle O'Callaghan," she said, stepping forward and offering her hand, "and I know you don't know me, and I know this all probably seems quite strange, but I can explain. Could we maybe sit down somewhere? It feels like we've been traveling forever."

The men exchanged glances. " 'We'?" the one called Drustan said warily.

"Oh, for heaven's sake, Drustan," a petite woman with straight silvery-blond hair and fringy bangs pushed past the towering Highlander, "where are your manners?"

A second woman, also petite, but with long curly hair streaked with copper and gold, emerged from behind the other twin, and they both hastened forward to greet her.

"I'm Gwen," the silvery blonde said, "and that's my husband, Drustan. This is Chloe and her husband, Dageus."

"Pleased to meet you," Gabby said, suddenly feeling like the queen of grunge, confronted by the two beautiful women. Here she was in an elegant castle, with four elegantly dressed people, she'd been traveling nonstop for a day and a half—or at least she thought she had; the time zones had gotten her rather discombobulated—and four plane changes and hours of stressful driving later, she looked it. Her hair had slipped out of its clip hours ago and she could feel it poking straight up from her head in back, she had no makeup on, and even the wrinkles in her clothes had wrinkles. She shot Adam a withering look. "I can't believe you didn't tell me we were going to a castle and that all these people would be here. Look at me, I'm a jet-lagged, bedraggled mess."

"Um, excuse me, but who are you talking to? And you're not a mess," Chloe assured her. "Believe me, Gwen and I have been in our share of scrapes and felt bedraggled ourselves, and you're not bedraggled. Is she, Gwen?"

Gwen smiled. "Hardly. Bedraggled is being in the full throes of nicotine withdrawal, and after a week on a bus with a group of senior citizens, falling into a cave, and landing on a body."

"And then getting tossed back a few centuries, with no idea of what's going on," Chloe agreed. "Naked, too, weren't you?"

Gwen nodded wryly.

Gabby blinked.

"I gave you my plaid," Drustan protested indignantly. " 'Twas ne'er my intention to send you back bare as a wee bairn, Gwen."

Gwen gave her husband a loving glance. "I know," she said softly.

The one called Dageus tossed his head impatiently. "All of which is neither here nor there. To whom do you speak that we canna see, lass?"

Tossed back a few centuries? Naked? What? Good heavens, were these people like Adam's half-Fae son, displaced in time? Her own life, her little corner of the Tri-State was looking increasingly normal to her with each passing day.

"Tell them, Gabrielle," Adam urged impatiently.

Blinking, Gabby nodded. "I have one of the, er... fairies here with me—"

"Tuatha Dé," Adam corrected irritably. "You're bloody well making me sound like Tinkerbell."

"One of the Tuatha Dé," she amended, with a wry smile. "He says I'm making him sound like Tinkerbell, but, believe me, no one could ever confuse Adam Black with Tinker—"

"Adam Black of the Tuatha Dé Danaan?" Dageus exclaimed, those exotic golden eyes widening.

"You know him?" To Adam, she said peevishly, "You didn't tell me they knew you."

"I wasn't certain if Dageus retained any memory of me, *ka-lyrra*. He was near death at the time, and I didn't know if Aoibheal would permit him recall," he said mildly.

"You mean, the Tuatha Dé Danaan that saved my husband's life?" Chloe exclaimed. "He's here with you?"

Okay, that threw her completely off balance. Adam had saved Dageus's life? When? How? Why? What was he doing, going around saving people's lives? What kind of fairy did that? None of the ones she'd ever heard of. Fairies didn't go around *helping* humans.

For heaven's sake, she thought, staring up at him, mouth ajar, *do I even know him at all?*

Damn the O'Callaghan Books. Had they gotten anything besides his immense sexuality right?

Adam smiled faintly and, with a gentle finger beneath her chin, nudged her mouth shut. His gaze fixed on her lips for a moment and he lightly traced the pad of his thumb over her lower lip. When he applied a gentle pressure, she was mortified to feel the tip of her tongue slip out to taste him. She hadn't meant to do it; she hadn't been able to stop herself.

His face went instantly taut with lust and he made a guttural sound in his throat. Nostrils flaring, he drew several slow breaths, then said tightly, "What, didn't read about that one in your silly *Books*, Gabrielle? Doesn't mesh with your preconceptions? Imagine that."

"Why didn't you *tell* me?"

"Would you have believed me?" he countered coolly. She winced.

"Hence, I didn't tell you." He let his hand fall from her face.

"Oh, do you see that?" she heard Gwen exclaim, as if from a distance. "She just disappeared again! This is *so* fascinating! And now she's back."

Gabby was still staring up at him when Chloe took her hand, gushing, "Oh, welcome, welcome, both of you. Are you hungry? Thirsty? What can we get you? And here, let us take your bags. So, er," she hesitated the briefest of moments, "I know this probably isn't the time for it, but just how old is Adam Black anyway? You see, I have a few questions about the Iron Age. Actually," she confided earnestly, "I have quite a few questions about several—"

"*Can* he eat and drink?" Gwen interrupted, with an utterly fascinated expression. "I mean, is he actually there? And, er... exactly where is there? Is he in another dimension or something? Parallel to ours, maybe?"

Dageus and Drustan exchanged wry looks and shook their heads.

Then Drustan stepped forward and slipped an arm around his wife's shoulders. Silvery gaze resigned, he said, "Why doona we just address whether or not the lass is hungry and let matters of history and physics bide a wee." To the general vicinity near Gabby, he inclined his head and said with quiet formality, "The Keltar bid you welcome, Tuatha Dé. The Old Ones are e'er welcome in our home."

Adam watched Gabrielle through nar-rowed eyes and, though he appreciated Drustan's formal welcome, was pleased that Dageus recalled him, and delighted that his *ka-lyrra* was finally beginning to see him for who he was, it was all currently doing little to appease him.

He'd not anticipated his reaction to seeing Gabrielle around the twins.

He didn't like it. Didn't like it one bit. There was too much testosterone in the room. And all of his—no inconsiderable amount—was invisible.

And knowing Drustan and Dageus were married wasn't doing a damn thing to ease his mind. Really, did she have to smile at them like that? Didn't she understand they were men and men were not to be trusted around a woman like Gabrielle, no matter how happily married they allegedly were? And Christ, he couldn't even mark his territory. Touching her in small, intimate ways failed to establish anything, because each time he did it, it only made her invisible to them.

He'd never hated being invisible more. Around normal men back in Cincinnati it had been of no consequence, but the Keltar were not normal men.

He toyed irritably with his empty tumbler of scotch, rolling it back and forth between his palms, eyeing the bottle on the sidebar.

Casting the MacKeltars a black look—which of course they couldn't see, but it made him feel mildly better—he stood, refilled his glass, and began pacing the library. It was a spacious, masculine room with cherry bookcases recessed in paneled walls, comfortable chairs and ottomans, a dusky rose marble fireplace, and tall bay windows. He circled it, absently examining books, listening while Gabby continued filling them in on their—ah, no, *her*—version of events to date. He'd tried to get her to tell it his way, but she'd seemed perversely delighted by the opportunity to tell the MacKeltars all about how her life had gotten so screwed up since his advent into it.

Gwen and Chloe were making sympathetic little noises, and he could just smell the bloody female bonding going on in the room. Everyone was bonding, except for the invisible person.

Bloody hell, he was hungry. But did he get to eat? No. Gabby had spoken for both of them, bypassing a meal, accepting a light snack in the library.

Shortbreads, candies, and nuts? A mortal body could expire of starvation on such meager fare.

And she'd not yet even gotten to the part where Darroc and the Hunters had appeared yet. Gwen and Chloe seemed fascinated by the notion of *Sidhe*-scers and had been asking dozens of utterly unnecessary questions about what it was like to be one. At this rate, it could take all night to get to the important parts—like what Adam needed them to do. If only he could speak for himself! He was beginning to wonder if she'd even manage to get it all wrapped up by Lughnassadh.

Currently she was elaborating about those idiotic, apocryphal O'Callaghan *Books*, and Chloe, antiquities lover and relentless bookworm, was trying to set up a time to come to Cincinnati to see them. Books. Faery was in danger, his queen was at risk, Darroc was trying to kill them, Hunters were on the loose, and they were talking about frigging books!

It mollified him only mildly to hear her say, "You're

welcome to see them, Chloe, but, frankly, I think my ancestors might have gotten a lot of stuff wrong."

About high damn time she admitted that, he thought, eyes narrowing, his gaze raking over her possessively. Willing her to look up at him. To make him feel less invisible.

But she didn't so much as cast a tiny glance his way, she was too busy answering yet another irrelevant question.

He was just about to stalk out and go help himself to something from the kitchen when Dageus said thoughtfully, "So 'tis the *féth fiada* he's cursed with that keeps us from seeing him?"

Adam's head whipped around. "What does he know of it, *ka-lyrra?*" he said, suddenly alert. Dageus was another human wild card, like his *Sidhe*-seer; the things he'd endured in the past year had changed him in ways of which none could be entirely certain. Had changed him so much, in fact, that when the present Dageus had encountered himself in the past—which *should* have canceled one of them out—it hadn't. Which was part of the reason the High Council had so firmly advocated his destruction. Of course, some among them had been driven by more nefarious motives, like Darroc.

"Yes, it is, and Adam wants to know what you know of it," Gabby related for him.

Dageus smiled faintly. "More than I e'er wished to. I used it myself to borrow a few rare tomes I needed not too long ago. We call it the magic mantle, or Druid's fog. 'Tis no' easy to wear; 'tis a chilling spell. There are two versions of it. The version the MacKeltars were taught, and the spell the Draghar knew—a much more potent, triumvirate enchantment, in the Tuatha Dé tongue. I ne'er used that version."

" 'The Draghar'?" Gabby echoed, frowning.

"For a time," Chloe explained, "Dageus was possessed by the souls of thirteen ancient, evil Druids who'd been banished by the Tuatha Dé to an immortal prison four thousand years ago. They were called the Draghar."

"Oh. I see." Gabby sounded quite unconvinced of her own words.

Chloe laughed softly. "I'll explain it all later, Gabby. I promise."

"Bloody hell, yes!" Adam exploded, stalking to Gabrielle's side. Closing a hand on her arm, he said urgently, "Ask him if he still retains the Draghar's memories, Gabrielle." During the time the thirteen dark Druids had possessed Dageus, their knowledge had been his, and they'd once been privy to virtually all Tuatha Dé lore. Adam had assumed that when Aoibheal had destroyed the Draghar, she'd stripped those memories from the Highlander's mind.

But what if she hadn't? If Dageus knew the ancient countercurse in the Tuatha Dé's tongue, he could terminate Adam's enchantment! No mere mortal could do it, nor could he himself, but a full-blooded MacKeltar Druid who knew the ancient words certainly could.

He'd be able to speak for himself, be seen again, be solid again, be able to make it unmistakably clear that Gabrielle was *his*.

"Okay, but they can't see me again, Adam. Stop touching me."

Stop touching me. Being invisible was making him feel impotent enough around the Keltar, and impotent was not a feeling Adam was capable of dealing with on any level, and her words provoked something fast and furious and primal in him. He was consumed with the sudden imperative to make her remember that not so long ago she'd been begging him to kiss her deeper, that he'd had his hand down her pants. Damn near inside *her*, and would have been there—with something far more intimate and personal than a hand—if they'd not been interrupted. That they had some serious unfinished business to attend to.

In one smooth motion, he tugged her up into his arms and crushed her mouth with a hot, savage kiss, plunging deep, claiming, saying with it: *I am your man, and don't forget it.*

Had she not yielded instantly, gone soft against him, accepting his kiss completely, he wasn't sure what he might have done. He was merely grateful that he didn't have to find out. In the library, invisible, with little to no foreplay was not how he wanted her first time to be. He wanted her first time to be an overwhelming, mind-numbing, perfect seduction that would brand her to the very core of her glowing golden soul.

Fortunately, she not only yielded, her knees did that little, utterly feminine buckling thing that made him feel like a veritable god among men, and he was able to make himself let her go.

When he did, she sank limply back into her seat, lips parted, eyes unfocused. She flushed, looking dazed, then shook her head abruptly.

He was pleased to see that Dageus and Drustan eyed her intently, then exchanged a thoughtful glance. Good, he'd finally marked his territory, at least a little.

"He wants to know if you retain the memories of the Draghar," Gabby said with another shake of her head, as if she were still trying to clear it.

Dageus nodded. " 'Tis why I brought it up."

"You do?" Drustan said, looking startled.

"Aye, though they've gone, their memories remain. Their knowledge is mine."

"Christ, you told me naught of that," Drustan growled. "*All* of their knowledge?"

"Aye. Masses of the stuff littering my mind. I spoke naught of it as 'twas of no relevance. With the Draghar no longer inside me, I have no temptation to use any of it. And the answer is aye again, I believe I can remove his curse. I, for one, would prefer to be able to see him. I doona care for this invisibility of his at all. 'Tis making me uneasy."

"*Yes*," Adam said, punching the air, elated. "Do it. Right now. Hurry the hell up." If he'd had the slightest suspicion that Dageus still possessed the memories of the thirteen, he'd have come here first, the instant the queen had abandoned him in London.

But he'd never imagined that Aoibheal might permit those memories to endure; so much of the Draghar's knowledge was innately dangerous, intrinsically corruptive. He snorted. His queen was slipping. When he was immortal again, they were going to have a long talk. Perhaps it was time he took a seat on her infernal High Council himself and got into the thick of things.

"He says, 'Would you please try?' " Gabby translated, tossing him a wordless little rebuke. He shrugged. Couldn't she understand his impatience?

"Is it forbidden magic?" Drustan asked Dageus.

"Nay. But 'tis the old Tuatha Dé magic. Not something we were necessarily given to use, though considering the queen left me it, well . . ." He shrugged.

"Do you feel 'tis dangerous in any way?" Drustan pressed.

"Nay, 'tis but a chant in their tongue."

"For Christ's sake, would you say it already?" Adam

hissed. "I need to be *seen*. I can't stand this bloody frigging invisibility."

" 'Tis your choice, brother. I leave it to your judgment," Drustan said.

After a moment's reflection, Dageus said, "I see no harm in it." Of Gabby, he inquired, "Where is he?"

When she pointed, Dageus rose and, circling the area she'd indicated, began to speak.

Or rather, Gabby thought, he opened his mouth and sound came out, but he wasn't speaking. It wasn't a single voice that issued from his lips but myriad voices, dozens layered atop one another, rising and falling, swelling and breaking. It was melodic yet chillingly dissonant, beautiful yet strangely awful. Like fire that one could crawl inside of trying to get warm, only to end up freezing to death in it.

It raised all the fine hair on Gabby's body, and she realized that if this was the old Tuatha Dé tongue, it was not a language Adam had ever spoken around her.

Whatever tongue he'd been speaking on those infrequent occasions wasn't this. This was a voice of raw power. Such sound could mesmerize, could seduce against a person's will. It was old magic, undiluted and pure. The kind she'd always imagined the Hunters possessed. A terrible magic.

As it built to a crescendo, she shuddered, closing her eyes.

"Easy, *ka-lyrra*; it's because you're a *Sidhe*-seer that it affects you so," she heard Adam say softly. "It's why I've not spoken my tongue around you. Your instincts to guard, to gather your people and flee, are being roused. In ancient days you would have heard us coming on the wind and secreted your villagers away. Breathe. Slow and deep."

She did as he said, pursing her lips and breathing through her mouth, trying to wait it out, hoping it would end soon. He was right, the mere sound of the ancient tongue was filling her with a bizarre kind of battle-readiness, a bone-deep urge to round up the MacKeltars and make them hide. Then to ride through the nearby towns, sounding the alarm.

Finally Dageus finished, and she heard Gwen and Chloe say simultaneously, breathlessly: "Oh, my God."

Gabby opened her eyes.

Drustan had risen to his feet and was scowling, an expression mirrored by his twin. Both were glaring at Adam—whom they obviously could now see. Then at their wives, then back at Adam.

Gabby absorbed the looks on Chloe's and Gwen's faces, and suddenly felt *so* much better about having had such a hard time ignoring the Fae all her life.

It isn't just me, she thought gratefully. She wasn't a woman of weak moral turpitude, a spineless, undisciplined fairy-abduction-waiting-to-happen; the Fae *did* have something magnetic and inordinately seductive, something women simply couldn't resist. Adam was affecting Chloe and Gwen in the same way he affected her.

And how could he not? she thought, seeing him anew through their eyes. He was nearly six and a half feet of powerful, gold-skinned Fae prince, his body sculpted of pure muscle, his long black hair spilling to his waist in a dark silky tangle. Clad in those tattooed jeans, boots, an ivory sweater, and leather coat, gold torque gleaming at his neck, he dripped dark, otherworldly eroticism. His chiseled face was savagely beautiful, shadowed with a few days' dark stubble. Ancient intelligence and barely banked sexual heat glittered in his exotic, dual-colored eyes. The faint fragrance of jasmine, sandalwood, and spicy man that always clung to him seemed suddenly to fill the room with his heady, intoxicating scent. She wondered, not for the first time, if there were some kind of chemical in the scent a Fae gave off that worked as an aphrodisiac on humans of the opposite sex.

He was, quite simply, a living, breathing fantasy, exuding an irresistible come-hither that held an intrinsic, unspoken caveat of danger. He had a come-and-get-me-baby-I'm-pure-trouble-and-you're-gonna-love-it kind of attitude that provoked a woman's most primitive sexual drives. Drew her even as she knew she should be running like hell in the opposite direction. Drew her, in fact, in some perverse way, *because* she knew she should be running like hell in the opposite direction.

And now that she was seeing the looks on Gwen's and Chloe's faces, she wondered how she'd managed to stay out of bed with him as long as she had.

For that matter . . . just how much longer she was going to be able to resist him.

For that matter, she amended irritably, as she watched Gwen and Chloe watching him, *why* she was. It sure didn't look like *they* would be.

"Holy cow," Chloe said faintly.

"No kidding," Gwen breathed.

The sexy Fae prince flashed them a smile that was pure devilish charm, sexy and playful and mischievous, briefly catching the tip of his tongue between white teeth, before his lips curved, dark eyes sparking gold.

Gabby groaned. She choked on it hastily, camouflaging it with a dry little cough. Her own private stash of eye candy had just been made available for public consumption and she didn't like it one bit.

Apparently she wasn't the only one.

"Are you thinking what I'm thinking, Dageus?" Drustan said irritably.

"Och, aye," Dageus said darkly. "You liked him better invisible too?"

"Och, aye."

"Should I curse him again?"

"Och, aye."

Adam threw back his head and laughed, eyes sparkling with gold fire. "Bloody hell, it's good to be back," he purred.

18

Dageus and Drustan weren't the only ones who'd like to see...er, rather, not see...Adam invisible again.

There were twenty-three females on the Keltar estate—not counting Gwen, Chloe, herself, or the cat— Gabby knew, because shortly after Adam had become visible last night, she'd met each and every one, from tiniest tot to tottering ancient.

It had begun with a plump, thirtyish maid popping in to pull the drapes for the evening and inquire if the MacKeltars "were wishing aught else?" The moment her bespectacled gaze had fallen on Adam, she'd begun stammering and tripping over her own feet. It had taken her a few moments to regain a semblance of coordination, but she'd managed to stumble from the library, nearly upsetting a lamp and a small end table in her haste.

Apparently it had been haste to alert the forces, for a veritable parade had ensued: a blushing curvaceous maid had come offering a warm-up of tea (they'd not been having any), followed by a giggling maid seeking a forgotten dust cloth (which—was anyone surprised?—was nowhere to be found), then a third one looking for a waylaid broom (yeah, right—they swept castles at midnight in Scotland—who believed that?), then a fourth, fifth, and sixth inquiring if the Crystal Chamber would do for Mr. Black (no one seemed to care what chamber might do for *her*; she half-expected to end up in an outbuilding somewhere). A seventh, eighth, and ninth had come to announce that his chamber was ready and would he like an escort? A bath drawn? Help undressing? (Well, okay, maybe they hadn't actually asked the last, but their eyes certainly had.)

Then a half-dozen more had popped in at varying intervals to say the same things all over again, and to stress that they were there to provide "aught, *aught* at all Mr. Black might desire."

The sixteenth had come to extract two tiny girls from Adam's lap over their wailing protests (and had stayed out of his lap herself only because Adam had hastily stood), the twenty-third and final one had been old enough to be someone's great-great-grandmother, and even she'd flirted shamelessly with the "braw Mr. Black," batting nonexistent lashes above nests of wrinkles, smoothing thin white hair with a blue-veined, age-spotted hand.

And if that hadn't been enough, the castle cat, obviously female and obviously in heat, had sashayed in, tail straight up and perkily curved at the tip, and wound her furry little self sinuously around Adam's ankles, purring herself into a state of drooling, slanty-eyed bliss.

Mr. Black, my ass, she'd wanted to snap (and she liked cats, really she did; she'd certainly never wanted to kick one before, but please—even cats?), *he's a fairy and I found him, so that makes him my fairy. Back off.*

But everyone seemed to have forgotten her.

Even Adam. Oh, he'd kissed her again once he'd been made corporeal, and it had been another of those toe-curling, breath-stealing, possessive kisses (and it had seemed to greatly alleviate much of the Keltar twins' bristling), but then he'd gone to sit by the fire and, shortly after that, the parade had begun and he'd hardly looked her way since.

And interspersed with the Maid Parade, Gwen and Chloe had been firing questions (bless their hearts, at least *they'd* seemed to recover nicely from Adam's impact; Gabby suspected this was due in large part to them being married to such extraordinarily sexy men), and Gabby had sat in silence, feeling as if she were slowly turning every bit as invisible as Adam had been. As if he'd not only cast off his curse but had somehow managed to cast it onto *her*.

Finally, his patience obviously fraying, Drustan had ordered the staff off to bed, firmly closed the library door, then, after a moment's pause, had locked it and leaned back against it.

Must you endure that all the time? he'd demanded incredulously of Adam.

Adam had nodded. *Though there are some*, he said with a glance in Gabby's direction, *who bash me a good one on first sight.* This said with a fine show of rubbing his lip, the one she'd split, and a faint insouciant grin.

She'd had to clench her hands into little fists to keep herself from leaping up and bashing him again. Merely for being Adam. For being so unforgivably irresistible. For being visible, damn it all. Why couldn't he have just stayed cursed? Was that so much to ask?

He'd *needed* her then. But no more. He could speak for himself; no longer was she a necessary intermediary. And there were dozens of other women who were clearly more than willing to supply anything he might *want*, at the merest seductive crook of a finger. She'd felt suddenly, inexplicably bereft.

Scowling, she'd feigned exhaustion, in no mood to deal with the feelings that watching other women fall all over him had provoked in her. In no mood to hang around and see if they might begin scaling the castle walls and breaking in through windows to get to him.

Gwen had torn herself away from the complex cosmology questions she'd been firing at Adam long enough to show her to a chamber.

Gabby'd been pleasantly surprised to find it was no outbuilding but a lovely suite of rooms on the second floor, with a stone terrace through French doors that overlooked a garden. After Gwen had hastened off, she'd been even more pleasantly surprised to discover a half-full decanter of wine on the bedside table.

She wasn't so happy about it this morning, however.

Nor about the fact that she'd ended up creeping out into the hall and purloining refreshments from two other "chambers" before she'd drifted off to sleep in a wine-sodden stupor.

She glanced at the bed and scowled. No wonder she felt so awful. It didn't look as if she'd done any sleeping there; it looked more like she'd done battle for what small part of the night she'd been passed out. The silky sheets were knotted, the down comforter was wadded, and two of the plush velvet bed curtains had been torn down from their hangings. She had a vague memory of being so tipsy that when she'd tried to get out of bed and go to the bathroom, she'd gotten tangled up in them and fallen.

She had another vague memory that she didn't like at all. She thought she might have cried last night. Over all kinds of stupid things: boyfriends and blown jobs and . . . fairies she couldn't figure out.

She'd caught herself picking up the phone, thinking of calling her mom at one point.

Right, to say what? *Hi, Mom, I really need to talk to you about this fairy I met? Gram's dead and I don't have anyone else?* Ha.

Come to think of it, she brooded, gingerly massaging her throbbing temples, she was afraid she might have actually managed to dial through before she hung up. She couldn't quite remember, but she'd just stepped over a phone book on the floor. And it was open to the international dialing page, and that wasn't a good sign.

With a morose little sigh, she pulled her hair back in a clip *very* gently, so all her tiny hair follicles—God, her head hurt—wouldn't scream too much in protest, then opened the door and stepped into the corridor beyond. She'd never been able to handle alcohol.

Aspirin, she needed aspirin.

A week ago, she brooded, striking off to the left (deciding after a moment's consideration that any direction was probably as good as any other in the labyrinthine maze of stone corridors) things had been so clear. She'd known exactly who she was and what her place was in the world.

She'd been an O'Callaghan, doing what she'd been raised to do, concealing herself from nasty, inhuman fairies, living a double life, and doing a bang-up job of it for the most part.

Then she'd been an O'Callaghan being tortured by one of those nasty, inhuman fairies, albeit an impossibly seductive one, in human form.

Then she was an O'Callaghan being protected by said impossibly seductive fairy in human form from some *truly* nasty, inhuman fairies.

And now she was just Gabby, currently staying in a dreamy, magnificent castle in Scotland with a Fae prince who did all kinds of non-nasty, non-inhuman things like tearing up lists of names, and returning tadpoles to lakes, and saving people's lives.

Not to mention kissing with all the otherworldly splendor of a horny angel.

A Fae prince whom virtually every woman in the castle wanted in her bed; and, from the looks of things last night, they weren't going to waste any time trying to get him there.

And life just sucked.

Adam fisted a hand around the panties in the pocket of his coat and closed his eyes, inhaling deeply, as if from such a distance he might somehow catch the scent of Gabrielle.

No such luck; nothing but a crisp Highland wind rushing by as he pounded across the field on the back of a snorting black stallion. And though the breeze was sweet, it was far from the sensual perfume of Gabrielle's private heat.

Those silky pink panties were one of several things he'd not been willing to leave behind in the hotel room. He'd only removed them from his pocket and tucked them in his bag because he'd planned on getting naked with his *Sidhe*-seer, and he'd not wanted to have to explain why he had a pair of her panties on his person, had she discovered them. He wasn't certain that was a thing a woman could appreciate.

Ah, but a man did. The soft, sweet, sultry scent of a woman caught on a silky bit of fabric that slipped so intimately between her legs, rubbing against that luscious mound, carrying that unique fragrance a woman only had *there*. A man couldn't breathe of such a scent behind a woman's ear or in the soft hollow of her throat, in her hair or in the small of her back.

Only if he was her lover did a man get to know that scent.

He'd known it since the night he'd pilfered her panties, and he'd been so damn close to it a few nights past. He was dying of impatience, about to explode if he didn't get to bury his face in it soon.

Not the panties. The real thing. Between her thighs, his face, his tongue, not just inhaling, but tasting. Feeling her writhe beneath him in ecstasy, feeling her come against his mouth. Lapping with his tongue, bringing her to peak again and again. Showing her all the pleasure he could give her, binding her to him in the most ancient and sure way a man could.

Unfortunately, other things had demanded his attention.

Not only had Gwen and Chloe hammered him with all manner of questions (many of which he couldn't find the words in their language to answer anyway, and some of which he'd refused to answer because such knowledge was still too far in mankind's future) but Dageus and Drustan had waited patiently until the wee hours for their wives to wind down and depart, then begun with questions of their own. He'd filled them in on all that had transpired, from the High Council decreeing Dageus be subjected to trial by blood, to his current straits.

Then, all-too-humanly tired, frustrated that Gabrielle was sleeping somewhere in the sprawling castle without him—they'd not been apart more than a few necessary minutes in days—he'd rather gracelessly imparted what he'd come for, and the twins had been less than thrilled.

You want us to bring down the walls between Man and Faery? Drustan had roared. *Are you blethering mad?*

Not that we aren't grateful for all you've done for us, Dageus had hastened to say, *but you just told us your queen nigh destroyed our entire clan because I broke an oath, now you're asking us to do it again?*

Hence, after a deep, dreamless sleep of a mere few hours (no matter that he was human in body, his Tuatha Dé mind still didn't dream), he *still* wasn't with his *Sidhe*-seer but out riding with the Keltar twins, as he had been all morning, pounding across the lush terrain, rehashing over and over again that he wasn't *really* asking them to break their oaths, he was only asking them to . . . delay fulfilling them.

Until the last possible minute.

Assuring them it would never go that far.

Realizing that were they to refuse him for any reason, he would simply sift stealthily up behind them and incapacitate them (and their descendant Christopher, who was also a Druid) if he had to, until Lughnassadh had passed. Because, by Danu, he *would* stop Darroc and he *would* preserve Aoibheal's reign and he *would* regain his power and he *would* see to Gabrielle's safety for the rest of forever.

In her defense—and all people were entitled to one, no matter how reprehensible their actions; that was one of the first things a person learned in law school—Gabby didn't plan to do it. There was no malice aforethought. Wanton and willful disregard? She might plead to that. But not to premeditation.

She was a good person. Really. Probably as much as ninety-four percent of the time.

Surely she could be forgiven for the other six percent?

It wasn't as if she'd left her room *looking* for the opportunity to malign anyone or indulge in a bit of character assassination.

But the opportunity presented itself (as wily opportunities to damn oneself frequently do), and she was hungover, and for the first time in more days than she cared to count, Adam hadn't been waiting with coffee for her the moment she'd opened her eyes. No, Adam had been God-only-knew-where, with God-only-knew-what-harem in simpering, adoring attendance. And she was grumpy, caffeine-deprived, and lost in the winding corridors of the castle.

So when she came up on the rear of a cluster of maids breathlessly discussing "Mr. Black" as they fake-dusted their way down the corridor, something with a small, mean soul reared its ugly head, baring pointy little teeth.

It didn't help that all five maids were young and attractive: a tall, leggy brunette, a shorter curvy brunette, a voluptuous redhead, and two willowy blondes. Nor that they were currently debating whether Adam was a foreplay man or a get-right-to-it kind of guy.

"Well, he likes foreplay," she was startled to hear herself say much too sweetly, "but he's so terrible at it that it makes you *wish* he were a wham-bam kind of man."

Five women turned to gape at her.

The leggy brunette regarded her skeptically. That she spoke with a sweet Scottish lilt only irritated Gabby even more. "Mr. Black? I'll not be believing that. That braw man's a lass's dream."

"A really *bad* dream maybe," Gabby heard her wayward, lying lips say. "The man can't even kiss."

"What do you mean?" the brunette demanded.

"Drool," Gabby said succinctly.

" 'Drool'?" the brunette echoed, frowning.

Gabby nodded, accepting that it was too late. She was in it, and she may as well do it up right and see it through to a Big Finish. What she might lack in character, she'd make up for with commitment. "Have you ever kissed someone who . . . well, it's like they open their mouth too much? And they get your face all wet, and by the time they're done kissing you, all you really want is a towel?"

The redhead nodded emphatically. "Aye, I have. Young Jamie down at the Haverton's pub." She made a face. "Ugh. It's disgusting. He slobbers."

"That's how Mr. Black kisses?" a slender blonde exclaimed.

"Worse," Gabby lied shamelessly. "He hardly ever brushes his teeth, and I swear the man wouldn't know what dental floss was if you tied a little ribbon of it smack around his itty-bitty, er... well, that's another matter. But, no, I shouldn't . . ."

"Nay, you should, you most certainly should!" a blonde exclaimed.

"Aye, don't be stopping there," the short brunette chimed in.

"You wouldn't be meaning his winkie, would you?" the redhead said faintly. "Oh, say it isn't so!"

Gabby nodded sadly. "I'm afraid it is."

"Just how itty and bitty?" the leggy brunette demanded.

"Well," Gabby said, sighing, "you know how big and tall he is?"

Five heads bobbed.

She edged closer, lowering her voice conspiratorially. "Let's just say he's not in proportion."

"No!" they exclaimed again.

"Afraid so." She could have left it at that, *should* have left it at that, but the green-eyed monster had a fistful of her hair, not to mention control of her lips. She was appalled to hear herself say "Take my word for it, the only one Mr. Happy is making happy is himself."

The leggy brunette eyed her suspiciously. "Nay, I'll hear none of this. Last eve I saw the bulge—"

"Socks," Gabby cut her off, barely managing to conceal her scowl. *How dare that woman be checking out Adam's bulge? I've hardly even given* myself *permission to do that.* "He stuffs socks down his pants. Though he prefers a banana if a nice green one is available. Says it gives the best firm impression. Says that since women wear Wonderbras, why shouldn't men enhance themselves too?"

"No!" Scandalized, the maids twittered, exchanging glances among themselves.

Gabby nodded. "It's true. I seriously considered suing the man for misrepresentation of material fact. Clothed, he might look like a dream, but out of those clothes, he's a nightmare."

The maids were all staring at her with varying degrees of shock and disappointment. Only the leggy brunette was still looking somewhat skeptical.

Gabby made a mental note to swipe a few bananas and deposit them in his room. She might have giggled at the thought had she not been so horrified with herself. Never in her life had she sunk to such depths. And apparently she wasn't quite done yet.

"You haven't noticed any bananas missing from the kitchen, have you? I'd keep a close eye on them if I were you. You might want to watch the sausages too."

And with that, she swept past them. Well, in as much as a hungover woman in jeans, a T-shirt, and tennis shoes (damn it, *why* hadn't she taken the slinky dress and heels from Macy's when she'd had the chance?) was capable of sweeping.

"For Christ's sake, Drustan," Adam said irritably, shifting in the saddle, trying to find a more comfortable position, knowing there wasn't one, because saddles hadn't been designed for men with immortal hard-ons, "you didn't even know that the purpose of your four feast day rituals was to uphold the walls between our realms until I told you. You thought they were just a heralding of the change of season and an affirmation of your commitment to The Compact."

"I ken it, and that fashes me more than a wee," Drustan exploded. "What if, in our ignorance, we'd failed to perform them in the past?"

"First of all, you never fail to keep an oath," Adam muttered darkly, "so I highly doubt that would ever have become an issue. Even if your whole clan were somehow wiped out, your bloody ghost would probably come back and bloody dance around the bloody stones. Second, it's not my fault your clan misplaced The Compact for so many centuries and you forgot the meaning behind the rituals. And third—this is really the only relevant part and it's what I keep telling you—" Adam said, enunciating each word tightly. Christ, his body hurt with wanting his *Sidhe*-seer. She was on safe ground. It was time. It was *past* time to make her his. How long had they been separated now? Fifteen mortal hours? It felt like a century. His skin was cold where, for the past few days, she'd been constantly pressed against him. "The queen will come, Drustan. She'll never let the walls come down. She'll come, demanding to know why you're not performing the ritual. Then I'll tell her about Darroc and all will be well. You'll perform the rites long before your twenty-four-hour window of time is up. And she'll be grateful, she *won't* be angry with you."

Christ, they'd been over this a dozen times. The Keltar Druids had from midnight on the dawning of the feast days of Imbolc, Beltane, Lughnassadh, and Samhain to midnight at the close of the feast day, to perform the necessary rituals. During that time the walls would thin, but they wouldn't collapse completely until midnight on the close of. For millennia uncounted, the Keltar had always performed their rituals at midnight on the dawning of.

When they failed to do so this upcoming Lughnassadh, once the walls began to thin, Aoibheal would appear, demanding to know what was going on. Adam was willing to bet she'd show by noon or shortly thereafter. There was no way she'd let the Isle of Morar be exposed, no way she'd let Fae realms rise up in the midst of human ones.

This was his one sure way to force the queen to appear. To bring down the walls between realms.

"And furthermore," he added darkly, "if you don't do this for me, there's not going to be any frigging Compact to uphold anymore. If Darroc overthrows the queen, he'll spill mortal blood in a heartbeat. Then you won't have to bother with your oaths; there won't *be* any walls between realms. You'll have a Tuatha Dé war on your hands, with the Unseelie roaming free in your world, and, believe me, the damage they could do in a mere matter of days would make your Black Plague seem like a pesky cold. In fact," he growled, "it will probably be *your* mortal blood Darroc will spill first, because he won't like that you possess so much knowledge of our ways. The two of you are a threat he'll want removed immediately."

"There is that," Dageus said, nodding his agreement and looking pointedly at Drustan.

"Is he always such a stick in the mud?" Adam demanded of Dageus, shooting a dark look at Drustan.

"Drustan's ever been overbroody about oaths and whatnot," Dageus said dryly.

"And it's a blethering good thing one of us is," Drustan said, casting Dageus a glare.

"Right, because if we *both* were, you'd be dead. Och, I forgot, so would I," Dageus said mildly.

Drustan's lips twitched for a moment, then he snorted and gave in to a laugh. "Point ceded, brother. Smartass."

"Learning more words from your wee wife, I see," Dageus noted, with an amused lift of a brow.

"I just did something so awful that I'm not sure I even know who I am anymore," Gabby blurted without preamble when she stumbled upon Gwen and Chloe MacKeltar; *finally* she'd found the center of the castle.

She hadn't meant to tell them that—really, she hardly even knew them, other than their brief conversation last night, which had consisted primarily of a recounting of recent events, nothing personal—but her mouth seemed to have its own bizarre agenda this morning, and she figured if she tried to zip it, she might explode.

Or worse, go find more wine, and she knew that was a really, really bad idea.

The MacKeltar wives were cozily ensconced in overstuffed chairs in a bright sunny room that opened off the second floor of the great hall, the east wall a bank of unbroken glass overlooking a lush tumble of gardens. They blinked up at her with warm smiles.

"Oh, come in! We were just talking about you," Chloe said, beaming, and patting a chair beside her. "Please join us. Have you had breakfast yet? There's coffee and pastries"—she waved a hand at the side table—"dig in. Gwen and I always breakfast in the solar; you can find us here every morning. We wanted to wake you, but Adam insisted we let you sleep. Said you hadn't gotten the chance to sleep in a real bed for a while."

The permanent scowl that seemed to have taken possession of Gabby's face eased a bit. He hadn't brought her coffee, but at least he'd *thought* of her. "Where is he anyway?" she asked peevishly, reaching for a buttery, golden-crusted scone.

"He went riding with Drustan and Dageus early this morning," Gwen replied. "They were talking nonstop in Gaelic as they rode out and it sounded pretty intense, so I think they might be gone awhile. What did you do that's so awful?" she asked avidly, plucking a clean cup from the table and offering it to her.

Sinking into a chair next to Chloe, Gabby poured herself a cup of coffee, heaped in sugar, and sipped greedily. Nice and strong, she noticed. *Thank you, God.* They waited patiently while she fortified herself, though by the time she'd finished her second scone, Gwen was tapping her fingernails against her cup.

Drawing a deep breath, Gabby began. Encouraged by their sympathetic responses, she ended up confiding the whole sordid debacle. Beginning with too much wine, skimming over the crying and the almost-phone-call, and ultimately to her confrontation with a contingent of the Maid Parade.

By the time she'd finished, Gwen and Chloe were laughing so hard they were wiping tears from their eyes.

"I can't believe I did it," Gabby said for the dozenth time. Blessed caffeine was thrumming through her veins, the scones had soaked up most of the sick feeling in her stomach, and the jackhammers in her head had died down to a dull tapping. She was beginning to think she might actually be able to take a shower sometime today. The mere thought of one when she'd awakened, the mere idea of little beads of water making contact with her tender scalp, had been more than she could bear. "Bananas," she said, appalled. "Do you believe I said that? I've never done anything like that. I don't know what got into me."

The moment she said "bananas" her hostesses started laughing all over again, holding their stomachs.

A very small, though bone-deep-embarrassed, smile curved Gabby's lips as she watched them laugh. It *was* kind of funny, or at least it would have been if it had been someone else who'd behaved so moronically. If her friend Elizabeth had done something so idiotic, she'd have laughed about it for months.

When they finally sobered, Chloe said softly, "Oh, please. What got into you was that last night every woman in the castle was looking at your man like he was their favorite kind of ice cream and they couldn't wait to devour him. Believe me, I can relate. Merely walking down a crowded street with Dageus can make me crazy some days. He and Drustan are hardly your average twenty-first-century men; women go nuts over them. The last time we were in Inverness some crazy romance author on a tour of the Highlands tried to get Dageus to model for the cover of one of her books."

Gwen nodded with a wry look. "It does get old. I nearly got into a bit of a tussle in a sporting goods store with a saleswoman."

But Gabby heard only one thing. "He's not my man," she told Chloe tightly. And wasn't that just the crux of the problem? "As a matter of fact," she added broodingly, "he's not really even a man at all."

"What on earth do you mean by that?" Gwen exclaimed.

"He's a *fairy*, Gwen." She couldn't believe she had to point out the obvious. Hadn't somebody told her last night that Gwen was a brilliant physicist?

"A male Tuatha Dé," Gwen corrected. "That's how

we think of them. Calling them fairies makes them sound like diminutive little things with wings. And they're not. They're just a different, highly advanced civilization, a race with vastly superior technology, but Adam's still every bit a man. Heavens, don't you see how he looks at you? If you have any doubt about what he is, look at that. That's pure man and nothing but."

Gabby went very still. "How does he look at me?"

Gwen and Chloe exchanged incredulous glances.

"Oh, for heaven's sake," Chloe exclaimed, "she's as bad as I was, isn't she, Gwen?"

"I think she might actually be worse," Gwen said dryly. "It's just a good thing the men are off elsewhere, because I can see we need to have a good long girl talk."

They rode for hours. It was early afternoon by the time they drew their mounts to a halt at the top of a vast, sweeping ridge. The sun had passed midpoint and begun its descent, and Adam was seething with silent impatience.

Still, no matter his mood, it was impossible to remain unaffected by the beauty of the Highlands. From their lofty vantage, the whole vale was spread beneath them like a scooped-out bowl between bens, at the heart of which sprawled Castle Keltar, looking tiny and faraway. Miles and miles of untamed, lush country stretched before them, dusted with the soft pastels of summer.

Adam inhaled deeply. How he loved this land. He'd always understood why the Scots had fought so fiercely to keep it. "Ah, she's lovely," he said softly, "Scotla is."

"Aye," Dageus agreed.

Drustan grunted, then sighed gustily, as if hours of talking and debating hadn't done it, but Adam's appreciation of their land had somehow resolved things for him. "We'll do it, Old One," he said. Grumpily. Clearly at irreconcilable odds with oath-breaking but conceding the necessity of it.

A quiet satisfaction spread through Adam's body.

That was what he'd been waiting to hear; the only thing that had been keeping him out on a horse, too far away from his woman. And with that victory, his thoughts turned with sharp focus to Gabrielle.

He knew just what gifts he would give her tonight. Tonight he would finally see his *ka-lyrra* in something besides jeans. Then in nothing at all.

Now he had seven glorious days stretching from here to Lughnassadh that he could spend with her, on safe ground, with no pressing concerns. Only the concern of sealing his claim to her. Of winning her body, mind, and soul. His desire for her was no longer about getting to experience sex in human form, it was only and all about simply getting inside her. Making her his. Being the one to turn those green-gold eyes all dreamy-sexy, the one to make her whimper, the one to make her shudder with pleasure. Who cared what form he wore, so long as he had her in his bed?

"Or, rather, not do it," Dageus was saying, when Adam tuned back in. "We'll sit back and let the walls come down. And we'll speak with our descendant Christopher and see to it he agrees."

Adam inclined his head, meeting the Highlanders' gazes with unspoken thanks.

"But hear this, Adam Black," Drustan added, "if all hell is to break loose a sennight hence, we'll be looking for you to fight at our side. We'll be expecting you to have our backs, as we'll be having yours."

Adam inhaled sharply as an emotion unfamiliar to him expanded in his chest. Drustan was looking at him as if he were just another man, a warrior to wage battle with them, to stand and hold against whatever may come. And he realized that beside them and beside his petite *ka-lyrra* he would stand. Even, if need be, against his queen.

"You have my word," he said quietly.

And when they both murmured swift acceptance of his pledge, that uncommon sensation, that strange pressure behind his sternum, expanded even more.

Gwen couldn't have been more right, Gabby reflected later that afternoon as she stepped out of the shower—she'd definitely needed some girl talk.

They'd talked for hours, whiling away the morning and most of the afternoon. The three of them had hit it off like old friends. She hadn't realized how desperately she'd needed to discuss things with someone. She'd been all alone with her thoughts since the moment Adam had burst into her life, and so much had happened so fast, and she'd not worked her way through any of it.

Gwen and Chloe had helped immensely. They were of the same age, and were a lot like her friend Elizabeth: smart (almost *too* smart), funny in a self-deprecating way, with big, generous hearts. And over the course of the day the three of them had curled lazily in the sunshine in the solar, talking nonstop

Gwen and Chloe had taken turns telling their stories

about how they'd met their husbands, and Gabby had listened, entranced.

Gwen had met Drustan first. She'd been on a holiday in Scotland when she'd fallen down a ravine and plunged through the bottom of the rocky crevice into a forgotten cave, only to land on an enchanted, slumbering Highlander from the sixteenth century (talk about *falling* for a guy). He'd sent her back in time to save him. But all hadn't gone well, and Dageus had broken his oaths to save Drustan's life so he and Gwen could be reunited.

And then Chloe had stumbled upon Dageus, or rather been stumbled upon by him, while he'd been holed up in a luxurious penthouse in Manhattan, searching ancient texts, trying to find a way to free himself from the thirteen evil souls possessing him.

Gwen had thought Drustan mentally unbalanced when she'd met him, with his talk of time travel and curses.

Chloe had thought Dageus a nefarious thief and hopeless womanizer. And she'd come to find out that he was possessed by purest evil.

Both had taken chances with their hearts, immense chances, against immense odds.

And both were deliriously in love, happily married, and living a dream. A dream that had tugged painfully at her heart when Gwen had brought her tiny, beautiful dark-haired twin daughters in to nurse, and Chloe had blushingly confided that she was expecting too.

And she'd not missed Adam's part in Chloe's happiness. Chloe had told her all that had happened in those dusty catacombs: about the showdown with the sect of the Draghar, how Dageus had taken a mortal wound in the process of defeating them and saving her. How she'd thought she'd lost her Highland love forever, and would have, if Adam hadn't given of his own life force to bring him back from the brink of death and see him returned to her.

That bore a lot of fascinated pondering in Gabby's mind. Just what motives had he been driven by? What thoughts had been going on in that beautiful dark head, behind those timeless, ancient eyes? What deep, unspoken feelings? Why would he stir himself to return a human man to his human lover? And at such a price?

For Chloe had also told her that Dageus had confided (when he'd finally come to bed for a few hours early that morning) that the reason Adam had been punished by his queen was because of his intervention to save the MacKeltars.

It was yet another thing he'd not told her—refusing to answer when she'd asked him twice before—but she could hardly blame him, because she'd not have believed it then.

She believed it now. And that knowledge was doing crazy things to her heart.

Now more than ever she wanted to know—who was Adam Black? Who was this big, underdisclosing, intensely sexual, surprisingly gentle Fae who seemed to spend more time with humans than with his own race? This Fae eminently capable of force, who never forced? This Fae who'd taken a stand for humans against his own kind?

More important, was all that fierce, guarded emotion in him reachable by a mortal woman?

That was the question that was making her feel shaky clear down to her toes. He was looking like every inch her fantasy prince. And it was scaring the hell out of her.

Before the afternoon was over, Gabby told her story in its entirety as well. It had been impossible not to. Gwen and Chloe were women who'd endured their own epidemics of otherworldly events; there'd been no need to hold anything back. Being a *Sidhe*-seer was only a moderately unusual thing from their perspective; it hardly even signified.

She'd told them how she'd been raised to fear the Fae, how her mom had left because she couldn't deal with her having the vision, how Gram had raised her, taught her to conceal her "gift." She'd told them what the O'Callaghan *Books* said about the Fae, and about how wrong she'd realized those books were—at least about Adam.

She'd told them how she'd given herself away that night she'd seen him, how he'd tracked her, and the many things he'd done since.

She'd finally admitted the fear she'd not, until that moment, admitted even to herself. That she would somehow survive all this, fall head over heels for him, only—unlike in her teenage fantasies—there would be no Happily-Ever-After. He would regain his immortality, secure her safety as he'd promised, then return to the Fae realm, and that would be that. After all, the universe would again be his oyster and, in the cosmic scheme of things, Gabby knew she was nobody's pearl.

It would be Game Over. Time up. No extended play. Just the haunting taste of an all-too-brief fairy tale left on her tongue, ruining her appetite for reality forever.

Well, first of all, Chloe had said gently, *I think it's too late, sweetie; you've already fallen.*

Gwen had nodded agreement. *But, second, and most important, Gabby,* she'd said softly, *the question you must ask yourself isn't, will you get a Happily-Ever-After? The question you need to ask yourself is, will you be able to live with yourself if you don't let yourself have a happy-now, and end up having had nothing at all?*

19

Gabby took her time with her hair and makeup that evening, a luxury she'd not been able to indulge for days. While they'd been traveling and sifting about, on those rare occasions she'd glimpsed a mirror—usually during a quick duck into a public rest room—she hadn't liked what she'd seen, so she'd not lingered. But tonight she had the assurance that they were on safe ground, there would be no unceremonious dips in lakes or falls from steeples, and she was determined to look good for a change.

Aspirin and a long hot shower had scalded away the last of her hangover. Chloe had invited her to drop by her chambers before dinner so they could find her something to wear, as they were nearly the same size. She was looking forward to wearing something besides jeans. Okay, she was looking forward to looking pretty around Adam; there, she'd admitted it. Really, a woman would have to be dead *not* to want to look good around him.

She brushed on lipstick and ran her fingers through her hair, letting it spill down her back, tugging a few long bangs to spike softly around her eyes. A smudge of smoky shadow at her eyes, a dab of mascara. A hint of shiny gloss on her mouth, enough to catch the light and do interesting things with it. Enough to draw a man's notice.

And that, she decided, eyeing herself in the mirror, was as good as Gabby got. Clothes would have to do the rest; she just hoped Chloe had something ultrafeminine and a smidgen provocative that she could borrow.

Opening the bathroom door, she stepped out into the adjoining bedchamber.

And froze.

Impossible, she thought, staring at the canopied bed.

Not that the velvet drapes were hung again or that the bed was neatly made—that was perfectly possible. A maid had obviously stopped in while she'd been in the shower, shaving her legs, smoothing on lotion, and fussing with cosmetics.

What *wasn't* possible was the slinky black dress she'd spent long minutes sighing over so wistfully at Macy's that was currently hanging between those drapes.

Nor, she thought, stunned, moving closer to the bed, the dainty heels she'd eyed so covetously.

Nor, she thought, eyes widening, that sinful bit of lacy bra and panties in her favorite shade of pale pink.

And, oh, my God, she thought breathlessly, *is that a box from Tiffany's?*

Clutching the lapels of her bathrobe, she glanced around the room.

There was no sign of him.

But on the air, faint yet unmistakable, was just a hint of the exotic scent of jasmine and sandalwood and spicy, seductive man, and she realized he'd probably sifted out mere moments ago while she'd been finishing up her makeup.

She reached for the box with trembling hands, opened it, and gasped, so stunned that she fumbled and nearly dropped it.

Nestled on a bed of velvet was a diamond choker and matching earrings, and she knew exactly where she'd last seen them. It had been back in Cincinnati, the night he'd brought her dinner from Jean-Robert at Pigalls. She'd left the office late, taken her usual path past Tiffany's to collect her car from the corner lot. There'd been a new window display up, and she'd been briefly captivated by the elegance of the simply set stones. She'd paused, gazing in the window at the matching pieces. Wondering, with feminine curiosity, what kind of man showered what kind of woman with such jewels. Wondering if she'd ever get so much as a diamond ring on her finger, or even a plain wedding band.

He must have been somewhere behind her, watching her.

Just as he must have been at Macy's.

I take care of what is mine, he'd told her when he'd handed her the keys to the BMW.

Indeed.

As she lifted the glittering strand of diamonds from the box, a small slip of paper fell out. She caught it as it wafted toward the floor.

Four words in ancient script, an arrogantly slanted scrawl.

Accept these, accept me.

Well, she thought, blinking, that was certainly direct and to the point.

She held the glittering stones in her hands for a long time, looking at them but not really seeing them. No longer really thinking but opening her heart, feeling, wondering. Hearing an echo of Gwen's words: *Will you be able to live with yourself if you don't let yourself have a happy-now, and end up having had nothing at all?*

Eventually she placed the box back on the bed and slipped on the panties and bra.

Stepped into the clingy black dress, tugged it over her hips, and zipped the tiny side zipper.

Perched on the edge of the bed, she strapped on the dainty, sexy shoes.

Then she reached for the box, donned the earrings, and fastened the strand of cool stones around her throat.

Adam had just stepped out of the shower when he heard a soft tap on his bedchamber door.

He hoped like bloody hell it wasn't another maid. When he'd returned from his ride, there'd been dozens of them loitering about in the great hall. While he was accustomed to women throwing themselves at him, he wasn't accustomed to them staring with such unnerving intensity directly at his crotch. Hard. As if they were trying to see through the leather to what lay beneath, or rather, stood beneath, because the damn thing was never going to go down until he'd had Gabrielle beneath him at least a hundred times.

"Who is it?" he called warily.

When he heard the soft reply, his eyes flared, then narrowed. With a lazy smile and slow deliberation, he dropped the towel he'd just knotted loosely about his waist.

"No holds barred tonight, *ka-lyrra*," he murmured, too soft for her to hear. He'd not thought to see her until dinner. But she was here, outside his door, outside his bedchamber. She might as well have strolled up to the lion's lair, nicely basted in fresh, warm blood.

His mouth was suddenly fiercely dry, his breathing harsh and shallow.

Would she be wearing them? Was she ready to admit? To take him? This woman who'd been raised on the worst tales of him, some of which were completely true?

And she *knew* that. She knew he'd razed the Highlands after Morganna; he'd seen the look on her face when she'd asked him about the date Morganna had died. She knew that, for all the things that were inaccurate in her *Books*, there were some that weren't. She knew that in nearly six thousand years he'd done a thing or two to merit some of the bad press he'd received. Gabrielle was no fool.

Had she seen past it? Had she seen *him*?

Would she have those damn diamonds on? He was almost afraid to open the door and see, so badly did he want her, given completely, without reservation, tonight, now, this moment. He needed it. Felt like he'd been waiting six thousand years for it. Christ, what was happening to him? Had he ever felt like this before?

He realized he was glaring at the door and had no idea how long he'd been doing it. He shook his head, muttering a curse at his idiocy. For Christ's sake, he was Adam Black. Not some bumbling mortal lad.

"Come in," he called, and if it came out a little more guttural than usual, he deigned not to notice. He stood at his full height of six feet four and a half inches, legs splayed, arms folded over his chest, wearing nothing but the ancient gold adornments of his royal house.

The door opened slowly—he felt like it was opening in slow frigging motion—but then there she was, and he felt as if someone had slammed a fist into his gut.

He was pleased to see she appeared to be suffering the same sensation.

She froze, her lovely green-gold eyes flying wide. "Y-y-you're...n-n—" she sputtered. Tried again, "Oh. Heavens. My. Goodness." Wet her lips. Took a deep breath. "*Holy shit, you're naked.* And oh—OH!" Her gaze dipped then flew back up to his face, and her eyes went even wider.

A smile of pure masculine triumph curved his lips. "Ah, yes," he purred. "And you, my sweet Gabrielle, are wearing my diamonds."

Gabby stood in the doorway, her heart hammering wildly.

Two-hundred-pounds-plus of gorgeous naked man stood before her, and he was so savagely, intensely beautiful that she couldn't tear her gaze away. Had to remind herself that oxygen was good for a girl, *so breathe, O'Callaghan*. She looked up and down, up and down again, little breaths slamming together in her throat.

Abruptly, she knew that after this night she was never going to be the same again. Nothing was ever going to be the same. Oh, yes, the man could define himself as the dawning of an epoch if he wanted to. There was, quite simply, before Adam and after Adam.

He stepped forward, moving with sleek animal

grace, a predatory glint in his dark gaze. He was hunter and she was food. And from the look in his eyes he was going to devour her.

He stalked to her, towering over her, staring down, reaching out to lightly touch the choker at her neck with his fingertips. "You know what this means," he said softly, intensely. "Mine. You accept it. You're mine. No, shush." He pressed a finger to her lips. "Don't say a word. Just let me look at you. I've been waiting to see you in this dress."

Circling behind her, he pushed the door gently closed, and she heard the metallic clicking of tumblers as he locked it. He padded slowly around her.

"Christ, you're beautiful, Gabrielle. Do you know how badly I want you? Do you know what fantasies I've been playing through my mind about you? Do you know how many times I jacked off, trying to get rid of this bloody eternal hard-on? Knowing that the only thing that was going to help was you?"

He padded another slow naked circle around her. "And now here you are. In my chambers. Locked in. And you're not getting out until I say you are. And I may never say it."

He paused behind her, leaned close, front to her backside, rubbed his cock against her ass in that sexy dress. The dress looked every bit as good on her as he'd known it would, clinging to every lush curve. Felt good too. Breath hissed between his teeth at the contact; it was so excruciatingly pleasurable that it burned. He sucked in a sharp breath and yanked himself back, knowing that if he touched her again like that it would be all over.

"And those shoes," he purred, his gaze dropping down over her ass, down the shapely curves of the

backs of her thighs, to her slender ankles with those little dainty straps tied around them.

"I watched you looking at them in Macy's. You've
got the sweetest legs and ass, Gabrielle. When I first
saw you in Cincinnati, you had on shorts and san-
dals on your feet. Even your painted little toes turned
me on."

He circled around in front of her. Her eyes were
wide, deliciously unfocused. Her lips were parted
and she was panting softly, her chest rising and falling
gently.

He pressed the tip of his finger to her lips, pushed inside. She closed those lush lips on it, sucking, and such
raw heat lanced through him that, for a moment, he
couldn't move. He finally managed to withdraw his
finger, sliding it slowly from that luscious pucker, then
traced a damp path over the shape of her mouth, across
her jaw, down her neck, to the lush valley of her
cleavage.

He should seduce her, he should woo her with
kisses, he should gently entice, lead her slowly yet inex-
orably down the path to her ultimate and costly capitulation.

But it was too late; he'd waited too long, and there
was a thing he could no longer deny himself. A thing
he'd been thinking about too much while riding today.
A thing he needed. Right now. And it pissed him off,
the hold it had on him, how savagely he wanted it. To
know the taste of her, to have her on his tongue, captured in his immortal memory. If somehow, for some
reason, she managed to stop him this night, at least
he'd have gotten this.

"For the record, Irish," he informed her tightly, just
in case she got the wrong idea, "I kneel to no one."

Then he dropped to his knees at her feet, shoved her dress up, gathered a fistful of silky material in each hand, and pushed her back against the door, pinning her to it by the fabric.

Gabby leaned weakly against the door, gasping for breath. The exotic scent of him was filling her nostrils, making her dizzy. Merely looking at him naked had gotten her so intensely aroused that she knew what he was about to find—she was wet; she was so wet she was almost embarrassed by it. She was ready right now; she didn't even need a kiss, or any other foreplay, for that matter. She certainly didn't know if she could survive what it looked like he was about to do. She just wanted him inside her. When he'd circled her like some big dark beast, talking to her, telling her how much he wanted her, she'd nearly begun begging.

And now he was on his knees between her legs, her dress rucked up to her waist, exposing her to him, naked but for a lacy scrap of silk slipping between her legs.

Oops, make that naked, she amended with a half-laugh, half-sob, as he dragged that lacy bit of fabric from her body with his teeth, tugging it down, down, teeth grazing her lightly, pausing to nip, scattering tiny little love bites over her skin, sending waves of chills skittering up her spine.

She felt drugged, drunken, intoxicated on passion. She had no idea how she'd managed to put him off this long, or why, and was suddenly astounded at how much time she'd wasted.

"I'm going to taste every inch of you before this night is through," he purred.

And then he began making good on that promise, with long, hot, velvety strokes of his tongue up the insides of her thighs. Lazy sweet nips on the plump inner parts of her legs, hot, openmouthed kisses on the delicate skin of her hips. He left no inch of her skin unkissed, unnibbled.

Then a hand was pushing her legs apart and his dark head was between them. When he flicked his tongue over the tiny bud nestled in soft folds, she grabbed great fistfuls of his silky, dark hair and shuddered, leaning weakly back against the door.

"Stay standing, *ka-lyrra*. If those sweet knees give out and you come down on the floor, I'll fuck you right there."

She let her knees buckle instantly, barely smothering a laugh.

"Aw, bloody *hell*, Gabrielle, I wanted this to *last*," he cursed, rolling instantly with her, catching her, going down beneath her to absorb the impact of her tumble.

But she was beyond niceties, she'd been waiting a lifetime for this. Couldn't wait one moment more. Sprawled atop his great, big, naked body, she wriggled against him until she'd cinched his hot, hard erection right where she wanted it, the swollen ridge of him riding with delicious friction against her. God, she was so close, a few good rubs . . .

"Oh, no," he hissed, instantly understanding. "You are *not* getting yourself there. Not without me inside you the first time."

"Then I'd suggest," she panted, "you hurry up and get inside me."

He made a choking sound, a husky, erotic-sounding laugh-growl. "Ah, Gabrielle," he purred, gripping her by the hips and rolling her beneath him on the soft carpet, "I'm never going to get enough of you, am I?"

"Not if you keep going so *slow*," she snapped testily.

"Spread your legs," he demanded. He stretched his body the full length of hers, supporting his weight on his forearms, kneeing her legs wider for him. "Lift them around my hips."

She obeyed instantly.

"Lock your ankles. This isn't going to be easy."

A delirious little shiver rocked her at his words. She knew that. She'd known it the first time she'd felt him pressed up against her bottom, there in Cincinnati, the morning he'd burst through her door, and it had been one of the things wreaking havoc with her senses ever since. All of her boyfriends had been big, tall men. She liked big men, always had, liked a bit of dominance. And Adam Black was big and bad to the bone, all around. She'd told the maids the truth, sort of; he *wasn't* in proportion, he was larger there than a woman would expect. "Somehow, I don't think anything about you is ever easy," she managed to gasp out.

"No it's not, but I think easy would bore you, *ka-lyrra*. I promise you I'll never bore you."

And then his hand was between her legs, a finger slipping into her sleek heat, pressing in, pressing upward, searching for her barrier. Then two fingers, and she was only dimly aware when he breached the thin membrane, the fleeting pain eclipsed by the pleasure of him moving inside her. Her hips arched helplessly up, wanting more, needing, aching for all of him.

And then his hand was gone and the thick head of his penis was nudging against her soft folds, and he was pushing himself inside her. She mewled, a whimper of distress, trying to adjust, wiggling, trying to accept, but he was too big and she was too tight.

"Easy, Gabrielle. Relax," he gritted.

She tried, but she couldn't; it was instinctive to resist, and they waged a silent sexual battle for a few moments, where he hardly gained another inch. Her muscles were bearing down on him, resisting the steely intrusion.

He sucked in a hissing breath through clenched teeth. "Gabrielle, you're *killing* me; you have to let me *in*."

"I'm *trying*," she wailed.

With a muffled curse, he abruptly shifted her, pushing her legs apart and up, resting her ankles on his shoulders, tilting her pelvis up and back, ruthlessly exposing her.

Fisting a hand in her hair close to her scalp, he tugged her head back and slanted his mouth hard over hers, taking her in a deep, soul-claiming kiss, his hot, velvety tongue probing, retreating. She was too stunned by the kiss, by the fierce, possessive savagery of it, to tense when he impaled her, which was, she realized, precisely why he'd done it.

He drove himself deep inside her with one slow, smooth, relentless penetration, filling her so completely that she screamed into his mouth, but he kept his lips sealed over hers, swallowing the cry. He stayed like that for long minutes, in her to the hilt, thoroughly invading every soft warm crevice of her, but not moving, just kissing her, his hot tongue tangling with hers. He was so large that it took long minutes for her to adjust, to ease and accommodate. Long minutes while he stayed still, occupying his territory, not surveying the perimeters until she was whimpering against his lips, begging him to move. Now that the pressure felt good, she was feeling an entirely different kind of pressure, that needed *lots* of moving to sate

"I'm in you," he purred. "Ah, Christ, I'm in you."

Then—*finally*—he began moving, an erotic little circular motion of his hips—not a thrusting but a slow deep rubbing inside her. Grinding himself into her, backing off just a bit, grinding again, each time nudging the tight bud of her clitoris with exquisite friction.

His intense, slow movements abraded some crazy spot inside her she'd not even known she had, and all her muscles clenched again on him, locking, shuddering, and when she came it was like nothing she'd ever felt before, an explosion so deep inside her, so shatteringly intense, that a visceral cry was torn from her throat.

"Bloody hell," he roared, his whole body going tight. He clamped his hands down on her hips, trying to back off, to pull out, not anywhere near ready to come yet, but it was too late, the way her body was closing around him was more than he could stand and he exploded inside her.

Hours later, Adam propped himself up on an elbow and stared down at Gabrielle, pondering what made beauty.

He thought he was beginning to understand. It wasn't symmetry of features; it wasn't perfection. It was uniqueness. That which one person had that no other possessed. That which was only their own. Perhaps Gabrielle's nose was like a thousand others, but they weren't on her face, with her eyes, with her cheekbones and hair. Nor were those noses graced with her many expressions, crinkling so charmingly when she laughed, flaring so haughtily when she was irritated.

He'd run the gamut of her expressions tonight. He'd seen her demanding, aggressive with lust, eyes glittering wildly as she'd arched and bucked beneath him. He'd seen her soft, sweetly yielding when he'd taken her from behind, on her hands and knees in front of the full-length mirror in the boudoir. He'd held her head back by a fist in her long silky hair so he could watch her face in the mirror. Watch those slanted green-gold eyes narrow and gleam like a cat in heat as she purred with pleasure. Watch her full breasts swaying as his heavy testicles slapped rhythmically against her ass and thighs. Watch her watching him do it to her. He'd seen her dreamy and lost as he'd licked and lapped her to peak after shuddering peak. And he'd even seen her looking almost frightened as he'd wrung yet one more delicious shudder from her.

If he'd had his full Fae power he would have eased her virgin soreness; as it was, he'd had to stop because she couldn't take any more. So he'd gently cleansed her as she lay sated in bed, built up the fire, then gone down to the kitchen for food, realizing they'd missed dinner. In fact, dinner had been over for many, many hours.

He'd run into Dageus in the dim, shadowy kitchens, where the Highlander had been pilfering ice cream from the freezer. The younger Keltar twin had taken one look at him, laughed, and said, "I doona suspect we'll be seeing you for a few days, will we, Old One?"

"You'll see me by Lughnassadh," Adam had replied with a devilish grin. "And quit calling me Old One. I don't call you Young One. Adam. It's just Adam."

"Aye, 'tis Adam, then," Dageus had replied easily.

As Adam had padded barefoot back up the cool stone stairs in the castle, toting a tray laden with food, his human body sore in places he'd not known a man's body got sore, he'd suffered another of those sudden sharp pains in his chest and had nearly dropped the tray. He'd had to stop and lean against the balustrade, gasping until it passed. He'd realized it was a good thing he would be getting out of his mortal body soon, because something was clearly wrong with the one Aoibheal had given him.

By the time he'd gotten back to the bedchamber, she'd been sound asleep, sprawled unselfconsciously across the bed, her nude body gleaming softly in the firelight. She was a vision of tangled blond hair, sex-flushed skin, and lush curves, a vibrant mortal, golden glow against silver satiny sheets.

Christ, she's amazing, Adam marveled, standing at the edge of the bed, staring down at his slumbering woman. Trailing the pad of a finger over the firm high peak of a breast. Even unconscious, her body reacted, the rosy nipple tightening. With a muffled oath he forced himself to drop his hand and back up a step, or he'd have his mouth on that nipple again, dragging the edge of his teeth across it the way he'd found she liked. And he'd hurt her, and he refused to hurt her.

She'd responded to him with all the pure, unstinting passion that he'd sensed lurking within her. All that fire she'd freed and turned on him, openly, without restraint, wanton to the core, and he'd reveled in it, soaked it up, gloried in it. She'd made him feel things he'd never felt before. Things he could spend immortal centuries pondering and perhaps still not fathom.

And for that gift you'll take her soul?

He flinched, shrugged it off. What—did human bodies come burdened with human consciences? *I'll give her immortality in exchange.*

You'll give her the choice? You'll tell her?

Not a chance in hell, he retorted silently.

If Gabrielle was to be his own private Eden, there would be no apple of knowledge proffered. Adam knew full well what had happened to that *other* Adam. A little knowledge always got a man booted out of the Garden.

He would not watch Gabrielle O'Callaghan die. He'd watched too many humans die. She was his now. She'd made her choice. She'd come to him, accepted him.

It would take a far better man than he to let her go where he could never follow.

Dageus smiled as he slipped through the darkened castle, one slightly melting pint of ice cream in his hand. He'd developed quite a taste for the modern-day treat, and a liking for teasing Chloe with the cool creaminess of it against skin scorching from his kisses. Licking it from her lips, her nipples, the svelte hollow of a hip.

They'd been making love for hours. Desire was in the air, the castle nigh smelled of romance. Tupping rode the night breeze and he was glad of it.

For if ever a man needed the healing touch of a woman, it was Adam.

Being possessed by the Draghar had changed Dageus in many ways, ways he was still trying to understand. He'd been systematically sorting through the vast amounts of knowledge they'd left inside his skull, extracting what could be used for good.

One of his most recently developed skills was that of deep-listening. He'd not yet told Drustan he could do it, was still learning to control it.

He'd never been able to manage it before, that

meditative Druid regard his da had so excelled at, that listening that could peel away lies and see to the truth of a matter, to the heart of a man.

But in the past months of wedded bliss he'd discovered a new quietude, an inner peace that, coupled with the thirteen's knowledge, had opened his Druid senses.

He'd deep-listened to Adam Black today when they'd ridden out, needing to know if he was speaking truth about his reasons for bringing the walls down. If the Keltar were to be breaking oaths again, Dageus had to know it was for a just cause. He'd delved lightly and in that shallow penetration had learned that Adam spoke true.

But then he'd sensed something else, something he'd not expected to find in an all-powerful immortal, not even one temporarily diminished; something he'd recognized, and he'd not been able to resist opening his senses wide and probing more deeply.

What he'd heard in the ancient one's words—in what he'd said and in those spaces between what he'd said and not said—had stilled him to the core.

Once Dageus had thought himself a lonely man. Before he'd found his mate, before Chloe had pressed her wee hands to his heart and pledged herself to him with the binding vows.

But now he knew that what he'd thought of as loneliness he could compound by thousands of years and multiply by infinity and still not manage to quantify that darkness that lay so deceptively still within Adam Black.

Strange days, he mused, pushing open the door to his chamber, when the Tuatha Dé walked among them in human form.

Er... sort of.

For that was another unexpected thing he'd discovered about their otherworldly guest.

Adam was, as he'd said, no longer exactly Tuatha Dé.

Nor, however, was he human.

20

Gabby didn't leave Adam's bedchamber for three long, blissful days and nights. Three perfect, incredible days and nights. She abandoned herself to them, to him, completely.

Oh, they didn't make love the entire time, her body—so delicate in comparison to his—couldn't have withstood it.

But there were many ways to give and take pleasure, and he was a master of them all. They spent hours in the shower, lazily bathing each other, exploring each other's bodies, tasting and teasing. Hours that she feasted on gold-velvet skin, rippling muscles, and silky black hair spilling across her naked body. More hours where she was spread on a rug before the fire while he rubbed her down with scented oils, making playful comparison of her to a mare that had been ridden too hard.

Sliding up behind her, riding her again. Rubbing her down again. More bathing, more playing in bed.

The only time he left her was to get food. Days and nights of eating and sleeping and sex. No woman, she decided, had ever lost her virginity more fantastically. There were many long hours where she was precisely as he'd said she would be: too languorously sated even to move. Convinced he couldn't possibly arouse her again; yet aroused in a heartbeat from a mere gold-flecked dark glance from beneath dusky lashes and slanted brows.

She felt as if she'd slipped into some netherworld of crystals and heather-scented fire and sizzling eroticism. Though she'd not noticed at first, too fixated on the vision of the great, dark, naked man, she'd finally realized that his chamber was called the Crystal Chamber because it housed crystal sculptures of various fanciful beasts. Unicorns and dragons, chimeras and phoenixes, gryphons and centaurs dotted the mantels, side tables, and chests. Dainty prisms hung in windows, more suspended above the hearth, catching the firelight and turning it to brilliant splashes of color.

Ornate silver-framed mirrors hung on the walls amid lovely tapestries, and dark, beautifully carved mahogany furniture graced the suite. Plush lambskin rugs were strewn about the floor. The bed was a masterwork of antique craftsmanship, topped with satiny sheets, plump down ticks, and a plush black velvet coverlet. It sported four posters the size of small trees (posters to which he'd tied her hands at one point, kissing and tasting her, driving her wild with need).

There couldn't have been a more fitting place for her to sleep with her Fae prince than this suite, surrounded by improbable creatures of legend, her improbable legend of a lover gilded by firelight, dappled with rainbow hues, rising above her, dark face taut with lust.

For those three days, she felt as if they existed in a place out of time, out of space, a fairy bower wherein nothing but the moment mattered, and the moments were so exquisite that, for a time, she forgot everything.

No questions spilled from lips too enchanted with kissing. No worries tumbled through a mind too intoxicated by lovemaking. No thoughts of tomorrow intruded.

There was now, she was happy, and that was enough.

On the fourth day he roused her while it was still dark outside, bundled her nude body warmly in a down comforter, and sifted them repeatedly until at last he stopped atop a mountainous outcropping.

Perching with irreverent grace on the edge of a sheer thousand-foot drop, he cradled her in his arms and they watched the sun come up over the Highlands, their breath frosting the chilly air.

It began with the merest kiss of gold on the far misty horizon, slowly burned off the fog, turned to a rosy-orange fireball, then bathed the hills and valleys in gold.

And as they sat on top of the world while the day was being born he told her of his plan: the why of the rituals the MacKeltars performed on the feast days and what would happen if they didn't perform them; that they'd agreed to hold off on Lughnassadh, a few days hence, in order to bring Aoibheal to MacKeltar land; that when she came, Adam would apprise her of Darroc's treachery and secure Gabrielle's safety as he'd promised.

He said nothing about what might happen between them then. No words of any future beyond that time.

And she didn't ask, because she was a big, fat coward. Falling for a fairy prince in human form was one thing.

But an immortal being? With all kinds of powers? Adam was overwhelming in human form. She couldn't imagine him in his natural state.

She wasn't sure she wanted to see him in it. She wanted things to go on like this forever. She didn't want any changes. Things were perfect as they were.

Adam with unlimited power could be terrifying.

Anyone with unlimited power could be terrifying. *She* could be terrifying with it.

So she refused to follow that line of thought any further. There was no point in speculation, it would only drive her crazy. So many things could happen, so many things could go wrong. She would deal with what came to be when it came to be. For all she knew, maybe Adam couldn't really protect her, and the queen would kill her or turn her over to the Hunters, and it would all become a moot point anyway.

There was a sobering thought.

And all the more reason to savor the now.

Which she did for the rest of the day, rolling across the bed with him, laughing and teasing and mating wildly.

Until dusk.

When the gloaming came, he bundled her up again, sifted them back to that high place, and they watched while the sky went violet, then black, and the moon rose and the stars came peeping out.

"I've seen thousands of these Highland dusks and dawns," he told her. "And I never get my fill."

She tipped her head back, staring up at the black velvet sky pierced by glittering stars.

And she started thinking about thousands of dusks

and dawns, about immortality and living forever, and before she could stop herself she blurted, "Why didn't Morganna take the elixir of life?"

His body stiffened instantly. He turned her roughly in his arms and stared into her eyes a long moment.

Then he kissed her and kissed her until she was breathless and no longer thinking about Morganna and immortality.

Though it would come back, that question, to gnaw at her.

"The two of you are cheating!" Dageus scowled at Chloe and Gabby.

"We are not," Chloe protested indignantly.

"You are too," Adam said. "I saw Gabby tilt her hand so you could see it. It's the only reason you keep beating us."

Gabby arched a playful brow. "Sounds to me like somebody who's used to being immortal and all-powerful just can't handle losing at a mortal card game."

Adam shook his head, smiling faintly. She was irrepressible. And she *was* cheating. Had been for the past two hours, but he'd been letting it slide until Dageus had pointed it out. He'd found it rather amusing that the Highlander wasn't catching on, too distracted by the steamy looks Chloe kept shooting him, or the way his petite wife would wet her lips and smile to jar his concentration.

He hadn't needed any such looks from Gabby. Her mere existence jarred his concentration. He'd thought the past week might have burned off some of his edgy, relentless desire for her, but it had in no way diminished it. Perversely, the more he bedded her, it seemed, the more he needed to bed her again.

He would have kept her all to himself, until the very dawn of Lughnassadh, had Gwen and Chloe not come pounding on the Crystal Chamber door a few days ago, informing them enough was enough and they really should socialize with their hosts, at least during part of their days. Surely that wasn't too much to ask?

A blushing Gabrielle had insisted they venture forth. Had given him a quick lesson in human manners, a lesson he'd not liked one bit. He loathed the idea of sharing her with anyone, for any amount of time.

But Gabrielle had been resolute, and so the six of them had spent the past several days hiking the Highlands during the day, dining in the evening, and drinking and playing cards or chess or some such human game into the wee hours. And Adam had done his damnedest to wedge all his desire for her into the time it took the moon to bridge the sky. Christ, he'd begun to hate the dawn.

Not since his days with Morganna had he lived on such an intimate daily basis with humans, and never had mortals welcomed him so completely as these. (Apart from the maids—those he just couldn't figure out; he'd never seen a bunch of women more obsessed with his groin: For some bizarre reason a curvy redhead kept offering him bananas, and the other night at dinner, a blonde serving maid had stabbed a knife in a plump sausage before plunking it on his plate with a downright baleful glare.)

But the MacKeltars treated him as if he were one of them. Ribbed and jested with him as they did among themselves. Thrust their wee hairns into his arms and made him hold them. He'd not had a baby in his hands for over a thousand years, had never had one spit up on him. Regurgitated formula was hell on silk and leather, but then he'd caught the look in Gabrielle's eyes and decided tiny Maddy MacKeltar could spit up on him all she wanted.

They even got testy with him when they felt he wasn't being forthcoming enough about himself. In the past few days he'd talked of things, shared experiences he'd shared with none before. His own kind would have scoffed, and mortals had never truly seen him as one of them, never freed him so completely simply to be, without censure or preconception. Not even Morganna. He'd always been one of the Fae to her, and his son had never welcomed him at Castle Brodie, refusing to acknowledge him as his father.

But here, in this enchanted time, he was Adam. A man. Nothing more. Nothing less. And it was a completely fascinating thing to be.

He glanced about the library. Drustan and Gwen were playing progressive chess near the fire, laughing and talking.

Their tiny, beautiful dark-haired daughters were slumbering nearby, waking occasionally to be fed.

Gabby and Chloe were laughing, insisting to Dageus that they would never cheat, how could he think such a thing of them?

The great clock above the mantel chimed the hour eleven times.

In one hour Lughnassadh would begin. And the walls between realms would start to thin.

And he would sit here in the castle and wait for the queen.

By the close of day tomorrow, at the very latest, Aoibheal would be warned, Darroc would be revealed for the traitor he was, the realms would be safe, and Adam might very well be his immortal, all-powerful self again.

His petite *ka-lyrra*, however, would continue aging day by day.

And he would have to stop that.

He glanced at Gabrielle. She was nibbling her lower lip, shooting Chloe a mischievous look over her hand of cards. Around her there was—as there was around each human in the library—that infernal golden glow. That glow that ever made of him an unstable magnet, drawn in spite of himself, repelled despite his efforts to cozy near. That which lured him, that which he could never touch or understand.

He inhaled deeply, exhaled slowly. Tossed back a swallow of scotch, savoring the way it burned his human throat as it never had in his Tuatha Dé form.

For the first time in his existence he wished for an ability no Tuatha Dé possessed. Though they'd learned to move backward to certain degrees in it, and forward again to their present (though never beyond that; legend held there was only one race that could navigate what was *yet* to be, but Adam gave little credence to such legends), not even the queen herself could stop time.

"Halt!" hissed Bastion.

The Hunters stopped instantly. "But we've got his scent. He's in these hills, very near here," one protested.

Bastion grimaced. "There are wards. The queen protects this land. We dare not cross them."

"But Adam Black and his human crossed them," the Hunter said impatiently.

"Should we summon Darroc?" another asked.

Bastion shook his head. "No. There's nothing Darroc

can do so long as Adam hides behind wards. We wait. We watch for the first opportunity. Then we summon Darroc. We'll not lose our chance again. The Elder won't move against the queen until this enemy of his is gone."

And more than anything, Bastion wanted Darroc to move against the queen, to topple her from her throne. This brief time of roaming the human realm again had awakened all his senses, sloughed away the boredom and ennui of his Unseelie hell. Reminded him of how alive he felt, how good it was to be a Hunter. How many delicious humans there were to prey upon.

He'd not blow this chance. Nor would he give the Elder a chance to screw things up again with his lust for vengeance. He'd summon Darroc only at the last possible minute, and if Darroc didn't kill him fast enough for his liking, Bastion himself would see to Adam's death.

21

Aoibheal paced a tract of silica sand on the Isle of Morar, staring out at a frothing turquoise sea, her iridescent eyes flashing.

Time, usually of no relevance to her, a thing of which she was, indeed, scarcely aware, had suddenly become a pressing concern.

A short amount of it ago, she'd sensed an unfamiliar sensation, a growing lack of cohesion in the fabric of the realms she'd created for her race. Because she'd not felt such a thing before, she'd not immediately comprehended what it was.

The walls between the realms of Tuatha Dé and Man were thinning.

It took her yet another amount of time to pinpoint the origin of distress in the weft and weave of worlds: The Keltar Druids had not yet performed the ritual of

Lughnassadh, the ancient rite that was to be completed at break of the feast day, as it had been for millennia.

She shook her head, astonished. By Danu, would they test her mercy again?

She narrowed her eyes, looking not outward but inward, stretching her far-vision across time and place. Seeking which Keltar was failing her now.

Stunned to find it was the same ones. Again.

Stretching farther to know the why of it . . .

She snapped ramrod straight, eyes wide with disbelief.

"*Amadan*," she hissed. "How *dare* you?"

Perhaps even more to the point, how *could* he?

She'd stripped him of everything, rendered him powerless—or at least she thought she had—unable to be seen, heard, felt. She'd consigned him to a vile existence, insubstantial as a ghost, and cast him into the human realm. Banished him, cut him off, denied him even the merest glimpse of his own kind.

She'd chosen the parameters of his punishment carefully, to force him to taste the bitterness of the human condition with none of the attendant sweetness, to cure him of his foolish fascination with mortals once and for all.

Her repeated indulgence of her favored prince—the only one of her people who ever managed to surprise her, and surprise was nectar of the gods to a sixty-thousand-year-old queen—had cast her in an unfavorable light with both her courtiers and her advisers. Not to mention the eternal cleaning up after him she was obliged to do.

The High Council had been insisting she take action for centuries and, after his most recent defiance, she'd had no choice but to agree. Adam had argued against her in front of her court and council, a thing she could never permit, lest her sovereignty be questioned, lest she be blatantly challenged. Though she was the most powerful of the Seelie, that power was hers only so long as she held the support of the majority of her people. That power could be taken from her.

She'd been certain fifty or so years of such punishment would be enough to make him grateful to be Tuatha Dé, to bring him to heel, to stop him from meddling with humans.

She'd not believed it possible for him to find a way to meddle in the form she'd given him.

Oh, how wrong she'd been. As always, if a loophole existed, her iconoclastic *D'Jai* prince found it. And in a mere few months' time. There he was, on the Keltar estate, and there was no doubt in her mind that he'd created this problem. Even cursed and powerless, he'd somehow found a way to do something to keep the Keltar from performing the ritual.

She stretched her senses again, feeling for dimensional faults. The ramifications of the thinning walls would first be felt in Scotland, then would spread quickly to Ireland and England. It had, in fact, already begun. The effects would radiate outward until, by nightfall, hidden Tuatha Dé realms would rise up all over the world in the midst of human ones.

By nightfall, any Tuatha Dé walking among humans in anything less than full human glamour would be exposed.

By nightfall, even the silica sands of Morar would gleam palely beneath a human moon.

Dimensions would bleed into one another, temporal portals would open. The Unseelie would be freed.

In a nutshell, all hell would break loose.

———

Adam was sitting with Gabrielle in the great hall, in the waning afternoon light, when he sensed the queen drawing near. *About bloody time*, he thought. Even he'd begun to get a little edgy waiting, wondering what was taking her so long.

He had no words for how he sensed her, was, in fact, rather surprised he could, being human and all, but there was a tensing in his body, a pressure inside his skull. He tightened his arms protectively around Gabrielle.

Hours ago, he'd insisted the MacKeltars leave the hall, get out of the castle—over their strident protests—persuading them it was wiser they be elsewhere, as Aoibheal would be furious when she arrived.

He'd kept Gabrielle with him. He would protect her against the queen's wrath, however need be, but he didn't want the distraction of vulnerable MacKeltars too.

A fierce gust of wind kicked up suddenly, extinguishing the fire in the hearth, then the air was drenched with jasmine and sandalwood, and Aoibheal was there, shimmering before them.

"Oh, God," he heard Gabrielle whisper, awed.

"My Queen," Adam said, rising instantly, bringing Gabrielle up with him, an arm around her waist.

Ah, yes, Aoibheal was furious. She was in high glamour, so terrifyingly beautiful that, even for him, she was almost impossible to look at, shimmering brilliantly, lit by the radiance of a thousand tiny suns. Though her form was essentially human, her body chillingly perfect, nude beneath her gown of light, there was nothing human about her. Pure power pulsed in the air, the presence of an immense, ancient entity.

"*How dare you?*" Her words reverberated through the great hall, steel striking off stone.

"My Queen," Adam said swiftly, "I would not have taken such extreme measures were your welfare not at risk. Gravely at risk."

"I'm to believe this is about me, Amadan? You would have me interpret your latest—and I must say by far greatest—act of defiance as a selfless act?" Mockery dripped from her voice.

She was using part of his true name, not Adam, but Amadan. Ah, yes, she was pissed. "It *is* about you," he said. A pause. "Though if you were inclined to reward me, I would not be averse."

"Reward you? What would I be rewarding you for? Do you have any idea what you've done? Do you know that already humans have begun slipping through the fabric of place and time where the old magic lies fallow?"

"The dolmens have opened?" Adam was startled.

"Yes."

"Well, why the bloody hell did you wait so long?"

She gave him such an arctic glare that he was surprised his skin didn't ice. "How am I at risk? Speak. Now. Fast. With each passing moment, I grow more inclined to punish you further than hear you out."

"Darroc has made an attempt on my life." *There. Face that, Aoibheal,* he thought, *and restore me to immortality as you should have months ago.*

The queen stiffened. "Darroc? How do you know that? You can no longer see our kind."

"*I* saw him," Gabrielle spoke then.

Adam glanced down at her, tightening his arm around her. Her eyes were narrowed, her face was averted, yet she was actually managing to peek at the queen from the periphery of her vision. The queen had chosen high glamour deliberately, knowing humans couldn't focus on it. But she didn't know Gabrielle, he thought with a flash of pride; she was strong, his *ka-lyrra*.

Aoibheal didn't deign to acknowledge her. "How?" she demanded of Adam.

"She's a *Sidhe*-seer, my Queen."

Aoibheal's eyes narrowed. "Indeed." She cast a raking, imperious glance over Gabrielle. "I believed them all dead. You do know that by the terms of The Compact that makes her mine."

Adam stiffened. "She helped me gain an audience with you so I could warn you that Darroc is plotting against you," he said tightly. "In exchange for acting as my intermediary, I assured her safety."

"*You* assured? You had no right to assure anything."

"My Queen, Darroc has brought forth Hunters from the Unseelie kingdom. There are a score or more in his service."

"Hunters? *My* Hunters? You jest!" The breeze swirling through the great hall gusted, bitterly frigid, licking around him.

Adam's breath frosted the air with tiny ice crystals when he said, "It's no jest. It's true. The second time he attacked, he didn't bother to conceal himself or his Hunters. I saw them myself."

"Tell me," she commanded.

Speaking briskly, he told her all, from finding Gabrielle, to approaching Aine and her companion, to Darroc's first attack and subsequent one.

"You saw all this, too, *Sidhe*-seer?" the queen demanded.

Gabrielle nodded.

"Tell me exactly what you saw."

Watching the queen with that half-averted gaze, Gabrielle told her what she'd seen in detail, describing the Fae involved.

"And we both know," Adam concluded when Gabrielle fell silent, "there's only one thing Darroc could have promised the Hunters to sway their fealty from you."

Aoibheal spun in a swirl of blinding light. She was silent for a time.

Beside him, Gabrielle was tense, breathing shallowly. He could feel the unease in her small body and realized that she was seeing the kind of Fae she'd been raised on tales of. The queen was truly formidable—there was no other word for it. Awe-inspiring, ancient, forbidding, alien, incredibly powerful. He only hoped his *ka-lyrra* would remember that he was not like his queen. That Tuatha Dé were no more like unto one another than humans were.

Finally the queen turned back to him. "Darroc is a High Council Elder. One of my strongest supporters, staunchest advocates."

"For Christ's sake, lip service, no more! Will you *never* see through that?"

"*He* has never left my realm to play with humans."

Adam bit back a caustic, *No, just Hunters,* and remained silent.

"He has served on my council for thousands of years."

Again he said nothing. He'd told her what he had to say; he knew she understood the ramifications of it. He knew also it would be difficult for her to accept that one of her Elders had betrayed her.

"I have forbidden any Seelie to bring forth the Unseelie for any reason, under threat of a soulless death."

"Gee," he couldn't resist saying dryly, "you think maybe Darroc forgot?"

"Don't think *I've* forgotten the bad blood between the two of you!" she hissed.

"I'm not the one walking with Hunters!" he hissed back.

Another silence. Her fury at him was easing, turning toward another as she digested his news. The air was slowly beginning to warm again.

"And for this you had the Keltar fail to perform the ritual of Lughnassadh that keeps the walls between realms intact? You took it upon yourself to risk our worlds colliding?"

"It was the only way I knew to gain your ear. To warn you. No matter that my queen had chosen to punish me, I could not permit an enemy to attack her without doing all in my power to protect her. I will always protect my queen. Even," he added pointedly, "when she has stripped away my power to do so. Besides, it's not as if I didn't try to find Circenn first. It occurs to me now that perhaps you were the reason I couldn't find him."

"Perhaps I was," she agreed. "Perhaps he and his family have been enjoying an extended holiday on Morar."

Adam shook his head, lips curving in a faint sardonic smile. "I should have known."

She stared at him a long moment. "I must have proof of this. I must see this with my own eyes. I must carry firsthand vision back to the council."

Adam shrugged. "Use me as bait."

"And you seek what in return?"

"The honor of serving you," he said smoothly. "Though, there is also the small matter of the return of my immortality and full powers."

"There is something you owe me. I'm waiting."

A muscle leapt in Adam's jaw. "I said it in the catacombs, mere moments after you cursed me."

"I would hear it again. Here. Now."

Adam's nostrils flared. With an imperious incline of his head, he said, "I see now that countering you before the court might have been ill-advised, my Queen. I acknowledge that a show of my fealty might have better served you. It is possible I might have endeavored to find a more appropriate venue to air my concerns."

"And counted yourself fortunate I bothered to hear you at all."

Adam said nothing.

"Don't think I missed all the 'might haves' in that 'apology.' You still have not admitted you were wrong."

"I believed at the time that there were those among your council who had personal motives for advocating trial-by-blood. I was concerned then that they plotted against you. It would seem I was right."

Aoibheal smiled faintly. "Ah, Amadan, you never change, do you?" She eyed him measuringly. "You will leave protected land. You will make your way back to where he first found you."

"Yes, my Queen."

"The two of you will leave in the morning, then."

"You mean, I will," he corrected.

"Don't tell me what I mean. I said what I meant. You and the *Sidhe*-seer."

"I said *I* would draw him out. Gabrielle isn't—"

"Gabrielle? Lovely name. You sound fond of your human. You wouldn't be about to argue with me, would you? You wouldn't be about to try my patience further, when I've yet to tidy up after your most recent mess?"

Adam stopped mid-word; when he spoke again his voice was carefully dispassionate. "When the *Sidhe*-seer," he rephrased, "agreed to act as my intermediary and help me find a way to contact you, I promised her safety in exchange. She has risked herself to aid us, we who hunted her people for so long. Her assistance has helped preserve your reign and the safety of all the realms. It has long been our custom to bestow gifts upon mortals who aid us. I promised her we would leave her in her own world when all was done, alive and well, free of any Tuatha Dé persecution, assuring her safety and that of those she loves."

"Grand promises from such a powerless Fae."

"Would you make of me a liar?"

"You do that often enough yourself."

Adam bristled. There'd been no need to say that in front of Gabrielle.

Silence stretched. Then the queen exhaled softly, a silvery sound. "Reveal this traitor for me and I will uphold your promise to the human, but I warn you, make no more, *Amadan*."

"Then you agree she should remain here. On Keltar land."

"I said that I will uphold your promise. But she goes with you. Darroc might wonder at her absence and not show his hand. If he has betrayed me, I want proof and I want it now. Before he acts against me and makes those in my court think it possible." The queen moved in a swirl of radiant light. "I will be watching. Lure him out for me and I will come. Show me Hunters at my Elder's side and I will restore you to your full power. And let you decide his fate. You'd like that, wouldn't you?"

Adam jerked his head once in a tight nod.

A rush of sound spilled from her lips in Tuatha Dé tongue. Beside him, Gabrielle shivered intensely.

"You will wear the *féth fiada* until this is done, Amadan."

"Bloody hell," Adam muttered savagely. "I *hate* being invisible."

"And, Keltar," Aoibheal said in a voice like sudden thunder, with a glance up at the balustrade. "Henceforth I would advise against tampering with my curses. Perform the Lughnassadh ritual now or face my wrath."

"Aye, Queen Aoibheal," Dageus and Drustan replied together, stepping out from behind stone columns bracketing the stairs.

Adam smiled faintly. He should have known no Highlander would flee, only retreat to a higher vantage—take to the hills, in a manner of speaking—waiting in silent readiness should battle be necessary.

Gabby went limp beside him with a soft *whoosh* of breath.

The queen was gone.

22

Early the next morning, Gabby and Adam packed to leave Castle Keltar and catch a flight back to the States.

As Adam was invisible again, they would be traveling cloaked, and Gabby was surprised to realize she was rather looking forward to it. There was a certain intriguing impunity one felt, concealed by the *féth fiada*. There was also the fact that it meant they'd be touching constantly, and she simply couldn't get enough of touching him.

Immediately upon the queen's departure yesterday, Dageus and Drustan had performed the ritual of Lughnassadh. Once the walls were again secured, they'd sat down and rehashed the afternoon's events, with Gabby serving as Adam's intermediary.

She'd been surprised by how wired with excitement Chloe and Gwen had been to see—sort of, out of the corners of their eyes as well—the queen of the Tuatha Dé. It seemed Chloe had felt quite cheated that Dageus had encountered her once before and had failed to take a complete accounting of her.

Their reaction—one not of fear but of interest and curiosity—had served to solidify her new slant on things. Yes, the Tuatha Dé Danaan (as Gabby was now calling them) were otherworldly, different, but not the heartless, emotionless creatures she'd been raised to believe they were.

As Gwen had said, they were another race, a highly advanced race. And though the inexplicable could be frightening, learning about it went a long way toward allaying one's fears.

Further toward that end, the MacKeltars had taken her, with the once-more-invisible Adam in tow, to the *other* Keltar castle last night, where Christopher and Maggie MacKeltar lived, and shown her the underground chamber library that housed all the ancient Druid lore, dating all the way back to when The Compact had first been negotiated.

Gabby had gotten to see the actual treaty between the races, etched on a sheet of pure gold, scribed in a language no scholar alive could identify. Adam had translated passages of it, emphasizing the part about *Sidhe*-seers: that "those who see the Fae belong to the Fae," yet they were not to be killed or enslaved but permitted to live in peace and comfort in any Fae realm they chose, their every desire met, except, of course, for their freedom. *I told you we didn't harm them,* he'd said.

On the way back to Dageus and Drustan's castle, while Chloe and Gwen had been talking about the queen again, Adam had insisted Gabby convey his irritation with them for leaving by the front door and circling straight around to the rear entrance of the castle to sneak back in.

I told you we expected you to have our backs if the need arose, Drustan had reminded him through her. *I also told you that we would be having yours.*

And when Gabby'd passed on those words, she'd glimpsed a flicker of emotion in Adam's dark gaze that had made the breath catch softly in her throat.

How could she have ever thought that Adam Black felt no emotion? Even the queen had displayed emotion. *That* was a fallacy in the O'Callaghan *Books* she'd be swiftly amending. Along with about a zillion others.

Still, she could understand how her ancestors had gotten it so wrong. If she'd had to go on the mere appearance of Queen Aoibheal, or of the Hunters, or even of Adam, without ever having interacted with them, without having come to understand so much about their world, she'd have thought the same things.

But she knew so much better now.

She'd spent another scorching, delicious, decadent night in Adam's arms.

He was the kind of lover she'd never imagined existed, not even in her most heated fantasies. And she'd had some pretty darned heated ones.

He was inexhaustible, alternately tender and wild, playful, then staring into her eyes with deadly intensity. He made a woman feel as if nothing existed but her, as if the entire world had melted away and there was nothing more pressing than her next soft gasp, her next smile, their next kiss.

He'd still spoken no words of either feelings or future. Nor had she.

Though the queen herself had guaranteed Gabby's safety when this was through, she was having a hard time seeing past their date with Darroc. She knew she'd not be able to truly draw a deep breath until it was over.

Then she would face her future.

Then she would try to decide—assuming she had any decision to make, that he didn't simply abandon her once he was all-powerful again—how in the world a mortal and an immortal could have any kind of life together.

"**Promise you'll come back. I mean it, and** *soon*," Gwen demanded, hugging her tightly. "And you have to call us and let us know the *minute* Darroc shows up and this is over. We're going to be worrying. Promise?"

Gabby nodded. "I promise."

"And bring Adam back too," Gwen said.

Gabby glanced at her tall, dark prince. The day had dawned swathed in a thick white fog, and though it was already ten in the morning, none of it had burned off. And how could it? If there was a sun anywhere in the sky, she certainly couldn't see it. Above her, the world had a solid white ceiling. Beyond Adam, who stood a dozen feet away, near the rental car they'd arrived in, was a white wall.

Adam. Her gaze lingered lovingly on him. He was wearing black leather pants, a cream Irish fisherman's sweater, and those sexy Gucci boots with silver chains and buckles. His long, silky, black hair spilled to his waist, and his chiseled face was unshaven, dusted with a shadow-beard. Regal gold glinted at his throat.

He was heart-stoppingly beautiful.

She glanced back at Gwen and was horrified to feel a

sharp sting of tears pressing at her eyes. "If he's still in my life, I will," she said softly.

Gwen snorted and she and Chloe exchanged glances. "Oh, we think he'll still be in your life, Gabby."

Her meticulously erected defenses on that very topic trembled at the foundation. She stiffened mentally, knowing that if she wasn't very, very careful, she could turn into an emotional basket case. If she let herself feel even the tiniest of the many fears she was suppressing, they would all break free. And there was no telling what she might do or say: The Banana Incident, case in point. Emotion did unpredictable things to her tongue. Bad, bad things.

Despite her resolve to keep her fears at bay, she heard herself say plaintively, "But *how*? For heaven's sake, he's going to be immor—"

"Don't," Chloe cut her off sternly. "I'm going to share something with you," she said with a glance at Gwen, "that a wise woman once told me. Sometimes you have to take a leap of faith. Just do it. Don't look down."

"Great," Gabby muttered. "That's just great. It sure seems like *I'm* the one having to do all the leaping."

"Somehow," Gwen said slowly, "I think before all is said and done, Gabby, you won't be the only one doing it."

"Turn left," Adam instructed.

"Left? How can you even *see* a left in this pea soup?" Gabby said irritably. She could barely make out the road ten feet past the hood of the compact car. But it wasn't just the fog that was aggravating her; the farther they got from Castle Keltar, the more vulnerable she was feeling.

As if the most magnificent chapter in the Book of Gabrielle O'Callaghan's Life was coming to a close and she wasn't going to like what she found when she turned the page.

She understood now why her friend Elizabeth, with her near-genius, analytical mind gave wide berth to murder mysteries, psychological thrillers, and horror stories, and read only romance novels. Because, by God, when a woman picked up one of those steamy books, she had a firm guarantee that there would be a Happily-Ever-After. That though the world outside those covers could bring such sorrow and disappointment and loneliness, between those covers, the world was a splendid place to be.

She glanced irritably at Adam. He was looking at her. Hard.

"*What?*" she snapped belligerently, not meaning to sound belligerent but feeling it to the core.

He said softly, "You aren't falling for me, are you, Irish?"

Returning her gaze fixedly to the road ahead, Gabby clenched her jaw, incapable of speaking for several moments, her stomach a stew of emotions, a veritable pressure cooker about to blow. She muttered a few choice words Gram would have shuddered to hear.

"*Why* do you keep asking me that?" she snapped at last. "I'm really *sick* of you asking me that. Do I ask you that? Have I ever asked you that? That is *such* a patronizing thing to say, like you're warning me or something, like you're saying, 'Don't fall for me, Irish, you helpless, weak little woman,' and what's with this frigging 'Irish' bit? Can't you call me by name? Is that one of those depersonalizing touches? Like it removes you a bit from the immediacy of the moment, somehow makes me less of a human being with feelings? I'll have you know, you arrogant, overbearing, thickheaded, underdisclosing, never-ask-me-any-questions-because-I-sure-as-hell-won't-answer-them-to-*you*-O-mere-mortal prince, that I took my fair share of psychology courses in college, and I understand a thing or two about men that applies to ones who aren't even of the human persuasion, and *if* I were falling for you, which I'm here to tell you I'm not, because falling implies an ongoing action, an event that's taking place in real time, here and now—"

She broke off abruptly, on the verge of revealing too much. Too wounded, too uncertain of herself, of him, to go on.

Inhaled. Puffed her bangs from her face with an angry breath.

Long moments unfurled and he said nothing.

Gritting the words slowly, she said, "Why didn't Morganna take the elixir of immortality? I *need* you to answer this."

The silence stretched. She refused to look at him.

"Because immortality," he said finally, slowly, as if each word were being forcibly pried from his mouth and was paining him more deeply than she could possibly know, "and the immortal soul are incompatible. You can't have both."

Gabby jerked and looked at him, horrified.

He slammed his fist into the glove box. Plastic exploded as his hand went right through it. Half the little door dangled for a moment on one hinge, then fell to the floor. His lips curved in a bitter smile. "Not what you expected to hear, eh?"

"You mean, if Morganna had taken it, she would have lost her immortal soul?" Gabby gasped.

"And Darroc thinks humans aren't very bright." Dark sarcasm dripped from his voice.

"So, er...but...I don't get it. How? Does a person, like, have to hand it over or something?"

"Humans have an aura surrounding them that my kind can see," he said flatly. "The immortal soul lights them from within, makes them glow golden. Once a human takes the elixir of life, that soul begins to burn out, until there is nothing of it left."

Gabby blinked. "I glow golden? You mean, right now, as I'm sitting here?"

He gave a bitter little laugh. "More intensely than most."

"Oh." A pause while she tried to collect her thoughts. "So, do they change, the humans who take it?"

"Ah, yes. They change."

"I see." The utter lack of inflection in his reply made her deeply uneasy. She suddenly had no desire to know *how* they changed. Suspected she wouldn't like it at all. "So then, that means our *Books* were right about the Tuatha Dé not having souls, doesn't it?"

"Your *Books* were right about many things," he said coldly. "You know that. You knew it when you took me as your lover. You took me anyway."

"You really don't have a soul?" Of all he'd just told her, she found that the most unfathomable. How could it be? She couldn't get her brain around it, not now that she knew him. Things that didn't have souls were... well, evil, weren't they? Adam wasn't evil. He was a good man. Better than most, if not all, she'd ever met.

"Nope. No soul, Gabrielle. That's me, Adam Black, iridescent-eyed, soulless, deadly fairy."

Ouch, she'd said that to him once. Seemed a lifetime ago.

She stared into the fog for a time, driving on auto-pilot.

And she tried not to ask it, but she'd just begun to believe that maybe the Tuatha Dé weren't quite so different from humans, only to find out that they were, and she couldn't stop herself. She had to know *how* different. Precisely what she was dealing with. "Hearts? Do the Tuatha Dé have hearts?"

"No physiological equivalent." Bored-now voice.

"Oh." Upon discovering how erroneous so much of the O'Callaghan lore was, she'd pretty much ejected the bulk of it from her mind, tossed it out with her many preconceptions. But parts of it had been right after all. Big parts.

More driving. More silence.

You're not falling for me, are you, Irish? he'd said.

And she'd had a minor meltdown because that was precisely the problem. She wasn't falling. She'd *fallen*. As in, past tense. Way past tense. She was hopelessly in love with him. She'd been building a dream future for them inside her head, embellishing it with the tiniest and most tender of details.

Gwen and Chloe had been absolutely right, and Gabby'd known it herself, even then. Just hadn't wanted to admit it. Just as she hadn't wanted to admit that the reason she'd wanted so desperately to know why Morganna had refused the elixir was because Gabby had been secretly hoping that he would fall in love with her, too, she could become immortal, and they could love each other forever. They could have an eternal Happily-Ever-After.

But she wasn't stupid. Ever since he'd told her about Morganna refusing the chance to live forever, she'd known there had to be a catch. Just hadn't known what a whopper of a catch it was.

Immortality and the immortal soul are incompatible.

Though she'd never considered herself a particularly religious person, she was deeply spiritual, and the soul was, well . . . the sacred essence of a person, the imprint of self, the source of one's capacity for goodness, for love. It was what was reborn again and again on one's journey to evolve. A soul was the inner divine, the very breath of God.

And his elixir of life reeked of Faustian overtones: *Here, take this and you can live forever, for the small price of your immortal soul.* She could almost smell the acrid brimstone of hellfire. Hear the rustle of unholy contracts scribed on thick, yellowed parchments, signed in blood. Feel the breeze from the leathery flapping of winged Hunters coming to collect.

She shivered. She didn't count herself a superstitious person, yet it got to her on a visceral level. Made her blood run cold.

A soft bitter laugh cut into her thoughts. "Not interested in living forever, Gabrielle? Not liking the terms?"

Oh, that tone was like nothing she'd ever heard him use. Wicked, cynical, twisted. A voice truly befitting the blackest Fae.

She glanced at him.

And sucked in a sharp breath.

He looked utterly devilish, his black eyes bottomless, ancient, cold. Nostrils flared, lips curled in something only a fool might call a smile. He was, at that moment, every inch an inhuman Fae prince, otherworldly, dangerous. This, she realized, was the face of the *Sin Siriche Du*; the face her ancestors had glimpsed on long-ago battlefields, as he'd watched the brutal slaughter, smiling.

"Didn't think so." Silky sarcasm dripped from that deep, strangely accented voice.

A dozen thoughts collided in her mind and she floundered mentally, trying to figure out where to step next in this conversation that had started out so innocuously, only to become such a quagmire.

He looked so remote, so detached, as if nothing could touch him, as if nothing she could say would matter anyway. And a little doubt niggled at her: Was this, then, how he was when he was fully Tuatha Dé?

She couldn't believe that. She *wouldn't* believe that. She *knew* him. He was a good man.

Leap, Gabby, an inner voice whispered. *Tell him how you feel. Throw it all on the line.*

She swallowed. Hard. Were Gwen and Chloe here, she knew they would echo that counsel. They'd taken such leaps, and look where it had gotten them. Who was to say it wouldn't work for her?

There was only one way to find out. Nothing risked, nothing gained.

She drew a deep, fortifying breath. *I love you*, she whispered the words in her mind. She hadn't had a lot of practice with those words, had only ever said them to Gram, and long ago to parents, both of whom had gone away. She wet her lips. "Adam, I—"

"Bloody hell, spare me whatever sniveling excuses you're about to offer," he snarled. "I didn't frigging ask you to take the elixir, did I, *Irish*?"

Tears filled her eyes and her teeth clacked shut. Oh, she hadn't needed that reminder! She was all too aware of that fact. And that he'd never said so much as one word about any kind of future together. Nor a single word that seemed to hint at any degree of commitment or emotion. Oh, there'd been sweet words in bed, even out of it, but none of those things to which a woman was so attuned, those seemingly casually spoken phrases that hinted at a tomorrow and a dozen tomorrows after that. No mentions of an upcoming holiday, or a place or thing he'd like her to see. No subtle words that were really subtle pledges, testing the water, seeking like response.

Not one.

Her declaration clotted in her throat. And suddenly she couldn't breathe, couldn't sit in the car with him one moment more.

She slammed on the brakes, jammed the car into park, and hopped out onto the road, walking blindly, scooping angrily at fog. The external environs too accurately mirrored her internal landscape: Nothing was clear, she couldn't see ten steps ahead of her, couldn't get a fix on where she'd just been.

Behind her, she heard his car door slam.

"Stop, Gabrielle! Come back here," he commanded roughly.

"Just give me a few minutes *alone*, okay?"

"Gabrielle, we're not on Keltar land," he thundered. "Come back here."

"Oh!" She stopped and turned abruptly. She hadn't realized that. When had they left Keltar land?

"No," a cool voice said as Darroc stepped out of the fog between them, "you're not, are you?"

Then Darroc was turning toward Adam, and she heard a sudden, sharp, short burst of automatic gunfire.

And Adam was flinching, jerking, great splashes of red spreading across that cream fisherman's sweater, his dark head flying back, arms outflung. Falling back, going down.

And Hunters were closing in all around her.

She felt their talons on her skin, felt a broken sob clawing its way up her throat.

And then she fainted and felt no more.

Ah, ka-lyrra, I look at you and you make me want to live a man's life with you. To wake with you and sleep with you, argue with you and make love with you, to get a silly human job and take walks in the park and live so tiny beneath such a vast sky.

But I will never stay with another human woman and watch her die. Never.

—FROM THE (GREATLY REVISED) BLACK EDITION OF
THE O'CALLAGHAN *Book of the Sin Siriche Du*

23

Gabby raised the plastic shade over the plane window and stared out into the dark night sky.

Alone, hence visible, she'd had no choice but to book a flight, putting it on her credit card. The only flight available had been the red-eye, and she had three lengthy layovers to look forward to, in Edinburgh, London, and Chicago.

When she'd regained consciousness, she'd been lying in the road.

Alone. With a sick, horrid feeling in the pit of her stomach.

Watching the man she loved being brutally shot had been the purest hell.

She'd heard the bullets ripping into his body with dull, wet sounds, she'd seen his blood spurting, and—if it had indeed been only an illusion courtesy of the queen, as she prayed it had been—the look of pain and shock on Adam's face had been stunningly, horrifyingly real.

She'd forced herself up on shaky legs, trembling, desperately looking around for someone to tell her that it hadn't really happened. That the queen hadn't really let him die.

But there'd been no one there to reassure her. Only thick, swirling fog and aching silence.

Apparently, Faery was done with her.

There wasn't even any blood anywhere; no sign that anyone had ever been on that road but her.

So what, she'd raged, shaking her fist at the dense bank of clouds above her, *I don't even get to know what happened? That's bullshit. If you think I'm just walking away without explanations, you are so wrong! Where is Adam? What happened? Show him to me! Tell me he's okay!*

But walk away, or rather drag her miserable self away, was exactly what she'd finally ended up doing.

She'd been out of her head for a time. She'd raged and shouted until her throat was raw, until she was capable of making only broken croaking sounds. She'd stalked and paced and stomped until her legs had given out, until she'd slumped against the car, then slid to the ground in exhaustion.

She'd huddled, shivering in the chilly fog while the day turned to night around her, waiting.

Absolutely certain that at any moment Adam would "pop" in, flash her that lazy-sexy smile, tell her he was okay, then finish the stupid, awful conversation they'd been having.

She would tell him that she loved him. And somehow everything would be all right. So, he didn't have a soul or a heart. So, he was physiologically different from her, sprung of an alien race. So, she could never become immortal.

So what.

She would take what Morganna had taken: a life with him. Whatever she could have of him. They could make things work, she knew they could. It might not be her idealistic teenage fantasy, but it would be enough. It would be far better than having nothing of him.

Fourteen hours later it had dimly penetrated that she couldn't sit in the middle of the road forever. That she was stiff and cold and hungry and needed desperately to go to the bathroom.

That she was slowly going crazy sitting in the dark by herself, torturing herself with imaginings.

Surely the queen hadn't let him die. Surely Aoibheal wasn't so callous, would never sacrifice one of her own. Surely she'd swept him away and healed him. Surely she'd kept her word and restored him.

But those "surelys" weren't entirely comforting, because *if* he was okay and restored, then where was he?

If he was okay, how could he just leave her sitting in the middle of the road, with no answers, no matter how messy of an argument they'd gotten into?

Unless, unless, unless . . .

Oh, the "unlesses" just sucked!

Unless he hadn't really cared about her at all.

Unless it had all just been a brief diversion for him.

Unless she'd never been anything more than a means to an end.

No. She refused to believe that. Just as she refused to believe he was dead.

"He's okay," she whispered to herself. "And he's going to come back. Any minute now."

Any minute became any day became any week.

Gabby moved woodenly through time. Detachedly going through the motions, void of passion, an automaton.

Though, upon returning home, a part of her had wanted nothing more than to barricade herself in her house and hide, to curl in bed with the covers snug over her head, there was a bigger part of her that harbored a special and very personal hatred of quitters, of people who just gave up and left.

It was something she could never permit herself to do.

So the very next morning after returning to the States, she'd gone in to work at Little & Staller, acting as if she'd never even been gone.

And just as she'd figured, no one had bothered to clean out her desk. Cases were still stacked every bit as high and haphazardly as ever they'd been. Cleaning it out would have taken time, and all the interns at Little & Staller were overworked. Besides, anyone foolish enough to clean off another person's desk inevitably got stuck with their caseload.

No, her desk would have sat untouched until one plaintiff or another had called, demanding to know why their case hadn't been heard yet. Until some fire had needed putting out.

Without saying a word to anyone, she'd walked in, plunked her double-shot espresso on the desk, sat down, and begun working on arbitrations. Woodenly. With brisk efficiency. Refusing to think about anything but the case at hand. Losing herself in her work. In the innocent people who needed her to help them, needed her expertise.

And when Jeff Staller had stalked over, red-faced and blustering, furiously demanding to know where the hell she'd been—and was she some kind of idiot to think she still had a job after disappearing like that?—she'd merely glanced coolly up at him and said, *Have you taken a good look at my win ratio? You want to fire me? Fine. Fire me. Say the word.*

It had been nearly a month since their little confrontation and he'd still not said "the word."

And she knew he never would.

Funny, she was dead inside, yet Jay had commented just the other day on how "together" she seemed. How great she looked, and he didn't know where her new confidence had come from, but, *It's kick-ass, Gabby. You're really rocking.*

She'd smiled faintly, bitterly amused by the irony of it: how not giving a shit about anything came off looking like confidence. It occurred to her that perhaps she should try interviewing with TT&T again.

But she didn't, because change was more than she was capable of dealing with at the moment.

Besides, at Little & Staller, she'd developed a routine that kept her nicely numb.

And if, on occasion, a sneaky little memory of a stunningly gorgeous Fae prince perched on the wall of her cubicle slipped past her tightly erected defenses, she quashed it immediately.

Filed another case. Asked for more work. Became a veritable arbitration machine.

She slogged through the days, pretending they weren't made of wet concrete and she wasn't wearing lead boots. Pretending that each step didn't require Herculean effort. Pretending it wasn't taking all her will merely to force herself to eat, to shower, to get dressed each day.

She lost weight and, in an effort to kill time she might have otherwise been tempted to spend thinking (there would be no thinking, no, none of that at all!), she used some of her suddenly superfluous escape-the-fairy fund to refurbish her wardrobe. She bought new clothes. Got her hair cut, started wearing it in a sexy new style.

A part of her knew she was only staving off the inevitable. Knew eventually it was going to catch up with her.

Knew that at some point she would have to face one of two inescapable facts:

A) The queen had let Adam die.

B) Adam had used her.

Bottom line was, she intended to avoid facing either of those two heartbreaking options for as long as she possibly could.

24

Adam was in a vile temper.

Not only had the queen let him get shot—and he'd suffered every ounce of burning agony involved in it, the bite of each and every bullet—she'd yanked him out of the human realm, tossed him back to Faery smack into the middle of the Tuatha Dé Danaan's High Council chambers, healed him but *not* restored him, then confined him to those chambers until she'd returned.

And when she'd returned—what felt like a bloody aeon later—he'd been forced to sit through the entire blasted, infernal, formal hearing, to testify to all he'd seen and all Darroc had done, to answer the most minute and ridiculous questions, all the while seething with impatience to get back to Gabrielle and do what he now understood had to be done.

"Bloody hell," he hissed, "are we *finished* here yet?"

The heads of eight High Council members turned to regard him with imperious, offended stares.

It was impermissible to speak out of turn in council. An unspeakable insult. An unforgivable breach of ritual court manners.

Screw the council. Screw court manners. He had things to take care of. Urgent matters. Not piddling courtly crap.

Adam shot an irritated glare at Aoibheal. "You said I could decide his punishment and that you would restore me. Get on with it already. Restore me."

"You speak with a mortal's impatience," Aoibheal said coolly.

"Maybe," he growled, "because I'm stuck in a mortal form. *Fix* me already."

She arched a delicate brow, shrugged. Spoke softly in a rush of Tuatha Dé words.

And Adam sighed with pleasure as he felt himself changing. Becoming himself again.

Immortality.

Invincibility.

A veritable demigod.

Pure power thrumming through his . . . well, he no longer had veins. But who needed veins when there was splendid, glorious, intoxicating power at his very core? Energy, heat, prowess, strength. All the possibilities in the universe at his fingertips.

And, bloody hell, it felt good. *He* felt good. There were no aches, no pains in Tuatha Dé form. There was no weakness, no hunger, no weariness, no need to eat or drink or piss.

Absolute power. Absolute control.

The world again at his disposal, again his favorite toy.

"Now you may cry sentence, Adam," Aoibheal said.

Adam pondered Darroc in silence.

Aoibheal whispered a soft command and suddenly the Sword of Light, the hallowed weapon capable of killing an immortal, the blade with which he'd long ago scarred Darroc, appeared in her hand.

And he knew that she expected him to demand Darroc's immediate soulless death. It was what he, too, had believed he would claim.

But suddenly that seemed far too merciful. The bastard had tried to kill his petite *ka-lyrra*, to extinguish the life of his passionate, sexy, vibrant Gabrielle.

"Do it," Darroc snarled, staring fixedly at him. "Get it over with."

"A soulless death by blade is too good for you, Darroc."

Darroc snorted. "You live like a beast in a cage, and you no longer even see the bars. I was only trying to free you, free us all."

"And enslave the human race."

"They were born to be enslaved. By their very nature. Weak, puny things."

And there it was, Adam realized with a faint smile, precisely the sentence the arrogant Elder should bear. "Make him human, my Queen. Condemn him to die in the human realm."

The queen laughed softly. "Well spoken, Adam; we are pleased. Both fitting and fair."

"You can't do this to me," raged Darroc. "I will *not* live as one of them! Bloody kill me *now*!"

Adam's smile deepened.

Aoibheal moved forward, speaking in the ancient tongue, circling around the Elder, faster and faster, until but a radiant swirl of light spun on the floor of the chamber.

As Adam watched, the light grew blindingly intense, then suddenly Darroc and the queen reappeared.

Adam eyed his ancient nemesis curiously. There was something...different about him. His human appearance was somehow unlike Adam's human appearance had been. But what? Rubbing his jaw thoughtfully, he scrutinized the ex-Elder.

Tall, powerful, beautiful as all the Fae. Long gold-shot copper hair spilling to his waist. Chiseled, aristocratic face etched with disdain. Copper eyes glittering with rage—ah, his eyes! They were human eyes, with no unnatural iridescence or fiery golden sparks flickering within them.

And, although Darroc still presented an exotic, stunningly masculine beauty only rarely glimpsed in the human realm (and then usually immortalized on stage or screen), he no longer had that brush of otherworldliness that Adam had never lost. Despite an ineffable sense of ancientness, Darroc would pass as human in nearly any quarter.

"I don't get it," Adam murmured. "He looks different than I did."

"Of course he does," said Aoibheal. "He's now human."

"Yes, but so was I."

The queen laughed, a silvery sound. "No you weren't."

Adam blinked. "Yes, I was; you made me human yourself."

"You were never human, Adam. You were always Tuatha Dé. I merely played with your form a bit, made you as close to human as I could get you without actually transforming you into one of them. I heightened your senses, made you believe you were mortal. You yourself had diminished your essence by healing the Highlander. But you were never human. It's the one form I cannot shapeshift our people between. Once I give a Tuatha Dé a human form, it is irreversible. What I just did to Darroc can never be undone. No one and nothing in all the realms can prevent him now from dying, human and soulless. A year, fifty years, who knows? He will die."

"But I felt human feelings," Adam protested.

"Impossible," Aoibheal said flatly.

Adam frowned, confounded. But he'd *felt* them. He'd felt pain in his chest where he'd thought he'd had a heart. He'd gotten a sick feeling in the pit of his stomach whenever Gabrielle had been in danger. He'd suffered human feelings. How was that possible if he'd never been in human form?

He shook his head abruptly, scattering the questions from his head, to puzzle over later. There were far more important matters to which he needed to attend. And quickly, before Aoibheal decided to constrain him in some new fashion for some ridiculous reason.

While the queen was occupied with summoning her guard to escort Darroc to the human realm and bring in her consort Mael, whom Darroc had betrayed as his accomplice, Adam quietly tensed to sift out.

Suddenly the queen's head swiveled in his direction and she snapped furiously, "You will stop that this *instant, Amadan D—*"

But she'd spoken too late to compel him—he was already gone.

     Adam went first to the Queen's Royal Bower.

Once before he'd stolen the elixir of life from her private chambers.

Now he did so again.

A tiny glass vial containing a tiny amount of shimmering silvery liquid.

And as he sifted about, displacing his residue before heading for Cincinnati, he reflected on those last moments he'd spent with Gabrielle.

You're not falling for me, are you, Irish? he'd asked. And she'd blown up at him.

Launched into a furious, rambling diatribe that hadn't made much sense to him, possibly because he'd tuned most of it out upon realizing after the first few sentences that there'd been no "yes" in there anywhere and she hadn't sounded remotely as if she'd been leading up to one.

And then she'd demanded to know why Morganna had refused the elixir of life, and something inside him had snapped.

Christ, it was always souls. Souls, souls, souls. And his great, big fucking lack thereof.

He could have offered her a pretty lie—he'd fabricated several smooth ones for just such an occasion— but anger, defiance, and an age-old hurt had filled him with a wildness, a need he'd been unable to deny.

To cram his reality down her throat. To say, *This is what I am, for Christ's sake, is it so bloody awful?*

See me. *See* me!

And she'd seen him.

Ah, yes, he'd *forced* her to see him.

And she'd gazed at him with horror in those lovely green-gold eyes. Those eyes that only the night before had been dreamy with passion, soft and warm and inviting. Those eyes that had made him feel every inch a man, more alive and at peace and at home than he'd ever felt in his entire existence.

And that was when he'd finally understood.

He'd been a fool with Morganna. He'd made a huge mistake.

He had no intention of making the same one with Gabrielle.

Now that he was all-powerful again, he would erase Gabrielle's memory of his admission. He would eliminate all those facts that she'd found so distasteful, wipe them cleanly from her mind.

Then he would slip her the elixir of life. And he would whisk her off and keep her blissfully occupied, keep her enchanted by whatever means necessary, for as many years as it took for her immortal soul to burn out.

And when her soul was finally gone, she would no longer even *feel* those parts of herself that made her try to cling to it. She wouldn't even know to miss it.

And she would be his *forever*.

As long as she possibly could turned out to be exactly one month, seven days, and fourteen hours.

Gabby would have made it longer, but once again, she was undone by yet another diabolical iced cup of coffee to go.

To her credit, she did briefly contemplate that giving up her addiction might greatly simplify her life. Still, by the time she'd arrived at that conclusion, it was too late.

Friday night. Date night. She stayed at the office late, knowing couples would be walking the streets of her neighborhood this evening, holding hands, talking and laughing, enjoying the light kiss of fall in the early September air.

Classes had begun again, and though her load was heavy, she'd kept her job at Little & Staller, rearranging her hours around her class schedule, in a desperate bid to stay busy enough that she couldn't think.

Upon leaving for the evening, she ducked into Starbucks and grabbed said dastardly iced coffee before going to retrieve her shiny BMW from the upscale paid lot she'd treated herself to with a bit more of her escape-the-fairy fund.

She slid behind the wheel, pretending the faintest scent of jasmine and sandalwood did *not* still linger in the plush leather interior.

Part of her had wanted to sell the car, to erase that reminder of Adam from her life, the same way she'd packed up the crystal and china he'd left on her dining room table, his T-shirt, and all the gifts he'd given her, and tucked them away in a trunk in the attic.

Unfortunately, she'd needed something to drive and the thought of selling the car and trying to buy a new one was more than she could dredge up the energy to even contemplate doing.

Just like returning the seventeen phone messages Gwen and Chloe had left in the past week would have taken too much energy.

It seemed the note she'd sent them a few days after she'd gotten home hadn't been enough. Granted, it had been brief: *Gwen, Chloe, things didn't work out like I hoped. But I'm okay, just real busy at work. I'll call you sometime. G.*

She knew what they wanted. They wanted answers. Wanted to know what had happened with Darroc, with Adam. She didn't have any answers to give them.

She hadn't gotten the Happily-Ever-After they'd gotten, and she simply couldn't face delving into her misery with such shiny, happy people. People who had all those things she'd hoped for: devoted husbands, beautiful babies, lives rich with love and laughter.

They would want answers about *her*. They would want to know how she was *really* feeling, and once they had her on the phone they wouldn't permit any evasion. Their empathy and kindness would unravel her. She knew that the day she called them back would be the day she fell apart.

Hence, she wasn't calling them back. Period. *Not falling apart. Not on the meticulously controlled agenda right now.*

And if they arrived unannounced at her house, as they'd threatened in their message last night, well... she'd deal with that then.

Ten minutes later, Gabby pulled into the alley behind her house. Exhaling gustily, she slung her purse over her shoulder, grabbed her briefcase, her gym bag, a teetering stack of files that hadn't fit in the briefcase because she needed a *lot* of work to get her through the weekend sane, then balanced her coffee on top of it all, wedging the plastic lid firmly beneath the underside of her chin to hold it all steady.

She made it all the way into the living room before losing control of the unwieldy load.

Files slipped one way, the briefcase the other, then the coffee went, tumbling from beneath her chin, bounced off an end table, knocked over a pile of books and magazines, and drenched it all with dark, iced liquid.

Cursing under her breath, she began snatching coffee-stained files from the floor.

And that was when she saw it.

Since the day she'd gotten home from Scotland, she'd been avoiding the turret library, refusing to go in, in no frame of mind to be able to even so much as glimpse the O'Callaghan *Books of the Fae*.

Not even noticing that all this time the *Book of the Sin Siriche Du* had been lying on the end table near the sofa.

It was now facedown in a puddle of coffee.

It was going to be ruined!

She pounced on it, snatched it from the thick, muddy spill of icy liquid, and frantically dabbed it off on the sofa, heedless of the mess she was making of the flowered upholstery.

Thumbed it open to assess the damage.

And as Fate—which Gabby was seriously beginning to believe was wont to masquerade as seemingly innocuous cups of coffee—would have it, the slender black tome parted to a page that hadn't been there before.

His elegant, arrogant, slanted cursive. She read it once, twice, a third time, flinching as the words slammed into her.

I will never stay with another human woman and watch her die. Never.

And there it was.

Her answer had been there all along.

No, he didn't die. He'd *chosen* not to come back.

An anguished cry built in her throat and she tried desperately to swallow it, but she'd been swallowing her feelings too long. Day after day she'd been denying the pain in her heart, managing to stay in a state of limbo by arguing the case to herself that so long as she accepted no outcome, there was nothing to grieve.

She could no longer pretend. He was gone. And he wasn't coming back.

Tears stung her eyes, blinding her. Clutching the book to her chest, Gabby sank to the floor, sobbing.

Because she was a *Sidhe*-secr, because he knew the *féth fiada* didn't work on her, and because he had an irresistible urge to spy on her unseen for a few moments before completing that for which he'd come, Adam popped into Gabrielle's kitchen a dimensional sliver beyond her perception, the tiny bottle of elixir cupped loosely in his hand.

He inhaled. Ah, he'd missed this, the scent of her! A faint, utterly feminine scent of vanilla and heather and sunshine.

The house was dimly lit, and he moved through it, seeking her. She was here, he could feel her.

Ahead of him in the living room, a light was on.

He stepped into the doorway and there she was. Sitting cross-legged on the floor with her back to him. Beautiful as ever. Dressed in a trim-fitting, short-skirted black suit (by Danu, he'd missed those sweet legs! — especially wrapped around his waist), with sexy little heels on her feet. Jacket nipped in at the waist, accenting her hips and full breasts.

But she looked different. Frowning, he stepped into the room, circling to her side. Thinner — he didn't like that at all. He liked his woman built like a woman. Liked the way she'd been before, soft and nicely rounded. Christ, how much time had passed? he wondered. He always lost track of it when he was immortal; time passed at a slower pace in the Fae realm than it did in the human one. Her hair was styled differently, too, but that, he decided, eyeing her, looked sexy as hell, though he couldn't quite get a good look at it with her head down like that and all of it spilling around her face.

A soft, wet sniffling sound came from behind the silky curtain of hair.

He cocked his head, moving to stand before her, looking down.

Was she crying?

Just then she raised her head, and Adam sucked in a breath at his first glimpse of her face. Her eyes were red and swollen, her cheeks tear-stained, and she looked so fragile and heartbroken that it pierced him to his very core.

Who had hurt his woman? What bastard had made her cry? He'd kill the SOB!

Then he realized that she was holding a book in her lap.

His book.

Had *he* made her cry?

As he watched, more tears spilled down her cheeks, dropping onto the soft black leather of the tome. She traced her fingers lightly over the cover. "Damn you, Adam Black," she whispered.

He snorted. Yeah, well, he'd heard that often enough to last an eternity.

Scowling, he began to reach down, to place his hands on her head, to sift through her mind and strip from her that which he should never have told her to begin with.

Reached. Hesitated. Drew back. Cursed himself softly. Reached again.

She spoke then, her voice thick with tears. "I love you, damn it," she said brokenly. "I love you so much and it's killing me. God, I was so stupid. You never cared about me at all, did you? How am I supposed to go on?"

Adam jerked, reeling backward, hands fisting at his sides. He scarcely felt the tiny glass vial imploding in his hand with a soft tinkle of glass.

For a long moment, he couldn't move. Just stood, stunned.

She knew he was Fae.

She knew he had no heart or soul.

She knew he'd done heinous things, and she'd just said she loved him.

She loved him.

Bloody hell, she *loved* him.

Never *cared* about her? Was she *crazy*? It was all about her! Every bit of it! Every action he'd made, every thought he'd had since that night he'd first seen her had been all about her! Not for a single moment had she been out of his thoughts. She was *inside* him. Part of him now.

How could she not know that? With every gift he'd chosen for her he'd been saying it. Every time he'd buried himself inside her body he'd been trying to tell her! It had been in his every kiss, his every touch, silent, because he'd not wanted words thrown back in his face. But even in his words it had been there.

Sort of.

In the peculiar way human males spoke of such things. Or so his millennia of spying on them had taught him.

How could she not have known that every time he'd said, "*You're not falling for me, are you, Irish?*" it had been his declaration that he *was*. Bloody hell, even back there on the train he'd known it.

Known he was doing the stupidest thing possible. Falling for a human. But he could no more have stopped himself from falling for her than he could have stopped that train from hurtling to its destination.

You're not falling for me, are you, Irish?

That had been her cue to say "*Um, well, maybe I am a little,*" and then he could have said, "*Well, um, fancy that; maybe I am too.*"

Simple, concise, direct male communication. Right? Wasn't that how men went about it? Had all his spying been on skewed samples of the population? Had he misinterpreted what he'd observed?

She loves me.

He was awed by it, stilled by it.

He glanced down at the shimmering silver liquid dripping from his fist.

And a moment of crystalline clarity shivered around him, settled into his being.

He opened his hand and slowly relinquished what remained of the vial. With a flexing of Tuatha Dé will, he consigned the spilled elixir and broken vial to a faraway, forgotten dimension where it would hopefully do no harm.

He finally understood that Morganna had been right all along—he *hadn't* loved her.

Love would never imperil, never vanquish another's soul.

The intense pressure behind his sternum was suddenly back, that seizing in his chest, that tense feeling in his stomach. The sensations built and spread, and he nearly doubled over from the intensity of it. And he suddenly apprehended the sum of his existence as nothing more than a culmination of a series of events destined to lead him to a specific bench on a specific night at a precise moment.

To this woman.

He stared down at Gabrielle.

She was sobbing, head bowed, face buried in her hands.

In her grief, she glowed even more brilliantly golden; passion being the seat of the soul. She was so beautiful with that divine radiance illuming her from within, the very essence of who and what she was. He felt sick to think he'd nearly taken it from her. He could never take Gabrielle's soul.

Nor, however, could he stand to watch her die.

Nor, however, was he willing to live without her.

Which left him, he realized, only one other option.

25

Queen Aoibheal eyed the spot where only moments before the last prince of the *D'Jai* had stood before her in her Royal Bower.

Adam was gone now. Gone to the human realm.

She sighed, feeling weary to the very core of her being. She'd argued with him, she'd bribed, she'd threatened. But nothing she'd said had succeeded in swaying him.

This is the sentence you chose as punishment for Darroc's crimes, Adam — yet now you would request it for yourself?

Yes.

You know the transformation cannot be undone! I cannot save you should you change your mind. Unlike your other adventures, there can be no last-minute reprieve.

I understand.

You will die, Adam! One mortal life—and none can vouchsafe how long—then gone.

I understand.

You have no soul. You won't be able to follow your Sidhe-seer when she dies.

I know.

By Danu! Then, why?

So calmly he'd stood before her, so composed. So regal and beautiful and so—she'd come swiftly to understand—very far beyond her reach.

I don't want to live without her, Aoibheal. I love her. An elegant shrug. *More than life itself.*

That was so utterly inconceivable to Aoibheal that she'd been momentarily unable to fathom an argument to counter it.

Make me human, Aoibheal.

As she'd paused, trying to decide if she should continue arguing, or simply confine him somewhere—in the belly of a mountain, perhaps deep beneath the ocean—until the *Sidhe-*seer was long dead, he'd knelt before her, without a trace of his trademark arrogance and pride.

Her vainglorious, impetuous, wild prince had bowed his head. Humbly.

And he'd said a word she'd not heard pass those beautiful, sensual lips, not once in six thousand years:

Please.

In that moment, she knew she'd lost him.

That if she did anything other than grant his request, she would make of him—her most favored prince—her greatest enemy. Not that he could harm her, considering how much more powerful she was (though, given how unpredictable he was, she wasn't *entirely* certain of that), but if she had to lose him, it would not be to hatred of her. She would yield him to another woman first, despite the sting of it.

Aoibheal closed her eyes, her hands clenching into delicate fists. Had she imagined, for even a moment, when she'd chosen his punishment, that things might come to such an end, she'd never have punished him. She would have resisted her Council's counsel and plotted her own course.

As she would do henceforth—in light of the recent betrayal by those closest to her—Council and consort, no less. She no longer had Adam to watch her back.

"Ah, Amadan," she whispered, "I shall miss you, my prince."

Gabby shook her head as she guided the sporty roadster down the alley behind her house.

A man in a Lexus had followed her halfway home from the grocery store, hopped out at a red light, and tried to give her his phone number.

Men had been hitting on her like crazy lately.

It's because you're so obviously not interested, Chloe had said the other night on the phone. *To many men, it's a challenge they can't resist—a pretty woman who doesn't care.*

Oh, please, it's just the car, Gabby had replied, rolling her eyes. She really *was* going to have to get rid of it. It was attracting all the wrong kinds of men. Not that there were any right kinds—she'd had a taste of fairy tale, and after that, no mere man could ever hope to compare.

She'd finally returned Gwen's and Chloe's numerous phone messages a week ago—that awful night that she'd found the *Book of the Sin Siriche Du*.

She'd been crying so hard when Chloe had answered that she'd not even been able to manage a "hello."

But Chloe had immediately known it was her, and Gwen had picked up on another line, and the MacKeltar wives had cried with her, from across an ocean. They'd tried to coax her to come back and stay with them for a while, but Gabby wasn't ready to see Castle Keltar again.

She might never be ready to see it again. She'd spent the most glorious days and nights of her life in that castle, lost both her virginity and her heart in the Crystal Chamber. She'd worn his diamonds there, become his woman there; she'd perched atop a sheer cliff in the arms of her Fae prince and watched the day being born.

Merely thinking about it brought a mist of tears to her eyes.

Nope, definitely not ready to go back to Scotland.

Gathering her groceries, she set the car alarm and hurried up the steps to the back door. She was just slipping the key in the lock when the door was pulled open from the inside so abruptly that she stumbled inward with it.

Smack into a rock-hard body.

She jerked, flailing backward. The groceries slid from her suddenly limp arms, and her eyes flew wide.

"Hello, Gabrielle," Adam said.

Her knees buckled.

"Stop *manhandling* me!"

"I'm not manhandling you," Adam said mildly, taking full advantage of Gabrielle's prone position to run his palm over her luscious, shapely behind. The moment she'd begun to go down, he'd swept her up and tossed her over his shoulder. "You swooned. I merely caught you."

"I do *not* swoon. I have never swooned in my entire life," Gabrielle shouted, thumping him in the back with her palms. "And that's *my* bottom, not yours, so quit touching it!"

Adam laughed. Ah, how he'd missed his fiery *ka-lyrra*! "Possession is nine-tenths of the law, Gabrielle. Seeing as how your bottom is currently in my hands, not yours, I believe that makes it mine." With a wicked grin, he rubbed her enticing, upturned rump, dipping intimately into the cleft between her cheeks.

"*Oooh*—that's the most ridiculous line of reasoning I've ever heard! What is that—fairy logic? Nine-tenths arrogance, and one-tenth brute force? Put me down. What did you do? Get in trouble again? Need a little *Sidhe*-seer help? Well, too bad. Go *away*."

He patted her bottom and continued to tote her through the house at a swift pace, making for the stairs. "I'm never going away, *ka-lyrra*," he purred, savoring the soft, supple weight of her against his body. It felt like a century since last he'd held her.

"Sure. Yeah, right. Go ahead, make some more empty fairy promises. I'm not falling for them this time. I'm not playing whatever stupid game you've got in mind. You can't just walk out on me, only to pop back in whenever you feel like it. There's no Open Door policy here. Hey—take me back downstairs! What do you think you're doing? Where are you taking me?" she snapped.

He turned his face into her and nipped her thigh with a playful love bite. "To bed, Gabrielle."

"I *so* don't think so," she hissed, promptly launching into a tirade about how he was *never* going to bed with her again. That she may have been gullible once, but she wasn't anymore. That he'd cured her of *all* her illusions. Wriggling like a wee hellion over his shoulder, she icily informed him that she had no interest whatsoever in having such a heartless bastard in her life to *any* degree, that she hated him, and that she only wished he were mortal so he could die and burn in hell for all eternity.

When he tossed her down on her bed, it knocked a bit of the breath from her, which gave him time to say, "You hate me, Gabrielle? That's a bloody shame. Because I meant it when I said I'm not leaving. I'm never leaving. I'm in love with you."

His *ka-lyrra* went still as stone, her mouth frozen open in a desperate bid for breath. Her throat worked convulsively. Then, with a great, indrawn screech of air, she launched herself at him, a flying, hissing female catapult of fists and tears.

It occurred to him, as he went crashing down to the floor beneath her, that he might well *never* understand women.

Gabby lay on the floor in Adam's arms, her head spinning.

He'd let her pummel him until she'd exhausted herself. He'd let her rage and yell and weep, enduring it all in patient silence until—crying so hard she couldn't breathe—she'd begun hiccuping uncontrollably. Then he'd rolled her onto her side, pulled her back against his powerful body, wrapped his arms around her, and held her until she'd calmed, whispering soft reassurances in her ear. "Shh, sweet. Be easy, love. It's okay. Everything's okay."

Love? Adam was saying the L-word? Into what impossible fairy tale had she fallen?

"Am I awake? Is this a dream?" she whispered.

"If it is," he whispered back, "I ask only that it go on forever. Not the crying part," he clarified, "the holding-you-in-my-arms part." He turned her gently then, to face him.

She buried her face in his chest, sniffling, trying to understand what was going on. Afraid to believe she was awake. Afraid that the moment she let herself believe it, she would wake up. Find herself alone in bed, in her big, silent house.

"Look at me, *ka-lyrra*," he said quietly.

With a little sniffle, Gabby tipped her head back and met his dark gaze. And frowned, bemused. She'd been so stupefied to find him in her house that she'd not really taken a good look at him. Something about him was different. But what? His eyes?

"I love you, Gabrielle O'Callaghan."

The words slammed into her; she stared at him mutely.

He kissed her then, his mouth slanting hard over hers, his velvety tongue gliding deep. And she gave herself over to it. Dream or not, it was real enough for her. She was in his arms and he was saying he loved her and if she was asleep, she just hoped she could stay asleep forever.

Even his kiss was different, she realized dimly, as her body flared to frantic, sizzling life in his arms. It held a touch of urgency that had never been there before. It was no longer shaped by immortal leisure but held a very human desperation, a mortal hunger and passion.

And it shook her so deeply that she went wild, kissing him back fiercely, pushing him back to the floor, clambering on top of him, burying her hands in his hair. Kissing and kissing him, with weeks of grief and longing and need.

How their clothing came off, she had no idea, only knew that moments later they were both naked on the floor of her bedroom and she was beneath him, and he was pushing inside her.

And she was alive again. There was blood in her veins, not ice. There was a heart in her chest, not—

"Adam," she gasped, stunned, "I can feel your heart beating." She'd never felt it before. Even though he'd been human, not once had she ever felt the powerful thud of his heart beneath her palm, the throb of a pulse at his neck.

And she'd never even noted their absence until this moment, when she *was* feeling them.

He drew back, his darkly beautiful face taut with lust. "I know." He flashed her a brilliant smile. Then he began moving inside her and she forgot all about a heartbeat she'd never felt before. Gave herself over to pure sensation. And the turret bedroom was filled with the wild, impassioned sounds of a woman and her Fae prince making love.

Later, Adam told her everything.

Well, nearly everything. He omitted that he'd almost taken her soul. And since she didn't know that he'd tricked them to begin with, he didn't bother mentioning that he'd told Circenn and Lisa the truth about the elixir of life, then taken them to the queen so she could restore them to their mortal state.

He'd made amends as best he could. He refused to b

damned for wrongs righted, or for things he'd "almost" done. He wasn't the man he'd once been.

He told her what had become of Darroc. He told her how time moved differently between the realms, and that he'd never meant to leave her alone for so long.

Speaking quietly, holding her close, he told her how he'd realized that there was no way he would be able to stand living with her and watching her die, as he'd done with Morganna.

The moment those words left his lips, Gabrielle tensed in his arms, jerked from his embrace, and shot straight up in bed. "Oh!" she hissed, eyes flashing furiously. "Then, what did you come back for? Are you telling me you're *leaving* me again?"

He shook his head hastily, and explained that—although he'd believed he was human—he'd never been. That the queen had only made him *think* he was mortal to punish him. He told her what the queen had said about such a transformation being irreversible for a Tuatha Dé.

And he told her that he'd finally realized that, since he couldn't bear to live without her, yet he couldn't bear to watch her die, there was only one choice left to him.

"The reason you can feel my heartbeat, *ka-lyrra*, is because now I really *am* human. It's for real this time."

Gabby's eyes widened and she stared at him, her lower lip trembling. "But you just said it's irreversible."

He nodded.

"You mean, you're going to *die*?" she whispered.

Cupping her head in his hands, Adam pulled her down for a deep, possessive kiss. "No, *ka-lyrra*, I mean, I'm finally going to live. Here. Now. With you." He drew a breath. "Marry me, Gabrielle. I'll give you the life you've always wanted. I can now. I'm human, just like you. Let me be your husband and give you babies. Let me spend the rest of my life with you."

"Oh, God," Gabby breathed, tears welling up in her eyes, "you gave up your *immortality* for me?"

He caught her tears with his tongue as they slipped down her cheeks, kissing them away. "No tears, Gabrielle. I have no regrets. Not one."

"How can you say that? You gave up *everything*! Immortality. Invincibility. All that it is to be a Tuatha Dé!"

He shook his head. "I *gained* everything. Or at least I'll think so," he growled, suddenly impatient, anxious, "when you give me a bloody answer to my bloody question. How many times are you going to make me ask you? Will you marry me, Gabrielle O'Callaghan? Yes or yes? And in case you're still managing to miss the point, the correct answer is 'yes.' And, by the way, anytime you'd like to tell me you love me, I wouldn't mind hearing it."

She pounced on him delightedly, straddling him, slipped her hands into his hair, and kissed him. He luxuriated in the bliss of her sweet body, closing his arms around her, his tongue gliding deep, tangling with hers.

"I'm going to take this as a yes," he purred, catching her lower lip, tugging playfully at it.

"I love you, Adam Black," Gabby breathed. "And, yes. Oh, abso-*freaking*-lutely *yes*!"

FIVE YEARS LATER

EPILOGUE

Gabby finished unloading the dishwasher and cocked her head, listening. The house was quiet; their two-year-old son Connor was already down for the night. Soon she would go upstairs, kiss their daughter, Tessa, good night, and lead her husband off to bed.

Professor Black.

She shook her head, smiling. Adam couldn't look less like a professor, with his chiseled face and those sexy dark eyes and that long black hair, not to mention that rippling, powerful body. He looked more like... well, a Fae prince masquerading as a professor, and doing a rather shoddy job of it at that.

When he'd first told her that he intended to teach history at the university, she'd laughed. *Too everyday, too plebeian*, she'd thought. *He'll never do it.*

He'd surprised her. But then, he often did.

He'd planned everything out so carefully. Before

he'd petitioned the queen to make him human, he'd established a detailed human identity for himself as an extremely wealthy man with vast bank accounts and a thousand acres of prime land in the Highlands. A human identity complete with all the necessary paperwork and credentials to permit him to live a normal life in the human realm.

And when she'd gently scoffed at his announcement of his choice of career, he'd waved those credentials at her—transcripts from the top universities in the nation, no less (of course, he'd made himself brilliant)—and gone off and gotten himself a job.

He'd developed a reputation as a renegade in the field, with all kinds of controversial theories about things like who had built Newgrange and Stonehenge and the true origin of the Proto-Indo-European tongue.

Students had to register for his classes a year in advance.

And she, well, she had her dream job. She and Jay and Elizabeth had opened up their own law firm and just this year had finally begun pulling in the kinds of cases she'd always hoped to represent. Cases that mattered, that made a difference.

They'd begun a family immediately, neither of them had been willing to wait. Time was far too precious to them both.

And, oh, he made beautiful babies! There was Tessa, with black hair and green-gold eyes; Connor, with blond hair and dark eyes; and yet another on the way.

She pressed a palm to her abdomen, smiling. She loved being a mother. Adored being married to him. She doubted any woman had ever been more completely and unconditionally loved.

She knew her husband would never stray, so highly

did he value that which he'd waited nearly six thousand years to know, so precious was it to him: love. She knew he would be there with her until the very end, that he would cherish each wrinkle, every line in her face, because in the final analysis they were not a negation of life but an affirmation of a life well lived. Proof positive of laughter and tears, of joy and grief, of passion, of *living*. Every facet of being human was amazing to him, each and every change of season a triumph, a taste of unbearable sweetness. Never had a man lived who savored life more.

Life was rich and full.

She couldn't have asked for more.

Well . . . actually . . . she amended with a little inner flinch, she could have.

Though most of the time she looked at Adam and just felt awed and humbled that this big, wonderful man had given up so much to love her, sometimes she hated that he didn't have a soul, and sometimes she wanted to hate God.

And she had a dream, a silly dream perhaps, but a dream to which she clung.

They would live to be a hundred, until long after their children and grandchildren were grown, and one day they would go to bed and lie down facing each other, and die like that, at the same moment, in each other's arms.

And this was her dream: that maybe, just maybe, if she loved him hard enough and true enough and deep enough, and if she held on to him tightly enough as they died, she could take him with her wherever it was that souls went. And there she would do what was in her blood, what she now knew she'd been born for; she would stand before God, a *brehon*, and she would argue the greatest, the most important case of her life.

And she would win.

"I don't understand, Daddy," Tessa said. "Why did the rabbit have to lose his fur to be real?"

Adam closed the book, *The Velveteen Rabbit*, and glanced down at his daughter.

She was tucked in bed, blankets to her chin, staring up at him. His precious Tessa, with her oodles of shiny black ringlets tumbling around her chubby angelic face, with her quick mind, and incessant curiosity, and her daddy's heart wrapped oh-so-snugly around her chubby little finger.

"Because that's part of becoming real."

"*Eew.* I don't want to be real. I want to be pretty like the fairy queen. Oops"—she clapped a tiny hand over her mouth—"wasn't 'posed to say that."

In the doorway, Gabby gasped softly, and Adam glanced up immediately, arching a brow at her, a silent question in his eyes.

I've never told her anything about fairies, Gabby mouthed. *Have you?*

He shook his head. They'd both assumed Tessa wasn't a *Sidhe*-seer. Gabrielle hadn't seen a single Tuatha Dé since that day Darroc had ambushed them in Scotland five years ago, and they'd assumed Aoibheal must have stripped the Fae-vision from the O'Callaghan line.

"What fairy queen, Tessa?" Adam said softly. "It's okay, you can tell me."

Tessa eyed him doubtfully. "She said you'd get mad if you knew she came."

"I won't get mad," he assured her, smoothing her tousled ringlets.

"Promise, Daddy?"

"Promise. Cross my heart. What fairy queen, sweet?"

"Ah-veel."

Adam inhaled sharply, glancing at Gabrielle again.

"Does Aoibheal come to see you, Tessa?" Gabby said softly, moving into the room, joining Adam on the edge of Tessa's bed.

Tessa shook her head. "Not me. She comes to see Daddy. She thinks he's pretty."

Adam bit back a laugh at the look his wife shot him then, her eyes narrowed, dainty nostrils flared. She all but growled. He loved that she got a little jealous sometimes, adored her possessiveness. Suffered from his own fair share of it where his petite *ka-lyrra* was concerned.

"Pretty, huh?" Gabby said dryly.

"*Mmm-hmm,*" Tessa said, rubbing her eyes sleepily. "But I can't see it no matter how hard I try."

Okay, now, that miffed him a bit, Adam thought, disgruntled. Before Tessa had been born, he'd pored over piles of parenting books, determined to be a good father. He thought he'd been doing a fine job, but wasn't his daughter supposed to have stars in her eyes whenever she looked at him? At least until she hit her teens? (And then God help the man who tried to date his daughter!) So, he had a few tiny lines around his eyes that hadn't been there before, he was still a handsome man! "You don't think I'm pretty, eh, Tessa?" He tickled his daughter's neck, right behind her ear, where it never failed to make her limp with laughter.

" 'Course I do, Daddy." She giggled. Then she gave him a thoroughly four-year-old look of exasperation.

"But I can't see what she sees. She says only fairies can."

Adam's heart skipped a beat.

It *couldn't* be.

Could it?

"Oh, God," Gabby said weakly, her gaze flying to his. She pressed a trembling hand to her mouth. They stared at each other for a long moment.

Adam nodded, wordlessly encouraging her to ask the question they were both thinking. He'd ask himself, but he couldn't seem to find his tongue.

He knew of only one thing he'd been able to see around humans when he'd been a fairy that humans couldn't see. He could scarcely breathe with wanting it so badly. With aching to be able to follow his wife from this life, into countless others. Five years ago, when he'd wed Gabrielle in a romantic Highland ceremony, the MacKeltars had offered him the use of their Druid binding vows: those sacred vows that united lovers for all eternity. He'd refused to say them—not because he hadn't longed to with every fiber of his being—but because it would have been to no avail, as he'd had no soul with which to bind himself.

Breathlessly Gabby said, "See what, Tessa? What can fairies see that you can't see?"

Tessa yawned. Snuggled deeper into the covers. "That Daddy's all glowy and golden."

Adam's mouth worked, but nothing came out.

"Adam glows golden?" Gabby said faintly.

Tessa nodded. "*Mmm-hmm.* Ah-veel says now he's just like you and me, Mommy."

Gabby made a soft choking sound.

For a long moment Adam couldn't move. He just sat on the edge of Tessa's bed and stared at his wife. She stared back at him, wonderingly, her eyes misting with tears of joy.

Then the enormity of it electrified him, galvanized him into action—there wasn't a moment to waste! If, by some miracle, he'd been gifted with a soul, he wanted it bound to Gabrielle's *now*.

Hastily dropping a kiss on Tessa's brow, Adam turned out the light, scooped Gabrielle up into his arms, and carried her from the room, hastening down the hall to their bedroom.

"*Ka-lyrra*," he said urgently, "there's something I want you to do with me. Vows I want to exchange, but you must know that they will bind our souls together for all eternity. Are you willing? Would you have me forever?"

Laughing and crying at the same time, she nodded.

Exultantly Adam deposited her on her feet, placed the palm of his right hand above her heart, and rested his left above his own. "Place your hands on top of mine, Gabrielle," he commanded.

When she did so, he spoke with quiet reverence and conviction:

"If aught must be lost, it will be my honor for yours. If one must be forsaken, it will be my soul for yours. Should death come anon, it will be my life for yours. I am *Given*."

Smiling up at him, her eyes sparkling with joy, she repeated the vows, and, the moment she finished, emotion crashed over him so intensely that it nearly brought him to his knees. He felt the bond quickening inside him, heating his blood with fierce passion, as their souls were united for all time.

Backing her against the wall, he buried his hands in

her hair, slanted his mouth over hers, and kissed her hungrily.

He had a soul. He knew love. He was pledged to his soul mate forever.

And Adam Black was finally truly immortal.

ABOUT THE AUTHOR

KAREN MARIE MONING graduated from
Purdue University with a bachelor's degree in
Society & Law. Her novels have appeared on the
New York Times, USA Today, and *Publishers Weekly*
bestseller lists and have won numerous awards,
including the prestigious RITA Award. She can be
reached at www.karenmoning.com.

Can't wait to read more of Mac's adventures? Catch the next book in Karen Marie Moning's sizzling Fever series. . . .

FAEFEVER

by

Karen Marie Moning

Coming from Delacorte Press
October 2008

KAREN MARIE
MONING

FAEFEVER

FAEFEVER
Coming October 2008

"I keep expecting to wake up and find it was all a bad dream.
Alina will be alive,
I won't be afraid of the dark,
Monsters won't be walking the streets of Dublin,
And I won't have this terrible fear that,
tomorrow dawn just won't come."
—Mac's journal

Part One
BEFORE DAWN

PROLOGUE

I'd die for him.

No, wait a minute . . . that's not where this is supposed to begin.

I know that. But left to my own devices, I'd prefer to skim over the events of the next few weeks, and whisk you through those days with glossed-over details that cast me in a more flattering light.

Nobody looks good in their darkest hour. But it's those hours that make us what we are. We stand strong, or we cower. We emerge victorious, tempered by our trials, or fractured by a permanent, damning fault line.

I never used to think about things like darkest hours and trials and fault lines.

I used to fill my days with sunning and shopping, bartending at the Brickyard (always more of a party than a job, and that was how I liked my life) and devising ways to con Mom and Dad into helping me buy a new car. At twenty-two, I was still living at home, safe in my sheltered world, lulled by the sleepy, slow-paddling fans of the Deep South into believing myself the center of it.

Then my sister, Alina, was brutally murdered while studying abroad in Dublin, and my world changed overnight. It was bad enough that I had to identify her mutilated body, and watch my once-happy family shatter, but my world didn't stop falling apart there. It didn't stop until I'd learned that pretty much everything I'd been raised to believe about myself wasn't true.

I discovered that my folks weren't my real parents; my sister and I were adopted; and despite my lazy, occasionally overblown drawl, we weren't southern at all, but descended from an ancient Celtic bloodline of *sidhe*-seers, people who can see the Fae—a terrifying race of otherworldly beings that have lived secretly among us for thousands of years, cloaked in illusions and lies.

Those were the easy lessons.

The hard lessons were yet to come, waiting for me in the *craic*-filled streets of the Temple Bar District of Dublin, where I would watch people die, and learn how to kill; where I would meet Jericho Barrons, V'lane, and the Lord Master; where I would step up to the plate as a major player in a deadly game with fate-of-the-world stakes.

For those of you just joining me, my name is Mac-Kayla Lane, Mac for short. My real last name might be O'Connor, but I don't know that for sure. I'm a *sidhe-*

seer, one of the most powerful that's ever lived. Not only can I see the Fae, I can hurt them and, armed with one of their most sacred Hallows—the Spear of Luin, or Destiny—I can even kill the immortal beings.

Don't settle into your chair and relax. It's not just my world that's in trouble; it's your world, too. It's happening right now, while you're sitting there, munching a snack, getting ready to immerse yourself in a fictional escape. Guess what? It's not fiction, and there's no escape. The walls between the human world and Faery are coming down—and I hate to break it to you, but these fairies are *so* not Tinker Bells.

If the walls crash completely . . . well . . . you'd just better hope they don't. If I were you, I'd turn on all my lights right now. Get out a few flashlights. Check your supply of batteries.

I came to Dublin for two things: to find out who killed my sister, and to get revenge. See how easily I can say that now? I want revenge. Revenge with a capital R. Revenge with crushed bones and a lot of blood. I want her murderer dead, preferably by my own hand. A few months here and I've shed *years* of polished southern civilities.

Shortly after I stepped off the plane from Ashford, Georgia, and planted my well-pedicured foot on Ireland's shore, I probably would have died if I hadn't stumbled into a bookstore owned by Jericho Barrons. Who or what he is, I have no idea. But he has knowledge that I need, and I have something he wants, and that makes us reluctant allies.

When I had no place to turn, Barrons took me in, taught me who and what I am, opened my eyes, and helped me survive. He didn't do it nicely, but I no longer care how I survive, as long as I do.

Because it was safer than my cheap room at the inn, I moved into his bookstore. It's protected against most of my enemies with wards and assorted spells, and stands bastion at the edge of what I call a Dark Zone: a neighborhood that has been taken over by Shades, amorphous Unseelie that thrive in darkness and suck the life from humans.

We've battled monsters together. He's saved my life twice. We've shared a taste of dangerous lust. He's after the *Sinsar Dubh*—a million-year-old book of the blackest magic imaginable, scribed by the Unseelie King himself, that holds the key to power over both the worlds of Fae and Man. I want it because it was Alina's dying request that I find it, and I suspect it holds the key to saving our world.

He says he wants it because he collects books. Right.

V'lane is another story. He's a Seelie prince, and a death-by-sex Fae, which you'll be learning more about soon enough. The Fae consist of two adversarial courts with their own Royal Houses and unique castes: the Light or Seelie Court, and the Dark or Unseelie Court. Don't let the light and dark stuff fool you. Both are deadly. However, the Seelie considered the Unseelie *so* deadly that they imprisoned them roughly seven hundred thousand years ago. When one Fae fears another, be afraid.

Each court has their Hallows, or sacred objects of immense power. The Seelie Hallows are the Spear (which I have), the Sword, the Stone, and the Cauldron. The Unseelie Hallows are the Amulet (which I had and the Lord Master took), the Box, the Sifting Silvers, and the highly sought-after Book. They all have different purposes. Some I know, others I'm not so clear on.

Like Barrons, V'lane is after the *Sinsar Dubh*. He's

hunting it for the Seelie queen Aoibheal, who needs it to reinforce the walls between the realms of Fae and Man, and keep them from coming down. Like Barrons, he has saved my life. (He's also given me some of the most intense orgasms of it.)

The Lord Master is my sister's murderer; the one who seduced, used, and destroyed her. Not quite Fae, not quite human, he's been opening portals between realms, bringing Unseelie—the worst of the Fae—through to our world, turning them loose, and teaching them to infiltrate our society. He *wants* the walls down so he can free all of the Unseelie from their icy prison. He's also after the *Sinsar Dubh*, although I'm not certain why. I think he may be seeking it to destroy it, so no one can ever rebuild the walls again.

That's where I come in.

These three powerful, dangerous men *need* me.

Not only can I see the Fae, I can sense Fae relics and Hallows. I can feel the *Sinsar Dubh* out there, a dark, pulsing heart of pure evil.

I can hunt it.

I can find it.

My dad would say that makes me this season's MVP.

Everybody wants me. So I stay alive in a world where death darkens my doorstep daily.

I've seen things that would make your skin crawl. I've done things that make my skin crawl.

But that's not important now. What's important is starting at the right place . . . let's see . . . where was that?

I peel the pages of my memory backward, one at a time, squinting so I don't have to see them too clearly. I turn back, past that whiteout where all memories vanish for a time, past that hellish Halloween, and the things

Barrons did. Past the woman I killed. Past a part of V'lane piercing the meat of my tongue. Past what I did to Jayne.

There.

I zoom down into a dark, damp, shiny street.

It's me. Pretty in pink and gold.

I'm in Dublin. It's nighttime. I'm walking the cobbled pavement of Temple Bar. I'm alive, vibrantly so. There's nothing like a recent brush with death to make you feel larger than life.

There's a sparkle in my eyes and a spring in my step. I'm wearing a killer pink dress, with my favorite heels, and I'm accessorized to the hilt, in gold and rose amethyst. I've taken extra care with my hair and makeup. I'm on my way to meet Christian MacKeltar, a sexy, mysterious young Scotsman who knew my sister. I feel *good* for a change.

Well, at least for a short time I do.

Fast-forward a few moments.

Now I'm clutching my head and stumbling from the sidewalk into the gutter. Falling to all fours. I've just gotten closer to the *Sinsar Dubh* than I've ever been before, and it's having its usual effect on me. Pain. Debilitating.

I no longer look so pretty. In fact, I look positively wretched.

On my hands and knees in a puddle that smells of beer and urine, I'm iced to the bone. My hair is in a tangle, my amethyst hair clip bobs against my nose, and I'm crying. I push the hair from my face with a filthy hand and watch the tableau playing out in front of me with wide, horrified eyes.

I remember that moment. Who I was. What I wasn't. I capture it in freeze-frame. There are so many things I would say to her.

Head up, Mac. Brace yourself. A storm is coming. Don't you hear the thunderclap of sharp hooves on the wind? Can't you feel the soul-numbing frost? Don't you smell spice and blood on the breeze?

Run, I would tell her. Hide.

But I wouldn't listen to me.

On my knees, watching that . . . *thing* . . . do what it's doing, I'm in the stranglehold of a killing undertow.

Reluctantly, I merge with the memory, slip into her skin . . .

1

The pain, God, the *pain*! It's going to splinter my skull!

I clutch my head with wet, stinking hands, determined to hold it together until the inevitable occurs—I pass out.

Nothing compares to the agony the *Sinsar Dubh* causes me. Each time I get close to it, the same thing happens. I'm immobilized by pain that escalates until I lose consciousness.

Barrons says it's because the Dark Book and I are point and counterpoint. That it's so evil, and I'm so good, that it repels me violently. His theory is to "dilute" me somehow, make me a little evil so I can get close to it. I don't see how making me evil so I can get close enough to pick up an evil book is a good thing. I think I'd probably do evil things with it.

"No," I whimper, sloshing on my knees in the puddle. "Please . . . no!" Not here, not now! In the past, each time I'd gotten close to the Book, Barrons had been with me, and I'd had the comfort of knowing he wouldn't let anything too awful happen to my unconscious body. He might tote me around like a divining rod, but I could live with that. Tonight, however, I was alone. The thought of being vulnerable to anyone and anything in Dublin's streets for even a few moments terrified me. What if I passed out for an hour? What if I fell facedown into the vile puddle I was in, and drowned in mere inches of . . . ugh.

I *had* to get out of the puddle. I would not die so pathetically.

A wintry wind howled down the street, whipping between buildings, chilling me to the bone. Old newspapers cartwheeled like dirty, sodden tumbleweeds over broken bottles and discarded wrappers and glasses. I flailed in the sewage, scraped at the pavement with my fingernails, left the tips of them broken in gaps between the cobbled stones.

Inch by inch, I clawed my way to drier ground.

It was there—straight ahead of me: the Dark Book. I could feel it, fifty yards from where I scrabbled for purchase. Maybe less. And it wasn't just a book. Oh, no. It was nothing that simple. It pulsated darkly, charring the edges of my mind.

Why wasn't I passing out?

Why wouldn't this pain *end*?

I felt like I was dying. Saliva flooded my mouth, frothing into foam at my lips. I wanted desperately to throw up but I couldn't. Even my stomach was locked down by pain.

Moaning, I tried to raise my head. I had to see it. I'd been close to it before, but I'd never *seen* it. I'd always passed out first. If I wasn't going to lose consciousness, I had questions I wanted answered. I didn't even know what it looked like. Who had it? What were they doing with it? Why did I keep having near brushes with it?

Shuddering, I pushed back onto my knees, shoved a hank of sour-smelling hair from my face, and looked.

The street that only moments ago had bustled with tourists making their merry way from one open pub door to the next was now scourged clean by the dark arctic wind. Doors had been slammed, music silenced.

Leaving only me.

And *them*.

The vision before me was not at all what I'd expected.

A gunman had a huddle of people backed against the wall of a building, a family of tourists, cameras swinging around their necks. The barrel of a semiautomatic weapon gleamed in the moonlight. The father was yelling, the mother was screaming, trying to gather three small children into her arms.

"No!" I shouted. At least I think I did. I'm not sure I actually made a sound. My lungs were compressed with pain.

The gunman let loose a spray of bullets, silencing their cries. He killed the youngest last—a delicate blond girl of four or five, with wide, pleading eyes that would haunt me till the day I died. A girl I couldn't save because I couldn't fecking *move*. Paralyzed by pain-deadened limbs, I could only kneel there, screaming inside my head.

Why was this happening? Where was the *Sinsar Dubh*? Why couldn't I see it?

The man turned, and I inhaled sharply.

A book was tucked beneath his arm.

A perfectly innocuous hardcover, about three hundred and fifty pages thick, no dust jacket, pale gray with red binding. The kind of well-read hardcover you might find in any used bookstore, in any city.

I gaped. Was I supposed to believe *that* was the million-year-old book of the blackest magic imaginable, scribed by the Unseelie King? Was this supposed to be funny? How anticlimactic. How absurd.

The gunman glanced at his weapon with a bemused expression. Then his head swiveled back toward the fallen bodies, the blood and bits of flesh and bone spattered across the brick wall.

The book dropped from beneath his arm. It seemed to fall in slow motion, changing, transforming, as it tumbled end over end to the damp, shiny brick. By the time it hit the cobbled pavement with a heavy *whump*, it was no longer a simple hardcover but a massive black tome, nearly a foot thick, engraved with runes, bound by bands of steel and intricate locks. Exactly the kind of book I'd expected: ancient and evil-looking.

I sucked in another breath.

Now the thick, dark volume was changing again, becoming something new. It swirled and spun, drawing substance from wind and darkness.

In its place rose a . . . *thing* . . . of such . . . terrible essence and pitch. A darkly animate . . . again, I can only say *thing* . . . that existed beyond shape or name: a malformed creature sprung from some no-man's-land of shattered sanity and broken gibberings.

And it *lived*.

I have no words to describe it, because nothing exists in our world to compare it to. I'm glad nothing exists in our world to compare it to, because if something did exist in our world to compare it to, I'm not sure our world would exist.

I can only call it the Beast, and leave it there.

My soul shivered, as if perceiving on some visceral level that my body was not nearly enough protection for it. Not from this.

The gunman looked at it, and it looked at the gunman, and he turned his weapon on himself. I jerked at the sound of more shots. The shooter crumpled to the pavement and his weapon clattered away.

Another icy wind gusted down the street, and there was movement in my periphery.

A woman appeared from around the corner as if answering a summons, gazed blankly at the scene for several moments, then walked as if drugged straight to the fallen book (*crouching beast with impossible limbs and bloodied muzzle!*) that abruptly sported neither ancient locks nor bestial form but was once again masquerading as an innocent hardcover.

"Don't touch it!" I cried, goose bumps needling my flesh at the thought.

She stooped, picked it up, tucked it beneath her arm, and turned away.

I'd like to say she'd walked off without a backward glance, but she didn't. She glanced over her shoulder, *straight at me*, and her expression choked off what little breath inflated my lungs.

Pure evil stared out of her eyes, a cunning, bottomless malevolence that *knew* me, that understood things about me I didn't, and never wanted to know. Evil that celebrated its existence every chance it got through chaos, demolition, and psychotic rage.

She smiled, an awful smile, baring hundreds of small, pointy teeth.

And I had one of those sudden epiphanies.

I remembered the last time I'd gotten close to the *Sinsar Dubh* and passed out, and reading the next day about the man who'd killed his entire family, then driven himself into an embankment, *mere blocks* from where I'd lost consciousness. Everyone interviewed had said the same thing—the man couldn't have done it, it wasn't him, he'd been behaving like someone possessed for the past few days. I recalled the rash of gruesome news articles lately that echoed the same sentiment, whatever the brutal crime—*it wasn't him/her; he/she would never do it.* I stared at the woman who was no longer who or what she'd been when she'd turned the corner and entered this street. A woman possessed. And I understood.

It *wasn't* those people committing the terrible crimes.

The Beast was inside her now, in control. And it would retain control of her until it was done using her, when it would dispose of her and move on to its next victim.

We'd been so wrong, Barrons and I!

We'd believed the *Sinsar Dubh* was in the possession of someone with a cogent plan who was transporting it from place to place with a purpose, someone who was either using it to accomplish certain goals or guarding it, trying to keep it from falling into the wrong hands.

But it wasn't in the possession of anyone with a plan, cogent or otherwise, and it wasn't being moved.

It was *moving*.

Passing from one set of hands to the next, transforming each of its victims into a weapon of violence and destruction. Barrons had told me that Fae relics had a tendency to take on a life and purpose of their own in time. The Dark Book was a million years old. That was a lot of time. It had certainly taken on some kind of life.

The woman disappeared around the corner, and I

dropped to the pavement like a stone. Eyes closed, I gasped for shallow breaths. As she/it moved farther away, vanishing into the night where God only knew what she/it would do next, my pain began to ease.

It was the most dangerous Hallow ever created—and it was loose in our world.

Creepy thing was, until tonight, it hadn't been aware of me.

It was now.

It had looked at me, seen me. I couldn't explain it, but I felt it had somehow *marked* me, tagged me like a pigeon. I'd gazed into the abyss and the abyss had gazed back, just like Daddy always said it would: *You want to know about life, Mac? It's simple. Keep watching rainbows, baby. Keep looking at the sky. You find what you look for. If you go hunting good in the world, you'll find it. If you go hunting evil . . . well, don't.*

What idiot, I brooded, as I dragged myself up onto the sidewalk, had decided to give *me* special powers? What fool thought I could do something about problems of such enormity? How could I *not* hunt evil when I was one of the few people who could see it?

Tourists were flooding back into the street. Pub doors opened. Darkness peeled back. Music began playing, and the world started up again. Laughter bounced off brick. I wondered what world *they* were living in. It sure wasn't mine.

Oblivious to them all, I threw up until I dry-heaved. Then I dry-heaved until not even bile remained.

I pushed to my feet, dragged the back of my hand across my mouth, and stared at my reflection in a pub window. I was stained, I was soaked, and I smelled. My hair was a soppy mess of beer and . . . *oh!* I couldn't bear to think about what else. You never know what you'll find in a gutter in Dublin's party district. I plucked the clip from my hair, scraped it back, and secured it at my nape, where it couldn't touch much of my face.

My dress was torn, I was missing two buttons down the front of it, I'd broken the heel off my right shoe, and my knees were scraped and bleeding.

"There's a lass that gives a whole new meaning to falling-down drunk, eh?" A man sniggered as he passed by. His buddies laughed. There were a dozen of them, wearing red cummerbunds and bow ties over jeans and sweaters. A bachelor party, off to celebrate the joy of testosterone. They gave me wide berth.

They were so clueless.

Was it really only twenty minutes ago I'd been smiling at passersby? Walking through Temple Bar, feeling alive and attractive, and ready for whatever the world might decide to throw at me next? Twenty minutes ago, they'd have circled around me, flirted me up.

I took a few lopsided steps, trying to walk as if I weren't missing three and a half inches of spike beneath my left heel. It wasn't easy. I ached everywhere. Although the pain of the Book's proximity continued to recede, I felt bruised from head to toe, from being held in the crushing vise of it. If tonight turned out anything like the last time I'd encountered it, my head would pound for hours and ache dully for days. My visit to Christian MacKeltar, the young Scot who'd known my sister, was going to have to wait. I looked around for my missing heel. It was nowhere to be seen. I'd *loved* those shoes, darn it! I'd saved for months to buy them.

I sighed inwardly and told myself to get over it. At the moment, I had bigger problems on my mind.